LIGHT NEEDLE

KA Barron

ISBN 978-0-473-37973-5 (Softcover)
ISBN 978-0-473-37974-2 (ePub)
ISBN 978-0-473-37975-9 (Kindle)
ISBN 978-0-473-37976-6 (eBook)

1

THE FLAT WHITE sky was all wrong. Rua looked around at the grass. It was long and dry. A line of hills rolled up and down in front of the horizon, green and criss-crossed with lines. Behind the hills was a blurred city. It was like trying to see something underwater when the water is neither still nor clear. As soon as she thought she could make out a detail, it would disappear and she would have to force herself to focus again. There seemed to be towers, some pointed, the others standing high above them and shining like mirrors reflecting a sun she could not see.

She felt as if she were looking at the city down a tunnel which was wrapped around her, yet far away and invisible at the same time. A breeze ruffled her long, black hair and she pushed it away from her cheek. She squinted at the city, willing her eyes to see past the smudging air. A movement in the grass caught her eye away in the distance. Out of the corner of her eye, the city had become a range of mountains. Perhaps it had always been mountains, but they flicked to a blur when she tried to stare at them. The grass moved again. What was there was hidden. And then it stood up.

It was tall and dark. She had seen one before. It was another iron wolf. It carried an axe which it held in both hands wrapped in gauntlets. It was moving towards her. Then she saw more in the hills. They were coming down the slopes making lines in the grass behind them. There was no sound, but she knew the iron wolf was coming for her. She was running, but her feet seemed to be stuck to the ground. Just lifting her knee took all her effort. It was like pushing against a wall. She gritted her teeth. She could feel the iron wolf approaching although now she could no longer see it. She could only see long grass all around her. There was nowhere to run.

She turned her head. The wolf was there, much closer now. She could not see the axe any more, but both of its arms were outstretched before her.

"Come to me," it said.

It terrified her. She strained against the bonds of the ground, flailing her arms to free her lower body. Then suddenly she flew forward with a shout. She was on her knees in the dark and tipping forward. She steadied herself on the edge of the bed. She could feel her heart beating. The dream clung onto her, the fear of it. The iron wolf with its outstretched hands.

She lay down again, listening to the darkness. The house seemed still, or was she imagining noises? What if the wolf had followed her? What if it was in the room now? She forced herself to look. The light of a new moon was shining dimly in her window. There was nothing in the room with her. She stood and lit a candle. She had to check the rest of the house.

She tiptoed out of her room peering into each of the other rooms as she went. She paused at her father's empty bedroom. It was times like this that she missed him most.

She was alone in the house. Of course she was.

"And what would you have done if you found one, Rua?" she asked herself, rolling her eyes. She returned to her room. Outside, the city was sleeping. From her bedroom window she saw a custodian's lantern pass the end of their alley and move on and felt reassured.

The dream was still vivid in her mind. She climbed back into bed, pulled the covers up and tucked her knees up to her chest. She felt afraid to fall asleep again in case she had the same dream. The moon was in the window, a star below it. She stared at them both. She would watch them until morning.

She watched them until her eyes closed and sleep reclaimed her.

2

THE CANDLE ON the hearth shook suddenly as the wind cut under the window pane, found a gap in the drapes and took the candle by the neck. A couple of sheets of paper lifted at the edges then settled back on the desktop. Simon Crowfoot looked up from his bookwork and tugged the heavy red material across the gap. He paused for a moment and listened to the rain pouring into the horse trough outside his window and pattering onto the cobbles around it. He stared into space, hypnotised for a moment by the noise, then he came to with a start at a sudden knock on the door.

It was late. He should have been in bed like the rest of the household. Who could it be? He was not expecting a caravan for a few days. Crowfoot put down his pen, put a marker in his accounts and carefully folded the book closed. Then he stood, picked up the candle and went over to the door.

"Who be there? It be late you know."

"Begging your pardon," came the muffled voice from beyond the door. "I know it be late, but it be John. I was caught out in the rain."

"John? I can hardly hear you. I thought you were in bed."

"I went out the back. Could you let me in? All the doors be locked."

Crowfoot sighed. He set the candle down on the shelf by the doorway, pulled at the bolts top and bottom, then opened it. The door swung open easily as the wind caught it. The candle flared and blew out. He looked at the tall shape outside, hooded against the weather.

"You be not -," he said, trying to swing the door closed, but it stopped, jammed against a booted foot. The figure outside shoved at the door and Crowfoot was knocked back, a gloved hand reaching to cover his mouth while the other pulled an arm behind his back. Crowfoot struggled and managed a muffled cry as two more figures came in the door and closed it behind them. One of them came over and grabbed Crowfoot's other arm. He was pushed down into an upright wooden chair by the wall. The third figure walked in more slowly. He stood and surveyed the dim room, saw the door to the stairs was closed, nodded to himself and turned to face the three men around the chair.

He pulled back his hood, revealing a gaunt face. Loose skin showed it had once known better fed days. A long wispy brown beard trailed from his chin. His eyes had a wild look.

The man in the chair watched him with wide eyes.

"I advise you not to call out, Mr Crowfoot" said the bearded man. "You would not want your poor wife to hear you. Believe me."

Crowfoot's eyes flicked to the door to the stairs, then back at the bearded man. He had not blinked since the men had entered. He nodded.

The bearded man looked at the first figure who had entered and gave one quick nod of his own head. The tall hooded man slowly moved his hand away from Crowfoot's face.

Crowfoot's mouth quivered as he tried to speak.

"I've no money in the house. But take what else you want. I don't want any trouble."

"We don't want your money, Crowfoot," said the bearded man. Then he bent over and stared at the seated man. "Although you've made a pretty penny haven't you?"

Crowfoot said nothing.

"Made a pretty penny dealing with devils."

Crowfoot began to shake.

"I...it..."

The bearded man shook his head.

"You have nothing to say, merchant. You have traded with the devil. You be bewitched and corrupt."

"I had to. They be our friends now. We need what they have – "

The bearded man put up his hand with a sharpness which stopped Crowfoot, although his mouth continued to move wordlessly.

"Condemned out of your own mouth. The devils be your friends? Well, well."

"I do have money here. I've remembered, I will tell you where it be. Spare me."

"I said I do not want your money. I do the Lord's work. He will provide."

"Mr Silver, he could tell us," said the taller hooded man.

"He already has," said the bearded man watching the merchant's eyes flick over to a tapestry of a running stag.

"Silver?" Crowfoot stuttered. "Jack Silver?"

The bearded man turned his eyes on Crowfoot, but said nothing.

"I thought you looked familiar... Surely you remember me. My carriers brought supplies to the Pits. Every week."

"Aye, and were you consorting with devils then too?" said Silver. "Do not play with me, Crowfoot. I do the Lord's work. His angels come to me in my dreams. 'Then they will know that I am the Lord, when I lay my vengeance upon them.' You should not have forgot the Lord for the love of devils."

Silver turned his back, giving a light flicking motion with his hand. The blade was on the merchant's throat in a second. It cut across quickly, a second mouth which gaped darkly in the gloom. Crowfoot's head fell back. The second hooded man wiped the blade on the merchant's shoulder then slipped it back inside his coat.

"Where be the safe, Mr Silver?"

"Behind that tapestry. Be quick. I will wait for you at the end of the street with the horses."

Silver pulled up his hood. He did not look at the merchant again, but walked to the front door, opened it and went out. The rain had stopped, but there was the smell of it on the cobbles and a dampness hung in the air. Water dripped from eaves and the night had turned very quiet. He began to walk down the dark street, his feet falling quietly.

Inside the merchant's house, the two men were already at the tapestry. The larger one tugged at it and it fell to the floor. Behind, in the middle of the wall was a small cupboard door. There was no handle in it, just a keyhole. The smaller man pulled out his knife again and tried to prise it into the gap between door and frame. He shook his head and turned to look at the body on the floor.

"See if he's got a key on him. Or check the desk."

The taller man stooped over the merchant. He pulled awkwardly at the heavy body. He found a leather pouch and tugged hard on it until it came away from the belt. It felt heavy in his hand. He opened it up and looked inside, fingering through the coins.

"Nah," he said and slipped the pouch inside his robe.

"Try the desk," said the other. The man walked across the room to the desk by the window, the smaller watching him. Then both turned at a creak. The door to the stairs had opened. For a moment they both saw a young man's face. It took in the scene in an instant, his face wide with shock. Then the door slammed shut. Both men leapt for the door. They grabbed the handle and pulled, but the door would not move.

"He's bolted it!"

"Then he'll not bother us. Find the key. Quickly. We can't stay much longer."

The smaller man returned to the door in the wall, while the other bent over the desk. He pulled open the top drawer.

"I've found a key!"

He brandished it in triumph. Then his look turned to one of surprise as the stair door opened again. He barely had time to notice the gun barrel before it exploded. He dived instinctively. There was a crash as the shot smashed the window.

The door slammed shut again.

"Enough. Get out!" said the smaller man. His companion needed no encouragement. The two of them ran into the street. The taller man's hood fell back as he looked behind him. Someone had followed them from the house. He thought he saw him raise his arm. There was another shot. It echoed around the quiet street off the stones of the big houses. His back muscles clenched in expectation, but it would have been a lucky shot indeed to have hit its target. He knew they were all but invisible now in the gloom of the street. They rounded a corner into the main road.

"See you at the Bull," said the smaller. The other nodded and ducked off down an alleyway. His companion vanished into the night, leaving the street empty. A cat jumped down from a roof and padded along the side of the road. It stopped and pricked up its ears, turning its head towards the side street from which the men had come. There was a sound of footfalls. The cat trotted around the side of the building and disappeared.

Half a dozen men came, coats swinging open above nightdress. They brandished pistols and a long-arm, a sword, a club. They stopped on the main road, one man holding up his arm and cocking his head to listen. Nothing. Nothing but the sound of water dripping from a gutter.

3

THE ROOM WAS scattered with men in twos and threes huddled over their cups and talking in a low hubbub. Nicholas Berwick went in swiftly, sweeping his eyes across the room as he walked to the bar. The barman watched him come. He was a broad man with a thick, bald head that ran into his oily neck as if they were one and the same.

"Evening trooper. What be you having?"

"Nothing tonight, Tom. I won't be here long. Just come to ask you some questions."

Tom squinted at him thoughtfully.

"If you be asking questions, you'll need a drink." He poured a cup from a jug in front of him and pushed it across to the soldier. "It be on the house, trooper."

"Lieutenant," Berwick corrected. "Thank you, but I can pay." He fished out a coin and placed it on the counter next to the cup. The landlord left it there.

"Suit yourself. Only being welcoming to the boys of the Order as all old soldiers should be."

Berwick thought the murmurings behind him had become a little quieter.

"There's been another killing," said Berwick.

"Aye, merchant wasn't it? I heard. I hear most things."

"Throat slit. Same as the others. Did you hear that too?"

"And that they were chased out."

"Before they could finish. So there was no sign this time."

"What sign?"

"The other two left a sign in blood saying 'Devil lover'."

Berwick heard the door close.

"You think it was the same eh, lieutenant?"

"They all had dealings with the delf."

"Serves them right then. Doesn't it?"

Berwick looked at the jug and took a swig from his cup.

"Be that a delf jug?"

"No."

"You don't let them drink in here do you?"

"I don't stop 'em."

"So were you open last night?"

"Of course."

"Did you see anything out of the ordinary?"

Tom smiled.

"I did. Look around you, lieutenant. The whole tavern be out of the ordinary. Old soldiers never die. They just go to the Bull and drink and tell stories. You'll be coming in here more often one day, once you stop wasting your time on being the watch. Go be a soldier again, man. This be not soldiering."

"Soldiers be for keeping the peace as well as fighting the wars."

"Not in my day, they weren't."

"Ah well," said Berwick as he lifted his cup to his lips again. "Times have changed now." He finished the beer and set it down. "Thanks for the chat."

Tom nodded and watched Berwick as he walked to the door, opened it and went out. Then he spat on the counter and wiped it with a grimy cloth.

"You be a disgrace to the Order," he muttered.

Out in the street, Berwick looked around. There were a few people loafing outside the tavern, but the street was quiet. Someone had gone out while he was talking, another had stayed. He had seen a man sitting on his own, but there had been no lone drinkers when he had walked in. There was no sign of him now, but there was any number of alleys and side streets he could have taken. He decided on left and walked quickly to the corner, then turned right.

A couple of old women were standing gossiping, washing bundled under their arms. A wagon carrying broken furniture trundled by and the women moved away without pause to avoid the splashing from the muddy roadway. Berwick walked down the road, looked casually over his shoulder, checked the women were still listening to each other eagerly, then stepped down a ginnel on his right. It was narrow, the buildings on either side leaned toward each other. The way was scattered with broken bricks and timbers and a sheet of canvas. He stepped over them and came out into a slightly wider alley amongst the tightly packed buildings. He turned right, found another, turned left, then right again and stopped before he reached the street at an archway.

He peered out carefully. He was just down from the tavern and across the street. He could see the door. He waited, hoping no one else would come down the alley and wonder what he was doing. He did not have to wait long. The door opened and a tall man in a brown smock emerged. He stretched and scratched his neck. Berwick heard him speak, but could not make out the words. One of the loafers pointed the way Berwick had gone. The tall man nodded, passed the other a coin and set off in the opposite direction. The loafer was up and in the tavern door before the tall man had gone three paces. Berwick pulled back behind the arch as the man walked by, but his eyes followed him as he went. The man took a side turning. Berwick casually stepped out and followed him.

Archbishop John Sibbald was praying, He had made himself a cross and in front of it he had placed the candles which never flickered, for Limbo was outside the count of the time he had known. He stared into the bright depths of the flame and lost himself there. His breathing became deep and slow. He waited while his thoughts calmed and ceased their relentless flitting. Where they had once been like unruly children running, skipping and noisy, they gradually returned to their seats, sinking out of sight as the light filled his mind. All there was, was the still flame of the candle.

There he rested, floating in the void of light and silence. There he knew he was in the presence of the creator. The Archbishop loved to lose himself. In Limbo there was nothing to distract him. In Limbo, there was nothing to fear.

It had been in one of these times that he had first heard the whisper of dreams as their threads wove a little more of Limbo. It was a chorus of whispers which rose and fell like wind running through treetops or the waves rolling onto a stony beach.

He had begun to pick out individual threads against the new cloth of turbulent thought. Some of these were clearer than others.

It was Silver who he heard first. Silver had called out to him. He had heard him through his dream proxy which had taken on his form when the first host of Limbo had entered the corrupted lands of Outreterre and Unama. Now he could find Silver almost at will. Silver opened his mind to him and it was indeed as soft and easy to mould as silver. He had made a willing pupil after the upstart arrogance of the perfidious Thomas Rodon, the Judas.

In Silver's dreams, he had learned something of the world, albeit through the haze of Silver's mind. He could plant ideas in Silver's head which grew as he awoke.

This time there was something different. He dreamed of a man in a grand church before a stone carving of the Cross of St Collen. He could see clouds below the church and through them were glimpses of a great and glittering ocean.

4

RUA WAS IN the office at the back of the shop, doodling in the margin of the accounts book when she heard the shop door open. She stood and went out. A thin puoli with sagging skin and ruffled hair came in and leaned on the counter.

"Good afternoon, Edwin. What can I help you with today?"

"I need something for my head."

"What is wrong with your head? It looks no worse than usual."

"I am not in the mood for your jokes, Miss Rua. I am not sleeping well. What can you give me?"

"You are not the first today who is not sleeping well. It must be the close evenings."

"I have a fine breeze of an evening. There are two windows in my room. No, I keep having dreams that keep me from sleeping."

Rua cocked her head.

"I say dreams, but they are hard to describe. I wake up suddenly with a sense of fog and a feeling that something is in the fog. I have it every night. It is a dark fog and there is something in it. What can you give me to stop me from dreaming? I just want a long sleep with no dreams. I am afraid to sleep in case I dream it again."

She screwed up one eye.

"Are you testing me because father is not here?"

"What are you talking about? I want some powders, not a test."

"You and John Malakki have hatched this between you to see if I prescribe the same thing. I have been doing this since I was small, Edwin. I would have thought you could trust me now."

Edwin closed his eyes and breathed in.

"I need to sit down. I have no idea what you are talking about. I have never doubted you could make as good a mixture as your father. So sell me the powders and let me go home to my bed."

"Are you saying you and John have not spoken of this?"

"I have not seen John for a couple of weeks."

"But he talked about the same thing. He talked about something in a blackness coming for him. He said it was like the blackness moved and it was white and dark at the same time. Said he keeps dreaming it too and his nights are unsettled."

"He said that did he?" Edwin looked puzzled. "He is having my dream. I must talk to him about it."

"I have some made up from earlier today. I made a large batch because so many people seemed to be sleeping badly."

"Are they dreaming too?"

"Yes, but John described his."

She made him up the powder, took his payment and watched him thoughtfully as he left the shop. Whenever the shop was empty, she would go back to the office and search through some of the books on the wall behind the desk and some of the notebooks in the drawers. She found nothing that satisfied her. When evening came, she closed up and walked down the lane, along two more streets and across the square until she came to Rosa's house.

Rosa was slender with long brown hair. She hugged Rua and invited her inside.

"This is a nice surprise. Have you eaten?"

Rua shook her head.

"Then join us. You must be bored of eating on your own. Your father should hurry back."

"I am worried, Rosa."

"What about? Come up to the roof and we can talk."

They climbed the stairs and emerged onto a rooftop terrace covered in plants. Similar roofs surrounded them, giving an impression of a large garden with the parapets of each building looking like an intricate labyrinth among them.

"This last week, there have been many customers coming to the shop complaining they cannot sleep. Many of them complain of dreams and today, two described the same dream to me. They said it made them wake up frightened."

"Well that is nothing," said Rosa. "I had a very vivid dream. A creature with a wolf's head was running at me. I woke up quite frightened. It has happened twice. What is the matter?"

Rua was staring at her with a look of horror. She took her hands in her own.

"Was the wolf wearing armour?"

"Yes, chain mail. It was black."

Rua put her hands to her mouth, her eyes were wide.

"Rua! Tell me. What is the matter?"

"I have been having dreams too. That was why I was worried. But mine was like yours!"

"Really? That is strange."

"It is more than strange. Everyone is having dreams. No, not everyone. Only puoli. No other customers are coming to me about it. At first I thought nothing of it because theirs were so vague, but the number of them frightened me."

"But Rua, we have always dreamed and dreamed vividly. Could it be coincidence? Perhaps we have talked of wolves and armour or something."

"We have never talked of that. And we have never had the same dream before. Yes, we dream vividly. Father said we dream of Limbo and beyond."

"If your father was here he would simply tell you we have it worst because we are first generation."

"Yes. But I have searched my parents' books. There is no record of sickness that leads to dreaming like this. There is some kind of sickness of dreams, but we have it worst. We need to find out how it has spread. I cannot continue giving out powders for dreamless sleep. It is not healthy."

"They will pass. They are frightening, but they are only dreams. Now then, forget your dreams for the night. Let us have a happy evening and you can dream of that. You should stay the night. Mother loves to have you and we can make up another bed in my room and talk all night and not sleep and dream at all."

"I would love to stay, but I need my sleep. I must work tomorrow."

"Your father would not begrudge you a late start though would he?"

"He may not, but the dreamers might."

"Ah you. Come on. It must be time for dinner. I can smell it. Let us go down and see what is afoot in the kitchen."

5

BERWICK REACHED THE edge of the trees and reined in his horse. A few hundred yards ahead of him, trotting across the open grass below the crest of the hill, a man was riding. He appeared to have no idea he had been followed. Berwick watched him reach the crest and stop. He stood up in the saddle and looked down into the valley on the other side. Berwick knew it contained woodland scattered with open heath. He was either looking out for someone, or perhaps making sure it was safe to go down.

Berwick looked about him. Even once the man had gone over the other side of the hill he would still be dangerously exposed. To his right the trees reached up to the top of the hill which leaned back to meet them. It would provide him with some cover, so he trotted along inside the edge of the trees and up the slope. When he had gone as far as the trees stood, he dismounted, wrapped the reins loosely around a branch and, bent into a crouch. He scurried up the short slope to the narrow crest which ended where part of the hillside had once fallen away and left a low bluff above the grass beneath it.

He peered over the top. The rider had just reached the bottom. He passed behind a woody bush with small green leaves and under a knot of trees. Berwick could see a clearing ahead of him. In the middle he noticed some stones which appeared to have been rolled out of a circular shape. A patch of bare earth showed where a fire had once burned.

The man emerged from the trees into the clearing, looked about him, then threw his short cloak over his shoulder and dismounted. The horse immediately began to crop at the grass. After a while, he sat down on the ground with his arms resting on his knees and his chin on his arms. Berwick lay and watched, only looking over his shoulder a couple of times to reassure himself that his horse had not wandered off.

He was just thinking of going back to fetch his water when the man in the clearing stood and looked off into the trees. Berwick peered down, but he could neither see nor hear anything. Then two more horsemen entered the clearing and dismounted.

One was shorter than the man who was waiting and had broad shoulders and short, thinning hair. The other was a slighter figure. He wore a long coat and his hair and beard were unkempt. They all shook hands and sat down. Then, a minute or two later, all three suddenly looked around. Berwick held his breath and ducked his head down. The urge to look again was great, but he was afraid they would be looking up at him if he peered over again.

He caught the sound of a voice and a jingle of harness and risked a look. They were climbing up into their saddles and in a moment had trotted off under the trees.

Berwick cursed under his breath. Had they realised he was following them? Which way would they go? He scanned the valley, concentrating on the open patches of heath. For all he knew, they had simply ridden under the trees and stopped again. Perhaps he should sidle down into the valley and see if he could see them through the trees, but he knew immediately this would be foolish. They could even be watching the hillside to see if anyone came down.

Then he saw them, just for a moment. They seemed to be taking care to stay under the trees, but he had caught their movement through a thinning of leaves. They were heading in the direction of the Melion road. If they were, he might be able to follow them obliquely and come out on the road at a different point, although he would have to take a guess as to which way they would go once they reached the road.

He returned to his horse, took a quick swig from his water bag and pulled himself up onto the saddle. He trotted quickly to the crest of the hill and down the slope until he reached the trees. As he rode, he looked around him, listening out for the sound of other horses in case the three men had turned back. He put his hand out to touch the butt of his long-arm and felt the comforting firmness of the pistol in the holster at his side.

For much of the ride he had to lean down against his horse's neck to avoid the low branches of the trees. He watched the slope of the ground as he went, following it to maintain his direction in the wood. He knew that if he kept the slight upward slope on his left, he would find his way out to the road which occupied a wider valley onto which this opened.

He estimated the distance and added on a little to compensate for the longer route he was taking. He reached the road a little after he had expected. He could see it beyond the trees, a good, cobbled Roman. There would be other traffic on it and he would not look quite so obvious if his quarry spotted him. He rode casually out of the trees onto the thick, long grass by the roadside. As he did so, his eye was caught by movement on the road to his right. Just coming around the bend, a single rider came trotting towards him. His hand moved instinctively to his pistol, but moved away again when he recognised the thick, buff jacket of a soldier. As the soldier reached him, he eased his speed and came to a stop.

"God be with you," said the soldier. He was young and the shine of sweat was on his face from his ride.

"And with you," replied Berwick, his fingertips touching his temple in salute. "I be Lieutenant Berwick. From Collenium. What be your unit?"

"Melion regiment. Carrying dispatches."

"Good. Would you take another for me?"

"Of course, sir. Would you write or have me remember it."

"I have no paper, so I will tell it to you. I be pursuing three men. They be suspects in the murders in Collenium."

"I've heard of them. That news has travelled quickly."

"They be on this road somewhere. Did you pass anyone?"

"I did. Maybe half an hour ago. And it was three men."

"One tall, one broad, one with long hair and a strange look about him."

"Them? They be the murderers?"

"I don't know for sure, but they've sure got something to hide and they dropped some evidence which should witness them to the killings. I need help. There be three of them and I be alone. Could you send for help? I hope they will keep to the road now, or you will not find me again."

"Don't worry. Galloping will find you. They be not going fast. Very gentle on their rides them. You follow and the men of Melion won't be far behind."

"Thank you, trooper."

The soldier nodded and was off again, getting his horse up to a canter as he rode on down the road. Berwick knew the town was only a few miles distant. He hoped help would soon be with him, but for now, he would need to follow on his own and hope for the best.

He put his horse into a trot and set off in the direction the soldier had indicated. It was late afternoon and the sun would soon drop below the treetops. It took him about half an hour to catch up with the three riders. As soon as he saw them, he slowed the horse to a walk and continued to follow from several hundred yards behind. He hunched forward like someone half asleep who was letting the horse find the way, but he would look ahead of him from under his brows.

After a few minutes, one turned casually to look back down the road. Neither of the others looked back, nor did they alter their leisurely pace. Berwick relaxed and continued to follow.

They had been going for nearly an hour when Berwick realised the light was beginning to fail. He had reached a bend and the three had briefly been out of his sight, but as he went around, there was no sign of them. The road ahead was empty. The trees on his right came to a stop and gave onto open fields which rose up to a wooded knoll. He looked about him, trying not to move his head too much. Where had they gone? The trees on his left were low and scrubby and he could see that they too ended not so far ahead. Had they turned to the fields to spend the night?

He did not want to stop walking for fear they were watching from cover somewhere, but he looked around at the ground for clues. There were fresh horse droppings. They were just off the road in the grass to the right. The only cover beyond it was the wooded knoll. They must be on there. He would need to wait for the soldiers to arrive from Melion before he made a move, but he would need to turn back without making it obvious from the knoll.

"Looking for someone?" came a voice from behind him. His hand leapt to one of his pistols. "Easy soldier or I'll put a hole in you."

He put his hands up.

"Slowly now, take the butt by two fingers of your left hand. That be right. Lift it up and drop it on the ground. Good. Now the other. Slowly I said. I can't miss from this range. Now dismount. Slowly. Good. Move sideways away from that horse. Now you can turn around. Slowly."

Berwick turned around. There were two men. They had come out of the trees from across the road. One was tall and had pulled his hood over his head, but he could still see a strong jaw with a rough beard on it. The other had the long hair and straggling beard. He reminded Berwick of someone, but he could not place him.

There was no sign of the third until he heard the sound of a horse approaching from the direction of the knoll.

"Why be you following us?" asked the man with the long hair.

Berwick said nothing.

"Have we done something wrong, soldier? What could we have done that a loyal soldier of the Order of St Collen could possibly have a problem with? Or perhaps you want to join us?"

"I do," said Berwick.

The bearded man laughed, but only the lower half of his face moved.

"I do," he mimicked. Then he stared at Berwick with an intense look that made him want to look away. "I think you be a traitor. A betrayer. A Judas. Hmm? Judas hanged himself from a tree. Would you do that? Be you a devil lover too? Verily, you be a devil lover. Outreterre be surely diseased. The canker is spreading. The whole body will be infected if I do not act."

Berwick heard the horse behind him stop and a man dismounted. He heard his pistol being picked up from the ground.

"Use his bridle," said the bearded man. "Take him into the trees."

Suddenly strong arms grabbed him from behind and pinioned his own arms behind his back. The man behind him pushed him forward. A pain shot through his shoulders and he was forced to stagger forward.

Then he heard horses' hooves in the still air of the dusk. It was coming from around the bend.

"Off the road!" said the bearded man urgently. "The trees!"

The tall man froze, confused for a moment, then went forward to take Berwick's horse. He tugged on the reins, but it whinnied and pulled its head back.

The hooves were louder. Berwick looked hopefully at the bend, then was shoved roughly forward again. Only the support on his arms stopped him from falling, He was at the edge of the road now. A branch of a tree jabbed him in the face and he tried to move his head away. The contrary movement sent another stab of pain down his shoulder. Then the soldiers appeared.

There were two or three dozen of them, in pale brown buff jackets with steel grey helmets. As they came around the bend, the officer leading them raised his arm and they slowed.

The four men on the road stood frozen, looking at the troopers, but their feelings were different.

"Perhaps you should let him go," said the officer, meaningfully, walking his horse towards them.

The unseen man behind him let go his arms and Berwick took a step forward, swinging his arms to free them from the grip which had held them.

"Be that him?" the officer asked of a man next to him.

"It be."

Berwick recognised the dispatch rider he had met before.

"You seem to have run into a little trouble, Lieutenant," said the officer.

"These men be murderers," Berwick said.

"I am Captain Benedict of Melion. Do you have proof of that?"

"Soon. And I have a purse they dropped. It came from a murdered man."

"I didn't drop anything!" said the taller man. Berwick did not see the sharp look which Silver gave him.

"We'll take them from here."

"I'll come too."

"No need, son. This be Lord Giles's manor. And besides. I think there be enough of us to look after these three."

"Captain, I've been following these men for two weeks..."

"Well done, Lieutenant. And who knows where it would have got you if we'd not come along. I'll take it from here. You may take your horse and your weapons, which you appear to have mislaid, and go."

Berwick stared sullenly at the captain for a moment. He felt like a new trooper again. He felt the eyes of the rest of the soldiers on him. He turned, bent down self-consciously to pick up his pistol, pulled himself up onto his horse and rode past them the way he had come. He would camp in the woods. The next day he would be back in Collenium.

Richard Denham sat straight up in bed. He realised he had thrown off the covers.

"What are you doing?" Helen mumbled beside him in the dark.

"Sorry. I was dreaming. There was someone scratching in the dark. They were on the other side of...something."

"Mmm," she said, not really awake.

Richard slid out of bed, hesitated a moment before touching the handle then opened it. The moon shone in through the landing window. He went back into the bedroom and brushed the curtains aside, peering out into the back garden. Nothing. Of course.

"What are you *doing*?" said Helen, struggling to stay asleep.

"Someone was trying to get in," he said. "I just... I just wanted to make sure they hadn't."

6

CAPTAIN BENEDICT LED the three men into the great hall. Lord Giles was sitting over a ledger with a goblet of wine at his side. He wore a long crimson jacket in the evening cool. He looked up as the men entered and his hand went to his goatee beard. He leaned back.

"Take those two away," he gestured vaguely at the tall man and the broad man. His voice was meaningful yet understated. It suited the cat like way in which he moved. "And cut his hands loose."

The captain nodded at one of the guards who put a knife through the cords around Silver's wrists, then he gestured to the six soldiers to leave with the two men. He stayed standing at the back.

"Mr Silver. You've changed."

Silver looked slowly over his shoulder at the captain. The officer had a face which looked as though it had been hacked out of wood and his scalp had been scraped hairless.

Giles watched him.

"I hear you've been having dreams."

Silver continued to say nothing.

"Come now, Silver. Why don't you sit down and tell me about them."

"You believe in dreams?" Silver asked.

"I surprise myself as to what I believe in these days, Silver. We have lived in an age of wonders. I hear you've been having dreams. I also hear you seem to have fallen into a little trouble. But let's not mind that. Why don't you tell me about your dreams?"

Silver stayed silent. He looked carefully at Giles.

"Jack, you need friends at the moment. These be troubled times when our once proud country kneels at the feet of devils. We be dealing with the devil, be we not? He has entered our house and left a disease which is rotting the fabric of our once strong country, where even soldiers of the Order be persuaded to do the devil's work."

As Giles spoke, Silver's eyes began to gleam. His hands began to shake and he lifted them, palms upward.

"My lord, your words be succour to my reeling soul. I thought I was a lone voice crying in the wilderness."

"No, Jack. There be other voices, but they do not speak out. They be torn. They have a devil on one shoulder and an angel on the other, but the devil talks louder. Now, Jack, your ways be interesting and have had some effect, but I thought your preaching was more effective than your practice. *That* has merely created the wrong kind of attention."

Silver attempted to look puzzled.

"You know what I mean, Silver. Let's not bandy words. That enthusiastic young man Mr Benedict left in the roadway this afternoon was not stupid. But, as I say, let us put those activities behind us. I have heard about your preaching, but I would like you to tell me. I've not heard it for myself."

"Some people say I be mad, my lord."

"Many mad people speak the truth, Silver. I don't care if you be mad. Tell me what you have been preaching."

Silver weighed up the request for a few moments, trying to see where this was going. He decided it could do no harm. It was merely what he had been saying to gatherings across the land for some months now.

"Seven years ago, the year when we would finally fulfil God's purpose and defeat the devils, the Archbishop prepared the Pits and sent a darkness over the land. I was given the honour of keeping the Pits and a host of devils were put in my care. The Archbishop came and entered Limbo, taking devils with him to find the way back to Christendom. While he was gone, I was beset by devils and overcome." He paused and swallowed, his face in his hands. "I shudder to think of it still how I failed the Lord. But the Archbishop sent a host from Limbo of all the Order who had died. They returned to Outreterre to save us. But the cunning of the devils and their sorcery banished them back to Limbo."

"I know all this. I was there."

"Yes, yes. But I was at the Pits. I met my lord Rodon on the way and he told me to beware of the coming of the host. I was filled with fear, God forgive me, and I hid in the woods by the road when they came. From my hiding place, I could see their armour and their flags and the cross of St Collen." His voice dropped to a whisper.

Lord Giles found himself drawn in by the words of the bearded man which were spoken now in little more than a whisper.

"And at their head, riding a great white horse, I saw the Archbishop. He rode at their head dressed all in white. He was like one transformed. His face was stern and implacable. But I was afraid of that great multitude and I stayed hidden as it went by me. And when I later heard that the sorcerers of the devils had corrupted the minds of our own people and pulled their souls out of them to fling at the avenging host of the Lord, I marvelled at their power and I hid in the hills."

His body seemed to hang with dejection as it remembered that time and the lines in Silver's face deepened. Then suddenly his frame became more animated and he looked up, into Giles's eyes.

"It was during my time in the wilderness that the dreams came. It was my forty days and forty nights, but no devil came to tempt me. No, an *angel* came to succour me in the night. It was dressed in bright steel and bore the cross of St Collen on its sable surcoat. It called me by my name and I was filled with hope and fear. It came to me every night until one night it did not come. Instead, by my bed of earth and stones, the Archbishop came to me from out of Limbo. He spoke to me in my dreams."

Lord Giles breathed deeply. He recognised theatricals when he saw them, but he also saw that Silver believed in himself entirely.

"His Grace told me he was alive. Yes, alive, but that he had been trapped in Limbo by a sorcerer. Through prayer he had searched for a way out and through prayer he had found my sleeping mind. I dreamed of him on many nights. Do not think this was one single revelation, my lord. It was not. Don't think I believed it myself at first. May God forgive my lack of faith. But to dream the same dream every night? Who has done that? There be always some difference. These dreams said the same things and continued the theme."

"And what was that theme, Silver?"

"That there were other men in this benighted world, other men of the Order. The men of the Parting who had taken the ships and sailed away more than five hundred years ago. His Grace told me I must find them, for they would be uncorrupted by the filth of these devils. He told me that echoes had reached him in his dreams of a city in the clouds where proud men walked the towers and battlements. He told me that it lies far to the south, across the sea which only the devils may now cross.

"He told me I needed to cross the sea, that I should find money to make that crossing. So I found friends. I hope you treat them well. They were once soldiers themselves."

"They be taken care of. Where be this place of men? How do we get there?"

"His Grace told me we must bend the devil's ways against them. I remember him saying such things. It was how he created the darkness out of the despair of the devils themselves. It was one way I knew his words were true and it was really him speaking to me out of Limbo. He told me the devils themselves could take me across the sea and that I should follow the clouds which would lead me to a city in their midst."

Giles's eyes narrowed in thought.

"The only place to the south of which I have heard is Naadu. It be a land rich in salt and iron. Our merchants speak of it." He tipped his head. "Or in some cases, thanks to you, *spoke* of it." He smiled briefly and without humour. "But that be a city of devils and it lies in a desert which they say be itself in another world. You have to pass through a great gloom to reach it."

"It be not Naadu. It be another place, but he did not know its name. He has only seen echoes reaching out to Limbo and he has tried to reach them, but cannot. Still he strives to be released. But there we will find allies in our struggle against Satan. The prodigal sons will return."

Giles sat back in his chair. Then he nodded to the captain who moved off to a table at the side of the room.

"Well, Silver, these do indeed sound like the ravings of a man who has spent far too much time on his own in the woods." He held up his hand as Silver opened his mouth to speak. "But I came across something which I believe may interest you."

The captain came over and held out a small packet of soft cloth. He placed it in Silver's hand. Silver weighed it in his hand and looked at Giles quizzically.

"That came from over the sea. Acquired through dealings with the devils. Open it."

Silver looked at it without trust as it lay in his hand.

"Open it. It won't hurt you."

Silver lifted his other hand and moved aside the cloth until a silver object lay on an open cloth in his palm. It was almost as long as his palm and was made of silver. It was a cross in the shape of a sword. Silver looked up at Giles, a new light spreading behind his eyes.

"The cross of St Collen," he said.

Archbishop John Sibbald was praying. He was floating in the void of light and silence. Then something disturbed it. It was loud, but muffled, yet the dream was passing through as if pulled by a needle through fabric.

He had encountered it before, felt it like an open door which he could walk towards and enter. He had not sought it out like he had those other minds who had known him in Limbo. It came past him oblivious to his watchfulness, rushing past his awareness, blundering through, groping aimlessly for a world beyond the world where Outreterre lay.

He could smell it was wandering. It was confused. He had become used to the colours of dreams of human and the colours of those of the delf. This was like neither and both. It felt like the dreams which came at him from both worlds. He could discern two threads. They shone brightly against a blur of the same colours in tones which seemed to have a common theme.

Once he could recognise them, he realised they were often there against the tapestry of dreams. He searched them out and tried to follow them and listen to them. At times, they reached briefly through the worlds. That fascinated him, for if he could find a way of breaching the worlds, he would be able to do the work which had been planned for him.

7

A SHEEN OF rain lay across the paving slabs of the courtyard and it gleamed as the sun struggled to shine through a veil of cloud. Berwick's boots crunched across the wet stone as he walked towards the door on the far side. It was half open and occasional shouts escaped from it. As he went closer he heard the sound of metal on metal. There were two men fighting. Berwick stood in the doorway looking at the large empty room. Long-arms and swords lined the wall.

He watched the men as they exchanged a few blows, then the one with his back to him paused and pointed out a problem with his younger opponent's technique. He was breathing harder than the older man and his hair hung wet on his forehead which glistened with sweat.

They both wore loose white shirts open at the neck. They stood en garde once more and began to duel again. Berwick stepped inside to see better and the man facing him looked up and, before he knew it, had the other's sword point at his throat.

"You be easily distracted. And easily killed," said the young man's opponent. He dropped his sword, rocked back on his heels and turned to see what had caused the distraction.

"Lieutenant Berwick, I should have you appear suddenly more often. It be a useful trick to ensure I win each time."

"You don't need tricks, Mr Rodon," Berwick replied.

"As you grow older, you need all the tricks you can muster, believe me." He turned to his student. "I think you've had enough for this morning. We will try again this afternoon."

The man bowed, gathered up his jacket and left.

"Now then, Berwick," said Rodon, his hand on the trooper's shoulder. "How can I help you?"

Berwick pulled the door closed behind him and spoke quietly.

"I be worried about Lord Giles."

Thomas Rodon's eyebrows raised with mock surprise.

"Any reason more than usual?"

"I've been following some suspects. Three men I think were involved in the murders. I followed them onto the Melion road. I'd already met one of Lord Giles's troopers and sent him for help, but the three men jumped me."

"Ho. But you lived to tell the tale."

"Lord Giles's men arrived or I don't know what would have happened. They took the men into custody but wouldn't let me go with them. Their captain said they would deal with it."

"And when was this?"

"More than a week ago."

"Well we've heard nothing from Lord Giles."

"That be the root of my worry."

"Then we will ask Lord Giles to bring the men to Collenium that they may be tried."

"I went to do just that, but Lord Giles's steward told me that he was gone."

"Gone? Gone where?"

"The steward seemed reluctant to tell me. Told me it was his master's business and not that of a soldier. But I questioned some farmers who told me they had seen Lord Giles riding out a few days before with a troop of horse. They were heading south. I tried to follow, but my tracking skills are poor. The last reports I had of them were that they were going south still."

"That be a strange business. But how do you know the prisoners were with him?"

"I don't. But when I asked, the steward told me he had no idea what I was talking about and fair slammed the door in my face."

"Strange indeed. Even from Lord Giles. So why come to me?"

"Who else should I come to? In matters such as this, I need someone I can trust. These murders are showing a clear divide between those who want a return to war and those who value the peace."

"Aye. You cannot change the hearts of all. Maybe not even if they had lived through what we have lived through. But what were you thinking?"

"We should follow them."

"You said you don't know where they went."

"There be nowhere else they could have been going save for Unama. I think they were riding for the ford."

"What mischief would Lord Giles have in Unama? If he rides in there with an armed band, who knows where it could lead."

"Indeed. And it be mixed up with those three. And there be something else. I recognised one of the men I was following. It only came to me after I had lost him. I woke up in the night and remembered his face, but he be much changed. It was Jack Silver who was beadle at the Pits. His hair and beard have grown long."

"Interesting. I would like to know more, but we cannot wander freely in Unama and ask questions of the delf about an armed band of the Order. We must seek help. We must go to visit our old friends at Kunnaslaki. They will know the whereabouts of Raul Hunter. I haven't seen him for some years. He came here once after the treaty, but would not stay long. He would be able to track them and knows many delf who could help us and explain our purpose."

"When can we leave?"

"As soon as I have written a note to your captain for your special release. Go fetch your horse. We will eat and leave."

Berwick had always believed Thomas Rodon was suspicious of Lord Giles. His alacrity at responding to his concerns proved it. He walked briskly across the courtyard. The sun was pushing itself through the cloud and the stones seemed to be sweating.

8

SOLIMO OPENED THE door to the toolshed. Inside it was dark. He felt surprised and turned to walk back into the garden, but the garden was no longer there, only darkness. He felt the familiar panic. He was in the Pits again. He looked around him, swinging his head from side to side rapidly, but he had the odd sensation that his head was not moving. It made no difference. There was still only darkness around him.

He began to sense something. Shapes, a feeling, he was uncertain, but the darkness contained something and he knew it was not the delf. He knew they were gone, back to what was left of their homes. He was alone here.

He began to back away. There was something coming. There was a larger presence behind the darkness, like a shadow approaching a closed door.

"Devil," it whispered. "I know you be there. I can almost see you."

His eyes flew open. He saw the two candles and realised he had gripped the bed sheets in his fists. He released the sheets and looked at the candles. He pulled the blankets up, rolled onto his side and curled up defensively.

"Good morning, Solimo," said Mondo as Solimo entered the funnel room. "We can harvest together today for a while. The moon is still high."

"I would like that," said Solimo quietly. He hung up his coat by the door and walked over to his station. In the middle of the room, the polished base of the light funnel dropped from the ceiling to the three cylinders on the floor. They pointed out from the funnel at equal angles. Mondo was sitting at the end of one, pedalling slowly. Solimo sat on one to his left and began to pedal to the same rhythm.

In the windows which ran around the top of the high walls, the night was beginning to glow. They pedalled in silence for a few minutes. Solimo felt the eyes of the older delf on him and looked up. Mondo's eyes stayed on him.

"Why are you staring at me?"

"Did you have the dream again?"

Solimo looked down. He was ashamed.

"It is nothing to be embarrassed about."

"How can I be afraid of the dark?"

"Many delf are afraid of the dark and you have good cause."

"I am a light keeper, but I sleep with two candles like a child."

"It is not for me to judge you. I was not in the pit as you were."

Mondo might not judge him, Solimo thought, but others would if they knew. He was supposed to take away the darkness of others. Was it that which haunted him? Did he take on the darkness of others when he healed them? The Light Doctor had never spoken of it, if she had. Perhaps she had meant to, but there would never be any lessons from her again. She had been killed.

"Just take a hold of the dream, Solimo. It is your dream."

Solimo turned to face him. He stopped pedalling.

"What is the matter?" Mondo asked.

"What you said. That is what makes it terrifying. I had not realised until now. I thought I was used to them, but of late I have struggled again. I am not sure it *is* my dream. I feel as though the dream belongs to someone else."

Mondo frowned at him.

"Yes. That is it. I cannot control the dream. I am afraid to."

"I think it will help you if you weave a sun wraith," said Mondo. "If you are to become a Light Doctor, you need to be able to weave the sun, learn how to control."

"I can never do that. And I can never be a Light Doctor. I am only a healer. You should be the Light Doctor."

"But I am not much of a healer. That is what you do and what Light Doctors do, but you need to master the sun if you are to succeed. Perhaps it would help you with these dreams."

"Maybe," said Solimo thoughtfully. He turned over the next thing he was going to say in his head. Mondo could see he was still thinking and waited. "There is something else about these dreams. They have not always been like this. Usually they are just of the darkness. But of late, there has been a different element to them.

There is a voice. There is someone there in the darkness. They are coming for me. They call me devil."

"Is it just the dream or something else?" asked Mondo thoughtfully.

"I think...it is something else. There is a presence in the dream. It calls from within the dream itself."

9

AN INVISIBLE HAND of wind stroked the grass around him. Raul finished inspecting the steer's hoof and slapped its rump. It trotted off and Raul stood, putting his hands on his hips and arching his back to stretch it after bending over.

The two horsemen caught his eye immediately. They were still two ridgelines away, but their dark shapes stood out against the green and the sweeping shadows of clouds. He tried to make out details, but they were too far away. He was still wary of being caught in the open, even after these years of quiet. It was a habit which had formed over decades and it was unlikely to leave him.

His own horse was behind him and his long-arm was in the saddle holster. He never rode out without it. He told Esella that it was only for shooting game, but he doubted she had ever believed him. He glanced back at the light tower on the hill over his left shoulder and then at the farmhouse over to his right with its line of young trees to windward. The riders dropped below the ridge and he stood by his horse waiting for them to reappear. The breeze swept past him, the thick grass leaning over to mark its passage.

The riders crested the next hill and he could see now that they were men. This was unusual. As he watched them, he decided they were heading for the tower. He did not feel alarmed. He usually trusted his instincts, but it was still sensible to be cautious. He jumped up on his saddle, turned his horse and set off down the dip in the land between the hill on which he stood and the light tower's.

They had noticed him. He saw their heads turn towards him. They were dressed for travel, and he could see they were armed. Both wore brimmed hats and long leather waistcoats. Each had a coat rolled behind them. They looked familiar and as he rode closer, they turned and came towards him. He could see they were smiling.

"Just the man we be looking for!" he heard called across the space between them. The man. He knew it was a figure of speech, but because of it he decided to stop and wait with his hands resting on his saddle front. The two men were still smiling as they came up to him, but he did not.

"Do you remember us?" asked the younger.

"I do. I do not forget a face. Even a man's. Particularly a man's."

Berwick looked affronted by the remark, but the older man seemed to take it in his stride.

"You are Nicholas Berwick," said Raul. "And you," he said to the older man, "are Thomas Rodon."

"Raul Hunter, we are here in friendship and to ask for your help."

Raul looked at the older man with the short beard. These men had once been his enemies, but had become his comrades in arms as they had fled through Limbo, united by their need to escape the Archbishop and his goblin army.

"Well then. You had best come for something to eat. That is my place behind me," he gestured to the house with his head. He saw the two men exchange a look, then he turned and led them to the house. He could guess what they were thinking: how had the hunter become a herdsman. It had been a difficult change for him too at first, although it had been gradual enough. He had started out visiting, leaving them game to eat. He had returned to Metsakant less and less often, always finding a reason to return to Kunnaslaki.

Then on one visit, Esella had asked him about a small herd of cattle that had wandered near the tower. The keepers had asked about them to neighbouring homesteads, but no one knew anything about them. It was assumed they had escaped from somewhere. Perhaps they had been wandering since the war, since the army of the Order had crossed the Styx ready to take Unama in the name of their god. They had a wild look about them.

When Esella had asked for his help to look after them, he knew the keepers would have been better off asking the local herders. Despite that, he had not turned down her request for help. Neither was the kind to talk about the bond that had been growing between them. Raul admitted it to himself that only slowly. He had looked after himself since before he was fully grown and only himself. Living near the borders where freebooters would sometimes come through the mountains from Outreterre raiding, life could be precarious. He liked to be able to move as he wished and to take matters into his own hands as he wished as well. He would not consult with anyone and there would be no one to miss him if he did not return from any of his forays. He had known loss as a child in the Tanglewoods of northern Metsakant.

So years had passed for them to become open with each other; years as the truce between the two races had held. It had been a hope against hope, but even Raul had let down his guard just enough. If anything happened, when the truce broke, they would be ready for it together.

The two men shook Raul's hand as they entered. It was an unfamiliar custom to him. He was unsure as to whether to grip firmly or weakly, but followed their firm holds and pointed to the chairs at the table.

It was warm inside, sheltered from the cool breeze and heated by the hearth. A pot hung over it and he ladled out some stew and poured water from a jug. As an afterthought he served a bowl of stew for himself before sitting opposite them.

The younger man looked frustrated, but the older was patient and Raul allowed himself a smile at the difference between the two. The older smiled in return.

"Thank you for the food and the welcome."

"We always welcome travellers who come in peace," Raul replied.

"This cottage be new be it not? I don't remember it from before."

"I built it four years ago."

"Still in the old style," said Berwick, eyeing the narrow windows.

"Old habits die hard. Or you can call me cynical."

"The peace has held," said Berwick.

"Are you still a soldier, Nicholas Berwick?" he asked.

"That I be, but – "

"Then perhaps you are cynical too," said Raul.

"Berwick helps to keep the peace," said Rodon. "You be right, not all men wish to keep it. Berwick be one who holds those..." he paused, searching for the words, "rogue elements in check. And that be why we come here."

Raul put a spoonful to his mouth, but said nothing. Rodon took it as invitation to continue.

"We have had some murders in Collenium. They be men who have traded with the delf or worked with them. It seems to be the same killer. He leaves a note saying - " he paused, "'Devil lover.'"

A weary smile passed over Raul's face.

"The third time, there was no note, but they were interrupted. Berwick here had some suspicions and began to follow a man he suspected. He led him to two others. He was following them when they were taken into the custody of one of our lords, Lord Giles. Perhaps you remember him?"

Raul shook his head.

"He be a man who never had much time for anyone but himself. But no one has been brought before the courts. And Lord Giles and a contingent of his men appear to have left Outreterre and have come south into Unama."

Raul had stopped eating.

"To do what?" he asked.

"That we don't know."

"But you suspect it is nothing good."

"Let's just say it be an unusual thing to do."

"But there are just two of you."

"I didn't want to enter Unama with what looked like a war party," said Rodon. "One of those be bad enough."

Raul nodded.

"But we need to find those men," said Rodon.

"How many?"

"I don't know for sure. Maybe twenty to thirty."

"So why have you come to me?"

"I assume they will try to keep away from where people live, so I will need a tracker. And I need a delf to help us so that we can help you. I be under no illusions as to how the delf still look on us. We will get nowhere without a friend."

"If they cause trouble, we will see to them," said Raul.

"That I do not doubt, but not without loss of life and I don't want it to escalate. I don't want to risk the peace."

Raul nodded again, slowly. Berwick spoke.

"I think Lord Giles be sheltering the murderers. It wouldn't surprise you to know not everyone wants the peace. Power be shifting away from the lords to the merchants. The soldiers be bored. The Lords still drill their regiments. I think we could see a return to the civil wars."

"Well, fighting amongst yourselves kept you off our backs for centuries. Perhaps we would welcome your squabbling," Raul said.

Rodon shrugged. "Would you like to risk it?"

A door opened at the back of the house. The heads of the three turned to see who it was.

"Esella, did we wake you?" Raul asked.

"It does not matter." She looked at their guests, recognition and surprise showed in her face. Rodon and Berwick stood and bowed their heads slightly.

"Excuse us, we did not know you were resting."

"I am hungry," she said, her hand going to her swollen belly.

Berwick grinned. "Congratulations," he said. "When be it due?"

"Four months," Raul said. Berwick looked surprised. "We do not grow our children as quickly as you." Raul explained. "We do not rush."

Esella looked suspiciously at the two men.

"Have you seen Solimo yet?"

"No, we saw Raul before we reached the light tower," said Rodon. "We were hoping the light tower would have news of where to find Raul. We had not realised he would be here."

Solimo was more welcoming than Raul. He opened his arms to them.

"How long are you staying?"

"We do not want to impose," said Rodon.

"And where else would you sleep. We can offer you a bed instead of a hilltop. We are old friends. Come in, sit down, tell us your news. Mondo is in the funnel room, but he will be pleased to see you as well."

"Mondo hardly knew us," said Berwick.

"No, but he saw what you did. He was there when you stopped the Order from shooting on the delf and when our alliance was first forged."

"Or forced."

"It was a common cause. It showed us how similar we are."

"Well, I don't think Raul sees it that way," said Berwick. "He hasn't changed."

"He has. He has mellowed."

"In sooth?"

"And what of you?"

"Oh," said Rodon looking away for a moment and placing his saddle bags on a stool. "Experiences change a man."

Solimo watched him and saw the sadness in his eyes. Rodon had perhaps changed the most out of any of them. Once the

Archbishop's right hand man, he had betrayed his trust to save Solimo and the Mage and indeed both Unama and Outreterre. Solimo caught Berwick's eye.

"Well," said Berwick. "Do you still grow the best fruit I've ever tasted?"

After the men had left, Esella confronted Raul.

"What is going on Raul?"

"I may be going away for a little while."

Esella frowned.

"How long?"

"Not long. They just need some help in tracking down these men."

"And what will happen when you find them? No more fighting Raul. You are going to be a father."

He touched her cheek.

"I need you here." She took his other hand. "I know you are restless. I just want it to be someone else who helps these men. They are trouble."

"These men have been our friends. If they are worried, then it concerns all of us. And I owe it to all of us to do what I can for them."

"You miss being free."

Raul took both of her hands in his.

"I will not lie to you. I do miss my wandering life sometimes. But it is a different life to the one I live now, and I would miss this if I lived another. I will miss you."

"Go then, Raul Hunter. I cannot stop you and do not want to. Just make sure that whatever you do is for the good of our baby."

"I will come back," said Raul.

"No one can see the future," Esella said.

10

BERETSKA'S PORT WAS busy. A crowd of fishing boats were lined up on two sides of the rectangular harbour, crammed together like beetles. Some were being unloaded from the morning's catch, others were being prepared for the evening. Crewmen walked the decks and called out to each other.

On the other side of the harbour were the bigger ships, three masted and high sided for the most part, loading and unloading cargo or dealing with repairs, the piers piled with crates, sacks, rigging and stacks of planks.

Berwick and Rodon surveyed the scene as they stood holding the reins of Raul's horse. For the men, it was their first time at the harbour on the southern coast of Unama. Ahead of them, the long arm of the harbour wall reached across. Beyond it, on a headland jutting above a tumble of foam washed rocks stood the smooth-sided stone tower that was both light tower and light house, gathering the light and using it to guide the ships in. From its wide base, it rose twice as high as Kunnaslaki.

Raul was talking to a man in a smock who was supervising the loading of the closest cargo ship.

"I don't know about you," Berwick said, "but I feel like everyone be looking at me."

Rodon grunted.

"It looks like that fellow might know something," he replied.

The delf was pointing along the wharf to another ship. Raul nodded and returned to the two men.

"Well?" Berwick asked.

"You not feeling comfortable?" Raul smiled, not without relish. "That is how a delf feels every time we enter Outreterre."

"I be sorry for it," Rodon replied. "Things will change, given time."

Raul raised an eyebrow, but said nothing.

"I am told that the master of that ship at the end knows who they sailed with. We should talk to him."

The master in question had a wild mane of hair and a face of salt spray gutters. He watched them climb his gang plank with a frown and once they were on his ship, he looked at the men suspiciously and at Raul with curiosity.

"Beretska is becoming popular with the Order," he sneered.

"That is why we are here," said Raul. "You are Qatiko Master?" The sailor nodded. "We have heard you know something about a party of men who came this way. A large party."

The master spat onto his deck.

"And what is your interest?"

"We believe that amongst them are some who are wanted for murder."

The master raised an eyebrow. "Murder? Of who?"

"Of men."

The master rolled his eyes.

"Is that supposed to upset me?"

"They were all merchants who traded with the delf," said Rodon. "Do you know of these men? Have you seen them?"

The delf looked at Rodon for a while, as if sizing him up, enjoying trying to make him uncomfortable. Rodon endured the stare. He had stared down worse than this.

"Yes. I have seen them," the master said, wearying of Rodon and speaking again to Raul.

"They wanted to charter my vessel. I told them they could swim."

"Why did you turn down the business?" asked Berwick.

"I have plenty of business and have no need of carrying thirty armed men and their horses on my ship, however much they offered me. I do not like them and certainly would not trust them."

"So what happened?" Raul asked.

"Well they tried someone else. And they found someone, a master I had beaten to a cargo. This one," he nodded his head to the crates still visible in his forward hold. "As you can see, it wasn't due for a while, so he thought he was getting one up on me taking them sooner. He needed something to pay his crew and decided to risk it. I told him to take the weapons off them first."

"Did he?" Rodon asked.

"I think he did. He was smart even if he had no principles," the master showed his teeth in a false grin.

"Do you know where they were bound?"

"I do," the master replied.

There was a pause during which the three travellers realised they were going to have to press for further information.

"May we ask where?" Rodon asked.

"You may," the master said with mock politeness. "And indeed I will tell you because we delf like to be helpful. They sailed for Naadu and I suppose Sata Utimaak."

"How do you know it would be there?" Rodon asked.

"It is where we mostly sail. Closest and cheapest port. Mind, I have been to some of the others if I think the Naadu will not give me a fair price. Being the closest can make them think they can take advantage."

"Is that where you are going?" asked Raul.

"It is."

"And may we come with you? I offer my weapons to you now for safe keeping," Rodon said.

The master laughed.

"Two men and a delf. A small posse to chase a large one? Do I have room for three lunatics on my ship?"

He contemplated their faces. Berwick noticed Raul was becoming frustrated.

"Your quarters will be cramped, but I will take you because you make me laugh. I will be sorry I will never hear the end of your tale."

"Thank you," said Rodon.

"And I will take your weapons, Mr Order," said Qatiko. "Make sure you remember to ask for them back when you reach Naadu. You need to stand at least a fighting chance."

"When do you sail?" asked Raul.

"On the tide tomorrow just before first light."

"Then we will see you tomorrow morning."

The master nodded. The conversation was over and they walked down the steps to the main deck and made their way back down the gangplank. The master walked over to the side and leaned on it with his elbows.

"Better bring your own provisions," he said. "I am not used to carrying passengers."

The three said nothing until they had reached their horses.

"I don't think he liked us," Berwick said.

"I think he liked us well enough," Rodon said, pulling himself up onto his saddle. "He would not have taken us otherwise. Come. Let's find a store and decide what be good eating for a sea voyage."

"He treated me almost as if I were you," said Raul. "A new experience I put myself through to find these fellows of yours. I hope they are worth the chasing. I have a child on the way and I would hate to leave you alone over there."

"We will manage without you if you need to go home," said Rodon. "You have led us this far."

"Do not worry. You have convinced me these last days of travelling that there is something amiss. And besides, as the sailor said, you will need help with Giles' men. I assume you have a plan for that?"

"A plan?" said Rodon. "No, I have faith in God."

"Then I hope *he* has a plan," Raul said wryly. "Come, I saw a likely store as we were coming down the street back there. Let us go and spend your money."

Archbishop John Sibbald was praying. He was floating in the void of light and silence.

How long he stayed in the light, he did not know. Time mattered little. But once he had immersed himself in the brightness for a time, he began to think. He thought unhurriedly. It was like a mason choosing the best block of stone to begin to chip at, or the woodcarver selecting the piece of wood of the right hardness and grain. Then he would make with his mind, his thoughts flowing into his own dream as he passed from meditation to sleep like someone enters mist, first as stray tendrils and then realising it is all around him.

In his sleep, the images remained, they crossed over from deep meditation to dream sleep like two oceans meeting and mixing. It became easier the more he did it.

The Archbishop awoke. The return to wakefulness was smooth and without the sudden transition and surprise of wakefulness that he had already half forgotten. Sleeping in Limbo was a luxury and a challenge. He was lying below the frozen candles and the cross, where he had sunk at some point, his head resting on the floor.

He lay for a moment, collecting his thoughts. This was lore the Mage had not dared to perform. The last mage had been too much of a coward to sleep. His dreams had been filled with fears, driven by his guilt and corruption so that when he slept, he had surrounded himself with the armies of his enemies and trapped himself in his own despair. The Archbishop was cut from better cloth.

He stood and turned to see what he knew would be there. For a moment he was proud of them. Then he gave thanks to God and asked for forgiveness for his moment of misplaced vanity. With every dream he added to the host of the Lord's vengeance.

They filled the room and were identical in their black chain mail and hauberks, each bearing the silver sword cross of the Order of St Collen. He did not know why he had chosen the heads of wolves for them. The idea had come seemingly unbidden, perhaps a surfacing memory of an image, a precursor to the tormentors which would scourge their souls in the afterlife. After all, that was where these soldiers of Christ would send their enemies.

He looked at the creatures, freshly birthed from his dreams, gripping two headed axes in gauntlets of steel. Their jaws hung open, showing red tongues and sharp teeth. These were the hounds of corruption and they would seek it out and destroy it wherever he sent them.

11

IT WAS A wet fog and it clung to the stone pier and made the decks of the ship slippery. Lord Giles steadied himself with one gloved hand as the ship lifted up and down, the water slopping between the hull and the pier. He could not wait to be on land, but he would see his men off the ship before he went himself. Silver was the first, his beard matted from the fog. Captain Benedict came up beside him. He tilted his head at the delf crew who made no attempt to hide their staring as the men walked their restless horses down the gangplank.

"They'll tell others where we've gone."

"Good. Let them see we be here. Let them watch us take the road."

He looked around at the few indolent locals sitting around the harbour. It was much quieter than Beretska because it only served shipping from Unama. "The locals will anyway. We will let them – " He paused as a thickset delf in a long, leather jacket crossed the deck towards him.

"You'll be happy to be rid of your troublesome cargo, eh Master?" Giles said to him.

"I think you will be happy to be rid of this ship. Your brave men do not like the sea."

"We are merely unused to it. I think they were concerned for their horses. Horses need exercise after all."

"They will have that. It is nearly a day's ride to Utimaak, but you will soon be clear of the fog. It usually stays on the coast and rolls away by midday. Sometimes though it blows right inland all the way to the escarpment." He raised his eyes to the mast. "Look now, the sails feel the wind before we do. We will soon catch it and leave you."

"I be sorry there was no cargo for you to take back."

"Are you sure you will not come back with us now? This is your last chance to come with us. There may not be another ship for weeks prepared to take you."

"I be touched by your concern. Don't worry about us, Master. We will take our chances."

"Keep a watch out for the light." He pointed to a tall, thin tower with a ladder of pegs winding around it which stood proud of the surrounding warehouses. "That would be lit when a ship is moored. It will tell you if a ship be in. They light them all the way inland to Utimaak, but with no cargo to trade today, I do not believe they will light it."

"No indeed," Giles said.

Giles did not like the look in the Master's eye. It bespoke of a mind thinking in another direction to the words.

"But of course it would be sensible to light it if you thought there were natives here with a cargo ready to ship."

"No, no. They are not expecting us. We could wait for nothing. We are best catching the offshore wind and riding it back north."

"You know best, Master. My thanks for bringing us safely to harbour, but I see we be the last aboard. I look forward to seeing you again soon."

The trooper captain caught his eye, but Lord Giles ignored him and walked over to the gangplank. Without looking back, he descended to the quay, took the reins of his horse from the man who was holding them out to him, climbed up and turned to Benedict who had just mounted next to him.

"Lead on, captain." He raised his voice a little. "To the sights of Naadu!"

The men turned in behind, their long brown coats hanging down across the backs of the horses. Then two by two the cavalcade rode into the fog. The master watched them go until he could no longer hear the hooves, then he turned to the rest of the crew.

"Make her ready. We sail inside the hour."

The master had been right. It took very little time to leave the fog behind. The riders emerged from it quite suddenly into a wide flat waste of sand dotted with the occasional low clump of rough plant.

The plain rose gradually until it came to a rocky range which ran parallel to the coast some distance inland. The road led towards it.

The company halted. Silver rode up beside Lord Giles.

"The devil said Utimaak was along this road, in those mountains, Silver. Are you sure that be not where we should be going?"

"My dreams tell me to go south, my lord."

Lord Giles looked south along the wall of fog which billowed down the coast as far as they could see.

"That does not seem to be a wise direction to take."

"Have faith, my lord. There be men in the south. Even if you don't have faith, believe the evidence of your eyes that the Lord has given unto you!"

Lord Giles turned to the captain.

"How much water do we have?"

"If we be sparing, a few days. The devils told me the coast be not hot and there be streams which run down from the ranges. My lord, we know there be water at the harbour. We will turn around when we be half way through our water if we've found no more. Don't worry. The men be with you."

Giles nodded. "Then we ride south."

As he spoke, a wind rolled down from the ranges across the coastal plain. The fogbank stirred and began to visibly shift back towards the sea.

"Ride fast. We must be out of sight by the time the fog reaches the sea. We musn't risk those devils seeing us. I want no one to follow us."

With a kick of his heels Lord Giles was off. His men followed, their coats flowing behind them.

None of them had ever seen a land so barren. To their right, the waves crashed interminably on the shore. They were not used to the sea and for many of them it was a source of endless fascination, a moving world without any end which kept coming and coming. In the mornings it had disappeared in the wall of fog which rolled in overnight. They took care to camp far from its damp chill, but it provided one benefit. The rocks of the coast would become soaked with the wet and early in the morning, puddles would form at their bases. Where these were deep enough, the men refilled their skins and bottles.

Their path was not a straight one. Sometimes the coast crept in towards them, sometimes they had to make their way inland or towards the sea to avoid ground that was too stony for the horses, or when one of the dry gulches that came down from the mountains proved too steep to take the horses into. Then they would work their way up it or down it until they found a place suitable to cross.

After three days, as the men prepared the evening meal, Giles, the captain and Silver held a conference.

"How much further must we travel, do you think?" Giles asked.

"It will be there in sooth," said Silver.

The captain ignored him.

"It will be many days hard riding this way, however far it be. There must be a road."

"One would hope, but what makes you so sure?" asked Giles.

"Naadu trades with the south. Many days away. I got that much from the devils on the ship. They didn't seem to know how many days, or didn't want to tell me. Where there be regular trade, there be roads."

"Perhaps they trade by ship."

The captain shrugged.

"Maybe. But the master said this was a shipwreck coast. I would put a road over there, hard up to the mountains away from that fog, away from this God forsaken land."

"Very well. In the morning you will send two men to scout the land and report back to us what they find." He turned to Silver. "I don't suppose your dreams gave us any more precise instructions?"

"The city be in the clouds, my lord."

"Of course. Which would seem to suggest we be going the wrong way and should really be going straight up in the air. No, I think seeking a road will be best. We shall continue along the coast until they meet up with us again."

The scouts rode off in the morning, while the others continued. In the evening the horsemen met the scouts who were on a rising hillock waiting for them. They brought news.

"There be a road, my lord. It be even and wide enough for wagons, but we saw no one. We made good speed on it. It be why we were here before you."

The road was as good as the scouts had suggested and their speed doubled. They found water in streams which trickled off the mountains and lost themselves in the dust. Each day they rode in silence and the weather became warmer the further south they went. They broke the monotony with hunting the small rodents which ran amongst the rocks at the base of the mountains.

It was around midday on the eighth day from the harbour that the captain raised a hand and the horsemen stopped. He pointed into the shimmering distance at a dark, rippling shape. They were no longer alone on the road.

"I would suggest caution, my lord," said the captain.

"Mmm," Lord Giles replied, but said nothing more as he sat in thought. The captain watched him.

"We should leave the road now and watch them pass."

"They will already have seen us as we've seen them. Let's continue. We be but strangers on the road and they will have news."

And so they continued, the shape separating out into many as they came closer to each other. Gradually the shapes resolved into horses and men and a larger, shaggy haired beast with a sad face which the men did not recognise. These were loaded with goods wrapped in cloth.

"Devils," muttered the captain to Giles as he looked at figures escorting the caravan. "Devils from a deeper part of hell."

The delf had skin of a deep bronze and they wore their black hair tied and knotted on top of their heads. They eyed Lord Giles's party with sullen curiosity until one rode up from the rear. He had a fleshy face and wore a loose hooded coat of faded brown.

"My lords," he said and touched his hand briefly to his forehead. He cast a glance over them all and his gaze swiftly found Lord Giles. "I hope you travel well. I am Merrimis of Utimaak."

"I be Lord Giles of Melion."

The delf touched his forehead once more.

"Bright day to you. It is midday and we are met. Let us honour the high sun and eat together."

"You be kind, but we have little to share. Only some meat and dry herbs."

"Then today the rain falls on you because we have bread and oil and spices and fruit of the forest which will taste of your home."

He paused and cocked his head. "But you said Melion. I do not know this place. Is it far to the south of Linana Pivaki?"

"Far. But I gratefully accept your offer."

Merrimis made a show of looking around, then gestured to the side of the road.

"Let us eat here." He turned and clicked his fingers. The delf began to jog about and move the animals off the road. Then they unpacked long sticks bundled with a kind of brown material from the sides of the pack animals. Soon these were erected into tents with open sides and supported at four corners with poles.

The delf unwrapped parcels of food and laid them out on blankets in the shade of the shelters.

"He does not seem surprised that we be men," said Benedict.

"Indeed. Offer them our meat," Giles said to the captain who took some of the rodent to Merrimis. He touched his forehead, flicked his eyebrows up and smiled broadly.

"You are kind, but please keep this for tomorrow. You still have a little way to go after all. Please sit with us and eat your fill. We have plenty."

Some of Giles's men were slow to eat. They looked at the food with suspicion. Silver refused to touch it, but Giles and the captain made a point of eating it as if they did so every day. The meat was dry and spiced and the vegetables were pickled. Platters of nuts were passed around and the delf took handfuls. Some of the men followed suit.

The two groups ate in silence, the men sometimes looking curiously at their hosts. Merrimis watched Silver for a while, then turned to Giles.

"This man is not eating, but he is very thin. You should make sure you feed him."

Giles cast a casual look at Silver.

"My apologies. My friend eats little at the best of times."

"It does not matter. I will not force him to eat. In the desert it pays to be able to eat less."

When they had finished eating, the delf dug their fingers into the dust and rubbed their hands together as if washing them with the sand. Two of them collected the platters of nuts and the trays of meat and pickles. Then all stood.

"Lord Giles, I am a trader, so I could not help but notice your fine horses. I do not know their breed. Would you trade some with me? I am sure I will have something that would interest you."

"We don't trade our horses. We have a long way to ride."

"Perhaps you could learn to ride our doka," Merrimis replied, gesturing towards their beasts of burden.

"You don't seem to like riding them yourselves," the captain said flatly. Giles shot him a rapid glance, but Merrimis smiled.

"It is true they are not the fastest ride, but they travel long and carry much more than a horse. It is no matter."

"How long are you out from where you began?" Giles asked.

"From Linana? This is our third day. You will be there tomorrow on your horses. Do you not know the road?"

"We don't travel it often."

"No. You do not look like merchants. We must be on our way." He turned and whistled to his crew who began to round up the caravan from its grazing. "Lord Giles, it was a pleasure to meet you on the road. I wish you safe travel."

"The same to you."

The delf touched his forehead and backed away a few steps, then turned and jumped onto his horse. The soldiers watched the horses and doka amble past them, then they too pulled themselves up onto their saddles.

"One more day and we will be in Linana," the captain said. "Where do you suppose that is?"

"Tomorrow will tell us."

They rode on and as the afternoon passed, they found the road and the rocky hills beside them bent towards the sea. They realised they were now travelling westwards from the line of the coast they had followed before. The way began to climb and they could see the long line of breakers leading off to the south. At the same time, the air began to grow damp again as they realised they were entering the edges of the fog bank. The road was rising steadily now, but it was still of a good condition. In places the pale yellowish rock had clearly been cut away to make the way straight and wide enough.

It bent back on itself as it climbed and they found themselves fully in the fog. They donned their coats as protection from the damp which draped itself around them.

In the dusk, they found a flat area of rock off from the road on the elbow of a bend. Black marks on the ground and scattered piles of round stones indicated that they were not the first to have rested there. They made themselves as comfortable as they could and went to sleep.

Silver woke suddenly with his beard glistening with droplets of water. The fog was still around them and muffled all sound. His dream was still with him.

"I have dreamed!" he said.

The soldiers stirred themselves, scowling at Silver for the sudden awakening and cursing at the wet in which they found themselves.

"What did you dream, Silver?" Giles asked, rather crossly. He was beginning to be irritated by this bearded wretch.

"It was the Archbishop. He came to me. He said he was close. He said the way between the worlds be thin. He thinks there be Christian men here. He was reaching out a hand to me. He said I could almost pull him through."

The captain looked at him, expecting something more, but Silver appeared to have finished. He stifled a frown and stood up, shaking his coat and beating at it to remove some of the fog which had condensed on it.

They broke camp quickly and were soon on their way. The road continued to rise through the fog. It was disconcerting to be unable to see the way ahead and the path behind vanished into the greywhite. There were more bushes here and low trees grew out of the rocks, encouraged by the moisture until the vegetation was thick and green. A few of the men tried to talk but their voices sounded unusually loud in the thick silence, so they stopped and rode without speaking.

The air quality changed quickly. The fog thinned and blue sky could be seen through it. Another turn of the road and they were above the fog. They marvelled at the ruffled ocean of white just below them which drowned the land. Away to the south and west, the chain of hills broke away from it. Now they could see that what they had taken for hills as they rode at their feet was actually the base of an escarpment. It marked a break in the land which became green as it turned inland, but further north it turned into scrub and then desert.

Ahead of them, the road rose more gently. They came to a small grassy plateau where they stopped for a while and let the horses rest. Its edges dropped back into the cloud. Ahead, the mountain continued to climb, but thick forest covered its slopes, separating the grassy plateau from the higher reaches.

As they waited for the grazing horses, with only an occasional whinny to break the peace, one of the men pointed. Across the road towards the trees was a gateway, the doors of which stood open. Squat stone towers emerged from the rocks around them on either side. There was no sign of life.

Lord Giles turned to Silver.

"Was this in your dream?"

Silver shook his head.

"Let's go," he said.

They remounted and went through the gate. The quality of the stonework was good. The gates were old, but well maintained. The road continued up a narrow cutting into which the gate had been strategically placed, then it opened out so that forest was on either side. The trees were thick with shiny leaves and the undergrowth was lush.

Now they rode as if expecting to meet someone. They would glance around casually, each hoping not to look as though he were nervous, but each one apprehensive. The road continued to curl up the hill in long bends which prevented them from seeing further than a couple of hundred paces ahead at any time. It was becoming less steep, that much was clear.

By midday the forest had changed and grown more stunted. Rocks and boulders began to emerge from amongst the foliage. High white cloud covered the blue sky, scattered here and there with lower grey scraps. In the mid-afternoon the men of Melion came out of the trees.

Before them was gently sloping grassland dotted with dark grey rock. It sloped up to a plateau of the same rock which was completely crowned by a city wall dotted by regularly spaced towers. Inside the walls, they could see a tower which rose taller than the others. Spreading from the top bloomed a gleaming bronze flower, open to the sky, open to the light.

The horsemen stopped below the city. Lord Giles heaved a deep sigh and turned to the captain, exchanging a look with him. Then he looked behind him for Silver.

"Your dreams lie to you, Silver. This be a city in the clouds, but those look like devil towers to me."

Silver shook his head silently. His mouth moved. This could not be. His dreams had led him this far.

"But my dreams told me there would be a city..." His voice tailed off. "Here be that city. Here be that city."

He looked up at the sky.

"Why did you bring us here, oh Lord?"

"We followed a road, Silver." Giles spoke scathingly. "There be always something at the end of a road. And in the world of devils we should have realised."

He closed his eyes and shook his head. Fury burned in the eyes of the captain and there were mutterings from the men.

"Surely we do not go in?" said Benedict. In reply, Lord Giles lifted his eyebrows in resignation.

Then the city gates opened. A line of riders in shining breastplates rode out. The men shifted uneasily on their saddles, their mounts stepping back and to the side, feeling the uncertainty of the men. The riders formed a line in front of the gates. Every other one held a lance from which a pennant fluttered.

"My lord!" came a hiss from behind.

All the men turned. There were figures in the trees on both sides. Each was pointing either a crossbow or a long-arm at Giles's troopers.

12

QATIKO MASTER HAD said it would be a week's sailing if the weather was with them. From the moment the ship left the protected waters of Beretska harbour, this started to sound like a very long time. Neither Rodon, Berwick nor Raul had been to sea before.

Firstly, there was the land pulling away from them to become a thinner line against the sky before disappearing altogether. Then there was the constant rolling of the deck beneath their feet. The wide horizon and huge sky was both beautiful and unsettling.

They spent their first day learning their way around the ship, apologising for being in the way and watching the arcane mysteries of sailing as the crew heaved on ropes, furled and unfurled sails and went about their business.

The ship creaked as they sat around the cramped cabin Qatiko had let them use. There was freight stored at one end of it and they had hung their bags and coats on this. Previously, their silences had been filled with riding or eating. Now they were alone in a small room, Berwick felt uncomfortable with silence even if neither Rodon nor Raul appeared to feel the same way.

"It be good to see you Raul, you know. And to see you so happy with Esella. I did not really know her," he said on their first evening as they sat down to a meal of cold chicken they had bought in Beretska.

Raul merely grunted in reply.

"How long have you been together?"

Raul shifted in his seat and Berwick wondered if he was prying. He realised he had not learned much about whether delf engaged in this sort of conversation.

"We were very slow," Raul said, not lifting his eyes from the table. "I did not make it easy. It had been a while since I stayed in one place very long."

"All the same," said Berwick, "it be good to see a man settle down."

"A man, maybe," said Raul.

"Sorry, I mean a delf. I mean anyone." He cursed himself for making such a blunder when he knew how sensitive Raul was. "My family has a farm. It will go to my older brother. That be why I joined the regiment. But one day I would like to farm too."

"Why?" asked Raul.

Berwick was about to answer when he realised that he was not sure what he was going to say. He smiled at his own pause.

"It be what I know. It be what I've always thought I would do, I suppose."

"It is not what I was brought up knowing, although I spent some time on a farm when I was a lad, after my father was killed by the Order."

Once more, Berwick was lost for words. Rodon was not.

"I be sorry about that. How did it happen?"

Raul fixed Rodon with his eyes from under his brows.

"The raid on northern Metsakant. He was a light keeper. I was away and when I returned, he was gone. I never even said goodbye."

Rodon looked down, then back at Raul.

"I be truly sorry, Raul. I cannot undo the past, but I can wish it undone."

"This is no great peace," he replied. "You ironheads forced a delf to bring you here all those years ago, then a delf saves you from annihilation. Why he did that I do not know. And your people are not grateful. No one likes to be saved by those they hate."

Raul shrugged and went back to his dinner. Then he suddenly lifted his eyes to them.

"If it had been any other men but the two of you, I would never have come."

"Why do you say that?" Rodon asked.

"I am surprised you need to ask. Look at why you came to me. There may be peace between our peoples, but it is a sullen peace. I think the people of Outreterre were bullied into it."

"No," said Berwick. "They be grateful for the peace. They welcome what Unama has to offer. Collenium be the richer for it. It be a new world."

Raul scoffed.

"I have been to your Collenium. I have walked down your streets. I have taken those looks of disgust and scorn and hatred, been barged into the gutter. I have been ignored. This is your new world, your harmony is it?"

"These things take time," Rodon said. "They have lived for hundreds of years thinking the delf were something they should fear."

"I have given it time."

Raul looked away again, then stood up, paused for a moment as if there was something else he might say, then, taking his coat from the boxes, walked out of the cabin.

Rodon and Berwick looked at each other.

"He be right," said Rodon.

"I know. But it does need time. It needs a new generation. We just have to buy that time. It could so easily fall back into war."

13

THE OUTCROP LOOMED against the darkening blue sky. Almost all colour had been sucked from the rock by the sun setting behind it across the grey gravel plain. A gust of wind flurried through the camp out of nowhere, scattering dust and shifting the tent flaps so that they scratched at the canvas.

The man pulled his collar up further and shifted himself a little closer to the fire. The firelight accentuated the wrinkles around his clear blue eyes. The puoli on the other side looked past the man gazing into the flames. The pack of cobs had been sat silently around their fire, but they had stirred. He saw what they had seen.

"Hugh," he said to draw the other's attention.

The man looked up, caught his eyes and turned to see what he was looking at. Then he stood and turned to face the figure who was walking towards the tent as the last of the sun burned the tops of the rocky horizon. He wore a long ragged coat which was open at the front showing a tunic made of hide still bearing its original owner's matted hair.

"Welcome to our fire, shaman," said the man. He could see the cobs still watching. He grunted at them and they turned back to their fire.

The newcomer walked with determination, as if against a strong wind, and he stopped suddenly between the two tents and the fire. The delf's face was lit by the flames. It was thin and bearded and his eyes glowed fiercely. He bobbed his head a few times and pursed his lips. He looked only at the fire. It was a few moments before he spoke.

"The fire does welcome me."

Without further invitation he came nearer, dropping onto crossed legs to form a triangle with Grafton and the puoli.

"My name is Hugh Grafton," said the man. "This is Sam Atana. We come from Linana Pivaki."

The shaman looked up suddenly and stared at each of them in turn. Grafton was bearded, wiry and beginning to turn grey. The puoli was also bearded, but his hair was cropped so short, his scalp gleamed through the stubble of it.

The shaman nodded his head a few times before returning his gaze to the flames. Atana looked across at Grafton and raised an eyebrow.

"My wife's grandfather was said to be a shaman," Grafton ventured.

The shaman spat into the flames. It was unclear whether this was supposed to be an answer.

"Two alone in the desert with a herd of cobs," he said at last. Atana frowned. Grafton shook his head at him.

"We are philosophers. The cobs are my helpers."

The shaman coughed, then spat again.

"The stars give you answers," he said.

"That is why we are here. For the silence and the light."

"I am here for your splinter of the sun."

Grafton smiled at the image for his fire.

They had left the shaman sleeping in the open by the fire. He was gone in the morning.

"He was mad," said Atana as he and Grafton followed the cobs over to the rock carrying a wooden case between them. "He didn't make sense."

Grafton smiled. "I think you would forget how to make conversation if you lived on your own in the desert."

"Why do they do it?"

"So they can be alone when they want to be."

"No wonder the Naadu left the light alone if it is only the mooncast who keep it."

"I want to talk to him. They know things."

"He didn't look like he knew where his arse was."

"I think you're being unkind, Sam."

"I think you need to make your engine work today or I will die of boredom. And this place still makes me nervous."

"We're off the Naadu trade routes here. This is simply the middle of nowhere."

"If you spent as much time in the real world as you did in your books and inside your own head, you would know that nowhere in the deep desert is off Naadu trade routes."

"Well. We are harming no one."

They had reached the rock and a sheltered spot where there was a little bay in the steep rising walls of the outcrop. The cobs were removing a canvas sheet from a large object. It slid off to reveal a gleaming machine. It was long and mounted on a pivot which enabled it to swing from a vertical to a horizontal position. It was parallel with the ground. The end nearest to them was polished brass and contained a bulbous chamber which narrowed and entered a series of three cones, each of which became progressively smaller until they reached a long tube which came to a fine point at the end. Beside it was a great wheel which linked to the heavy, bulbous chamber by a set of cogs. It all sat on a sturdy chassis mounted on large, ridged wheels which were locked into position by brakes.

"The cobs are losing their enthusiasm too," Sam said.

Grafton inspected the machine, blowing imaginary dust off it and rubbing his fingers on slight scratches. He made some adjustments to a series of circular handles along the length of the tube, then prised open the lid of the wooden case which he and Atana had put down. He pulled out a couple of light sponges and placed them in the brass chamber.

"Let's try it again."

Then he turned a wheel on the pivot and rotated the device so that it was towards the base of the rock.

That evening they were by the fire once more when Atana looked up.

"Hugh, your shaman's back. He clearly enjoyed your company."

Grafton smiled. "It isn't often you come across intellectuals in the desert."

"Welcome to our splinter of the sun," said Grafton. The shaman cocked his head and looked at him.

"Your grandfather was shaman."

"My wife's grandfather. I never met him."

"The sun met him."

"The sun meets everybody."

The shaman made a noise in response which suggested everybody knew that already. Then he looked into the fire. Grafton did too. The branches and fire looked like a vision of Hell from the cathedral. All it lacked were demons and the damned.

Then a little sphere of flame lifted off from the top of the fire. It was the size of a thumbnail. It hovered above the flames, unaffected by the rising hot air. Then abruptly it peeled back on itself and exploded silently, small flames twisting away from the centre and fading instantly into nothing. The puoli and the man both looked at the delf who was still staring into the fiery caverns. The shaman spat into the flame, but said nothing. He continued to be quiet for some minutes until Grafton and Atana began to be uncomfortable. Atana grinned at Grafton. Conversation felt difficult now that they had this silent third party. Atana decided to challenge the silence.

"Shaman," he said, "why do you live in the desert?"

The shaman did not respond. Atana wondered if he had heard him.

"You live in a city if little lights."

Atana let the answer hang while he tried to unravel it. Grafton watched him with a faint smile.

"Your lights are little too," Atana said, gesturing at the stars.

"Your brain is little," the shaman responded in a matter of fact tone.

Grafton chuckled.

The silence drew on once more.

The shaman turned abruptly to Grafton.

"Here you can make light out of the darkness."

"Really?" Grafton asked.

The shaman shrugged.

"We are all lights in the dark," he said.

Grafton and the shaman were sitting deep inside the rock. Grafton had put out his lantern and wedged it under his leg so he could find it again.

"Sit. Say nothing," the shaman said. "Keep your eyes open."

And so they sat in silence in the darkness.

Minutes passed and stretched. Grafton felt as though his eyes were falling out of his head and being pulled into the impenetrable black.

"What can you see?" the shaman asked eventually.

"Nothing."

The shaman grunted.

"Look again."

Grafton searched the darkness.

"Still nothing."

The shaman grunted once more.

Thoughts rose and fell in Grafton's mind. Some of them passed by, others circled. Some thoughts stayed until he realised they had been moved on by others coming up behind.

At times he became aware that he had not been thinking at all and with that, the realisation that he was thinking once more. Then the prowling thoughts would begin again.

Then he saw a spark.

"What did you see?"

"What makes you think I saw something?"

"You moved your head."

Had he made a noise?

"I did think I saw something. A point of light. Only for a moment."

Grafton was becoming used to the shaman grunting at him, but he could not tell if the noise that greeted his comment was disgust or satisfaction. He became aware from the sounds next to him that the shaman was moving. Standing up perhaps.

"Dinner will be good," the shaman said.

"Are we leaving?" Grafton asked.

All the reply he had was the shaman's steps moving off the way they had come in. There was no light. He looked around to check, but the shaman was walking into darkness. He pulled out a tinder box from his jacket and lit his lantern. The cave revealed itself, leaping into view as if created at that instant. The shaman had already disappeared around a bend in the tunnel. Grafton stood and caught up with him.

"How could you tell where you were going?"

"I have been here before. I hold the light in my head."

Grafton and the shaman continued their visits for the next few days. He began to look forward to it after working with the needle. They had been visiting the cave for a week when he felt the shaman behind instead of beside him. He had not heard him move and he almost jumped when the shaman whispered in his ear.

"Hold the light inside your head. Remember light."

He said it like a whisper and the sound of it rumbled and rolled into Grafton's ear like a distant rockfall.

The flashes came suddenly. There were great bursts of them exploding silently around him. They emerged quickly, dim at first, but some of them became quite bright. There were dots. He made a puzzled noise. He tried to look at them, but they evaded him, always moving away from his searching eyes. He thought he saw curves and zig-zags.

"Now you see," said the shaman.

Grafton was spellbound. There was light in the dark although it did not illuminate the cave.

"Do you see what I see?" Grafton breathed.

"Light from the darkness," came the reply.

Even as the shaman dragged him back to the light, the flashes kept coming, only stopping as the daylight flew into the cave.

"What was that?" Grafton asked the shaman.

By now, Grafton was used to the shaman's delayed responses. They walked back out together and it was only as Grafton broke away to join Atana who was sitting by the fire stirring a pot squinting at his friend from under his eyebrows that the shaman finally replied.

"Light from the mind."

Grafton knew that was all the explanation he was going to receive.

Inspired by that first success, Grafton followed the shaman into the cave every time he went. The shaman did not object. Perhaps he even welcomed Grafton's company. The first time, the shaman had said "Want more." It had been unclear whether it was a question or to whom it applied.

Each time now, Grafton waited for the splashes of colour, the dots which danced and flashed at him. Then one time, it was different. He felt the shaman's thin rough hand touch his then grasp it urgently. His first reaction was to pull away, but the delf held on. And then he saw something in front of them.

There was a movement in the darkness, a stirring. It was turning. Somehow the darkness had a form and texture; there were lights. All around him now, he realised, the darkness was glittering and the glittering was swirling around him in a huge, sweeping circular motion. He could no longer feel the rock underneath him. He felt as though he were floating above some immense glittering whirlpool.

The lights were spiralling away from them now and all around him. Grafton realised he was inside the spiral. They were like stars, they were immeasurably far away. He felt very small and alone. Suddenly he felt very afraid. He wanted to be away from there, to hide in some small, dark box where he could feel the sides. He felt as though he were falling into an empty, infinite vastness.

Without any warning, it all faded. He realised there were no longer the spots of colour and that he was aware of the rock once more. The shaman let go of his hand.

For a few minutes they sat in silence. Grafton was shaken. He was trying to understand what had happened. He wondered if the shaman would explain, if the shaman even knew, but the shaman said nothing. Instead he could hear the delf's slow, deep breathing. Perhaps he was asleep.

"What was that?" Grafton asked. His words sounding strangely loud in the stillness.

Still the breathing.

"Shaman, what was that?" he asked again.

"Pretty," the shaman replied.

Grafton waited for him to say more.

"It was the dance of the cosmos," the shaman said after a long pause.

"But..." Grafton did not know what he was thinking. He was trying to understand. "Were we *there*?"

The shaman laughed.

"You *live* in the cosmos!"

"Yes, but were we *out* in it? How could we see it?"

"I used to go to the sea," the delf replied. "I would walk into it up to my waist. To wash. Or to stand. On the clear days, it never ended. I tried to understand all that water. It was too much."

He felt the delf's arm around his shoulders, smelt more strongly the animal smell of him.

"But now I have been out there. I know the sea is so small."

The shaman said nothing else. The arm lifted from his shoulders and he heard the shaman stand. Grafton did not light his lantern any more. He simply reached for the shaman's robe and held onto it, feeling his way in the dark until the glow of morning blinded them.

"What happened to you?" Sam asked as they emerged from the cave, Grafton still squinting in the dim morning light. Grafton shook his head and walked away from the camp along the edge of the rock.

Neither noticed the riders until they were almost in their camp. They had come around the side of the rock. There were about a dozen of them in pale, dusty clothes. Their leader swung himself down from the saddle with showy ease.

"A bright day to you," he said, bowing. "I am Eudinasis. I bring you greetings and an invitation from the Tafa Naadu to visit her in Utimaak."

"A bright day to you," Grafton replied. "I am sorry but we are engaged on important studies of natural philosophy which I would rather not interrupt. We would be happy to accept the Tafa Naadu's invitation on another occasion."

The leader of the riders smiled and bowed again.

"This is not an invitation." He gestured to the other delf. "These fellows can help you to pack up your camp."

14

MCCLURE COULD WATCH the sea all day. He did not care what mood it was in, it always fascinated him. Today it basked glittering in the sun. It lay, wide and blue across the bay which filled his view below the terrace café. He was sat right by the stone parapet, his iced tea and a closed paperback beside him on the table. It was a dog-eared copy of *The Cruel Sea* which he had picked up in a second hand bookshop. One of a surprising number in English. A faded blue cotton cap slouched on his head and tufts of white hair poked out above his ears. His grey-blue eyes squinted into the mid-afternoon glare, the lines around his face creasing upwards although his skin had grown indifferent to the effects of heat, cold, rain or wind.

He turned to watch someone who was coming up the hill. The lad was walking slowly, but steadily. He wore a brimmed felt hat and a backpack which sat easily on his shoulders. He walked as though the pack were not there. The cafe was at the crest of the hill and as he came level with it, he turned to look at the view, his hands on his hips, savouring the chance to rest and take it in at the same time.

The older man looked at the backpack and the lanky body under it. It was not overly large compared to many backpackers he had seen, but it looked well used. Then the lad turned towards the cafe and noticed the man. He grinned. It was a wide, easy smile.

"*Buenas tardes*," he said.

"Afternoon," said the man.

"Afternoon," the lad replied. "Am I that obvious?"

"Obvious enough."

"Great view isn't it? Worth the walk up."

"It's even better with a drink in the shade," said the man. "Come and have a seat."

The lad paused for a moment.

"Thanks. I will."

He moved with a confidence which belied his years. He dropped his pack beside the table and took a seat opposite the man.

"Phew, sorry. A bit sweaty," he said.

The man smiled.

"What would you like to drink?"

"Water would do for a start."

"And then what?"

He hesitated. "What's that?"

"Iced tea."

"Sounds good."

The man called over a passing waiter and gave him the order in Spanish.

"That sounded good," the lad said.

"I can sound good in quite a few languages," the man smiled, "if I pick what I'm going to say carefully."

"I can say hello, goodbye, please and thank you and count in several," the lad grinned back.

"Being able to be polite is very important, I always think."

"True. So before I'm too rude, I'd better introduce myself, seeing as you've just ordered me a drink." He stuck out his hand. "Charlie Denham," he said.

"George McClure," said the older man. "Are you inter-railing?"

"No, hitching. You meet more interesting people," Charlie said, before adding with a grin. "And it's cheaper of course."

"Did you hitch all the way down here?"

"I did. Well, I cheated to start with. Got a lift with some friends from home south of Paris, then did the rest in little hops. I walked over the Pyrenees. It was amazing."

"Really? That must have been something."

"Damn near killed me. Toughest walk I've ever done in my life."

It always amused McClure when young people talked about their lives as if they were long.

"How long are you away for?"

"All summer. Maybe longer. I've been trying to decide whether to go to uni this year or next. Dad says I should leave it a year. He's probably right."

"Dads often are."

"What about you?"

"Well I don't know how long I'll be away either. I've just retired you see."

"Cool. What were you doing before you retired?"

"A number of things, but most recently I was a priest. Still am. It doesn't stop you see."

"A priest?"

"Yes. I'm still human though."

"I don't mind," Charlie grinned. "You just don't look like a priest."

"What does a priest look like?"

"Hah! I don't know. A bit more…" he smiled again. "No, I'd better not go there. Ah, *gracias.*"

The iced tea and water had arrived and Charlie took advantage of the distraction. George waited until Charlie had had a long gulp of the water and a sip of the tea.

"If it helps, I wasn't always a priest."

"Really?"

"I was a sailor."

"Navy?"

"Merchant."

"Cool. Did you get about a bit?"

"Oh yes."

Charlie took another drink.

"I bet you've got some stories."

"A few. But you can see many places and still miss out on exploring the heart and soul of Man."

Charlie grinned and nodded.

"I suppose so, but I do a lot of thinking when I'm walking. What made you become a priest?"

"It's a long story."

The lad seemed to wait, as if hoping for the story, but George was not going to tell that story now.

"I remember the first time I came to Spain. It all seemed so foreign. Not like the Costa del Sol down the coast there."

"Yeah, I drove through it. Didn't appeal at all."

"I would have thought you would have enjoyed the nightlife and all the other young people," George said, but at the same time he did not believe his own words. Charlie did not seem to be the kind of lad who would go for that. You don't hitch your way down two countries to dance with other English people in a club.

"Not my thing really. I enjoy the road. Dad and me have been going on trips for years. Mum too sometimes, but usually just Dad."

"Why's he not with you now?"

"Well he couldn't spare the whole summer for a start. Besides, he said it was time I went out on my own."

"And how are you finding it?"

"A bit lonely at times. But I also like being on my own. I think it would just be nice to whistle up a few mates when I wanted some company. You know, to share the view with."

George smiled at him without speaking and took a sip of his own drink. Yes, it was good to have someone to share the view with. He felt jaded next to this lad who sat with his boots stretched out before him ready to take on the world, but invigorated too. A summer before him and a pack on his back. What glorious freedom.

Raul was prowling the deck when he came upon Berwick leaning over the gunwale staring at the sea.

"You spend much time here," said Raul.

"It fascinates me. It's so…" he fumbled for the words. "It's so big. It moves all the time. And to be honest it frightens me. I think if I keep an eye on it, it won't get me in the back."

"So why are you doing this? Why are you so keen on getting these men?"

Berwick glanced at Raul to see how seriously he meant the question.

"Because it's the right thing to do," he said. "I don't like what those men did. I don't like how they think."

"You used to think like that."

Berwick nodded. He was silent for a while. Below him, waves crested and vanished under others, slapped together and were subsumed into the ocean as if they had never been. "It's something I have to do. It's atonement."

"What do you have to atone for?" Raul said, scoffing. "You were just a kid. It is Rodon who needs to atone for what he has done. A lifetime of it."

"And he's trying to, but I can't speak for him." He paused again. Even Raul could tell there was more to come.

"I killed a delf once. In cold blood."

Raul stared at him.

"Richard had found him in Lord Lyell's garden. He was a garden
delf who had escaped. We thought he was dangerous because he
had been in the light. We thought he would be able to summon
demons. The Archbishop told us to take him out of sight. Out of
sight of Richard. And - " Berwick stared relentlessly at the sea. "I
stabbed him."

He could see it all. He could smell again the damp, cool
morning and see the dank corner near a lean-to containing firewood
where they had dragged the delf and killed him without any fuss
and with barely a second thought. The second thoughts came weeks
later when he had spent time with delf and Solimo in particular. He
had seen something more than devils with a hatred of humans.

"He looked at me when I did it. He was frightened and he did
not understand." He turned to Raul. Raul's face was impassive.
Berwick thought he had said too much. "So was I."

Raul inhaled deeply. Berwick saw he was gripping the side of the
ship. His whole body had become tense.

"Your Archbishop truly is not so holy as he would like to think,"
Raul said. "Why would he have you murder out of sight of Richard?
Because he knew it was murder, that is why."

"It was." He was shaking his head. "It was murder. I don't deny
it. But it was so easy. I was taught to think that delf wanted to kill
us, but now I don't want more to think like I did. It's so easy to
hate. We can't all go through what I did to change me."

He wanted Raul to understand. He realised that he needed Raul's
forgiveness.

"That's why I'm doing it. It's not going to change the world, but
hopefully, it'll help a little. Help your people and mine."

Raul was not looking at him any more.

"What about you, Raul? Why are you helping us? You don't look
like you believe the peace will last."

"I came because I could get the chance to kill more ironheads,"
Raul replied slowly. "I will grant you that much: I have not been
able to do that these last seven years."

15

ONE OF THE riders from in front of the gates came forward. He was escorted by a lancer on either side, their faces shaded by the brims on their helmets. Giles tried to look at a pennant, but they were all drooped down the lances in the still afternoon air. The three stopped.

"Who are you?" said the middle rider. It was abrupt, expecting an answer. Giles was unused to being spoken to in this way. Nevertheless he swallowed his pride.

"I be Lord Giles of Melion."

"Melion?"

Giles nodded in a small bow. "At your service."

"Throw down your weapons."

The captain cast a sideways glance, his cheeks twitching.

"Calm yourself," Giles muttered.

"I can as easily take weapons from dead bodies, but I would rather not kill the horses," said the rider.

Giles shrugged. Then he unhitched his sword and let it fall to the ground. He took his long-arm from its holster and dropped it beside his sword. Then he pulled the two pistols from his belt.

He sensed hesitation from his men.

"We cannot bow to these devils!" hissed Silver.

"There be no future in martyrdom," said Giles. "Put down your weapons. This be not our time to fight. Do it now."

The men did as they were told until the ground around the horses was littered with guns and swords.

"Ride forward," said the lead rider from the city.

The troopers did as they were instructed. As they did so, the line of riders curved down on either side to meet them, forming an alley and an escort towards the gates.

As they rode between them, Giles looked at the faces which looked back at him impassively. Skins varied in colour from a pale red to a sandy brown. From what he could see behind their helmets, their faces were fine boned in some cases and wider in others. Some were like no delf he had seen before, but they had travelled far. Who knew what other forms of devils existed in this world?

They rode towards the gate and the walls rose up at them.

"Dismount and move away from your horses," came the command in the now familiar voice. Slowly the troopers obeyed, taking their time out of a mixture of apprehension and rebellion.

"And now, welcome to Linana Pivaki."

They passed beneath the arched gateway and its thickset tower and emerged into a small walled courtyard. There were watchers on the walls. On the far side, on the left, was another gate. The riders corralled them towards and through it. They emerged into a street. They could see faces through windows, but it was otherwise deserted.

The leader of the city's riders dismounted. He gestured towards a blocky building next to the gate.

"Lord Giles of Melion, step inside." Then he looked at the men. "You will wait here."

Giles cast an unconcerned look back at his men, then went through the door as he was instructed. The leader followed him in, removing his helmet as he did so and tucking it under his arm. Two of the dismounted soldiers came in beside him and stood on either side of the door. Giles was aware of them, but did not turn around. The leader walked past him and stood behind a desk.

"Please sit," he said.

Giles tried not to stare. The person in front of him was blond and had tanned skin. He was a man. Silver had been right.

Giles sat, wondering what he would say. Up until this point, he realised, he had never really believed what Silver had been saying. He had always assumed there would be another explanation.

"Where is Melion?"

"Melion be in Outreterre," Giles responded quietly.

The man studied him.

"That would make you very unusual," he said at last.

"Indeed it would," said Giles and here he permitted himself a small smile.

"Can you prove it?"

"What proof would you accept? I have my ring."

The man held out his hand, but did so as if asking for the ring rather than ordering it to be handed over. Giles removed it from his finger, leaned forward and placed it in the man's open palm, carefully watching him as he did so. The man looked at it, then picked it up and studied it.

"The sign of the stag," he said, nodding. He handed it back. "I am Edward Clifford, captain in Wootton's Legion, the duty custodians of Linana Pivaki. If you are indeed who you say you are, I apologise for your welcome. We would always wonder at so large a group of armed men come to our doors, but times have been strange of late. Why are you come?"

"To find you. To find other men. We had thought ourselves alone in this world. Our histories tell us there was a parting and that some of the Order went over the sea. We never heard anything more and it has been assumed for many, indeed hundreds, of years that no one survived that voyage because no one came back. We heard rumours. I am an inquisitive man, so I decided to follow those rumours."

"You say no one came back, yet did anyone come to look for us?"

"I have. I cannot speak for my ancestors, but it be said there was no knowledge of seafaring in those that stayed behind." He tipped his head on one side. "Can you speak for yours?"

Clifford looked mildly surprised to be asked a question, then merely shrugged.

"They had reasons for leaving. There was a world to explore and a world to conquer. I always thought the lack of seafarers was an excuse for a lack of adventure. Why would they go back?"

Giles smiled. He did not want to divulge much until he knew more about Linana Pivaki.

"What about my men, captain? We have been travelling for many days and they be tired. Would you permit them somewhere to rest?"

Clifford stood.

"I am sorry. We shall see them accommodated. And then you will meet my father."

The room was shaped like an inverted, three-sided pyramid. Each wall was lined with stone benches which were half full of people on one side and nearly three quarters full on the other two.

A delf in a long white robe was sitting at the base of the pyramid. Her grey hair was short. She pointed to a fleshy man in a burgundy jacket.

"Senator Fitzwarren, you wished to raise a point about the Naadu?"

Fitzwarren stood, one hand clutching a sheaf of papers.

"Indeed I did. The leaders of my caravans are bringing me increasing reports of Naadu movements. They are coming further south, further east. They are encroaching on our territory and our trade routes."

Someone stood on the half full side. Her black hair was tied back behind her neck and she had her hands on her hips.

"The Naadu know the desert well," said the delf. "They go where our caravans dare not."

"Our caravans don't know the desert because they don't go there," Fitzwarren replied, irritated. "Standing idly by while others control the trade isn't what made Linana great as you will know from your history, Senator Koli."

"There were a number of things which made Linana great, Senator Fitzwarren," said a third senator standing up from his place in the third set of seats. "Its military power is only one of them."

"To what are you alluding, Senator Lake?"

"It was cooperation between delf and man."

Lake smiled and his pale brown skin and large honest eyes made his smile all the more annoying because it came from a face so perfect.

"Ah, but of course a puoli would say that!" said Fitzwarren. The lean man with short grey hair who was sat beside him put his hand lightly on Fitzwarren's arm and stood next to him.

"I think what Senator Fitzwarren is concerned about is that Naadu has no borders. They wander everywhere from the Fog Coast to the inland plains. If they continue to trespass on our trade routes, our trade and indeed our reputation will suffer. Really they should have been made a dominion years ago."

"Senator Clifford, long before your people came here, we were rubbing along very well," said Koli. "My cousin's cousin is a friend of the Tafa Naadu. It is through these connections that we are able to ply what you must admit is a very lucrative trade. Their goods come through us before they can continue further south."

Fitzwarren had been watching his friend, but at this point, he interjected.

"They have no choice. To avoid us would mean three times the journey to the southern markets. But if we owned their trade, it would be much more lucrative for us. You people are soft on your distant family connections."

The delf smiled.

"They have worked for thousands of years."

Clifford smiled too and signalled to Fitzwarren to sit.

"And the Republic of Linana Pivaki has worked better for hundreds of years since. This city would be little more than a collection of huts around a fort on a precipice were it not for the Republic. You, Senator Koli, enjoy luxury unheard of in your golden past. Look at the Naadu clans in their dusty towns and windblown tents. We could have so much more if we sent a legion or two across the desert and exerted a little more control. One clan at a time. The Tafa would understand. She knows that where there is competition, one side needs an edge."

"But Senator Clifford," said Lake, the puoli. "We could all be much happier if we cooperated more. You talk as if the clans are separate, but they work together closely benefitting from each one's strengths."

Clifford rolled his eyes.

"I would be much happier if they cooperated more, yes. Indeed, I would be much happier if you cooperated more."

"You would want me to vote that the senate sends an army into Naadu. But there are links between our peoples, even across the wastes."

"Then use those links so the Naadu see sense."

"You mean see your point of view," said the puoli senator. "Why do you not see ours? Why must we always see yours?"

Later, Clifford and Fitzwarren were standing outside the pyramid hall. They watched as a puoli and a delf walked past laughing.

"It is always the same," said Clifford. "The demi-delf are an upstart race."

"I've always said they should never have been given a place in the senate," the older man replied.

"Yes, Roger. We can agree on this all over again, but it doesn't change the facts. The demi-delf will vote with the delf. They're one and the same really. It makes a mockery of the republic when their collusion is so constant. We are a minority in our own republic."

Giles had said nothing about his conversation with Henry Clifford when he returned to his men, but he had smiled at them confidently. The men were led through the city on foot, still escorted by soldiers. They walked up paved streets. The buildings were made of the same yellowy rock as the mountain up which they had climbed. They were well made, many had shutters. Roof gardens merged with the plants which hung down or climbed up the walls. The streets were busy with people in loose clothing, open at the neck, often bare armed. The populace stopped and watched them as they rode by. There were both delf and human faces.

There were murmurings from amongst the men, but Silver lifted his head, closed his eyes and pressed his palms together.

"Thanks be to God," he said. "Forgive me my lack of faith. I hesitated but a moment!" He turned to Giles. "Will they help us?"

"It be too early to say."

When Clifford rode on ahead, Giles beckoned Benedict and Silver near him.

"His name be Edward Clifford. He be captain in a legion of custodians as he called them. There be certainly devils amongst them, but their leader be a man. There be something odd about this place."

Their route took them uphill towards a cluster of battlements which were strategically placed on a rock which rose higher than the rest of the city. It surrounded the nearest of what they could now see were three light towers.

Giles gestured to the imposing battlements.

"I must say, our cousins appear to have done very well for themselves."

Gates were opened. There were sentinels on the walls around them. Scrutinising their faces, there did seem to be both human and delf amongst them. The men were guided to a low building inside the citadel walls.

Clifford rode up to Giles.

"Lord Giles, if you would accompany me please. Your men will be safe and comfortable here."

"May I bring anyone with me?"

"You may," said Clifford.

Benedict had been watching the men in. He looked at Giles expectantly.

"Captain, you go with the men," said Giles. "Silver, come with me. Don't talk unless I tell you to."

Clifford took four of his guards and escorted Giles and Silver to a square building at the head of the wide courtyard in which they stood. They entered a great hall with timber beams and high windows through which light fell, illuminating three groupings of leather covered seats arranged in a triangle. Dust hung, twisting gently in the shafts of light. The room was empty of people and they passed through it to a staircase which wound up and emerged onto a wide stone balcony high above. The balcony appeared to skirt the entire building and gave views over the battlements and across the city.

They could see down the main roadway, along which they had walked, to the walls and the open ground before the trees began. Far below, they could see the fog bank poised in the distance for its nightly embrace with the land and a line of white surf on the coast.

Clifford led them around the side. To the southern end of the city they could see two great structures which rose higher than the other buildings. Clifford saw them looking.

"That is the warehouse district," he said. "Goods come in, goods go out. It makes it easier to combine caravans – and to charge duty – if we concentrate the storage of trade goods in one place."

They continued around and Giles and Silver saw that on the landward side, the west, the city sat level with the plain. Here the land was green and watered by two rivers. In the hazy afternoon distance they could make out a range of hills. The rivers joined not far from the city in the knot of a much smaller settlement.

Between it and the city was a reservoir, shining gold in the evening. It lay dammed up behind a high earthen rampart. A two tiered aqueduct led from one side of it to the south eastern corner of the city which, like the building on which they stood, rose higher than the rest of the plateau. The tamed river emerged in a low valley with wide flat banks which led into the city.

Immediately below them, the city sprawled across the mountain top, taking up all of the available space. Just outside the battlements of the citadel was a great cathedral, its twin towers rising higher than the light tower. It was a huge building, at least twice the size of St Collen's back in Collenium. Giles thought it strange to see them standing so close together. Silver leaned into Giles' ear.

"The house of the Lord cheek by jowl with a temple to Beelzebub, but see, the great cathedral rises higher!"

"Hold your tongue," Giles hissed, gripping Silver's wrist tightly. He sympathised though, it made him uncomfortable.

At least two thirds of the way across the city, a gorge cut a deep, wide gash from the sea, its rocky sides climbing steeply from the waves which churned inside it. The river which entered the city from the plain emerged from a tunnel to empty into the gorge in a waterfall.

Between them and the gorge was an area of grand structures, but the rest of the city was made up of lower buildings, many of them with rooftop gardens.

The two parts of the city were joined by two bridges thrown across narrowings of the gorge sides. They hung from ropes looped across the gap. On the left hand bridge, workers clambered around scaffolding making repairs.

The tallest of the three light towers stood between them and the gorge while a third stood on the far side, surrounded by further battlements. The shadows of the light towers fell across the city and that of the tallest jagged into the gorge and to the other side, stretching at that hour of the day even onto the trees which gathered on the edge of the plateau.

Already surveying this view, they found a man. He was clean shaven and had a line of grey hair around his bronzed scalp. He wore a long, loose shirt, belted at the waist, with wide sleeves which reached half way down his forearms. He watched them approaching and Giles saw intelligence in the man's eyes.

"My father, Henry Clifford, Senator of the Republic and Dominions," said the younger Clifford.

The older man extended an arm and smiled.

"Well, well. So the family finally comes to visit. My son tells me you are lord of Melion."

"In sooth. And this be Mr Silver."

The senator eyed Silver suspiciously. His hair and beard were unkempt and his clothes thin and fraying. For his part, Silver stared back with wild excitement, barely able to stop himself from speaking. Giles noticed the senator's suspicious glances.

"Do not be disturbed by my friend's appearance - " he began.

"He is a prophet," Edward Clifford interjected. His father looked at him curiously. "So say Lord Giles's men," Edward added.

Curse their loose mouths, Giles thought, but the older man was looking again at Silver.

"A prophet? And what is your message, prophet?"

"Retribution is at hand!" Silver exclaimed immediately without waiting for Giles's permission. "The Lord's wrath be on the heads of the corrupt. I be but a voice for he who comes after me." He suddenly leaned forward and grabbed the senator's forearm, staring into his startled eyes. "He comes out of Limbo. He will step out of our dreams and clasp you in his arms!"

"What do you say about dreams, prophet?" Henry Clifford said with a vehemence which surprised Giles. Edward too was looking intently at him. "What do you say about dreams?"

Silver was surprised and momentarily silenced, but then he spoke in a loud whisper.

"The Archbishop comes to me in my dreams. He told me to seek out the sons of the parting. In them lies our salvation from the corruption, from dallying with devils."

The Cliffords exchanged looks. Giles was thinking quickly. How could he regain control of this situation?

"I apologise. Mr Silver can be rather...intense..."

Henry Clifford relaxed and smiled.

"Never mind, Lord Giles. You must both come to my house for dinner. Edward, fetch Senator Fitzwarren."

They descended from the roof of the hall and made their way through the city. Their route took them past the foot of the second light tower.

"How did they build them so tall?" Giles asked, tipping his head back like a hood to see upwards.

"Oh yes, they are marvellously crafted," Clifford answered. The stonework was smooth and the tower grew out of a triangular block house at its base, narrowed towards the top, then bulged out again to accommodate the wide, bronze flower at the top.

"Why do you leave them standing?" Silver demanded. "They are pagan temples. They should be thrown down."

"Oh no," Clifford responded mildly. "They are important to the delf and have come to be important to us too." He held up his hand to Silver's open mouth which was about to speak once more, with a gentle smile. "Do not speak before the story is over, prophet. Once I have told it, you may make your judgement."

Silver's eyes narrowed, but he closed his mouth and shook his arm free of Giles' restraining hand.

16

CLIFFORD'S HOUSE WAS entered from the street. The front door gave onto an atrium which led to a quiet colonnaded courtyard containing a pool with fish. The main living area was upstairs and away from the noise of the street. At the back, large windows looked out over the gorge. On the opposite side, away to the right, the waterfall where the river ended rolled off the edge of the cliff, sending up spray and a cooling breeze. The last of the sun was shining on the tops of the falls and its golden light faded even as they were looking at it.

"Those bridges are a fine piece of engineering," said Lord Giles. "I do not understand how those ropes can take the weight."

"Oh it is quite safe. As you can see, we conduct regular repairs."

A fresh gust of cooler air came off the waterfall, bringing a freshness to the warm evening air.

For the first time, the guards left them, staying in the atrium. Giles and Silver sat down at one end of the large table with the elder and younger Clifford. An attendant came with cups and a jug of water, then clay goblets and a taller flask. Giles watched him and noticed Silver watching him too.

"Some vezi?" Henry Clifford asked.

Giles looked puzzled.

"It is a fine spirit. In the language of the mountains, it means water, but it is as far from water as you could care to find. It will put a fire in your belly and prepare it for food. Watch this."

Henry tipped a little of the vezi into one of the small glasses. Then he took a candle and angled it down so that the flame met the liquid. Then there was a blue flame in the glass. He picked up the glass quickly and blew into it sharply. The blue flame was extinguished. Then he tipped the glass back and emptied the contents into his mouth.

He smiled at his visitors.

"You can drink it without the flame first if you want. Don't let the flame burn too long. It'll burn up the vezi and could crack the glass with the heat.

Silver turned down the vezi, but Giles tried it with the flame. It had a sharp tang to it, but he felt its warmth as it went down his throat. He tried it cold too and decided he preferred the less flamboyant version.

Food was brought out, cold meats and cheeses. The cheeses were strong and hard and the meats lightly spiced. Senator Clifford asked them questions about their journey. It had been many years since he had ventured to Naadu.

"I usually go inland across the grass plains to the mountains. They make the most exquisite wines from the grapes in the foothills. You should visit. Are you intending to stay long?"

"We don't know," Giles responded. "We came to find other men of the Order."

"And so you have found us. Are we what you were expecting?"

"I don't believe I had any preconceptions, but perhaps I be a little surprised by all this," he said, gesturing generally about him.

At that point, the attendant came in again carrying finger bowls and towels. Silver stared hard at him once more and the attendant looked back at him and flicked a glance at the captain of the custodians. Giles caught the flicker of an eyebrow.

"He looks like no delf I have seen before."

"He is a puoli," said the captain of the guard.

"What devil be that?"

Edward smiled in response. "They are not delf." He paused. "They are half delf."

The visitors exchanged glances. Silver had stopped chewing.

"Part delf, part man."

Silver exploded. "What sins be these?" Food and spittle flew from his mouth.

"Be quiet!" snapped Giles. "Forgive him, I fear his wits have been turned from lack of sleep on the road."

Henry Clifford frowned and waved away the startled looking attendant.

"When we, our ancestors, first came here, we were few," Henry said. "They knew there was more of this world to see and that it was theirs to conquer. They defeated the first delf army which came their way, just as the Order did under Sir William. But this is not like Outreterre or Unama. This is a great continent. Even our dominions now do not stretch to its edge. The delf kept coming. So we made truces and alliances with our neighbours. We divided the delf amongst themselves. And they realised they could learn things from us. They never knew about ships. They sailed boats in the shallows off the coast down there, but up north, the shipping was in the hands of merchants of Naadu. They had all the trade along the north coast. They sailed further too, south of Linana. Here they avoided because of the fogs and lack of a harbour. We changed that, dredging a harbour on the coast. You came up the harbour road, but there are few ships from the north now. We opened trade routes to the south. We opened trade routes inland. We took caravans and knights across the plains and beyond the mountains."

He tilted his head on one side and looked at Silver.

"My friend, the delf in him is being bred out. It made sense. We were few and a long way from our kin in Outreterre. And so to tie them to us, we allowed the lowest men to breed with them. Delf breed slowly, as you'll know. But mixed with men, they breed almost as quickly as men. Our numbers increased as the puoli grew. The puoli bred amongst themselves. Now it is impossible to say how much blood of either race is in any one of them. The ruling families protected the blood of our fathers so now there are three races. Men, the puoli and the pureblood delf. And the further inland you go, the more delf there are. But they are all represented in the Republic. We have become strong until our influence has spread across the land. The legions of the Republic keep the peace across our dominions."

"Are you of these legions?" Giles asked Edward.

"Wootton's Legion is indeed a legion of the Republic. Soon I will be travelling again. Our time as custodians of Linana Pivaki is almost over. Last night, Kallick's Legion arrived. It is camped on the plain ready to take over. It is an honour the legions share by turns and a rest from their ceaseless watch over the dominions."

Giles welcomed the change of subject, anxious not to provoke Silver again and needing time to think about the revelations.

"Do the legions see much action?" he asked.

"These years there is little more than suppressing bandits and pirates. They are a deterrent and they give confidence to our merchants and trading partners."

"So now you know some of our history," said Henry Clifford. "But what of our ancestral cousins across the sea? Tell us how Outreterre has fared in the years gone by. We have heard little from merchants until these last few years when we have started to receive new goods."

Giles played down the internecine wars which had proceeded at intervals down the years in Outreterre. He talked more about the raids of light keepers on innocent families near the mountains than the mounted bands of freebooters who used to cross the Styx and raid the farms of northern Unama. He also talked about the recent reconciliation between delf and Order. They seemed to have heard about that in the news that passes along the trading lanes.

"We heard confused tales of combining your forces against a great host. Some said it was goblins, others that it was real devils out of Hell."

Giles smiled.

"I be sure you do not believe all tales that arrive on ships."

He turned the subject to farming and the viticulture to which their hosts had already alluded. At the end of the evening, the senator asked his son to escort Giles and Silver back to their men.

It was dark when they left. They had walked a little way from the gorge when they came to a junction where another road led off to the right. Lanterns caught their eye and shouts.

Edward Clifford stopped and stared up the road. He glanced at his two guards who both nodded.

"Come on," he said.

Without a word, Giles and Silver followed the soldiers up the street. There were people running towards them. They cast a fearful look at the soldiers and ran past. Clifford grabbed the arm of one.

"Is it another werebeast?"

The man nodded.

"The Cliffs Quarter?"

Another nod. Clifford let the man go and carried on. The soldiers followed him. Giles turned to watch the people go and his eye was caught by a light suddenly appearing on the highest part of the city where the tallest light tower stood. The door at its base had opened and figures were emerging.

Silver looked at the manor lord in alarm.

"My lord, what passes?"

"I don't know. Perhaps you had better wait here. I want to see what they be talking about."

"He said werebeast," Silver hissed.

Giles looked quickly up the road. He would have to run to catch up with Edward and the guards.

"Stay here and watch," he said, then ran after the soldiers.

There were no more people about. He could see lights behind shutters from some of the buildings. They had run up an incline and the road had begun to narrow. A fork in the road led off into two dark laneways. He caught up with Edward and his men. They had drawn their swords. Clifford heard him come up.

"What are you doing here?"

"I thought I could help."

"You – You have no weapon!"

Giles had not thought about it. He looked at his empty scabbard.

"Here, take these," said Clifford and handed him his dagger and then the pistol from out of his belt. "Look for a moving shadow, but don't trust the gun."

The eyes of the two soldiers were wide with fear as they glanced nervously into the shadows around them and crept forward. He realised he could hear his own breathing; the night was silent. What was this about werebeasts? Perhaps it was some kind of cob come into the city from the forest. Still, he was pleased for the weight of the pistol in his hand. The dagger felt pitifully small.

"Right hand fork," Clifford whispered. Giles could see the pale shape of his face turn to look at him. "Lord Giles, watch behind us."

They edged further up the street, peering into the darkness. Giles felt vulnerable walking backwards and not knowing the men to whom he was trusting his life.

The street began to bend to the right. Giles watched as the comforting sight of the end of the road giving onto the lit main thoroughfare disappeared from view. The buildings were larger here. Perhaps they were tenements or warehouses. As they rose around them, they seemed to close in, shutting out the sky. A few showed the dim glow of lantern light within, but none of it seeped onto the street. The moon had not yet risen and the stars gave no light.

Even as he saw a movement, Giles called a warning, but it happened too quickly. The shadow dropped silently. Perhaps it had been hanging from a building. How long had it watched them?

There was a gargled cry from his left and shouting. The soldiers were frantically calling out to each other in the darkness as they swung and looked about them. Giles backed away from the noise, slashing the knife in front of him until he found himself against a wall. There he stayed, his chest heaving from the sudden exertion and darting sharp glances into the shadows.

Then he saw light coming from the lane behind them, bobbing along as if being carried. A group came around the corner. Giles could make out nothing behind the lanterns and the torches. Then there was another light, a ball of bright light like the sun and a familiar shape formed. With terror, Giles realised it was a human form of bright, flameless fire. A sun wraith.

Daylight filled the narrow street. Opposite him, one of the soldiers lay still on the cobbles in a pool of blood with his throat ripped out. Clifford and the other guard were looking wildly about them. Clifford's sword arm hung limply and he was nursing it with his left. There was no sign of anyone, or anything else. Giles pressed himself back into the doorway, hoping the sorcerer which had summoned the sun wraith could not see him. But something was wrong here. Neither of the two soldiers paid it any mind.

Then the sun wraith lifted from the ground. Giles watched it and realised there was something climbing up the building right above his head. He dodged away from the wall and across the street, in his hurry, nearly stumbling over the body of the guard. He watched, squinting at the brightness as the wraith wrapped itself around the figure on the wall. It looked like a man, but there was something animal about its face. Then there was burning, but no sound. A dark shape fell from the wall and the wraith leapt away into the sky and hovered over the middle of the street.

Clifford and two of the newcomers to the scene went over to the fallen shape. They wore crimson capes emblazoned with a golden circle across which a cross was laid in white. The capes were belted at the waist and each man carried scabbards containing short, broad bladed swords. Each wore a helmet which wrapped around their face. Behind them, still holding the lantern, stood four soldiers dressed in the white shirts and breastplates which they had seen on the custodians at the front gate. The two in crimson removed their helmets and bent over the figure. They said something to each other. Then Clifford looked up at Giles and beckoned him over.

"Have you ever seen anything like that before?" Clifford asked.

Giles eyed the still hovering sun wraith, then joined Clifford across the street.

The creature on the ground was badly burned, but it was human in shape and he could see it had been wearing grey mail armour. Scraps of other material hung from it. But it was what was left of the head which amazed him. It was blackened, but there seemed to be the shape of a muzzle and teeth.

"No," Giles said. "I don't recognise it. What be it?"

"We don't know, but it's not the first."

The two men in crimson stood, and as they did so, Giles saw that only one of them was a man. The other was delf, but his hair was cut short like the men. It accentuated his fine, bony features. The delf's eyes passed over him without interest.

"Where did it come from?" he asked Clifford.

Clifford shook his head, then he staggered. Giles caught him as he fell.

"Help me here," he said to the two in crimson.

"He needs a physician. You should have waited for us."

"You be a light keeper, be you not a healer?" Giles asked.

"Light *keeper*?" said the other in crimson turning to him with a puzzled frown. "No."

He looked at the four soldiers who had accompanied him. "Burn this," he said, pointing to the creature. Then he looked at the dead custodian. "And him too." He looked over at the captain who was now leaning on Giles' shoulder. "How were you hurt? Let me see that wound."

He pushed up Clifford's sleeve. "That looks like a sword wound." He turned to the other guard, still standing dazed in the middle of the street. There was blood on the soldier's blade. "You will be more careful in future. Take your captain to a physician."

The man and the delf replaced their helmets and turned back down the street. Above them, the wraith was fading and the street returning to its darkened state. Giles helped the other guard with the weight of Clifford as they followed the crimson caped figures down the lane.

"If they be not light keepers, who be they?" Giles asked.

"Warders," the other guardsman replied as if it were obvious.

Giles decided to keep any further questions to himself. Further down the hill, they came upon Silver. He was relieved to see Giles.

"What happened?" he asked.

"Werebeast," said Giles matter-of-factly. "And then a sun wraith. Of course."

Silver looked at him strangely.

"Later," he replied.

It was late when Giles and Silver left Clifford with the physician. The custodian led them to the hostel where Giles' men had been put up. They were all waiting for them. The captain assured Giles that they had all been treated well, although there were still guards outside. Giles told the captain about their evening. When he talked about the warders, Silver's eyes bulged.

"Who wielded the demon?" he asked.

"I don't know which one. I had the impression that it could have been either."

"But that be heresy! Christian men should not practise sorcery!" Silver's eyes were flicking from side to side. "This city be cursed," he said. "That be why the Archbishop led us here. It was to show what will happen in Outreterre if we consort with the devils. This be a city of corruption. They have bred with devils and they deal in sorcery! We must leave."

"How can we leave? There be wonders here to be discovered. Don't jump to the purposes of your dreams after so short a time. Besides, I be not sure if we be prisoners or guests yet. No, we will stay for a little while and see what we can find out. There be much to be learned."

"Beware lest you succumb to temptation, my lord," Silver said.

"I will," Giles replied and patted him on the shoulder. "Now, let me see that our men's accommodation be all it can be."

He left Silver with his thoughts and went to see to his men.

Berwick was leaning on the side of the ship watching the sea. He was mesmerised by how the waves moved constantly, changing shape, rolling and shifting. The sea was a deep blue and the sky was paler, scattered with cloud. The deck heaved beneath him, a movement he had become used to and now enjoyed. He liked to stand and feel the muscles of his legs tense and flex to compensate for the movement. The sails were puffed up like a belly, occasionally drooping as the wind subsided for a moment.

Rodon joined him. His face was impassive.

"I thought I was a long way from home when we were in Beretska," said Berwick.

Rodon raised an eyebrow and nodded.

"What will we do if we catch up with Lord Giles?"

Rodon's mouth twitched as he considered the question.

"I haven't really thought that far ahead," he said at last. "A plan be of little use if you don't know where you will need to put it into action. We may come upon Silver alone somewhere, in which case the plan would be simple."

"Would we try to bring him back?"

Rodon frowned.

"We would try," he said.

"And what about Giles?"

"He be not a wanted man, but I be curious as to what he be about. I never did like him." He looked at Berwick. "In sooth, Silver does not interest me. I want Giles."

Berwick looked at the sea for a while and they were both silent.

"You keep me sane, you know, Mr Rodon," he said at last.

"Why do you say that?"

"I know it be right to try for peace between man and delf. But every time I be faced with a group of my comrades, I feel like an outsider. A traitor even."

"From all you meet?"

"Sometimes when I talk to someone on their own, their talk be different. They tell me they have nothing against the delf. But I wonder if they mean that or are dissembling."

"It be a long road to change centuries of hatred."

There seemed to be little answer to that.

"Have you spoken to Raul today?" Berwick asked.

Rodon looked up at the poop deck where Raul and Qatiko were having one of their regular good natured arguments. The little delf's eyes were invisible inside his baggy squint and it was hard to tell whether he was smiling or only grimacing into the sun and wind.

Rodon shook his head.

"Barely. But I think we have him to thank for the master's softening towards us. Last night's fruit was a pleasant complement to our salt beef and biscuit."

"You butter him up about his navigation," Berwick replied. "You'd think he was passing on the secrets of the creation when he tells you how he plots our course."

"His understanding of the position and movement of stars be astounding. At least to me. He seems to find his way on the sea as well as Raul does on the land."

"That be what makes him the master," Berwick shrugged.

They watched the waves sliding past with a brisk wind behind them, the keel ploughing through the waves and the waves shrugged off the ship and rolled uncaring back on their way.

"Will Raul see this through?" Berwick asked.

Rodon did not reply immediately.

"He has come this far. The turning point was Beretska. But we offered him what he wanted. A reason to go back into the wide world and also something to hunt. Ironheads to boot. I sometimes wonder if Silver and his friends be the only ones missing the war."

17

SOLIMO WAS PEDALLING when Mondo came in. The older delf watched from the doorway for a moment before quietly closing the door.

"Good evening, Solimo," Mondo said. "I was looking for you earlier."

Solimo smiled ruefully.

"I am sorry."

"Are you still worrying about the dreams?"

"Yes. No. More than that. But those dreams have stopped."

"Those dreams? Are you having more?"

Solimo nodded, then frowned. "Echoes of dreams."

"Whose?"

He shook his head.

"I do not know."

"Well you look tired."

Mondo climbed onto his saddle and began to pedal. They pedalled together in silence for a while. Then, all at once, Solimo stopped, climbed off his saddle, took his coat and hat from the hook near the door and went out.

"Good night!" Mondo called after him.

Solimo walked across the yard and out of the gate. There was still a faint glow in the west, but the moon was full and bright. At this time of night he felt that the world looked unfamiliar. It felt like another place rather than where he had lived for years. The hills rolled on towards the distant mountains, little more than a long low smudge in the north.

He walked away from the light tower and sat on the edge of the slope. If he looked to the right, he could see the cottage where Esella and Raul lived. A little smoke curled out of the chimney, unmolested by the still evening air. It was cool and he breathed in through his nostrils, filling his lungs slowly, holding it, then gently exhaling.

He could smell the grass. Somewhere a sheep bleated and another answered. Then it was silent again.

He looked at the moon. It hung large and low in the sky. He could see the shadows and shapes on its surface. He had wanted to be a light doctor for years, so why did he resist?

There was a sound from the cottage and a light appeared as the door opened and he could see Esella silhouetted. She tipped out a bucket, then straightened, looking towards him. She put the bucket down, closed the door behind her and started to walk up the hill. He watched her as she came towards him, one hand sometimes moving unconsciously to her belly.

He could not work out the look she gave him when she reached him, but he decided to say something to stop her looking at him in that way.

"It is too early for the star watch."

"I came to see you. I saw you on the hill and wondered what you were doing. You have been very quiet of late. Why have you stopped singing?"

"Have I?"

Had he? He had not noticed.

"Esella..." He stopped. What was he going to say? She waited without pressing him. Then she sat down beside him and looked out across the moonlit hilltops, keeping him company in the silence.

"You have changed," he said at last.

"I know," she replied.

"Was it Raul?"

She smiled faintly.

"I think it is the baby. It uses my energy. It is a better way to use it than anger."

"Do you think I could change?"

"What do you mean?"

"Can the light change you?"

"You know it can."

He was silent again.

"I am afraid of the light," he said. "I am a healer, but the light can also do harm. If I master the light, what could it do to me?"

He was aware of Esella breathing. It was slow and steady. It lulled him.

"Only what you let it."

He breathed in deeply again, feeling the air as it moved through his nostrils. What might he let it do if he had the chance?

"You are good, Solimo. You are the best delf I know. You are already master of the light of the sun for healing. It shines through you, Solimo. When you smile, it lights your face. You would never do anything but good with that power. You could not. The Light Doctor knew you could not. I do not know what you are really afraid of. Surely it is not the light."

"I am afraid of being without the light," he said. Suddenly he remembered the Pits where he had waited with the lost delf who had lived in darkness for years. "I lost the light once and I lost...myself. I love the light too much. It would consume me."

"Then why do you tempt yourself with it all this time? You are around the light constantly, yet you never weave it as it can be woven. It is liberating to weave the wraith, Solimo. It is like an extension of yourself, acting beyond you."

"It is a weapon, Esella. It kills."

"If you let it. If you need it to. It can also simply be a beacon."

There was silence between them once more.

"What if I failed?"

"*If* you failed?" She paused and stood up. "Then you will have learned something." She watched him for a reaction, but he gave none.

"Come home with me. I have made some dinner."

18

GILES RECEIVED A visitor in the morning. He and his men had had breakfast and were sitting around the courtyard in the sun waiting for something to happen. The men were in groups talking, whittling or drawing absently in the dust with sticks. The captain was pacing irritably and Silver was kneeling in the corner in prayer. Giles was sitting on a bench with one foot on an upturned wooden pail thinking about all that had happened to them.

A door onto the courtyard opened and Senator Clifford walked in. The men watched him, glad of something new to look at. Giles stood as the older man walked towards him.

"Good morning, senator," he said.

"And good morning to you, Lord Giles. I would like to thank you for being of service to my son last night."

"It was nothing. I merely helped him to the physician. Is he well?"

"He will be. But you talk of only part of the service you rendered. You went with him and his men where there was no need for you to go and you did so when you were unarmed."

"I was of little use to him. And perhaps had I realised the true nature of the situation I would have stayed safely behind."

The senator grunted. "If men truly understood the nature of the dangers they walked into, I feel there would be many more cowards. You are too modest. You went towards what you saw made others flee. That is enough and I thank you. The city should thank you."

Giles nodded in appreciation, then beckoned his captain to him.

"Sir, I would like to introduce my right hand man, John Benedict."

"Ah, you have the look of a military man," said the senator, taking his hand.

Giles smiled.

"He is indeed my chief retainer and knows a soldier's ways. But please, would you sit with us. I will fetch some chairs. Payton!" He called across to one of his men. "Find us some more chairs!"

Disturbed at his prayers, Silver stood up and walked over, concerned that he was missing something.

"Good morning, Mr Silver. It is good to see a man at his prayers."

"Aye. I trust you have been at yours this morning?" he asked gruffly.

"Silver, that's enough," Giles snapped.

Clifford waved his hand. "Don't worry, Lord Giles." There was a pause while Payton and another man brought extra chairs for them. Clifford settled himself. "He is right to suspect. I have not been at my morning prayers, but I do say some before I go to sleep. And last night I gave thanks for the safe deliverance of my son from the werebeast."

"It be a curse!"

"Is that what you believe?"

"Silver," said Giles in a warning growl.

"Please Lord Giles, I am not a man who is easily offended. And a prophet is not a prophet if he does not issue challenges. Few are welcomed by their listeners." He turned to Silver once more. "Speak, sir prophet."

"Indeed I will not hold my tongue when the Lord demands I speak out. You be cursed by God and this be His justice upon you."

"And what have we done to provoke the wrath of God?" the senator asked calmly.

"Need you ask? You have bred with devils and made a race of half devils. You have meddled in their sorcery and corrupted men in the ways of witches and sorcerers."

"That is not how we see it."

"Where else do these werebeasts come from? Why else do they come? But you can repent!"

"Mr Silver, I have already explained about the puoli. We prefer to think we are breeding the devil out of them."

"No no, you should not mock the Lord! Has He not warned you last night when one of the half devils tried to kill your own son?"

"While I feel a soldier should keep a clearer head, it was but an accident of the moment."

Silver leaned closer to the senator.

"There be no accidents. There be only God's will."

"Then perhaps I should explain about the light. It is true it is an art of the delf, but we have turned it to good and to further our power across the land. We have made war with the light and turned it into a powerful weapon. The delf way was to use it for defence in time of need and to use it for healing. We do not waste it on healing. Physicians can do that with their learning and ointments and potions. We formed the Knight Warders of the Light, who you saw last night, Lord Giles."

"And it be of them I speak. Tell me," Silver said, bending nearer so that the senator felt impelled to back away. "Tell me, senator, be the devils baptised? Be they Christians now?"

Clifford hesitated. "Why no, they are not. The delf do not understand the Word of God."

"No!" Silver said triumphantly. "Because they be devils and forever locked out from God's favour for their rebellion. Who did the creature kill?"

"A puoli soldier and two others it found in a house. It was first seen in a house. Just like the others that have come, the person killed has been sleeping."

"These puoli be an abomination in the Lord's eyes." Silver's eyes were round and he stared without blinking at the Clifford. "They must be erased from the earth. Man came to Faerie with a sacred mission to claim this world for the Lord. We have failed him time and time again. We be weak. God sends these creatures to you as a warning and a sign. You must repent your evil ways and seek forgiveness while there be still time. Do your priests not tell you this?"

"No, Mr Silver, they do not. They tell us that God is the light of the world."

"Aye, that he is, senator, but these be not true light, they be Satan's simulacrums of the Lord's blessed reality. They twist it to their evil purpose to create demons. How be that blessed? All your power and conquests be in vain because you seek conquest for your own sake. If you needed help, you had only to pray for God's help. But instead you turned to Satan and used his crafts and bred with his children. God's vengeance will always come. The Lord says 'The night be gone; the day be at hand. Let us cast off the works of darkness and put on the armour of light. Let us walk properly as in the daytime, not in orgies and drunkenness, not in quarrelling and jealousy.' "

"Mr Silver, a devil is but a fallen angel. Is God not a forgiving God? The power of the light is now with the Republic and we have brought into our power many dominions. We are fulfilling the hopes of those who first journeyed into Faerie."

"It be *not* what was intended! Our purpose here be to spread the Word of God and convert the heathen. If they will not convert, then they are to be cast into the flames!"

Clifford stood. Giles stood too, a worried look on his face. Clifford smiled at them both.

"Lord Giles, I'll tell you again. I'm not offended. Mr Silver gives me much on which to ruminate. I will go and pray and think about what you say. In the meantime, I hope you do not object if you try to keep your men to their quarters. You are of course free to leave at any time, but for the time being the city is nervous and while you are our guests I would like you to remain safe. I will speak to the senators and ask their leave to let you come and go as you please."

"Senator, I be grateful to you. We will, by your leave, stay, although I cannot say for how long. I would that we were able to provide you with some hospitality in return for your kindness."

"Perhaps that can wait until I visit Outreterre. I must admit, I have said before that you would deserve a visit when you came looking for us. We had always assumed that those we left behind were happy with their lot, for as you can see, our curiosity has led to greater things."

Clifford and Fitzwarren were seated in leather covered armchairs, each holding a goblet of vezi. They were sitting in Clifford's snug, a room with two walls lined with books, a third with a painting of a caravan of pack animals winding over the mountains and the fourth with a window looking out towards the waterfall.

"Roger, I have had a very interesting conversation with the prophet from Outreterre I told you about."

"What does he say?"

"He says the werebeasts are a curse from God."

"A curse?"

"That it is a punishment for creating the puoli."

"Could that really bring down a curse on us?"

"Well, it's taken many years."

Fitzwarren looked down at his glass.

"They've been very useful to us, the puoli. Where would we be without them? Surely God can't be angry with us."

"I was thinking as I came home. The werebeasts have only killed puoli."

Fitzwarren frowned and thought for a moment, his fingers reaching to stroke his beard.

"It's true. They have. What do you think it means? Are they cursed? Or have they become prey for something that has lurked unseen. No, it's really not possible. We've never seen anything like the werebeasts. They are not like the cobs, they wear clothes. They appear out of nowhere. Could they have come from the sea?"

"Then why do they come singly? No, there is some other reason. This prophet has given us the only explanation which I cannot immediately refute, although I simply struggle to believe it."

"On what grounds does he claim this knowledge?"

"He has dreams. He tells stories of a man, an archbishop who went into Limbo. I think it is to do with dreams and maybe those of the puoli in particular."

Fitzwarren stopped stroking his beard and looked up in surprise. Clifford nodded.

"Yes, Roger, it surprised me too, but I've no reason to disbelieve him. He at least clearly believes it and so does Lord Giles and he seems to me to be an intelligent man. But listen, I had another thought as I was walking home. We should isolate the puoli, for our sake. If these creatures are only interested in them, that would show us. And the loss of a few puoli would not be too much to bear. And in that time, we might discover where they come from. If we can save them from the werebeasts, they'll be indebted to us. And that would be very useful in the senate. They have inherited the delf sense of obligation."

"They have indeed," said Fitzwarren and he took a long thoughtful sip on his vezi.

Clifford was on his feet in the senate again.

"Some of you will know that my own son recently fought off a werebeast until the light guard arrived. One of his men was killed, bringing the total number of dead to sixteen at the hands of these creatures." He paused and surveyed his listeners. "Has no one else noticed that all of the dead are puoli?"

"But I heard your son was wounded by the beast," called out one of the puoli senators.

"He was injured, yes, but not by the beast. No, it was his other puoli guard, flailing in terror with his sword. It seems more likely that the beast was attacking him and in defending himself, he struck my son. Edward was at the front. He was the natural target, but the beast chose the two puoli."

There were murmurings around the room which were loudest from the puoli side as the senators discussed the insight.

"But why would these creatures try to kill us?"

Clifford held out his hands in a gesture of puzzlement.

"That I do not know. I have asked the knight warders to catch one that comes so that it can be studied. They have burned all the others. But until we find out, we need to protect you."

"What do you suggest? How can we protect ourselves?"

"We could put a guard on every puoli household in the city," Clifford offered.

"That is hardly practical. There would not be enough soldiers."

"Could we leave some undefended? Take the risk, at least protect some...although I would not be the one to choose."

"No, we could not do that."

A delf counsellor stood.

"They need the protection of a light tower."

"None are big enough to take all of them," the puoli replied. "Although I suppose we could make do for a while, even if it were uncomfortable."

There was silent thought around the room. Clifford sat down again and watched the others. He glanced across to Fitzwarren who returned the look, then turned back to the delf and puoli.

Then one of the youngest puoli senators stood. Clifford knew him to be one of the most recently elected.

"The Old Quarter is like a small fortress. It has the gorge on one side with the two bridges, the river winds across half its back facing the plains and the Tower of the Stars is a fortress within the fortress.

It would seem that would be the best of the towers. We could build shelters behind its walls. I am not a military man. Torko, you were a soldier. Is it defendable?"

An old puoli senator stood to respond. "I was only a sergeant, but yes, that is the oldest part of Linana for that reason. It was the easiest spot to defend."

"Then we should move us there."

Clifford stood again. "Before we go further with this, we need to make a decision on the use of the custodian guard."

"Some are puoli. Use some of them to protect us."

"I don't doubt it, but we need to obtain the backing of the senate first before we make that decision."

"Then shall I suggest a show of hands?" the delf senator suggested.

"Seconded," said the puoli who had begun the debate.

"Let us see the vote," Clifford said. Then he looked with satisfaction as every arm in the room was raised. As he sat down again, he could not help but catch the eye of Fitzwarren at the end of the row below him.

19

CHARLIE STOPPED ON a flat part of the track and turned to see where George was. He seemed pretty fit for an old guy, but he felt guilty striding ahead. He looked around at the outcrops of white stone and the forested valleys below. Small yellow flowers crowded at the base of rocks to escape the heat of the sun.

"It doesn't seem five minutes since I had your energy," George said as he caught up. "No one ever tells you what getting older is like. Suddenly everyone's younger than you are and you never noticed it happen."

"There's a little tree up there by that crag with a good bit of shade. We could have lunch there."

"You're a hard task master, Charlie. It's hours since breakfast."

"Yeah, but it's just starting to get really hot now, so aren't you glad we started early?"

George put a large, leather hand on Charlie's shoulder.

"Listen you. I've been getting up early for years. The only shock was finding you were prepared to get up early too. The youth of today. Full of surprises!"

Charlie chuckled.

"Come on. Home straight, old man."

"Watch it, sonny."

Charlie ran the last section of hill just to prove his point, then collapsed breathing heavily on the grass in the shade, sliding his pack off in the process. George seemed to move slower than ever, but there was a deliberate slowness and an affected nonchalance about his pace.

Charlie decided he would ignore the deliberate provocation and started extracting lunch from his pack: bread, cheese, salami and tomatoes. He took out his penknife and started to prepare sandwiches, slicing the crusty loaf across the middle. He had one ready by the time George joined him.

"Slow and steady gets the sandwich," George grinned.

Charlie made his own and they munched in silence, watching the shadows of clouds drift across the surrounding hills.

"If I hadn't met you, I'd never have thought of coming up here," George said as he finished his sandwich. "I would have kept to the roads in my little hire car. What time was that bus back tomorrow morning?"

"Ten o'clock. And from right outside the pension, which if this map is right, is just down in the next valley. That means we've got all afternoon to get down, but it would be a bit rude to rush it."

"Mm," George agreed, biting into an apple.

"This place reminds me of somewhere," said Charlie. "Except the trees are different."

"Where?"

Charlie was quiet for a few moments.

"A bit hard to explain." His voice tailed off. George looked at him. He seemed to be deep in thought.

"You'll know what Limbo is won't you?"

"As a priest you mean, and therefore expert in these things?"

"Yeah."

"It's where some people believe you go when you die while you're waiting for the last coming, or if you're a baby who dies without committing any sins. Kind of a waiting room. It's not even official doctrine. I think it's rubbish myself, dreamed up by medieval scholars to justify their existence. What on earth made you ask that?"

"Unlembien," Charlie said.

"Pardon?"

"Train of thought," he said. He paused. He had never talked about this to anyone. "I've been to Limbo."

"Well yes. The world of school behind you and the big wide world opening its arms to you in front. And here you are, sitting on a hill between the worlds."

"No. I mean, I've *been* to Limbo. Some of them called it Limbo. Or Unlembien."

Something about Charlie's tone of voice made George stay silent. He knew from long experience when someone was going to tell him something they thought was important.

"I've thought about it a lot. It was the land between the worlds. It was where dreams were made, or where they went. Or something.

Never really made any sense, but I just accepted it at the time." He was musing. He stopped, looked quickly at George and away again.

"Sorry, doesn't matter."

"Do you have something you want to tell me?"

"No," said Charlie, but in a way which denied finality. "Are all priests like you these days?"

"Like me? My parishioners used to tell me I was unique. They used to say I wasn't really like a priest, but I think priests are people and people are different."

"I agree with them. You're nothing like the only other priest I've met. But he was an archbishop."

"Oh ho!" laughed George. "They're another breed altogether. How did you meet an archbishop?"

"It's a long story."

"I like stories."

"A very long story."

"You said we have all afternoon."

"And you wouldn't believe me."

"Charlie, when you're a priest, it's your job to listen and not to judge. Or at least to reserve judgement for as long as you possibly can."

"I've never really told anyone about it except for Mum and Dad. Because they've been there too. I did tell Fraser. He's my best mate. But I don't think he really believed me."

"Try me," said George quietly.

"Should I call you Father George?" Charlie smiled, but his gaze was somewhere over the hills.

"If it helps."

"When I was eleven, I went to another world. I don't know how I got there except that it was through dreams. But it wasn't a dream. It wasn't. It went on too long. It was real. It was like this." He gestured around him. "It felt just like being here, except it was somewhere else. Dad was there too. And Mum. Later..."

Charlie was very quiet as they descended the hill a few hours later. George took up the rear again on the way down, feeling the strain on his knees and glad of the stick he had picked for himself that morning. He was quiet too. He was pondering the story Charlie had told him. It was a preposterous story, but Charlie clearly seemed to believe it. It was very strange, but he had found himself listening intently, gripped by the narrative.

Charlie had not asked him for his reaction. He had simply told the story. Once it was finished, a few minutes had passed in silence. George had been wondering what to say.

"That's a great story," George finally said.

"Yeah. But it's not just a story. It really happened to me. It made me. And changed our lives. All of us."

"I can hear that."

Then Charlie had shoved the remains of lunch into his backpack and had set off over the ridge and down the other side of the hill.

As they walked, George wondered what he should say. All sorts of theories passed through his head as they walked. Charlie had made it all up; it was from a book or a film; Charlie had been on drugs and hallucinated; it was some kind of cry for help; a way of dealing with a family trauma. But George also liked to think of himself as open minded. So a part of him did indeed reserve a space for the option that it was all true.

At the bottom of the hill, they reached a small village sitting by a river with a pretty little bridge curving over the waters.

"I'll buy dinner," said George. "I think I owe you something for your history."

"I don't mind if you don't believe me," said Charlie.

"We all like to be believed," George replied. "I believe *you* believe you went there."

"Cop out," Charlie grinned.

George was woken by a voice crying out. His eyes opened to the darkness of the pension room he and Charlie were sharing. It was Charlie. What was he saying? His head felt blurred as he struggled with the jolt of awakening. For a moment he saw a candle reflected in the window. Then in the dark, he could just make out Charlie's bed and Charlie crouched on it. Perhaps he was asleep. A cool draft crossed the room. Then something happened. Charlie moved, a shadow passed across the room.

George was awake now. He could no longer make out Charlie and the candle was gone. He thought again. There *was* no candle in their room and the window was on his side, not Charlie's.

He fumbled for his torch which he had placed on a chair beside his bed and pointed it across the room. It lit Charlie's bed and a pile of blankets. Charlie was not there.

20

RUA SWEPT THE last of the dust out the front door and paused on the threshold. The evening was quiet, the humidity beginning to ease with the onset of the night breeze. Her neighbour was coming up the cobbled alley, a sack over his shoulder, his bare brown arms taut with the weight. His silver hair was tied up on the top of his head. He noticed Rua.

"Rua girl. if you stand there any longer, I will get you in to do our sweeping."

Rua smiled. "If I swept your house, Alai, you would have twice the space you have now."

Alai chuckled and stopped when he reached her.

"Have you heard from your father?"

"Not for a while."

"Maybe you should go to Naadu yourself."

"Why?"

"You heard about the last werebeast?"

"I did. What happened?"

"They found it and destroyed it. But listen, it came from a puoli too. He was found dead in his bed, or the remains of him were. There was talk at the market about the puoli bringing these things."

"Why? They cannot blame us?"

"They do not know, Rua girl. I heard every rumour you could think of about why werebeasts would be looking for puoli."

A troubled look came into Rua's eyes. Alai put his hand on her shoulder.

"I did not mean to worry you. Only to warn you there is something going on. Come and stay with us tonight. Mara will not mind. And she will scold me all evening if I tell her I saw you, but you would not come."

"Thank you. You are kind, but I have already prepared dinner. You are only next door if I need anything."

"Right. You be sure to come by if you need to. Never mind the time it is. But I must get this flour home. I will feel this shoulder in the morning."

"Good evening, Alai. Moonshine on you."

"And you, Rua girl."

She watched him enter the door down the alley, then closed her own and walked over to her table. The family room looked very empty and for a moment she regretted turning Alai down. Then she thought better of it. She did not feel like talking and Mara would ask all sorts of questions she did not want to answer at the moment.

A pot was above her oven. She lifted the lid and looked in. It ought to be enough for a few days. She lit a candle then ladled a portion into a wooden bowl, took it to the table and sat down.

There was little to clear up and she sat for a while in the gloom with only the candle for light. She went to the door, opened it and looked out. She turned towards Alai and Mara's door. Maybe it would be pleasant just to go and talk. She missed that without her father. It would also stop her from thinking. Her thoughts were simply going around in circles. She listened to the sounds of the evening, listening for the alarm from the previous night, but there was nothing. All was as it should be. She closed the door, bolted it and went through into the shop.

The shutters were down, but windows high in the wall above them let in the evening light. There were shelves down each wall and in the middle of the room running at right angles to the shop front were more shelves, two sided, reaching up to chest height. She knew the shutters were latched, but she tried them anyway, then went into a small room at the back.

Inside was a desk which stretched the width of the room. There were drawers under it and cupboards above it. Light came from a skylight, so the room was still lighter than the shop. She sat down at the desk and looked at the book which lay open in front of her. In it were columns of writing and numbers.

Absent-mindedly she pulled a band from her wrist, reached behind her head and pulled her hair through the band and out of her way. Then she sat and studied the book, flicking back and comparing numbers, then scribbling some notes and calculations. She looked through the door into the shop, pushing out her lips thoughtfully.

Going back into the house, she made a final tour of the downstairs then climbed the steps to her bedroom.

As she lay in the candlelight, she tried not to think of her dreams. She wished she could have told Alai, but it would have only frightened him. Perhaps he would have called the custodians even, or at least asked her to leave. But it was ridiculous. Things could not come out of her dreams. These creatures were coming from somewhere else. Perhaps they were wild cobs growing bold and aggressive.

She watched the candlelight and began to hum quietly to herself to keep the silence at bay. She closed her eyes, then opened them again. The candle flame swayed gently across from her bed. She watched its darker centre hovering around the black wick. The flame seemed to grow in her mind as she focused on it. Then she thought of a tunnel. It was a little like her alley, only closed in and she could not see the sky. There seemed to be only darkness at the other end.

She heard something. She was being pulled forward. She could feel herself moving through the tunnel. She put out her arms to feel the sides. It was cold, like stone or metal. Something moved. It was on the ground. She could not tell what it was, a dark shape in the darkness. Fear gripped her centre, clutched at her insides. She tried to push herself backwards, away from it. Then it moved upright.

It spoke. She could not tell what it was. It spoke a word.

"Solimo?"

She pushed herself further away. She heard herself whimper.

"Is it you?" came the voice again. It was an insistent whisper.

She scrambled back. She must wake up. She shook herself. Then the voice was louder.

"Solimo? Where you dreaming? I was dreaming."

It was a male voice. She heard a sound, a movement, a breath, a shadow...

And she was sat up in bed, looking at the candle. Something rose behind it. Something else was in the room.

A cold prickle swept over her skin. She could not open her mouth. Fear pinned her to the wall.

"Who are you?" the voice said. The figure rose up and moved forward into the light. "Am I still dreaming? I'm not am I?"

It did not look like her other dreams. There was no armour, but it had the face of a young man. He looked puzzled.

"Don't be scared. I don't even know where I am. Is this Unama?"

Rua pressed herself back against the head of the bed. She felt very exposed. Where could she run to? She was shocked, but she did not feel the same terror that welled in her in those dreams. She stared at him. He had a bag in his hand. His eyes followed hers. He seemed to look surprised, then relieved, then he looked at her again.

"I'm sorry," he said, gently this time. "I don't want to scare you. It's been a long time since I was here. Look, I'll go."

Then he turned around.

"Where is it?" he said, his voice desperate. "The room's gone." He turned back to her. "I'm awake. I know I am. Aren't I?"

She still had not replied. She had been dreaming. He had been dreaming. What had just happened?

"How do I get back? How did you bring me here?"

"What are you?" she said at last. He looked human. How was he in her bedroom?

"I'm Charlie. From England. Have you heard of it?"

She shook her head and frowned a little. From England. She had heard of England from her father. It was where the Order had come from all those years ago, from another world.

"Are you a light keeper?"

Her eyes widened a little, but she said nothing. He knew about light keepers, yet he was from another world, or he claimed to be.

"Are you delf?"

She shook her head uncertainly. He had to be from another world, she had met him in a dream, but now he was here.

"What were you dreaming of?" His voice was insistent this time. She backed away a little more. He had said he had been here before. He knew about delf; he knew about light keepers.

"The neighbours will be here. They will kill you. I can shout," she said at last. Why had she said that? She did not want to frighten him, she wanted to talk to him.

"Don't shout. Please. I don't even know how I got here."

Rua found she was no longer afraid. She was shaken, but she was also curious.

"Look, I was dreaming of here. I was thinking about it all today. Were you dreaming? You must have been."

Charlie looked behind him. "We're both awake aren't we? There's no light funnel. You've stopped dreaming."

Rua nodded.

"I'm stuck here." There was a growing fear in his voice. "Can you sleep again? Can you dream the same dream?"

Rua shook her head slowly. It had been their dreams. Their dreams had met, somehow. Had she really done that?

"You must go now," she said.

"I can't go. I don't even know where I am! You've got to help me."

Then he shook his head in exasperation.

Had she really brought him here? She had never done that, she could not do it again. She wondered if her father would know what had happened. He had read so much.

"I'll go. I'll bloody find somebody."

He held up his hands, including the bag. She continued to watch him. He glanced at the door and sidled towards it. He kept his eyes on her and opened it with his foot. It was a clumsy move and he almost tripped. She was frowning now. She could not let him just leave. This was perhaps the most important thing that had ever happened to her. The things in her dreams had been frightening, but she had still felt they were only dreams. But if this Charlie could come out of a dream, maybe there was something else? She had to know. She needed to talk to him, to try to understand what had happened.

He went out the door.

Charlie was half way down the stairs when a sudden rapping sound made him jump. The sound came from the door at the bottom of the stairs. It had the look of an outside door. It sounded urgent. His blood froze. It was still dark outside.

The rapping began again.

"Custodians. Open up! Wake up!"

What was happening?

The girl was at the top of the stairs now. Charlie could see her in the gloom, her eyes widening. He was growing more alarmed.

"Who is it?"

There was a thump on the door and the latch rattled. Then they heard another voice. It was Alai.

"You make a great deal of noise. It is still early."

"Sunrise. We have many houses to get around."

"What is the matter?"

"All puoli must go to the Tower of the Stars," the voice outside replied. "You will be protected from the werebeasts there."

Charlie started to back away up the stairs towards the girl. Then she came towards him, brushed past and went to the door. She put her hand on the latch, then looked up towards him. She gestured quickly with her hand and he instinctively backed away into her room again.

He stood there, not knowing what to do. He could feel his heart pounding. He saw light creeping across the window sill and saw what appeared to be rooftops. Then he heard voices downstairs.

"Are you Rua Grafton?"

"Yes," said the girl.

"You need to get some things. We will be back in an hour. We are taking all puoli to the Tower of the Stars for protection from the werebeasts."

"Are there more coming?"

"Who knows? But the custodians and the warders can protect you there." There was a pause, then the voice added more quietly. "Do not worry. We look after our own."

He heard the door close and heard soft footfalls on the stairs. Then she was in the room again and looking at him. He looked back. She was short and slight with long, straight black hair, a small, wide nose and dark eyes.

"What do you know about werebeasts?" she asked.

Charlie frowned. "Nothing..."

"You came out of my dream."

"I think I came through it, not out of it...if I remember it right. What were those men after? Why didn't you tell them about me?"

"I don't know. You came out of my dream. They might have killed you."

Charlie felt the blood drain from his face.

"Why?"

Rua sat down. "No, they would not. They would not have thought that. They do not know."

Charlie was struggling to think. He was confused.

"Are you delf?" he asked.

She shook her head again. "I am puoli."

"What's that?" Charlie asked.

"My father is a man, my mother was delf."

"What? I didn't know that was possible."

She looked at him strangely.

"I just never knew of any delf and human having children."

"It does not happen much anymore. I am a first puoli. Most puoli have been puoli for generations."

They looked at each other.

"Where are you from?" she asked.

"Earth. England. But I've been here before. Or maybe not here."

"I have heard of England. My father used to tell stories about it. It is a magical place. Are you really from there?"

"I am. It's not magical, it's just...different. Where is this?"

"This is Linana Pivaki."

"Linana - ?"

"Pivaki." She looked around the room. "I need to get some things. I cannot think. You seem to be already packed."

"I just grabbed it automatically. I thought you were someone I used to know."

"Solimo?"

"Yes. He was a light keeper. He was delf. He was my friend."

She watched him. He wanted to know what she was thinking. Then she opened some drawers and took out a few items of clothing and stuffed them into a leather bag. She picked up the candle and went out of the room and down the stairs. He picked up the other candle and followed her. They went into a room lined with shelves. It looked like a shop. She went into the room at the back and opened a book and stood in thought looking at it. Then she closed it, opened a drawer and pulled out a smaller black book. She added this to her bag.

"I do not even know if I should take some food."

"Always take some food," said Charlie. "You never know where the next food's coming from."

She looked at him with a raised eyebrow. He felt as though she might be laughing at him. He didn't want her to laugh at him.

"That's just my experience," he shrugged.

"Well. I have some stew. Are you hungry? I made enough for the week. I cannot take it all."

"How long are you going for?"

"I do not know. But I am sure they will provide food."

A thought occurred to Charlie.

"What are the werebeasts?"

She shook her head and looked troubled, then she looked right at him.

"I dream of them. I thought you were one."

"I'm not."

"I know. They are frightening. I dreamed of them before they came. Rosa did too. She is my friend. They frighten her too. There is something wrong about those dreams."

"Isn't there someone you can ask? Is there a light doctor?"

"No," she said, as if it were obvious. "They are only in stories."

"I knew a light doctor," Charlie said. "But that's just a story now. She died."

He looked up, a frightened light in his eye. "She was killed by things from a dream as well. From Limbo."

21

RUA HAD HALF packed her bag. And then she stopped. She had just been explaining to Charlie what had been happening in the city. She felt he might understand what was happening and be able to give her advice.

"I'm not sure if I should go to the Tower of the Stars," she said.

"Why not? They'll be able to protect you there, that's what it's for, isn't it?"

That was not the answer she wanted. She had wanted certainty. He was just repeating what the custodian at the door had said.

"I don't know. It feels wrong. I've been feeling trapped."

"Seems like the best place to be would be a light tower."

"And what do you know about them from your world? There never were any in your world. Are there some now? I've never seen any in my dreams."

"You dream of my world?"

"Yes, sometimes. Father calls me a reacher. He says I could reach through if I really tried. He says he read that it happened when the first puoli were born. But after that, they were not allowed to marry outside the puoli and it stopped happening."

"So that's how you found me?"

It must have been, but reaching was one thing, actually linking the two worlds was another altogether.

"It's never happened before. You must be a reacher too."

"Well I'd certainly been thinking of here from last time. That was when I met light keepers. They looked after me when I was a child. But what are you going to do now? Go to the light tower?"

She tipped her head and twisted her mouth. It seemed to be what she did when she was thinking.

"We will go there to start with. And then we'll see."

"We?"

"Well I cannot leave you here, can I? You are my responsibility. And my father will be interested to meet you."

"I bet he would, showing up in your bedroom in the middle of the night," Charlie replied ruefully.

Rua chuckled. It was not the kind of laugh he had expected from her. He had expected something more girlish, but this was a free, confident chuckle. And her whole face lit up when she did so. Charlie wanted to get her to laugh again.

"They'll see I'm not puoli," he said. "Look at my clothes for a start."

He did look very strange. She went into her parents' room and came out carrying a long brown coat of light material.

"Put this on over your things. It has a hood too. Father wears it when we go looking for plants on the escarpment."

By the time she and Charlie left the house, there were other puoli from Rua's street waiting for the two custodians to return.

"Where is your father?"

"Naadu. He is away in the desert. He wanted to try something out away from the city. So he's gone out to a place we know on the edge of Naadu." She noticed Charlie's puzzled face. "It is a country far away to the north."

So he had missed Unama altogether, thought Charlie. His dream had reached out for the world that he knew and he had found it. But where he had thought to find Solimo, he had found Rua. Half delf, half human. How did that fit with what he had known before?

The early morning air smelled fresh and cool and it carried the scents from the flowers and foliage which crawled up the houses in vines. The sky was clear, but the sun had yet to climb high enough to shine into the street.

They joined the puoli. Rua knew them all and smiled at them. They smiled back nervously. Only one was talking, a small, older puoli with a worried face who kept pulling at his left ear.

"Oh there you are Rua," he said. "This is a strange business. A strange business. Do you think we will be safe at the light tower? Your father would have known would he not? He would have known. We could have asked him. These werebeasties, they are not right. They come in from the mountains you know. Must do. From the forest. Probably came in from Naadu. Brought in by some trader and left in the forest. That is just what they would do. Nasty business. I am losing even more sleep. It has me that worried. Have hardly slept a wink and it is worse since they came."

As he talked, he would look around at the others in the group for confirmation or validation. He received a few half-hearted nods, but few were saying anything.

Alai came out of his house.

"Rua girl, I thought that was your father for a moment."

"He is a friend. Came to help. His name is Charlie."

Charlie nodded at the delf and looked away again, feeling conspicuous. The delf merely smiled and seemed to think little of him.

"Have you food any with you? They should have food. Mara will make you some if you need it. This cannot go on long. You will be back soon when they stop these things coming in."

Two soldiers arrived. They stood on the corner and beckoned to the group who picked up their bags and walked over to them. Alai waved at them thoughtfully as they walked away.

The two custodians led them down the lane. There were more puoli threading down the main road when they joined it, and they joined the stream of people flowing through the city streets. puoli guardsmen walked alongside them, sometimes helping to carry bags or small children.

The Tower of the Stars stood tall on the north eastern side of the city. Light was creeping around the top of the funnel. As they crossed the city, it began to come alive and people would stop to watch them pass, delf and humans both. Most looked blankly at them or waved at people they knew, but a few looked hostile.

The closer they went, the more puoli joined them. Rua had never seen so many in one place. It felt odd to be in a crowd of people that was only puoli, apart from Charlie. He was walking quietly beside her, his head moving from side to side looking at the city and sometimes turning around.

"What are you doing?" she asked.

"Trying to remember where we're going. I always do that in a new city. It looks different going back the way you came, so I try to look at it from both directions. Besides, I've never been here before. I'm just looking at it. It's pretty cool. I love the plants growing over things. That's very delf."

"Could you do it less obviously? It looks odd."

"Sorry," he said and for a few minutes he stopped doing it.

116

She was glad he liked Linana.

They passed a higher rocky outcrop topped by battlements, a light tower and twin towers.

"Is that a church?" Charlie asked.

"Of course. The cathedral of Mary, the Star of the Sea."

"Do you go?"

"No. A few times. Father does not."

"Don't they make you?"

"No. I think most of the Christians go."

Charlie was surprised.

"So where are we? It's only been a few years since I was here and delf and humans were all set to kill each other. How is it this different? You talked about generations of puoli."

"That may be the case in Unama. We hear a few things from the trading ships, but you never know what to believe of the stories of sailors and traders. But this is not Unama and the humans here are not the ones you would have seen from Outreterre. Not for hundreds of years. My father's ancestors came from across the sea. From Outreterre. They wanted to explore, where the others wanted to stay where they were. They started out by fighting the delf, then ended up working with them. That is where the Republic started. Delf would not have thought of doing that sort of thing on their own. It is a human thing."

They walked only slowly across the city, moving at the pace of the slowest people in the front. There seemed to be no hurry.

"We're not going very fast. I thought people were afraid of these werebeasts."

"Yes, but they only appear at night."

"Can they survive daylight?"

Rua shrugged.

"They have managed to kill each one before the day came."

They emerged into a square. On the other side was a bridge across a gap. As they crossed it bridge, he looked down with amazement. The sea was foaming against the cliffs in the confined space and further along, a waterfall tipped over the edge, sending up a mist of spray. Beyond it was another bridge.

"That's impressive," he said.

They entered another square with a church on their right. Beyond the square the road led amongst buildings and another road turned off it climbing up to the gate of the Tower of the Stars. It was surrounded by a high wall with towers. The light funnel itself rose up tall in the middle from a much larger structure than he had seen in Unama.

"Looks more like a castle than a light tower."

"They all look like that," Rua replied. "I suppose it's what happens when delf and humans build together."

They came to a standstill. The delay was caused by the bottleneck at the main gate. The narrow road came to a terrace with balustrades which projected like a stage from the front wall and stood above the buildings backing onto the square.

When they finally reached the gate, each puoli was being recorded as they entered.

"What are we going to say for me?"

"I don't know. Your name?"

There were four guards on the gate. One was tall and gave Rua a broad smile, ignoring Charlie. Rua smiled back and Charlie unconsciously pulled himself up to his full height. He felt put out.

"Hey," said the guard. "Good morning. What is your name then?"

"Rua Grafton."

"Rua, lovely name."

Pathetic, thought Charlie.

"Why are you taking our names?" Rua asked.

"If anything happens, we can see if we have lost anyone. We will take good care of you here. I will see to it myself." He winked.

Charlie eyed the guard's thin moustache and beard scornfully.

"Where do you live? In case there happens to be another Rua Grafton."

"The Kettlewalk."

"I will see you around, Rua Grafton."

He turned to Charlie.

"Name?"

"Charlie Denham."

"Street?"

"The Kettlewalk," said Charlie.

"Ah. You together?"

"We're friends," said Rua. Charlie wondered what he would have said. The guard nodded slowly and gestured them into the courtyard of the tower.

It was already busy. Shelters were being erected on the open ground from wooden frames and canvas sheeting. Puoli were milling about or sitting in groups. Two shelters had already been completed. Family groups with younger children were being directed into the buildings against the main walls and custodians looked down on all from the tops of the perimeter towers.

"Right. What do we do now then?" Charlie asked. "Shall we have a look around?"

They walked slowly around the courtyard. Rua often greeted people she knew.

"You seem to know half the city."

"We have a lot of customers."

"What is it you do again?"

"My father is a physician. Amongst other things."

"Other things?"

"Oh..." Rua seemed to be searching for words. "He is also an alchemist."

"Really? Don't they make gold or something?"

"No," she replied, a little as though he were an idiot. He decided not to ask anything else.

When they reached one of the buildings, they made to go inside, but a guard put his hand out.

"You can stay out here. It is just those with little ones going inside."

They shrugged and carried on around.

"I think we should find ourselves a spot soon before it fills up completely," said Charlie. "How many people are they going to fit in here?"

Rua shrugged. "I don't know. There must be a few thousand in the city. Rosa!"

Another girl was approaching them. She was a little taller than Rua with longer brown hair and wearing a loose white blouse. She was smiling at Rua, but he noticed her glance at him. The two girls embraced.

"This is my friend Rosa. And this is Charlie."

She smiled at Charlie, but there was a quizzical look to it.

"You have never told me about Charlie before," she said.

"We only just met," said Charlie. "Hey, I'll just go for a look around. See you back here?"

Rua nodded. Charlie was sure he was going to be talked about and it would be easier if he was not there. He decided to count the people inside the courtyard. Counting passed the time, but people were moving about so much and more were coming in all the time that he soon gave up. All he knew was that it was very crowded.

People were still arranging themselves, setting out blankets and bags and making little camps for themselves, getting to know their neighbours and setting up shades against the sun.

Around midday the smell of food began to fill the courtyard. Kitchens had been set up around it, so he made his way back to Rua. She was just where he had left her, once he found the spot again himself. She and Rosa were reading. Rua looked up and gave him a quick smile. Rosa looked at him with interest which showed he had been explained to her.

"Find anything?" Rua asked.

"People," he replied. "And lunch, I think."

They queued for food. Rua had a wooden platter with her and Charlie pulled out a white enamelled tin plate from his pack.

"That's nice," Rua said.

"You think?" She hadn't seemed to be joking. "It's a camping plate."

When they sat down to eat, she was interested in his cutlery too.

"This is a very lightweight metal. What is it?"

"I don't know. Aluminium?"

"Is it special?"

"Not really."

"I have glimpsed your world in my dreams too," said Rosa. "Rua and I can see that far because we are first generation."

"Is that why you are friends?"

"Our parents were friends first. They naturally drew together when others shook their heads at a mixed couple. There had not been any for many years."

"Oh," said Charlie. He was not sure what else to say. "That doesn't sound very friendly of them."

"People can be small-minded with things they are not used to," said Rosa.

The two girls talked animatedly over lunch. They chatted about people they knew. Rua smiled easily, her whole face changing when she did. Rosa was more serious.

Charlie felt as though he was in the way, so went for another walk in the afternoon. He found a corner to sit and watch the puoli. At one time they had been half delf and half human, but now they were completely mixed after generations of inter-breeding. In general, they were of middle build or slighter. He was taller than most of them. Almost all had dark hair, but the colour of their skin varied from white to a dark bronze red, darker than any delf he had seen before. Deep brown eyes were common, but there were also some with paler brown or green eyes. These looked quite startling and there seemed to be no correlation between eye and skin colour. Green eyes seemed to be as likely on darker skin as light skin. He even saw some that were almost blond. In the main, they were a good looking people, he decided. Many had the fine bone structure and narrow faces that he had come to expect of the delf.

He was pleased to find Rua again in the afternoon. He wanted to have something specific to tell her about his afternoon, but all he could think of was the obvious observation about the sheer number of people.

Dinner was very similar to the meal served at lunchtime. Rosa was not there, but she came back after the meal, bearing a kind of cake which her mother had made. Afterwards, people sat talking quietly. Somewhere, instruments were playing. It felt like a music festival Charlie had been to the previous summer. They were sitting close together and Charlie could feel Rua's leg lightly touching his.

"Charlie, do you still have a father and mother?" she asked.

"Yes," said Charlie and suddenly felt guilty that he had not even realised that she had only ever mentioned her father. He assumed her mother was dead, or at least, no longer around.

"What do they do?"

"Dad runs outward bound training for companies and Mum's a call centre supervisor," he replied. Then he looked at her. She was staring at him. He burst out laughing. "I don't think you have either of them here. Dad kind of teaches people to look after themselves in the mountains and find out about themselves. Mum works at a place where, they...help people to save money."

"Is your world very different?" Rosa asked.

"Yeah, I suppose it is. Or my part of it is. Other parts of it are probably a bit more like this." He looked around. "But then your world has different places too. This is nothing like Unama."

He wanted to keep talking to her, but there seemed to be so much to ask and there were so many people around he was reluctant to do so in case people overheard. There were enough nervous people about with arousing any suspicion through strange questions and answers.

The sun went down. A couple of puoli nearby pulled out a flute and a stringed instrument which was plucked on the lap. Puoli in the group around them started to sing. It was a kind of wavering song which seemed to hang in the air like a hovering fly. Most of the songs seemed to be in a similar vein. Rua smiled as she listened and he watched her profile. It was flat with a small, thin nose. When she turned to see how he was enjoying it, she almost caught him looking at her. Perhaps she had seen, but she just smiled.

"Do you know any songs?"

"A few," she smiled, then turned back to the other singers.

There was a flurry of night time routines. Latrines had been erected and water was provided in large barrels. Rua and Charlie found a place to sleep under a shelter. Rosa was not far away, helping some friends with three young children. The evening was warm. Charlie had a sleeping bag in his pack, but was loathe to bring it out because he knew it would attract attention. Instead he slept in the coat Rua had let him borrow.

The ground was firm. He had spent a few nights on the road sleeping on hard ground and the night was mild. He was aware of the thousands of people all around him and it disturbed him. There was coughing, chatter, odd sounds of things falling or being knocked together, but gradually it began to fade away. Instead, he heard breathing around him, deep and slow. Rua was asleep. Lanterns hung silently on the walls. Flaming torches flickered and licked at the air on top of each of the towers.

He looked at the sky as the clouds began to clear and gave way to a night of stars. He saw the sentries on the towers. He pondered his day. He realised it was the first time he had had to really collect his thoughts. He was back. In Unama or at least the same world. He wondered how he had come through and remembered something Solimo had once told him.

"Dreams are the frayed edges of reality. Our worlds are linked by dreams. Every once in a while, someone dreams so vividly that a thread wraps itself around a thread from another reality. And there the worlds join. Some can do this deliberately. Others do it by accident."

Which was he? The accidental kind it seemed; and so was Rua. But now he was here, he needed to get home again. Solimo could have sent him home again. He wondered how he could contact him. Just how far away was he? Or could he return with Rua's help? That seemed doubtful. Unlike Solimo, she appeared to have no control over her dreams. She had talked about Knight Wardens. They sounded something like Light Keepers. He wondered if they could help him, although there was a climate of fear around strangers which he would need to negotiate. He was worried, but excited too. He had left home to travel and have experiences. Perhaps he had met George McClure for a reason so that he would dream of this world again. And as a result, he had met Rua and that was no bad thing.

He saw her in his mind smiling at him. She was very pretty, or at least he thought so. Perhaps it was an unusual kind of pretty that few others would find attractive. Either way, she did not carry herself as if she were attractive and he liked that. The surprising thing was that she seemed to accept him.

The thoughts circled his head and he realised the stars had faded. There seemed to be a mist in the air above the city. He felt cooler and wished again for his sleeping bag. Perhaps no one would notice if he used it now that they were all asleep. He mentally rehearsed climbing into it and feeling warm. Then he thought about waking up after everyone else and being discovered in it and the inevitable curiosity which would follow.

The ground shook. Just for a second. He was no longer thinking of his sleeping bag. Had the ground just shaken? Had he just imagined it? No, it was just one of those moments when you jolt awake as you fall into sleep. He relaxed again.

Once more he felt the shake. He sat bolt upright. He had not been asleep. The ground *had* moved, if only for a moment. His heart was beating faster. Perhaps they had earthquakes here. He looked around. From what he could see by the lights of the lanterns, no one else had moved. Perhaps he was in a seismic zone and this was normal for them.

Then the ground shook again. This time it did not stop for a few moments. Instead it eased but weaker tremors continued. Still no one was moving.

"Rua!" he hissed.

She did not move. How could she sleep so soundly? How could everyone sleep through it? Were they all that sleep deprived? He looked up at the towers. Surely the guards had noticed it? He could not see any of them.

The clouds had completely misted over. The mist had sunk into the courtyard itself. The shaking had become a dull rolling under his feet. It was a horrible sensation. It felt like standing on a floating pier, except he knew he was not floating. He bent over Rua.

"Rua, it's an earthquake! Wake up!"

He shook her. She slept on. He tried to remember what to do in an earthquake. Get under cover? Get away from things that could fall? He pulled on his boots then looked around for Rua's bag, locating it by her shoulder. He picked it up and tied it to his own pack, then put it on his shoulders. He had all he needed now.

The shelter above him had begun to sway. The rolling was increasing in frequency. Why was no one waking up? Was this a dream? It had to be; something odd was going on. He slapped himself in the face. It felt real, but he had been fooled by dreams before. He stood on one leg and tried to stand on his toes. The rolling made him lose his balance and he fell. He put out his hands and landed on a sleeping puoli.

"Ah, sorry!" he said automatically, but the puoli did not move. He continued to breathe slowly and deeply as if drugged, oblivious to the shaking.

Then the world began to lurch. Charlie heard cracking, a grinding roar. The funnel tower seemed to be tilting. He stared at it in stunned fascination. It was tilting! Then in slow motion the top portion slid, the funnel tower began to crease in the middle.

He did not think, he reached down and grabbed Rua by the arms. Then he pulled her onto his shoulders in a fireman's lift. She was much lighter than his teammates in rugby training at school. He began to run, trying to find a way through the sleeping bodies.

The funnel tower crashed into the courtyard. Dust billowed into the mist. Distracted, he tripped on a body and tumbled down, spilling Rua onto a sleeping couple. None of them were disturbed. Charlie turned back to look at where the tower had fallen. He was horrified. There had been people sleeping where it had come down.

The ground now felt as if it were part of a giant swing. He looked up madly at the walls and towers as the ground pitched beneath him. Still he could see no guards in the towers. He looked again. Something was wrong. It was the flames of the torches; there was something odd about their movement. It was slow and jagged and irregular.

Then Rua began to moan. She waved an arm. She was dreaming. Her breathing had speeded up.

"Rua, wake up! You're dreaming. Wake up!"

Something told him he had to wake her. He had a hollow feeling in his stomach. Suddenly the top of the tower nearest to him tipped off the stone beneath it. As it toppled inwards, it ripped away at the wall beside it, creating a great tear in the stonework. He turned away as the dust roiled past him. Then he pulled on Rua's arms again. He had to get out. He had to get out!

She was onto his shoulders once more and he was bolting for the pile of rubble before the wall. He scrambled up it uncertainly, balancing Rua's weight on his back. Twice he lost his footing with the shaking. He had to pause, lean and swing a foot forward with the ground as it spun. The earthquake felt as though it had been going on for an age. Rua was twitching and letting out strange little frightened noises. He was swearing now, a single stream of obscenity. It focused his mind. As he reached the summit of the rubble, he realised he was at an outer wall. There was no city beyond it, simply mist giving way to darkness. Without a backward glance, he leapt out into the night.

22

ONCE CHARLIE WAS beyond the walls, he felt safe from falling debris. The ground was still moving, but it seemed to have decreased in intensity. To make matters worse, Rua was making kicking movements with her legs. He gently laid her on the ground, then groped in the side pockets of his backpack. He found his head torch and put it on. He looked at Rua, the light shining in her face.

"Wake up," he said.

She groaned. Then her eyes blinked open, wide with fright. He realised all she could see was the light of his torch. He whipped it off and shone it in his own face.

"It's me. Charlie. You're safe now."

She took a moment to register what he had said.

"Something was coming," she said. "And I knew there were more over the hill."

"It's okay. It was just a dream. There's just been an earthquake."

"A what?"

"A really big earthquake. You can still feel it."

"An earthquake? What's that?"

"It's when the earth shakes."

"The earth doesn't shake."

"Well it bloody did tonight. But everyone slept through it. I was trying to wake you, but you wouldn't. No one would wake up."

"There was something coming. It was coming for me, but then it didn't need me because there was a big hole behind me."

"It's okay, it was a dream."

"It wasn't just a dream. It was real. It was trying to get in." She sat up. "Where are we?"

"Outside the walls." He gestured behind them. She looked and could see the gap in the walls from the dim light inside, but it was not clear. It was like looking through frosted glass. None of the rest of the city was visible from where they sat. Something moved across the gap and disappeared.

"We must get away from here," she said.

"What's the matter?"

"I'm not sure. Shine that light around us."

Charlie did so. It revealed rocks giving onto the thick forest.

"We can't get through there. We'll have to go back to the city."

"No. Not back to the city," Rua said.

"What?"

"I've got a bad feeling. We need to go through the forest."

Charlie shone the torch at the trees again. He felt wide awake.

"Does anything live in there? Wild animals I mean."

"No. Well, sometimes cobs, but rarely this close to the city."

"Great. Well at least I know they don't like torches. Can you walk?"

"Yes, I think so."

He stood and put out his hand. She took it as she stood. Then she swayed and grabbed at him. He put out both hands to steady her.

"Are you sure you're alright?"

"No, but it will pass. Come on, this way." She simply turned and headed towards the trees. "Come on," she repeated. "You lead the way. You have a lantern."

Charlie went ahead, found a gap in the bushes and went through.

"What way do we go?"

"Just go downhill. And try not to go too far to the right."

They scrabbled through the undergrowth. Once amongst the trees it was not so thick because the vegetation grew thicker on the edges where there was more light. Now Charlie could make out a way between the trees. Twigs and branches would whip him in the face and he took to walking with an arm raised to guard himself. Every minute or so he would turn to make sure Rua was still behind him. She was always there and was adopting the same pose with both of her arms.

The way sloped gently, but their flight through the trees seemed interminable. They could have been going anywhere. Eventually Charlie paused, pointed his torch at the ground, then turned it off.

"What is the matter? Why have you stopped?" Rua asked.

"I want to see if I can see anything."

He waited for a few minutes while his eyes adjusted to the darkness.

"Can you see anything?" he asked.

"I can see the trees."

"And I think it's a bit lighter over there. Or I might be imagining things." Charlie pointed away to the left where the darkness seemed less dark. "Let's have a look over there."

He kept his torch off and walked carefully. As he went, the light did indeed grow and they came to the edge of the trees. They pushed through the bushes and came out from under the foliage. Shrubs dotted the stony ground. They left the cover of the trees and looked around them. Less than a hundred metres ahead, a knob of rock rose above the trees. There were flatter sections amidst steeper faces. Charlie headed towards it.

"Let's get our bearings from up there," he said.

They walked up it, holding onto the rock for support in places. Once they were above the treetops, they turned to look around them. A few hundred metres away, to the west, the escarpment ended in a steep drop of deeper darkness. To the east was another darkness with a few lights grouped together in the near distance. Almost south of them was the city. What they saw astounded them.

The city was dimly visible on the high point of the range, its walls, buildings and towers silhouetted against the sky in which stars were twinkling. On the eastern side of the city, where the Tower of the Stars was sited, there sat a glowing fog. As it swirled, broken and ragged walls became visible before vanishing.

"What's that?" Charlie asked.

"I do not know," Rua replied. "Is that your earthquake?"

"Earthquakes only shake. Is it dust lit by a fire? It doesn't look like it."

"Fire flickers. That light is constant."

"It'll be from the light tower…" Charlie's voice tailed off even as he spoke. "But it doesn't look right."

"How are you an expert in the light?" asked Rua taking her eyes off the city for a moment and looking at the shape of his face in the night beside her.

"I'm no expert, but I've seen all the lights. I don't remember them looking like that, but it reminds me of something I can't put my finger on."

"Something is moving in there," said Rua, her eye caught by a shadow in the fog. "I can't tell what it is."

The shadow passed across the gap in the wall again. Then it paused and seemed to lean out of the fog for a moment. Rua gasped and flattened herself onto the ground. Charlie instinctively did the same thing.

"What's the matter?"

Rua was breathing harder.

"It was in my dream," she said.

"What?"

"It was in my dream. It was the same."

"But you hardly saw it. I couldn't see what it was."

"I saw it for long enough. It was a wolf." She looked at Charlie's face in the dull illumination of the distant glow. "It was a man with a wolf's head. They are in my dreams. They've been coming for me. Now they're here. Is it looking for me?"

"When you're awake?"

"I don't know."

Then a sudden look of concern came to her face.

"Rosa! She had the same dream as me!"

"About the wolves?"

She nodded.

"Do you want to go back?" he asked.

"I'm afraid to. But I'm afraid for her."

"You said yourself, you can't. And what could you do? Isn't the city filled with soldiers? They'll know what to do."

"You're right. The Wardens must deal with them. I am afraid to stay, but I'm not afraid of the desert."

"The desert?"

"To find my father. He will know what is happening, probably better than the Wardens. He has read more of the lore. He's in Naadu."

"Where's that?"

"North across the desert."

"How can we cross a desert?"

"I know where there's water. My father taught me how to find it and he also has caches of food and water in the places he goes to most often. And I know where we can find horses. You do ride don't you?"

"Actually yes," said Charlie, suddenly pleased with himself.

"We need to get to Akus. It is where the rivers meet. Not far. We should be there in two hours. Follow me."

Charlie had no choice. He pulled his pack on his back again and with a final look at the strange city behind, they were off down the slope.

23

HENRY AND EDWARD Clifford were on a wall looking towards where the Tower of the Stars had once stood. In its place was a half ruined circuit of wall filled with a misty dull grey light which glowed strangely in the dark city. They gripped the parapet as another tremor rolled under them. They had seen the light tower fall, but the tremors they were feeling outside the walls of the light tower did not seem strong enough to have caused it.

They had made their way to the citadel walls as the first reports had come in of what was going on. The gorge yawned below them a few streets away. The North Bridge stretched across the gap. Below, lining the street, hundreds of the custodian guard were formed up in squads facing the Old Quarter.

"Where is that light coming from?" Edward asked, as much to himself as to his father.

"The puoli must be dead. I haven't seen one come out since we came up here."

"They can't be dead. The shaking is all but stopped, it will be safe now to go in. I'll take the men in."

"You should be resting your arm."

"I promise you I won't lift anyone."

Edward went down from the wall and Henry saw his son walk out amongst the companies arranged below and call out orders. Then he watched the soldiers follow him at the double across North Bridge. They entered the streets below the Tower of the Stars and they disappeared from sight amongst the buildings, reappearing higher up, beside the wall. He led the troops to the broken gates which hung open, forcing the guardsmen to pick their way around fallen blocks of masonry.

From this vantage point in the citadel, Henry could see inside the walls of the Tower of the Stars. He could just make out Edward bending down to inspect the first puoli inside the compound. He and other soldiers then began to make their way around the other bodies. None of them appeared to move. More of the soldiers were inside now and they were fanning out amongst the puoli.

Suddenly Edward stopped in his tracks. The senator tried to see what had caught Edward's eye. At the far side of the courtyard, where the mist was thickest and the light brightest, there were shadows in the fog. Something was moving in there. A shape emerged. He peered at it. Had a puoli survived? He looked again. Something was wrong.

Edward was backing up. Custodian guardsmen all over the courtyard were standing now. He could faintly hear orders being shouted. The soldiers were forming up. The figure which had emerged was not alone. There were three of them, dark shapes with strangely shaped helmets. The soldiers had formed two firing lines. Those without long-arms were standing at the back, swords drawn.

The three figures were coming towards them. They moved quickly, but seemed to slow down as they came closer. Henry could see they were holding things in their hands. Could these be more werebeasts? He saw the flash of the long-arms moments before he heard the sound of gunfire. He saw the werebeasts stutter in their forward motion, but where he had expected them to fall, they did not. Instead they came on towards the soldiers.

The second rank of soldiers fired. Once more the creatures came forward. He must call the Knight Wardens. Two soldiers were already sprinting down the street outside the walls.

He could hear more orders and the soldiers behind the front ranks raised their swords and charged at the werebeasts. The creatures were swamped by the soldiers. He could not see what was happening. He thought he saw men fall. All he could see was confusion. Then the guards backed away. Some were on the ground, others were supported by their fellows, but the creatures lay where they had fallen. They had been dismembered, dark limbs scattered about them.

Edward called back his troops. He was shocked at how many were injured, or worse.

"Collect up their bodies," he called. "The Wardens need to inspect them."

He went up to the bodies himself with those he had ordered forward. Some picked up their fallen comrades. The others stood looking with disgust at the werebeasts.

They had the heads of wolves with black bristly hair. Their teeth were sharp and red tongues lolled from between their jaws. Like the other he had seen, they were wearing black chainmail. He bent down to feel it. To his surprise it would not lift. It was like the beast's skin. His hand recoiled in shock. In their gauntleted hands, now lying a short distance from the body, they carried ugly looking axes. But what puzzled him most was that there was no blood. The heads had been hacked at and they were maimed with slashes. Two had had their heads almost severed from the body, but there was no blood anywhere. He pushed one with his foot. He half expected it to move and look at him.

Four soldiers stood behind him. They watched in horrified fascination.

"Find blankets to carry them," he said. "Don't touch them. Use gloves."

He looked around at the puoli again. Sleeping. They had not been able to wake them. He could see them breathing, but they slept like the dead. He shivered.

His men picked up the torso of the first werebeast, rolling it roughly onto the waiting blanket. Its head lolled off its neck and the guardsman closest to it jumped back involuntarily. Then they began to pick up its limbs. They were about to pick up the blanket again when a voice just behind him called out.

"There are more of them!"

Edward Clifford looked up and there, emerging from the fog on the far side were more of the wolf men. Five, six of them this time. Then a seventh.

"Form up!" he called. He bent down and tried to wrench the axe from the hand in the blanket, but it would not come away and for a moment he was brandishing the whole arm. He dropped it and drew his sword again. Where were the Wardens?

The wolf soldiers came at them. They seemed in no hurry, but they walked with an unwavering purpose. The custodians fired volleys at them again. Once more, the creatures staggered backwards with the impact of the bullets, but kept coming at them.

Clifford directed his men into squads and sent them against individual werebeasts. They approached them with swords outstretched, but as they neared the beasts, the animals began to slash with their axes. The soldiers jumped back, surprised this time by the resistance.

"Back off! Back off!" the captain roared.

The soldiers backed away. Clifford picked up a rock from the ground that fitted into his hand and lobbed it at the nearest beast. The stone bounced off and the creature stopped and turned its head towards him.

"Back behind the gate!" he called. He did not want any of his men to face them unnecessarily. The first of his troops were retreating through the gate when the wardens arrived, their crimson capes billowing as they ran. There were ten of them and they were taken aback by the number of werebeasts.

"They're all yours," said Clifford, then he turned to a sergeant at arms. "I need pikemen, lancers."

The sergeant frowned at him.

"Pikes?"

"Use the ceremonial ones. In the armoury."

Then he turned to watch the Wardens. Two sun wraiths hovered in front of them already, their weavers standing at the front, their comrades ready behind to weave more if necessary. Suddenly the wolfmen charged. The sun wraiths whipped into movement at the speed of an eye and the four leading werebeasts collapsed, their hair and mail burnt, but the other three came on. The sun wraiths turned on them. They swooped at two of the werebeasts, but one of the creatures was missed and swung its axe at the nearest warden. He leapt back, but as the axe fell it crashed into his boot and he dropped to the ground, his face screwed up in anguish.

Another sun wraith flew from the hand of another of the Wardens. Within a minute, all seven creatures lay unmoving and burned on the ground.

The leader of the Wardens turned to Clifford.

"They were too close. If more come, we need to burn them before they come that close again."

"I have sent for pikes and lances. We need to keep them at bay. Long-arms are useless against them and swords are too dangerous, too close to them."

"Where are they coming from?" the Warden officer asked.

"I was hoping you would be able to tell me," Edward replied. "They came from out of that," he said and pointed at the opposite side of the courtyard where the fog was at its brightest.

The officer looked at the remains of the Tower of the Stars which was lying crumpled across the ground.

"Have you looked in there yet?"

Clifford shook his head. "Not yet." Then he turned to some of his men who were standing behind them. They nodded and walked off to see what they could find.

The Warden officer turned to his own men.

"Follow me. Be ready."

They began to walk across the courtyard and the officer noticed Clifford was following.

"Where are you going?"

"I'm coming with you. I want to see where they're coming from."

The officer looked down at Clifford's wounded arm.

"I think you should stay here. You cannot help us."

"I won't get in your way."

The officer shook his head. "Stay here. We will handle this. I don't want to have to worry about you."

They walked carefully across the courtyard, keeping a wary eye on the bright fog ahead of them.

The sun wraiths were fading and the wardens paused, wondering whether they should weave some more. They looked at their officer.

"Light up two," he said.

Then they walked into the mist.

Clifford watched them disappear and waited for them again. He expected them to come back a few moments later. They could only go as far as the wall which by his reckoning was no more than ten yards inside the fog. But they did not come back.

He exchanged puzzled glances with the men by his side. There was silence in the courtyard. Time appeared to be stretching out. Another tremor shook them. Clifford tensed his legs and regained his balance. Then he looked to his right to see a block of masonry lean slowly forward. At first he thought it would not fall, then, impossibly slowly, it tipped forward and floated down in a lazy rolling motion. A small cloud of dust billowed gracefully around it with equal slowness.

He turned back to the fog. It drifted in front of him. He wanted to know what was inside it. He realised he was walking slowly forwards. He must know what the Wardens were doing. A chill ran over him and the hairs stood up on his neck and down his forearms. He could no longer feel the warm evening air.

He walked closer, stepping over the sleeping bodies of puoli without looking at them.

He entered the fog suddenly. It was thick and he could barely see in front of him. He walked some more. He kept expecting to reach the wall, but he did not. It must have collapsed with the earthquake, but looking around, he could see nothing, only the flat stony ground.

The mist was thinning and he could see a kind of daylight. He could see hills and a forest. He stopped, frozen to the spot. Ahead was a grassy plain and low hills. Right in front of him were bodies, the bodies of dozens, perhaps hundreds of burned werebeasts. Amongst them were the ruined bodies of the ten Wardens.

And he realised the forest was no forest. He was out of the mist now and could see clearly. There was a great crowd of thousands of men with the heads of wolves. They stood dark and unmoving, but all their eyes were on him. And in their centre was a man on a white horse. He had long greying hair and a crimson cloak.

Clifford had no idea how long he stood there. It could have been moments or hours. Then he turned and fled back into the mist.

24

CHARLIE AND RUA walked across the humped ridge of the escarpment around the back of the forest until they came to a long, shallow slope. Rua led the way at an angle, following the edge of the trees until Charlie could see a few lights twinkling out in the darkness, the same he had seen from the knob on the ridge.

"That's Akus," said Rua. "We just head for those lights."

They walked through grass. Charlie could barely see it, but felt it swishing about his knees. He was disconcerted by the darkness.

"Do you know where you're going? I can't see a thing."

"Just follow me. The river is over there. You'd hear it before you fell in it."

She sounded as though she thought he was an idiot. Perhaps she walked around in the dark all the time. They continued through the grass, Charlie trying to walk as close behind her as he could, but he almost bumped into her when she stopped suddenly.

"Shh!" she said. "Did you hear something?"

Charlie listened. There was no sound, just the occasional whisper of a breeze across long grass. They set off again. Seeing she was nervous made him worry too. Perhaps there was good reason to be nervous and he was just ignorant of the danger.

The lights became closer and the vague shapes of buildings formed around them. Then Charlie could indeed hear the river as a rushing hiss.

Suddenly they were crunching on gravel as they entered the main street of Akus. It was empty apart from the two of them. They walked quietly down wooden boardwalks until they reached a wide two storey building. A light was on inside, left by the window.

"Tibo leaves that there in case a caravan comes through at night," said Rua. "He will be surprised to see me."

"What time is it?" asked Charlie.

Rua looked to the east.

"I feel it will be dawn within the hour."

She tried the door and it opened into a small antechamber where the lantern was sitting on a shelf by the window. There was another door on the far side. Rua went over to this and knocked on it three times. It took about a minute for them to hear movement, then a voice spoke on the other side of the door.

"Who is it?"

"Rua Grafton."

There was a noise of unbolting and the door opened outwards revealing a tall, elderly delf with his hair tied back and a candle in his hand.

"What are you doing waking me at this time? Wait – is your father home?"

"No," said Rua. "But I need horses. Two."

Tibo glanced at Charlie behind her. Rua saw the look.

"This is Charlie. My friend. We're going to look for my father."

Charlie could not remember when someone had looked at him so suspiciously before.

"At this time of night? Come back at lunchtime."

"Tibo, I need to find him. And I need to get out of Linana."

"Are you in some kind of trouble?" said Tibo. He looked both concerned and stern at the same time.

Rua tried to find the right words, but gave up. "I don't know. I hope he can tell me."

Tibo narrowed his eyes. "Will I get in any trouble if I let you have horses?"

"Not with the City," said Rua.

Tibo looked at her, then shook his head.

"If I were not so tired, I could think straight. I will probably regret this in the light," he muttered. "But remember Kallick's legion is camped by the river, so you might want to go around them. "Especially," he said with a raised eyebrow, "if you are in any trouble."

Without another word, he led them through a third door in the anteroom and down a corridor hung with leather and metal which gleamed in the light of his candle. At the end, they came to a door which opened into a larger room. Charlie could smell horse before the door was even opened and indeed there were a few snorts as they entered and Tibo lit a lantern just next to the door.

Light and shadows tipped across the room. It was a stable with stalls on either side. Tibo looked Charlie up and down, then walked off down the line of stalls. He stopped half way down and turned back to face them, looking surprised to see they were right behind him.

"Rua, this one will be good for you. The one at the end will do for your friend. I will fetch saddles."

He returned with a saddle and a lantern for Charlie, both of which he thrust at him. Charlie stood puzzled for a moment and realised he was supposed to know what to do with the saddle and harness. He had learned once, but it had been a while ago. He found the horse Tibo had indicated. She blew through her nose and shook her head as he came in. Charlie started to talk softly to her. He patted her neck. Then he lifted the saddle onto her back and tried to remember how to fix it on. It was unfamiliar and he wrestled with it, all the time muttering soft nonsense for the horse's benefit.

He heard the stall door open behind him. It was Tibo.

"What are you doing? Have you never done this before?"

"I have, but with a different harness. This one's a bit funny."

"There is nothing funny about my harness, boy."

He made some adjustments.

"There. And I hope you were watching." Then he pressed his face up close to Charlie's. "And you watch yourself with Rua. I do not know what you are doing and I do not know you, but I cannot help feeling you are why she is running like this."

"I can assure you I'm not the reason," said Charlie.

"I do not believe you. If any harm comes to her, harm will follow you," he said.

Charlie felt suddenly cross and foolishly brave. "No harm will come to her while I'm there to stop it. I promise you."

The old delf grabbed his wrist and looked him in the eyes.

"Promise me, do you?" he said.

Charlie nodded, disturbed by the delf's look.

"Well I will hold you to it, boy. But from the look of you, she will be the one stopping harm to you."

He dropped Charlie's arm dismissively and picked up a couple of things that he had put by the door.

"Some provisions," he said. "There is room in the saddlebags."

Then he walked over to the doors at the end of the stable and opened them. Charlie thought it had become lighter outside.

Rua was leading out her horse. Charlie did the same. Out on the street, Charlie pulled himself up into the saddle and tried to remember how to ride.

"Thank you," said Rua.

Tibo grunted. "I am still charging you," he said.

"Of course," she said.

"And if I do not hear word within three weeks, I will kill you both," he said.

"If that happens, I can't promise to pay," Rua smiled as she climbed easily into the saddle. Then she made a clicking sound with her mouth and rode forward. Charlie imitated the noise and his mare seemed in two minds about whether to stay or go. Tibo tapped her rear and Charlie followed Rua and caught up so that he was riding alongside.

Rua turned. Tibo was still standing by the open doors of his stable. She raised her hand to him, then turned back. Charlie looked at the horizon to his right. There was a paler light behind the hills as the sun's rays began to crawl up the sky. A thought occurred to him.

"How far's Naadu?"

"About eight days," she said. "Plenty of time to tell me how you know so much."

So that was how they spent their first day. For only the second time in his life, yet the second time in three days, Charlie told of how he and his father had separately found themselves in Unama and Outreterre. How his father had been befriended by the Order while Charlie had helped the delf to send a light funnel to his world. It was to collect light even after the Archbishop had made a darkness spread across Unama.

She listened quietly, interjecting a few times. She commented on his age, she asked about his father and mother. As she did so, he remembered again that she had only ever mentioned her father.

"What happened to your mother?" he asked.

"She died when I was a child. A sickness took her. My father brought me up, but perhaps I stopped being a child quickly as well. He is a very educated man. He was at the university, but he had to give it up when he married my mother."

"Why?" Charlie asked.

140

"Because she was delf and he is human. Puoli can marry puoli, but they don't like new puoli. Father said it is because of the dreams."

"What dreams? Your dreams?"

"Yes. Puoli of the first generation have very vivid dreams. We dream of both worlds even when men cannot dream of the world they came from. Father thinks the joining of the two races stirs up ancestral memories. Rosa does it too. That is how I dreamed of you, and you said you were dreaming of here, so I must have reached through to you without knowing you were there."

Charlie smiled.

"But I didn't always dream of the wolf men," she continued. "That is new. Anyway, my father had to leave the university, but it didn't stop him studying. He is interested in everything, in plants and medicine and history and light lore. I think he must have read every book in the university library."

Charlie talked of how he and his father had been united, then captured by the Archbishop and taken into Limbo. When he reached that part of the tale, she became very animated.

"You have been into Limbo too? Did you see any wolf soldiers? I never saw anything there before. I didn't know if I was seeing Limbo or your world unless I could see your world through Limbo. I've done that a few times."

"I didn't see wolves, but there were these other creatures. They were kind of like men but weird looking. If you dream something in Limbo, you actually create it. I did it myself with someone from school. It was scary. But these ones were like soldiers in armour, but not real people. And there were thousands of them. Someone called them goblins. They were horrible. I was terrified of them."

She became quieter.

"They sound like the creatures I have seen. The way you describe them, they do not seem quite alive. Do you think these could have been dreamed too?"

"I must say I hadn't really thought about it."

"But who could be dreaming them? Did you leave anyone behind?"

"Not that I know about. Even the Archbishop came out to lead his army, but he was killed along with it. But I haven't got to that part of the story yet. But I suppose someone else could have got into Limbo just like we did."

So he continued, telling her how they had met the Mage in Limbo who had been trapped there in his light tower with all his books since the coming of the Order and how they had finally escaped. How the Mage had funnelled the hope of human and delf through himself to create the light of hope, destroying the Archbishop's army which had been created from the Mage's own nightmares of fear and despair.

"You met a mage?" she exclaimed.

"Yes. Solimo always called him the last mage."

"There are no mages now. Father says there used to be mages in Linana as well, but that was before humans came. Now there are just the Knight Wardens and they only use the light as a weapon. He says there were many more uses of the light, just like you talk about, but they do not practise them in Linana anymore."

At the end of the story, Rua sat frowning into the distance.

"What's the matter?" Charlie asked.

"I'm thinking," she replied. "So those goblin soldiers you met, they had been dreamed by the Mage. I'm convinced someone is dreaming the wolf soldiers too." She turned round to face him. "And it must be the Archbishop. You didn't find his body because he was never there. If you saw him, it was just something he had dreamed. That was why you never found his body. It was destroyed by the light of hope along with all the others. You did say that the bodies of the other horsemen were not destroyed by it."

"That's right. I suppose it could be true. I've often wondered it myself, but now I hear you say it, it seems to make complete sense." Charlie was feeling stupid again.

"But why is he sending wolf soldiers into my dreams?"

"Because he can, probably. But I don't know how, the Mage never slept."

"Why not?"

"He was afraid of sleeping and creating more goblins. That's what he told us anyway."

"But what could he have done if he hadn't been afraid of sleeping?" Rua asked.

Charlie shrugged. "We never really had time to ask."

"What happened to him?"

"I don't know. He dreamed us back home, then he disappeared. I often wondered what happened to him. Maybe he went back to Unama. Solimo probably knows."

They continued riding a few moments longer, then Charlie looked up.

"That's what it reminded me of!"

"What?"

"The light on the Tower of the Stars back in Linana. It reminded me of Limbo."

Rua stopped her horse and looked at him.

"You're right. It was flat. There was no sun in that light. You could see, but there was no light. Were we looking into a dream?"

Charlie shook his head. "I've no idea."

"Father would know."

"Or Solimo. He could look it up in the books maybe, except all the best ones are supposed to be still in Limbo where the Mage took them."

"There are books in Limbo? My father would die to read those books." Then she looked horrified. "Could the Archbishop have read those books?"

"I suppose so. The Mage never talked about there being very much to do all day."

"We need to find my father. Now more than ever."

They rode until early evening. Rua stopped at a jumble of rocks which jutted out from the high section of the escarpment like a prow into the flatter highlands. She led the way through them until they came to a narrow cleft in the rock. As they approached, Charlie realised it was actually a cave mouth.

"This is one of the camps we use when we're out here collecting plants. It's big enough for the horses."

She slipped off and looked at the ground outside the hole.

"What are you doing?" Charlie asked.

"Looking for signs of wild cobs."

"Wild cobs?"

"They're rare along here, but I always check anyway. My father's are trained, but he always taught me to be wary of the wild ones. Come on, it looks clear."

She led her horse inside. Charlie stood up in the saddle and took a good look around at the rocks, half expecting one of the large eared ape-like creatures to leap out. But all he could see was the stone turning russet in the low sun. He climbed down, took his horse's reins and followed Rua inside the rock.

It was dry and cool and the walls leaned towards each other like a tent, coming together in a crack along the ceiling. The cave led back about thirty feet.

Rua tied the horses to a knob of rock at the rear, then came back to Charlie near the entrance.

"Did you make this?" he asked, pointing his foot at a ring of stones on the floor which surrounded a patch of fire blackened ground.

"Oh, there have been cobs here!" she exclaimed, startled. Charlie's eyes widened, then she chuckled. "Yes. That was us. We haven't been here for a few months, but the wind can't get in here."

"That's just as well. It was looking a bit stormy out there," Charlie said.

They ate a rather chewy rehydrated stew from one of the saddlebags. Charlie was picking at an irritating piece of food that was lodged in one of his teeth. He felt great satisfaction when he finally removed it.

"What did you mean about wild cobs? All the ones I met in Unama were servants of the Order."

"They can be trained, but usually only if you separate the children from the parents when they're very young. Father uses some to help him in his work. He's trained them to power his light needle."

"What's that?"

"He's been experimenting with light lore. No one's interested in Linana now, although he thinks the Wardens might not like him playing with light. That's why he's gone south. The needle is like a funnel in reverse, only much smaller. It can focus collected light still further. We worked on it together."

They talked a little longer until the fire burned down. They had no more wood to put on it and there was nothing left to do but go to sleep. It was almost completely dark in the cave, with just a grey slab of night sky breaking the total darkness of the inside of their shelter. Charlie thought of Rua lying nearby and looked at that grey opening. Lying down, he realised just how tired he was. Before he knew it, his eyes were closed and he was asleep.

Rua was sat on the step of Charlie's house as he walked down the street. As he approached, she turned her head and smiled at him.

"Hello Charlie," she said. It was only two words, but they seemed full of meaning. She loved him. It was clear.

A warm glow suffused him. Charlie opened his eyes and felt a sense of loss. A grey light entered the cave. It was early morning, he guessed. He turned his head. Rua was still asleep, her head turned away from him. He lay watching her for a few moments, then pulled himself out of his sleeping bag. One of the horses snorted and he glanced at Rua, but she slept on. Being careful not to make any noise, he walked softly outside.

The sky was overcast and there was a strong offshore breeze. He stretched and walked up the slope until he could look down over the sea. North and south, it stretched for mile after mile. The breeze was cool, but fresh. He went back down to the level of the cave mouth and hopped about on the spot to warm himself. He felt the need to move and exercise so he jogged around the rocks. He was interrupted by a call from Rua.

"Charlie! Where are you?"

He jogged around from behind a rock. She looked worried.

"What are you doing?"

"Just having a stretch. What's up?"

"I think someone's coming."

Charlie looked around automatically.

"Which way?"

"I dreamed it. Someone's looking for me."

"Your father?"

"No. I don't think so. I don't know, but I woke up feeling it was someone I didn't like."

"Are you sure it wasn't just a dream?"

"No, but I'm not sure I believe in just a dream any more."

"So who don't you like?"

"No one. I like everyone I know."

"Were there any of those wolf soldiers in it?"

She shook her head.

"Well that's a plus. Let's just have some breakfast and get going then. If there is someone after us, we'll still be ahead of them."

They rode all day. As the day progressed, the breeze grew into a wind. They saw no signs of life and whenever they stopped to look over the escarpment at the road, that was empty too.

That night, they had to sleep in the open, although they found a space out of the wind amongst the rocks along the top of the escarpment. There was nothing to make a fire out of, so they ate fruit and nuts and hunks of bread which was no longer fresh.

Rua was nervous as they prepared to sleep.

"You're worried about that dream again aren't you?" Charlie said.

"I am. You think it's silly don't you?"

"I don't. I've had a very open mind for years."

"But what if there is someone following us? What if I dream of the wolf soldiers again, and we're out here on our own?"

"Don't worry. Look, you're knackered. You go to sleep and I'll watch you. I can tell when you're having that dream about the wolves, you look scared."

"I'm afraid to. What if you don't notice?"

"I will. And anyway, you'll end up going to sleep some time anyway, so you might as well do it when I can watch over you."

Charlie liked that expression: watch over you. It sounded responsible and caring at the same time. The girl looked at him with those large brown eyes and he forced himself to look right back into them. I'd watch over you any day of the week, he said to himself.

"I will sleep then, but at the first sign of anything, you wake me. I will not mind if I was not dreaming it. Just wake me, whether you are sure or not."

"Deal," said Charlie.

"What does that mean?"

"I agree. I'll wake you even if I'm not sure."

"Good. Then I will sleep."

She lay back, pulled the coat over herself, curled onto her side and closed her eyes. Charlie watched her for a few minutes. Her breathing began to slow. Then he saw her eyes open. She turned her head.

"It will be boring to watch me."

"It won't," Charlie replied. "Really. I'll cope. Go to sleep."

"Wake me in three hours. Then you can sleep."

She turned back again. He watched her. Her breathing slowed. He could see her whole body relaxing into sleep. He knew she was gone. He relaxed too. She had really needed to sleep. He shifted his position. He had been sitting awkwardly, but had not wanted to move in case it disturbed her. He moved so his back was against one of the stones. His own coat was around him. He looked up. There was cloud across most of the sky, but through a break, he could see a couple of stars twinkling. He watched them until they blinked out behind the clouds.

He sat for a long time, lost in thought. It could have been an hour or two before the moon came up and gleamed through the cloud. Then it suddenly broke free and shone down brightly on the rocks around him. It felt very bright.

Rua made a noise and shifted. He looked down, startled, but her face looked quite calm. She had moved onto her back and he could see her whole face. He stared at her in the moonlight. He looked at her closed eyes, her eyelashes, her lips, the hair nestled around her cheeks. He stared at her lips. He wanted to kiss them.

"I'm in trouble," he muttered to himself.

He looked away, stood up and walked to the edge of the rocks to where he could see across the landscape. The moon tore its way through a thin patch of cloud and rode the silver smoke of cloud which washed around it. The moon lit the landscape strangely. There was no colour and the light created hard shadows which contrasted strongly with the brightness of the moon. He felt as if the world had changed into black and white through which he could somehow imagine colour.

Unearthly, he thought. Then another thought came to him, a thought which had occurred to him many times. Where was this place? He and his father had talked about it often and they had never come to a conclusion that satisfied them. They agreed it was Earth because the stars seemed to be the same, but beyond that, they could not decide.

He realised he was not watching Rua and turned back in a hurry. She had not moved and he was relieved to find she still wore the same calm expression. He made himself look away and study the rocks around their camp. He looked at the way in which the light fell on them and tried to count the different shades of grey. His eyes jumped from one rock to another trying to match up different shades to see if they were the same one. He could not decide. Eventually he gave up and his gaze returned to Rua.

She looked so peaceful. He wondered what it would be like to wake up and turn to see that face next to him. She had a squarish face and a pointed chin. He wanted to reach out and touch her cheek, gently touch it and look into those brown eyes which were hidden behind her eyelids. He thought of those eyes. He wanted to dive into them, be lost in them. What is it about eyes, he wondered.

"Oh God, you're an idiot, Denham," he muttered.

She opened her eyes.

"Did you say something?"

"Er…no. Just talking to myself. Keeping myself awake. You should go back to sleep."

"No. It is your turn. I feel good. What time is it?"

"I don't know, but the moon's over there now, if that helps."

"You let me sleep for over four hours."

"Did I? Sorry. Well you obviously needed it."

"You need some too."

"Yeah, maybe." He tried to sound casual, but he was dog tired and knew it.

"I will stay awake and keep watch."

He smiled ruefully. Then he too curled up on the ground. He turned to look at her. She was not looking at him and he was disappointed.

"Rua," he said.

She looked down. Those eyes. They were so dark in the moonlight.

"What?" she asked.

How long had that pause been?

"If you feel sleepy, wake me. You don't want to fall asleep without me watching."

"Do not worry. I can keep myself awake."

He turned back and closed his eyes. He could still see her. He wanted to open them again and see if she was watching him. Would she look at him as he slept? What did she think about him? Could she be thinking the same thing? No, don't be ridiculous. Why would she? In his mind, he watched her sleeping face. And in his dreams he watched it still.

He knew he had been dreaming of her because she had smiled at him just before he woke up. He woke with the disappointment of knowing he had just been dreaming and therefore it was not real.

The warmth of that smile stayed with him, but only as a haunting unreality.

He opened his eyes and sat up. Where was she? He looked around. Then he saw her perched up on the rocks looking at the view. The sunrise was streaking light across the sky. Of course she had been watching that rather than him.

"Dickhead," he said, shaking his head.

25

HENRY CLIFFORD WATCHED the space where his son had gone. Moments passed with nothing to mark them but the slow drift of the dull, white fog.

Then shouting. Mad, frantic shouting.

A man was running out of the mist. It was Edward.

"They're coming!"

It was shouted at the limit of his voice. He stopped as he saw the men of the guard watching him. He paused, gathered himself, then turned to face the fog once more. He drew his sword and waited.

He must have said something to his men because those behind him drew up in ranks, weapons at the ready. All but two. These went scurrying from the front rank back out through the gate and down the street.

The senator felt uneasy. He had never seen his son react in that way to anything.

He saw the soldiers stir. Something was coming through the mist. This time they came in serried ranks. They marched forward as the others had marched, slowly, steadily.

The soldiers charged and broke upon the wolves. He saw men go down. He saw them pressed back. He looked for his son. He could not see him.

The wolves kept coming. Then the guards fell back. Some turned and ran, others faced forwards, but walked backwards, forming a rear guard for their retreating comrades.

Henry had seen enough. He rushed out of the citadel, through the streets and onto the bridge towards the fleeing soldiers. He met the retreating guards on the far side of the gorge where they had paused to regroup.

"Where is the captain?" he demanded. He grabbed at a soldier near him. "Where is Captain Clifford?"

The man merely shook his head, then looking behind him, tore himself from the older man's grasp and ran on. Clifford followed the soldier's eyes and looked at the gate just as the last man in it was cut down by an axe. Then the beasts were onto the roadway. He had no weapon. He backed away down the street. Someone must come. He picked up a discarded long-arm, checked it was loaded and raised it to his shoulder. He picked out a target, and fired. All the beast did was pause in its walk as the bullet struck it.

There were bells ringing all across the city now. The alarm was up, but the enemy was already inside the walls. Clifford turned and ran down the street. The bridge across the gorge was ahead of him. A group of soldiers had gathered there. They saw him coming and began to call to him.

"Come on sir!"

They were beckoning him. He turned to look behind him. He had lost the wolf soldiers. The street was empty, but the phantom light from the Tower of the Stars leaked a glowing pool across the far end of the road.

There were sounds of shouting coming from over the bridge. A great company of guardsmen was there. They were led by cavalry, while the infantry came at the double. They bore swords, halberds and axes, pikes and lances. Alongside was a second detachment of knight wardens. The senator stood to one side as they swept past him on the bridge.

As he watched them go, he wondered what had become of the first knight wardens. They had not returned.

He could see the first animal soldiers appearing at the end of the road now. As he did, sun wraiths flew from the hands of the wardens and descended on the beasts which burned and fell at their touch.

There was a noise above him. There were men running along the rooftops. They were carrying torches. Then fire was shooting through the night as bolt after flaming bolt was fired by crossbowmen from their vantage point on the houses.

For the first time, the wolf soldiers wavered at this onslaught. The wardens stepped to one side and the cavalry charged into the werebeasts. The charge crushed the front ranks of wolves with its momentum, but they were not afraid of the horses and pushed into them regardless, swinging their axes.

Something about the wolves spooked the horses. They began to rear up, their eyes rolling back. They kicked out in fear. Several riders were thrown, but others found controlling their horse and trying to fight was too much. They rallied their mounts and pulled back.

Immediately, a phalanx of soldiers marched past, lances lowered and charged straight into the close-packed beasts who were still gathering themselves from the arrows and the sun wraiths.

But a strange thing was happening. There were wolves at the front of the invaders who were still moving but were not walking. Some burned, he even saw one with no head. But they came on. They were being pushed forward by those behind. Their march was relentless. Where a wolf beast fell, those behind merely stepped over it or carried it ahead of itself like a shield. Flaming bolts continued to rain down from above, but they were having little effect on the forward motion of the dense pack of wolves.

The weight of men behind the phalanx was itself pushing at the advancing beasts, but it was quivering now. Those at the front had nowhere they could go. Then the phalanx began to be pushed backwards itself. There was a cracking of wood as some of the lances splintered.

More sun wraiths lit up the street and tore into the front ranks. The phalanx stood back. Once more the wolves in black mail seemed themselves to go backward as the wraiths cut like a fiery scythe through their number.

Moments after, Clifford realised there seemed to be fewer flaming bolts than there had been before, a body fell from the top of one of the buildings. Clifford looked up. There were wolves on the rooftops. The bowmen were retreating, firing as they went. Two wolves plummeted down, rolling backwards, their chests cloaked in flame.

Henry had to find out what had happened to his son. He needed to know. He took hold of one man who was wide-eyed with fear.

"Did you see what happened to my son? To Captain Clifford?"

"I'm not sure. He was at the front when they came. I couldn't see. I haven't seen him, my lord. Maybe he's with the injured. They carried some off."

Clifford turned from the battle and hurried down the streets to the infirmary. The clamour of bells continued across the city. Passing houses, he saw fearful faces looking out of the windows. He heard hooves and a rumbling as around the corner came four cannon pulled by horses. They galloped up the road towards the bridges.

When he reached the infirmary, he did not need to ask where the injured men had been taken. A harassed orderly was carrying buckets and towels down a corridor. Drops of blood left their own trail on the floor. The senator simply followed.

He turned into a room lined with beds. Half of them were occupied, but all activity was around four of them which had been newly occupied. One of those had already been covered by a sheet. The man nearest him had lost half an arm and was shivering while the orderly held him and a nurse tried to deal with the stump. Clifford looked away and at the two other men. Neither was his son. He walked in fear towards the fourth and slowly lifted his hand to the top of the sheet. It hovered there for moments, his stomach lurching. He rehearsed in his mind what he would do if Edward was under that sheet.

He pulled it gently at first. It revealed dark hair...was it too dark? Emboldened he pulled some more and a delf face was revealed. His first thought was relief, then he felt revolted at the jaw which had been hacked away from the rest of the face. He covered the delf's face again and walked out of the room. His relief had been temporary. He still did not know what had happened to his son. If he was not still fighting at the bridges, he must have fallen inside the Tower of the Stars.

At that moment there was the distant thunder of cannon fire. As they went off, the bells stopped tolling. Indeed, there was no longer any need for them. The alarm had been raised. The city was racing to defend itself. His place now was with the senate.

Most of the senators were already there when he arrived. They wore the overly alert looks of the newly awoken. Only two of the sides were filled and Clifford realised that the puoli senators must all have been in the Tower of the Stars. There were many conversations going on, but all went quiet when a tall delf in a crimson cape entered accompanied by a broad shouldered man. He was bearded and grim faced. He wore a shining golden breastplate and had removed his helmet which he held tucked under his arm.

"What news, General Wootton?" called out Roger Fitzwarren.

"We are holding them at the bridges," Wootton replied. "They are impervious to long-arm. We don't know if it is their armour, but fire and cannon shot they *are* subject to. It appears they can be dismembered or burned. And of course, the Marshal's men are wreaking havoc in their number."

The delf nodded.

"The knight wardens are at the forefront of the counter attack. These wolf creatures have never been able to withstand the sun raiths and so it continues now."

"Marshal, I have heard it said that a detachment of knight wardens was overcome by the wolves."

"That we do not know. We know only that they are missing."

A murmur went around the room.

"Where are they from? Did they come in from the plain?"

"We will know more in the morning," replied the general. "At the moment, we are concentrating on containing the incursion."

"How many of our forces are employed?" the senator asked.

The general turned to face him.

"The whole of my legion is holding the gorge, except one battalion watching the other walls. We would expect Kallick's legion to be massing now near Akus."

"Expect? Don't you know?" the senator demanded.

"Sir, communications are not simple at night and with the enemy forces occupying the old quarter. If I were in the shoes of General Kallick, I would have had ample notice of the attack and the noise of the alarm would have carried to him without difficulty. There is no wind tonight."

"And may I remind you," the marshal put in, "that there is of course another squadron of wardens with the legion, as well as artillery. We have these wolves between the hammer and the anvil and we will smash them."

Senator Clifford did not reply, but he did not feel as confident as the marshal and the general sounded. He had seen the wolf creatures. They did not look like any enemy he had ever seen before. All the tactics the legions of the republic had ever used had not been tested before on creatures which could brush aside the work of long-arm as if they were pebbles.

There was a movement at the back of the hall and an officer entered. His face was sweating and his hair stuck to his scalp. He stood just inside the doorway and fidgeted where he stood. The two senior soldiers noticed him, but feigned no interest as they awaited further questions from the senate. However the senators were also watching the officer and the silence pointed only at him.

"I believe your officer there has news," said Fitzwarren with meaning. "Do not stand on ceremony with us before you receive it."

Wootton beckoned to the officer who came forward at once. The three heads bent together as the man spoke. Meaningful glances were exchanged, then the general faced the expectant senators again.

"The legion has taken up positions south of the bridges. The enemy is contained within the old quarter."

"You mean we have ceded the Old Quarter to them?" Clifford asked.

"We hold the bridges against them. I repeat, they are contained within the old quarter and our cannon and wraiths are keeping the bridges clear. Even as we do, their numbers are reduced further."

"We need answers about where they come from now," said the senator. "Until then, your claims that they are contained are baseless. The prophet who has come told us we would suffer divine punishment. Does this not begin to look like something supernatural?"

"Nonsense," said the general, but the senator thought he lacked conviction.

"You know your gods better than I," said the marshal. "I know the light and these creatures wither before it as all creatures do."

"Then you must continue with the light and throw them back to wherever they came!"

In the hostel courtyard in the west of the city, the men of Outreterre were pacing restlessly as they listened to the sound of cannons. A few had woken puzzled to the crackling of long-arm, but all had been roused by the din of the bells.

"What passes?" demanded the captain.

"It be the hour of retribution," Silver responded. He was stood in the middle of the courtyard, his arms open as he looked at the night sky above him.

"Will they simply leave us here?" asked the captain.

Giles raised his head from where it had been cupped on his chin.

"Do sit down. I am sure we will have a visitor soon if it be as Silver suggests."

The men gradually sat down, following Giles' lead, but they remained on edge. A rattling at the door brought them all to their feet. It opened and Senator Clifford entered with Fitzwarren.

Giles stood.

"Good evening, senator," he said. "We have been wondering when we would hear news. It be disconcerting to be locked away and hear sounds of battle."

"I apologise for my absence, but I have been otherwise occupied. My son is missing and I fear he's been killed." Clifford swallowed and continued. "As I explained to you yesterday, we had put the puoli into the Tower of the Stars compound in the old city where they could be protected. Something has happened there. We don't yet understand. There were earthquakes, then the wolf soldiers began to appear. First there were a few, then there were hundreds and now I believe thousands. My son disappeared fighting them."

"So they be here now? In the city?" asked Giles.

"They are. We have lost the old quarter to them, but we still hold the bridges and General Kallick will be advancing on them from the plain. They will be crushed between the two forces."

"Forgive me, senator," said Giles. "But you do not look convinced."

Clifford dropped his head for a moment.

"I confess, I am not. These creatures are not of this earth and I fear our arms may not be enough to hold them."

"They *be* not of this earth."

Silver had walked over and was standing behind the senator.

"They be not of this earth. They bring divine retribution and every blow you strike against them be a sin against God."

"I want you to see them," Clifford said to Silver. "Then you will see they cannot be from God."

"I will gladly look upon the terrible fury of God. You must make your peace with Him and shun these devils you call friends."

"Lord Giles, will you come too? And bring your captain. A military man's view is always welcome."

"What of my men?"

"I am sorry, but they should remain here for now. I am sure we could use more able-bodied men, but we are at war and the military authorities are in charge now."

156

Clifford led them back to the citadel. There was already a glow across the eastern horizon. The sound of gunfire continued sporadically as they went, but it seemed more distant.

"That is not from within the city," said Fitzwarren. "Our guns have stopped."

"It will be Kallick's. Perhaps the attacks on the bridges have been defeated and now it is Kallick's turn for victory."

There were guards on the gate. They saluted the senators and let them all through. The group climbed the stairs once more until, out of breath, they emerged onto the walkway. The entrance faced the east. Dawn was almost upon the city and the light funnel was already bowing to catch the first rays of the sun.

The group walked to the east and looked towards the old quarter. No one needed to be told where to look. The courtyard of the Tower of the Stars glowed distinctly. Below it, the two bridges could be clearly seen reaching across the blackness of the gorge. If there was an army in the old quarter, it was not yet easily visible. Any crowd would have blended with the shadows which still lay across the city.

Light shone suddenly from behind the distant mountains as the sun lit the eastern walls of the city a bright yellow. Then their eyes were caught by flashes and movement on the plain before Akus. They realised they were watching cannon fire and the blur of something in the air.

"There! Kallick's cannon and sun wraiths!"

They watched for a while.

"Be they holding them back?" Giles asked.

They had seen neither sun wraith nor cannon fire for some time.

"Perhaps it is nearly over," said the senator.

Then the sun rose further and struck the figures on the plain. A mass seemed to be moving. There were two: a larger one moving away from the city and a smaller one just in front of it.

"That be two armies," said the captain. "And one has been caught in the open."

The smaller force continued to move towards the lights of Akus and came to a stop with its back to the river. The larger force surrounded it, but stopped as well. Both forces had moved into the valley bottom where the river licked at the heels of the smaller force. Just then the sun spread across the city and beyond.

On the far side of the gorge, the roads were lined with massed dark figures. The bridges were littered with bodies. On the near side, partly hidden by the buildings in front of them, could be seen units from the custodian guard and at least one cannon.

On the plain, it quickly became clear what had happened. The larger force was dark, while the smaller, dotted with pennants, was hemmed in against the river.

"That is Kallick's legion," breathed Clifford. "We are undone."

26

THE RADIO WAS on, but it was almost drowned out by the rain beating at the windows. This weather wasn't good for business. He had just received another cancellation email. He could always offer orienteering or the mud run, but it had to be the right kind of groups for those to appeal, especially in the rain. He stood up to go to the kitchen to make himself a coffee and the phone rang. Another cancellation? He considered not even answering it, then perhaps they wouldn't be able to cancel. He picked up the phone.

"Is that Richard Denham?" said the voice. It was a solid, reassuring voice.

"Speaking."

"My name is George McClure. Father George McClure, if it helps," the voice hesitated, "although I'm not sure it will. Please excuse me for calling you. I don't want to alarm you, but I thought I should talk to you. You have a son called Charlie?"

"What's happened?" Richard asked, terrible thoughts already racing through his head.

"Perhaps nothing at all. I wasn't sure whether I should call you at all. He told me your company name, so you were easy to find. Have you heard from him in the last couple of days?"

"Excuse me, do I know you?"

"I am sorry, I should have said. I met your son in Spain. We went hiking together. He was very good, very patient with me. I'm not as young as I used to be. Then we were staying in a pension and in the morning he was gone."

"Why is that unusual?" Richard was suspicious and fearful now.

"He took his bag. But you see the room was still locked by a key on the inside. I can't see how he could have gone unless he jumped out of the window, but that was closed."

"What do you mean?"

"He said..." Again McClure hesitated. "I do apologise for bothering you, but he didn't seem like the kind of lad to just disappear."

"He's not."

"Richard, he told me a story. He said he had never told it to anyone. I don't know why he told me, although people do tell me things. Part of being a priest I suppose."

"What story?" Richard spoke quietly.

"About some travelling he did. You both did. An adventure." There was a pause at the end of the line. Richard sensed the man was waiting for a response. Richard gave him none and the man continued. "I must admit, I didn't know what to make of it at the time, although it was a good story."

"What story?" Richard repeated, more forcefully this time.

"About an unusual place you went to. And what makes me connect it, is that in the night, when I thought I was dreaming, I thought I heard Charlie call out the name of someone from that story."

Richard said nothing. He was waiting. He could feel his heart beating.

"Solimo," said McClure. "Does that name mean anything to you?"

"Yes," Richard whispered.

Richard did not know what he thought he could do, but he wanted to be where Charlie had disappeared. And he wanted to meet this man who had called him up. There were flights from East Midlands airport to Almeria. From there, he took a bus. He found McClure waiting for him in a cafe.

The older man stood up when Richard arrived and they shook hands.

"You look like him," McClure smiled. "What can I get you? I'm drinking iced tea."

"Thank you."

"How are you feeling?"

"Worried sick. And excited."

"Excited?"

Richard looked at McClure. He *did* look like a man he could talk to. "There might be a way back."

"To Unama?"

"I would be curious to see it again."

McClure nodded.

"You think we're making it up don't you?"

"No actually, I don't. Although I don't understand it. Look, I'm a priest, well, retired now, but I'm used to people struggling to believe in something."

He smiled and Richard smiled too.

"Do you think we should notify the police?" McClure asked.

"You would be a prime suspect."

"Naturally."

"No. I have a feeling about this. We should wait. I've emailed him and left messages on his phone, but I don't think he'll answer them. I think he's gone there, but I don't know how."

"Perhaps we should start with the pension then. We can go there in my hire car."

27

GRAFTON EMERGED INTO the daylight and squinted at the brightness of the sun. He could see there was someone standing there, but his eyes were still adjusting to the light and he put up his hand to shield them from the glare. The person laughed.

"Ha! You are becoming like a cob yourself with all this time underground, Grafton. Sit down. I have brought you some refreshment."

Grafton unbuttoned his woollen jacket, laid it on a rock and pushed his cap back on his head. Then he opened the door on the lantern he was carrying and blew out the light.

"Thank you, madam. Sam did not tell me the Tafa herself had come to see progress."

"Well I like to see things for myself as you know. I understand the reports of others better if I have a context of my own. Please sit."

Grafton could see the tall, heavy delf in her long, loose white robe and plaited hair. She sat herself on a stool and one of her two attendants brought Grafton a cup of water. Grafton sat on a pile of boxes by the cave entrance and gratefully accepted the drink.

"How are things progressing?" the Tafa asked while Grafton was still drinking. Grafton wiped his hand across his beard.

"Your visit is very timely. We've just exposed the first of the salt layers. It was a little deeper than the earlier projections suggested. Once we've cleared enough of the top level, you'll be able to mine further without any assistance from me."

The Tafa pouted.

"You want to leave me so soon?"

"Tafa, I did not want to come her at all, but your Eudenasis was rather persuasive."

"Have you not enjoyed the chance to test your needle?"

"That I have, but I disliked the feeling of being forced to do something."

"Oh you humans are so haughty. Any delf would make a point of helping their fellows."

"No one likes to be forced to help. They like to offer it of their own accord."

"Would you have done?"

"Perhaps, if you had asked. But now I wish to go home. We have helped you as much as we can."

"Your mighty machine could help make our work much easier."

"And you'd waste half the salt you mined. The temperatures are too high for the salt. You're better off digging that out the old fashioned way with a pick."

"You are very protective of your needle, but I am very impressed with it. It has saved me months of quarrying and all those months can be reckoned in real value of the salt trade. Naadu will become a new city so much faster and your efforts will benefit all."

Grafton smiled wryly to himself.

"You're a real philanthropist, Tafa, but I think you're talking more like a human than a delf."

"True, your ways of doing business are more..." she searched for words, "...intense than our own, but here in the desert I think we have always lived a more intense life. Where water becomes a thing of value, we look for value in other things too."

She looked around the cave with her hands on her hips. Then she frowned and reached for the lantern, staring at a patch on the wall just inside the tunnel entrance. She went over to it, moving the lantern about.

"There is some other mineral in these walls. It glitters."

"There are many minerals in these rocks," Grafton said. "I cannot say what value any of them may have to you."

"But what will you do with the Needle when you return to Linana Pivaki?" she asked him. "Even if it worked with that southern light, your wardens keep it all for themselves and they would never let you have any. We were made for a partnership we two."

Grafton looked up at her, wondering whether he should stand too. He decided to stay seated and compensated for his discomfort by leaning back on the rock wall behind him and being more relaxed.

"What little light I had I did indeed come by with some difficulty. You have it in abundance. And I must admit, I was concerned about further distilling the essence of light to cut rock. I felt as though I were debasing it in some way. But if it can be used to kill, why can it not be used to save labour. The old mages would have known what to do with it. But who says I'll continue to use the Needle? Maybe I'll just invest your payment onto another project."

The Tafa smiled knowingly.

"That would be a waste of your genius, Grafton."

Grafton flicked his eyebrows non-committedly. "I have a short attention span."

Then he stood and looked out past the jumble of rocks to the desert plain below.

"And you, Tafa, what will you do with all this salt? Linana Pivaki would like a piece of that trade. How will you keep them away?"

"I will give them a piece of the trade. They are the gateway south, but I think I can open up the gateway east. I believe the deposits are considerable and will be worth the investment of a route inland."

"That will eat into their control of the inland trade. You know there are factions in the Senate eager for an excuse to make an example of Naadu."

She shrugged.

"I realise. I will just have to trust to old ties and their respect for a business rival."

Grafton's eyebrows lifted again despite himself.

"Now," said the Tafa, "I hope you are rested enough and we can go below."

"Will you be warm enough?" Grafton asked, reaching for his jacket again. "It's much cooler down there."

"It will be a refreshing change," smiled the Tafa.

Grafton relit his lantern and they walked inside the cave mouth in silence. The air changed immediately to a dry coolness. There was room for them to walk side by side. The tunnel was roughly hewn at first, but then it gained a more regular shape. It widened and the walls became smooth. They gave an impression of frozen liquid. The Tafa ran her hand along them thoughtfully as they walked.

The tunnel tended downwards and every now and then there was a wider chamber where rubble was piled. At one point, the Tafa paused to look back. The tunnel mouth was still just visible, a small hole of light. She looked at her two attendants and smiled.

"How do you think you would like to work down here then?"

They smiled nervously. The Tafa grunted.

"When it comes to miners, I think I will need to turn to men or puoli like your Sam."

A sound came from below and they discerned pale green glowing eyes floating in the gloom. They reached another chamber and stood to one side. Six cobs loped up the tunnel and past them, their long, hairy arms pushing small carts laden with rock. The four watched as they went by. The creatures ignored them, their large ears pinned back to the sides of their heads.

"Would you use cobs?" Grafton asked.

"Could they be trained do you think? We delf have an inherent distrust of them, but I know you have used them since you came here."

"Of course. They are strong and I don't need to pay wages, just treat them reasonably and feed them."

"It is something I should consider I suppose, but it does make me uneasy."

They continued in silence, their boots crunching on the stony floor until they reached a final chamber. Two other lanterns were hanging on the walls and they illuminated a crowd of cobs busy hacking at the far wall with picks. Rock came away in lumps and landed at their feet where others would pick it up and drop it into more of the same kind of cart they had seen being pushed on the way down. They were moving slowly.

The light needle sat in the middle of the chamber. Sam Atana was making adjustments to the small wheels on its side as they entered. He straightened up when he saw the party approaching.

They came to a halt next to the machine and the puoli nodded and touched his finger to his head in a simple salute, but said nothing.

"Well, well," said the Tafa. "So this is the mighty Needle. It looks so simple."

"The complexity is inside," Grafton replied. "And the quality of your light helps enormously. It has an extra width to it that we don't find in the south. The light is passed through these smaller funnels and lenses. They are not true light funnels, but I have made what I can."

"When I heard you coming I thought you were bringing more light," said the puoli.

"But I do, Sam," said the Tafa and she turned to her attendants. They were both carrying backpacks which they removed and placed on the ground. Sam knelt and opened them. He carefully removed a pile of packages wrapped in oilskin.

"We will be able to start early with these tomorrow," said Sam.

The Tafa looked disappointed.

"Tomorrow?" she said. "It was a long walk just to *look* at the Needle."

"You want to see it in action?" said Grafton.

"Of course," said the Tafa. "I want to see how my investment works in practice. I think it will be even more interesting than the results."

Sam frowned and looked at Grafton.

"I think this should be our last lighting of the day. The cobs are exhausted," he said.

"I have never known a man worry about cobs so much. They are only beasts. They will sleep all the better tonight," the Taha said.

"They are higher beasts," said Grafton. "Have you known a horse use an axe?"

"No, but horses can work a treadmill, as I take that to be," replied the Tafa pointing at the large wheel.

"But not in the way this wheel works," Grafton answered. "I need greater speeds than a pony is prepared to run inside a wheel and I need the rate to build at the right pace."

He turned and looked at Sam.

"Very well, one last lighting."

There was a rumbling from behind them. The Tafa and her two attendants turned to see what the noise was with a little alarm.

"It is the cobs returning with the empty wagons," said Grafton.

Reaching the bottom of the tunnel, the cobs shoved the carts against the wall and began to gibber.

"Why are they making that noise?" the Tafa asked.

"They think I'm going to keep them working." Then he looked at the others who had stayed in the chamber. He held up four fingers. "Four. Wheel."

One of the cobs grunted to the others and the gibbering from the cart pushers stopped. They loped to a corner where they squatted and chewed on some meat which had been wrapped in leaves and took turns to drink from a stone bowl. All but four of the other cobs joined them.

Sam took three of the packages from the pile and unwrapped them. Inside each was a single square of thick, swollen material: a light sponge. Meanwhile Grafton went over to the needle and opened a door in the side of the chamber. He slid out a compartment and slowly opened a drawer in the side. Sam carried the light sponges to the needle. Grafton held the drawer out to him and he placed each one inside. Once all three were in, Grafton shut the drawer tight and fitted it back inside the needle's end chamber. He looked at the Tafa who smiled back at him expectantly.

The last four cobs stood waiting to the side of the chamber.

"They seem to know what is happening," said the Tafa.

"They know precisely what is happening," said Grafton. "They have done this procedure many times."

He turned to the cobs who were watching him.

"Up wheel, up!" he said.

The four cobs climbed into the wheel, one pair behind the other, waiting. Grafton nodded at Sam who moved the needle so that it was pointing at a part of the wall which was indented. He in turn nodded at Grafton who turned to the cobs.

"Walk," he said.

They immediately started to walk on the wheel, a slow lope. At first the wheel made a rumbling clank, but as they settled into a rhythm, it began to whirr.

"Nothing appears to be happening," said the Tafa.

"Wait," said Grafton. "Sam will start to open up the needle, feeding light to it gradually. Putting it simply, it contains a number of light funnels so that the light becomes highly refined. When it emerges from the end of the needle, it will be superheated and will be able to cut through the rock. In some rocks, it is then much easier to chip away the stone. In others, we can place gunpowder in the holes and blow the rock away. We've used both methods here."

The cobs not in the wheel showed no interest in what was happening. Most had finished eating and were huddling together to sleep.

The needle continued to whirr.

"More," said Grafton and the cobs on the wheel moved from a walk into an easy lope. The machine clanked as it shifted into the new speed, then settled.

"More," said Grafton again and once more the machine clanked as the cobs began a faster lope, keeping rhythm with one another.

This continued for a minute or two and then, quite suddenly, a tiny beam of light appeared from the point of the needle and shone on the rock wall in front of them. Within seconds, there was a sizzling sound from the rock.

The Tafa tried to watch, but instinctively shut her eyes to the glare.

"Don't look at it," said Grafton. "It's concentrated sunlight. It'll blind you."

"Indeed. But is it really cutting?"

"That is the sound you can hear."

Sam took control of the needle and started to slowly move it down across the rock. The cobs gazed ahead. The Tafa looked at them.

"So steady," she said. "Quite hypnotic."

Grafton looked at them too. He had forgotten. It was indeed hypnotic. Their motion was completely synchronised with each other and they moved as if they were a single eight legged beast. Grafton looked at them, imagining a single entity. He tried to discern any difference in pace, but there was none. They were moving together, a regular shuffle and click the only sounds. It was the rhythm of the wheel. He could no longer hear the wheel, only the rhythm. It seemed to be speaking words, the same ones over and over like a chant. Over and over. His eyelids began to weigh heavy. It had been a long day. He opened them wide again. His head felt light. He swayed and put his hand out to steady himself.

The cobs continued their relentless loping. Grafton's eyes lost focus as he stared at them, he seemed to be looking beyond them. Suddenly the cave was filled with a blaze of light as if the sun had come out underground. It was like a spray of light bouncing back from the focused jet of the needle.

The ground seemed to shift beneath Grafton and he lost his footing. He put his hand out and there was nothing there.

He realised he was lying on the ground. Had he blacked out? He looked up at the rough rock ceiling. He could see more of it than he expected. There was another light coming from somewhere. He sat up, looking around for the others.

The cobs had fallen out of the wheel and the light from the needle had faded. Sam, the Tafa and the two attendants were also on the ground, but the Tafa was sitting up and looking past him.

"What was that?" she asked. Then her eyes widened. "Did you know that was behind it?"

Grafton followed the Tafa's wide-eyed gaze. Where the rock wall had been at the end of the tunnel, there was now a gaping cavern mouth. They could see it gave onto a wide space which appeared to be lit. There was vegetation growing thickly up the far side of the space. Grafton frowned and pulled himself to his feet. The others groggily followed suit. The cobs were slower to move.

Grafton trod carefully towards the cavern entrance, leaning on the needle for support as he went past. He looked around at the walls. They were a quite different rock type, grey and smooth. He passed his hand across them. The floor too was smooth. He turned to the Tafa who was looking as puzzled as he felt.

"There was water here once."

"How could this have been here and we not know about it?" the Tafa asked. "A valley inside the mountains. But those plants..."

They were nearly at the lip of the cave now and could see they were inside a round opening in the ground. The sides of it were lined with boulders, as was the floor and thick greenery crawled over everything.

"It's all so different," Grafton breathed.

The Tafa was at his side now.

"Well this is a treasure," she said. She looked up. "Could this be a cavern? It must be."

They looked up above the rim of the bowl. Grafton shook his head.

"Those look like clouds."

"A mist. It is dim."

"It looks like a collapsed cave, but it must be huge."

The air was cold and moist with a fresh, green smell to it.

A movement caught Grafton's eye. A branch on the nearest bush had moved. There was something behind it. The Tafa was looking too.

"What was that?" asked Sam right at Grafton's shoulder. Grafton jumped.

"You keep quiet all day and choose now to speak?"

There was a sniffing from behind them. It was one of the cobs. It walked up past Grafton, its ears raised and its snout up in the air. It grunted, then opened its mouth and let out a snuffling bark.

"What can you smell?" Grafton asked.

The Tafa looked from Grafton to the cobs, then forward as the bush moved again. A figure emerged slowly from behind it. It was broad shouldered with long arms and large ears.

"A cob!" exclaimed the Tafa. "How did it get past us without seeing?"

"That's not one of my cobs," Grafton replied quietly. "Everyone stand still. That must be a wild one."

The two attendants went to pull out pistols from their belts.

"Please, no sudden movements," hissed Grafton. "We don't know how many are there." He paused. "And while mine are trained, they're still cobs. Be very careful."

The attendants' hands hovered by their belts.

"Do as he says," said the Tafa quietly.

The strange cob put its head up in the air and sniffed, never moving its eyes from them. Then it grunted. In response, from out among the bushes and boulders, more cobs appeared. Their eyes glowed green in the gloom.

The smell of cobs was strong; Grafton's others had crept up behind and were sniffing and staring past him. They began to bark in short coughs. What could have been replies came from the cobs beyond the cavern.

"Can they get up?" the Tafa asked.

"Yes, using those boulders they could be up in seconds."

The cobs were all barking at each other now and shuffling and flapping their arms.

"Back away slowly," said Grafton. "Do it now."

The four began to move, edging away from the mouth of the cavern. The two groups of cobs remained focused on each other, but neither moved any further forwards. They backed behind Grafton's cobs. They could no longer see the others down amongst the boulders. They kept backing until they reached the needle again.

"Now, I suggest we go back up the tunnel."

"What about the needle?" asked Sam.

"We will come back for that."

"I will put extra guards on the tunnel and a gate."

"We will need to separate our cobs from those wild ones," said Sam. "We need them for the needle."

"I realise that," Grafton replied. "We'll think about that when we're in a safer place."

They climbed the tunnel quickly, looking behind them to ensure they were not being followed. It was almost dark when they emerged. The Tafa turned to Grafton.

"Grafton, do you have weapons?"

"We have long-arms over there," he nodded towards where their tents were set up beside a sheltering rock.

"Good. I would like you to stay here with one of my men. We shall return to the city and I will send out some more men to guard this tunnel entrance and some carpenters to make a gate. When we are properly prepared, we will return to see what wonders your needle has revealed."

"Very well," Grafton nodded.

"Shoot anything which comes out," the Tafa said.

"I would be reluctant to shoot my trained cobs, Tafa."

"Then I will hold you responsible for the results of any escapes, Grafton," the Tafa replied. "I have an obligation to protect my people as well as to make money."

"I understand," said Grafton. He watched the Tafa and her attendant walk off to their horses tethered a short distance away. The attendant left with them looked nervous.

"Don't worry. We will light a fire by the entrance. That will deter them."

The delf nodded.

"Watch the doorway while Sam and I fetch some wood over."

He and Sam walked over to the pile of firewood heaped near their tent.

"I must go back, Sam, there was something very strange about that place I'm curious to understand."

"It did look odd. I am sure that was sky in there."

"I agree, but I want to go back in and have a look around. You will have to stay here, but I want to get in there before the Tafa's thugs go blundering about in there shooting at anything that moves."

"I would rather you did not," said Sam as he heaved an armful of wood up to his chest.

"It does make me nervous I admit, but those cobs didn't seem to care about us."

Sam grunted, but said nothing and carried his wood over to the tunnel entrance where the Tafa's attendant was already keeping an uneasy watch.

28

THE THREE WERE sitting at their breakfast when Qatiko's wrinkled head peered around the door.

"Come on up. I have a sight for you."

Intrigued, they followed him on deck. They were about to ask what they should be looking at when they turned towards the prow and saw for themselves. There was a wall of fog spread across the horizon like cloud floating on the water.

"What be that?" Berwick asked.

"That boy, is the fog that sits on this coast for most days of the year. A cold current runs down here."

"We be not going into it?"

"If you want to get to Naadu the short way, you are."

"But how can you see where you be going?"

Qatiko slapped Berwick on the back.

"Do not worry, horse rider. I can do it all from soundings. I know where I am now, for I know the time and I saw the stars before they faded with the sun. Naadu's port was located where it is because it had the only channel a ship can use. The rest is shallows where we cannot go."

They stood watching the monster come steadily closer and when they entered it, it was without warning. One moment it had been ahead of them, the next it was around them, damp and clinging. The wind all but dropped.

"We will make way only slowly in here, but we should pass through in an hour, maybe two. You should pack your things. This is your last day on board."

The riders had little to pack and they were soon back on the deck, eager for the eerie mist to clear and to see land again. Droplets formed on their hats and coats and the whole crew fell to talking in quiet voices as if there were others, unseen in the whiteness, who might hear them.

The world had become quiet and very small, where the rippling of the sea running alongside and the creak of timbers and flutter of sail sounded overly loud.

The quiet was punctuated at regular intervals as the sailor at the prow took soundings and called out the depth. Qatiko himself was at the helm, sailing from memory.

"That is the first time I have seen him concentrate," muttered Raul to his companions.

The other side of the fogbank was revealed to them as suddenly as it had enveloped them. Land appeared seemingly by magic. They were only a short distance off shore and the coast stretched in both directions, a straight line of waves rolling into a beach and an endless wilderness.

"Amazing," said Rodon. He turned to Qatiko. "You be a magician, master."

Qatiko winked, but did not reply. He only looked to make sure the crew was preparing ropes to tie up. Almost dead ahead was a cluster of buildings with a tall, narrow tower, and a harbour. A small ship carrying a single mast was moored in it and figures could be seen moving about. The boat had a high prow and low slung sides. It was unloading fish.

"Welcome to Sata Utimaak," said Qatiko. "Do not judge all of Naadu by this befogged outpost."

They came alongside the pier. A delf strolled along it and took a thrown rope without a word, then two of the crew dropped to the ground and helped tie up the ropes to iron rings mounted in the wall of the pier. Once they were settled, Qatiko called for the gangplank, then he extended his hand in welcome.

"Would your lordships like to be the first to land?"

They led their horses down the gangway and their feet and brains reeled at the solid, unyielding ground.

"If you are off to Naadu City, you could tell them I am arrived, or you may see them on the way." He pointed at the beacon tower. "In theory, the chain of these is lit whenever a ship comes in, but it does rather depend on the watchman at each beacon along the way being awake. Given nothing happens most of the time, I suspect the system is not quite as effective as they would wish, because a bored watchman is usually asleep, not staring into the distance in case someone lights the previous beacon. More than once they have had to send a rider into the city. So you can never be sure of timings, but it would save me a ride into that blasted desert. Just follow the breeze and the beacon towers down the road. Naadu City is in the escarpment."

"Thank you for your hospitality," said Rodon.

"Make sure one you of lives to come and tell me the tale," Qatiko said, then he turned his back and busied himself with the ship. "Right, have that hold unloaded and into those warehouses. The sooner it is collected, the sooner we can be on our way."

Raul, Berwick and Rodon saw no reason to stay any longer. They climbed onto their horses and set off down the road.

29

THE ROAD HEADED inland in a straight line through the stony desert. It was marked by a relative smoothness and hardness, its path being cleared of larger stones and devoid of any of the small, stubborn plants which insisted on making a home in the dust. It had a minor, but steady incline, so that over the day's ride, a reasonable altitude had been reached even before the escarpment barred their way as a rocky wall.

There was little to see as they rode except for the beacon towers spaced at regular intervals, each with their own stone hut. Each of these had been lit before Raul, Rodon and Berwick reached them. There was no other obvious sign of life as they passed any of them, beyond the flames in the beacons.

There was no breath of wind and the day had worn on into the early afternoon. Each of the three had their hats pulled down and the collars of their coats up to provide shade from the sun. Berwick would try to avoid looking ahead because the brightness of the ground hurt his eyes. He preferred instead to stare at the back of his horse's head. Alternatively, he would close his eyes, but this led him to doze off on a couple of occasions. He was embarrassed once by Raul and once by Rodon on being discovered asleep. It felt like sleeping on sentry duty. He did not feel he had Raul's respect. Despite the delf's obvious resentfulness of the men, he still detected that Raul respected Rodon. Rodon himself dealt with the conditions enviably, keeping the cool indifference to discomfort or his surroundings in general which was the hallmark of his behaviour.

Raul pointed up the road. The two men squinted for a few moments before noticing the distant dust and a shifting blob ahead which showed itself darker than the road surface. It turned out to be wagons pulled by doka. Two delf sat on the board of each, each one bearded and hooded. Their skin was a deeper bronze than Raul's. All the waggoners stared at the three of them as they rode by and some gave a nod, but they exchanged no other greeting. For their part, the three riders had little chance to salute the wagons because they were muffling their noses and mouths from the dust given off by the wheels. Someone must have seen from the beacons that Qatiko's ship had arrived and had sent these wagons to carry its cargo back inland.

They continued down the road, the escarpment becoming clearer. The rock was more orange in colour than the coastal plain. The empty road was strange to all three of them who were used to vegetation and passing others on the way.

As the road reached the escarpment, it veered to the left, following a fracture in the rock and around the bend they came upon Naadu City. Stone walls had been erected at the base of cliffs where nature had finished its natural defences, although the gates stood open. The city appeared to have grown out of the rock. Where it had not extruded buildings onto ledges which followed a road up the slope, it had been burrowed inside the ground with windows and doors carved into the living rock.

It was a shock to see so many people again. They stood in the street talking or sat in the shade. Some were tending small rooftop gardens and picking fruit from them, perhaps for an evening meal.

Berwick had never felt so far from home before. He felt impossibly foreign and exposed. These were of neither his land nor his race. He had no idea what these people were like beyond the fact that the likes of Qatiko were able to trade with them. For the first time, it occurred to him to wonder how they might receive him, a member of another race. Then he reminded himself he might not be so new to them: Giles and Silver would have passed this way. That they would be the ambassadors for his race only made him more nervous.

He looked over at Raul and wondered how comfortable he felt. Both he and Rodon looked relaxed and he envied them. They had passed through the gates now and no one had challenged them. Berwick looked up at the city growing up the rock on two sides. It rose high to the very top of the escarpment upon which he could see towers.

The road wound up the cliff and part way up it split and led off to the right and round into a jumble of rocks and inland. The only way onward was to pass through the city. He wondered what there was beyond it or whether this whole continent was a great desert.

Facing the main gates were several large, blocky buildings with flat roofs. Their only windows were long slit windows, boarded with wood. They reminded him of the fortified farm houses the delf built in northern Unama against the border raiders.

The road narrowed as it passed through them and bent first to the left and then the right before emerging into an open square. As they went through, Berwick had the feeling that they were being watched. He looked around him, but could see nothing but blank walls and there was no one watching from the roofs. If felt as though he were passing through a gateway again. It would not be possible to mount an assault through that dog-leg roadway without it losing momentum.

When they came into the square, there were the remains of a market. Stalls were bare and scattered about were broken boxes and scraps of cloth which blew around the legs of the stalls. It gave the square a desolate feel.

On the far side was a three storey building with balconies on the upper levels. On these were tables and chairs.

"Do you think that be an inn?" Rodon asked Raul.

"Shall we find out?" he replied. He rode across the open ground and dismounted at the front. The other two followed and Berwick leaned forward and took the reins of his horse.

"Wait for me," said Raul.

The front of the inn was covered by heavy matting with ropes on either end so that it could be lifted if desired. Berwick leaned forward on his horse and touched it. It was indeed woven, but it felt as firm as wood.

Raul had gone through an opening in this solid curtain and after a minute, he emerged again.

"It is indeed an inn. I have not said we would stay, but I have said we would like some refreshment."

They tied their horses to rails and made their way inside. After the brightness of the day, it was very dark. A young, quiet delf who made no attempt to either look at them or speak to them led them up two flights of dim stairs, their eyes adjusting as they climbed. Reaching the top, they were dazzled all over again when they looked to the front and the balcony.

The table to which they were shown had an excellent view of the square and a narrow view of the road back into the desert. To their left was the orange rock of the escarpment. To the right however, the lower section of the city was visible, crowding onto the flat land and looking like a single structure with hundreds of extensions. The shadows were lengthening and there was movement around doorways and terraces in the city.

The delf server returned carrying a tray with three cups and a jug. They had not ordered anything and to their surprise, the drink was hot. It had a sour flavour, but they found it quite refreshing. This was followed by a chewy bread filled with seeds. The server watched them try to chew it, then, without asking, took a piece from Berwick, dunked it in his drink and handed it back to him.

Rodon picked up a hunk of his own bread and while Berwick was still looking confused, put it in his own drink then put it to his mouth. Berwick did the same thing and found the bread far more palatable. The server disappeared and returned with some strips of cooked meat and vegetable on a woven platter, then some pieces of fruit. The meal was welcome after the repetitive food on the ship. It was flavoured strongly with herbs and spices.

They were half way through the meal when four delf came onto the balcony. There were three males and a female. They sat at the far end and were brought a similar meal.

"Stop looking at them," said Raul to Berwick.

"I think they be talking about us," he replied.

"That may be true, but do not look at them."

One of the delf stood up and walked towards them.

"Those are your horses below. Will you sell them?"

All three turned to face him.

"Why would we sell our horses? Would you have us walk?" asked Raul with a faint smile.

"I will give you a good price, you can buy something else to ride. There will be no need to walk."

"They are not for sale," said Rodon. "But thank you for your offer."

"You are all so polite," he said. "I never thought to see more of those horses so soon. If you change your minds ask for me. I am Merrimis. I apologise for disturbing you."

The three of them exchanged glances.

"So he has seen similar horses to ours. Could it be Giles?" Berwick asked.

"Perhaps," Rodon replied. "But I be not wanting to ask this early in our visit."

"Then how will we find out about our friends Lord Giles and Silver?" Raul asked.

"We have just had one person approach us because of our appearance. Perhaps we may find out things simply from walking about." He looked at the others and felt some sort of explanation was required. "They have been here for some time already and we don't know why they be here. There could be...interests which we do not understand and we don't want to blunder into them."

"You have a hunter's caution," said Raul.

"Thank you," Rodon replied.

They decided to take rooms in the inn for the night. The morning was cool as the city lay in the shadow of the escarpment. They were served breakfast on the balcony and sat watching the market which had been set up below. It was small and not all the stalls were in use. The server told them that the full market happened only once a week.

They went on foot to explore the city, first wandering through the market which sold fresh fruit and vegetables and some scrawny birds. They turned their attention away from the market and wandered deeper into the city. First they went through the jumble of streets on the ground. It was a maze of piled boxes interspersed by alleyways, stairs, tunnels and lanes. Sometimes they did not know if they would enter someone's house by accident or even where the boundaries of public and private space were. Vines, trees and creepers grew where they could, traversing many of the boxes. In places they had been trimmed neatly, in others, on the same plant, they had been left to run wild across walls and windows, feeling out wherever they had a mind to go.

They passed people along the way. Few spoke to them and if any did, it was merely a greeting, but many looked at them as they went by, particularly at Berwick and Rodon. Some sat in doorways or under awnings, others in small stalls tucked onto alcoves on the side of buildings. Children sometimes followed them, but ran off if Rodon turned his grim face on them.

There were signs of work in delf making things in cool, shadowy rooms and in noises of hammering and song which came from unseen workshops. At one point they came out on a wall amongst a range of small pits filled with liquids of browns, buffs and reds. A smell arose from it as the tanners plied their trade.

In this way they climbed and wound and followed where they would until they emerged onto a wider road. They looked back and realised they had climbed some distance as the lower city piled itself up against the escarpment like a stack of discarded crates. It reached all the way up to the road which led back and forth across the face of the rock. In places there were buildings dug into the rock only on one side, but in most places, the road had been cut so that there had been room to delve on both sides.

They continued upwards. Soon after their break, they passed through a larger section of stores, some selling metal goods, others had food laid out neatly on stalls. Every now and then, they would emerge at a point from which they could look down and see how the city spread further than they had at first thought around the foot of the rock like a pool of water.

They came at last to the top. Here there were larger freestanding buildings which formed an avenue. They had triangular doors and windows edged with brick. At the end of the avenue was a garden and behind it, a tall building built almost entirely into the rock with only a grand high entrance facade. On the top of the rock into which it was built was a tower. It contained a familiar large flower of metal reaching up to the sun which was pouring down strongly from a wide, blue sky.

"A light funnel," said Berwick. It seemed strange to Raul to see something so familiar in a place so foreign.

They walked through the larger buildings and came to the garden. It was filled with shade trees and shrubs grew thickly around the borders and under the trees.

In the middle of this garden sat a delf in a long white dress. She was talking to a small group of other delf and two more stood discreetly a short distance behind her. She looked up as she noticed them appear and must have said something because all other heads turned to face them.

"This looks like a much richer part of town," said Berwick. "Do you think we should be here?"

"No one seems to mind us," returned Rodon.

One of the group stood and walked towards the three travellers. He was tall and elegant and his hand rested on the pommel of a short sword. He touched his forehead with his right hand.

"Bright day to you. I am Eudinasis Steward. The Tafa would talk to you," he said.

The three exchanged glances, agreed without words and followed the delf into the garden.

The delf called the Tafa put down a sheaf of papers she had been holding on the bench beside her.

"I heard you were coming," she said. "You have been looking through the city. You are welcome."

She looked thoughtful and turned to the two men.

"And what do you seek?"

Rodon hesitated before answering.

"We are looking for some people who we believe came here."

The Tafa looked troubled.

"Do you know Hugh Grafton?" she asked.

"We do not," said Rodon slowly.

She relaxed a little.

"We seek men, a group of them. Have they been here?"

"A group of men, you say. Like yourselves?"

"Something like us," Rodon said.

"No. I would have known about those."

Rodon frowned. There was something about the way she spoke which made him suspicious.

"Why do you search out these men?"

There was a pause in which Berwick hoped someone else was deciding what to say. Rodon spoke first and he had clearly decided that the truth was the best option for the circumstances.

"We have reason to believe that amongst the group of men is a man or men who be wanted for crimes in my country. This delf," he said gesturing at Raul, "be known to us as an excellent tracker and given we were venturing into the lands of the delf, we thought that it would be wise to have a delf guide."

The Tafa turned to him.

"You are Unaman are you not?"

"I am," Raul replied.

"And what is an Unaman doing travelling with men?" She smiled sweetly as she spoke, but there was an edge in her voice. "This man must have done something serious for you to cross the desert to find him," she mused. She looked them up and down and said suddenly: "I have some work for you."

"We are not searching for work," said Rodon.

"That is not important. I have some work for you. It will suit the skills you have. A man has become lost. It is the man I said before,

Hugh Grafton. I would have thought you might have heard of him. I understood he was well known in Linana.”

Berwick tried not to avoid giving anything away with his expression. They were clearly being mistaken for someone else. This delf was not surprised at meeting men and indeed seemed to know what they were.

“He was mining for me in the mountain,” she continued, “and found a great cavern. Against my wishes he went inside and became lost. I sent in others to find him, but they have not returned either. So now I want you to find them.”

“I be sorry for your trouble,” said Rodon. “And thank you for this kind offer, but we be not in need of work and we have work of our own to do.”

“This is not a request,” said Eudinasis simply. “You will do this for the Tafa. This is our city and we are offering you work. Or are you spies? You walk around our city armed. Yes, I know what you have in your horses’ saddles and I know what is under your jackets.” He gestured quickly and they realised that other delf guards had come silently behind them.

“Remove your weapons and place them on the ground.”

The three complied, Raul slowly leading and the other two following. The Tafa nodded.

“When you have answers for me, then I will consider what to do with you. My guards will show you to the cavern.”

30

THEY WERE ESCORTED by the Tafa's soldiers along a road which led out of the city. They turned off it into a tangle of ravines which ran through the leading edge of the escarpment. They were littered with debris from where the cliffs had crumbled, but a track of sorts had been made through them.

Finally they came to a dead end where a narrow view looked off onto the coastal plain. On this cleared patch of ground were a tent and a series of shelters pitched against the rock. The shelters contained boxes and sacks. A door had been fixed into the rock and a squad of soldiers was sitting around it. There was a hatch in the door which was open and a guard was looking through it when they arrived.

The leader of the guards approached the squad's leader and started to talk to him. At the sound of his voice, a man emerged from the tent. Berwick looked at him, caught by his appearance. He was tanned and bearded and at first Berwick took him for a delf.

Eudinasis turned to him.

"Sam Atana, we have found someone to find your friend and our comrades. This one," he pointed at Raul, "is a delf tracker. The others you may know."

"I do not know them," Sam said. "But I am glad you have come."

Rodon raised an eyebrow, but said nothing. Raul frowned and followed Rodon's lead.

"Follow me and I will take you in and tell you what I know," said Atana.

The soldiers had already opened the door and revealed a passage heading into the rock. They passed through, followed by Eudinasis.

"What have you been told?" Sam asked.

"Next to nothing," Raul replied.

Sam caught the surly tone in his voice.

"Where are you from? You do not look like you come from Linana."

"We are travelling," said Raul. "Tell us what happened."

"My colleague and I were drilling through the rock. We cut through to a cave. Or at least the Tafa says it is a cave, but it looks like a valley to me and that I do not understand."

They passed through the gate in the rock and after a few minutes of walking down a tunnel, they reached a cave. Light was spilling into it from an opening in the far side and in the middle of it, pointing to the opening, was a strange brass object.

"It is what we use to drill with," said Atana. "You do not need to worry about it. The thing is, it cut through the rock to this place. The Tafa's men cannot find it going above ground, so it must be some hidden valley. I am sure they are simply incompetent. My colleague, Hugh Grafton went in on his own the day after we found it. We had cobs with us and they went in because there were some wild cobs in the valley. I thought we would be able to keep hold of the ones which were still asleep, but we lost them all. They would not have hurt Hugh, but I cannot say the same for the wild ones. They would not be used to people. I am told they are not used to seeing cobs in these parts."

Rodon was looking at the needle.

"Is this in any way like a light funnel?"

Atana looked away for long enough to give away an answer without saying anything.

"I need to tell you what I know about that valley," he continued. "We have not only lost Hugh. The Tafa sent some of her own soldiers in to have a look around and none of them have come back."

"This is sounding promising," said Raul with a snarling edge to his voice. He walked over to the opening and looked out. Rodon and Berwick joined him.

"That is amazing," said Raul. "It is so different." He looked at Sam over his shoulder. "How can the Tafa think this is a cavern? You can see the shadows from the sun."

"She has not been here since we broke through. It was late when we did it. Most of the cobs were asleep. It was supposed to be the last cut of the day."

"What be you drilling for?" Rodon asked.

"That is not important," said Eudinasis who had been watching the discussion. "I want you to find my men. I do not care about the cobs out there."

"We need *our* cobs back," said Sam to the officer, frustrated. "The Tafa wants them back. We need them to help run the needle. We heard gunshots after your guards went in. Our cobs might already be dead if your people had anything to do with it."

He turned back to Rodon, Raul and Berwick.

"It is important that you are careful about using your weapons. Do you know anything about cobs?"

"I know how to kill one," said Raul.

"Not these ones," said Sam. "They are special."

"You said most of your cobs were asleep at the time?" Rodon asked. Sam nodded absent-mindedly. "Was anyone else asleep?"

"No," he said. "Although..." he stopped.

"Although what?" Rodon pressed.

"There was something. The ground seemed to shake, or we all lost our footing. I thought perhaps I had blacked out because I realised I was on the ground. We all were."

Rodon looked at the other two, their eyes were widening. Sam was looking at them quizzically. Rodon beckoned him over to the cave mouth where they were all stood.

"Come and show me where you saw them go. I assume it was down these rocks?"

Sam went over and started to point into the valley.

"Where do you think this place is?" Rodon asked him quietly, his voice did not carry to the escorting soldiers beyond the needle.

Sam looked at him with narrowed eyes.

"What do you know about this place?"

"Has this happened before?"

"No."

"That is not Naadu out there. That is somewhere quite different."

"But how could they?" Raul asked.

"You two of all people should understand."

Sam was frowning at them now.

"What do you know?" he insisted.

"Not much, I assure you. But we will happily search for your friends. It looks like morning out there."

Sam looked again into the valley of rocks and plants.

"You are right. It does seem to hold and lose the light differently to back there, but I have not been permitted to come down here much. The soldiers prefer to stay at the top of the tunnel and will not let me come here alone."

Eudinasis had come up behind them, a suspicious look on his face.

"And if he has told you what he knows, he can return to the top of the tunnel and you three can go on," he said.

The two men and the delf stepped over the edge of the cavern and made their way down the boulders which led to the valley bottom. Their long-arms had been returned to them and were over their shoulders so they could use their hands when necessary. As they went, they looked around them, but the wide bowl appeared to be empty.

They reached the bottom and looked around at the rocks and the bluish green vegetation which lay across it. They sniffed at the air. It was much colder than Naadu.

"That smell…" said Raul.

"It be faint. The plants?" asked Rodon.

Raul shook his head.

"Which way then?" Berwick asked.

Raul looked at the ground.

"There are several tracks here. Most of them are cob. Two are not. One is a wide trail, the other," he pointed at a bush, "is narrow and made by one person. Which would you like to follow?"

"Both?" Rodon suggested. "The single one first. If that be this Grafton, he be alone and therefore in greater danger than armed soldiers."

"Very well, follow me. I will watch the ground. You watch my back."

Raul bent over inspecting the plants, looking at stems moved aside, crushed leaves, broken twigs and the marks of someone passing in the dark mud and green moss which filled the gaps between stones. As he went, the two men scanned the rocks. They were half way to the rim of the bowl when Berwick hissed.

All three stopped and followed his gaze. Away to their left, two cobs had appeared. They must have been watching them from behind some bushes.

"What are they doing?" Raul asked. "Why are they showing themselves to us?"

"You speak like a cob hunter, not a cob trainer," said Rodon. "Sam told us they had cobs with them which escaped into there. Maybe those are two of them."

"So can you speak to them?"

"Not at this distance," Rodon said.

Raul shrugged. "Keep an eye on them then."

They continued. Berwick watched the cobs. They did not move, but continued to watch them in turn.

They began to turn to the right, the trail running parallel to the edge of the bowl at a distance, then it stopped and headed straight for the steep sides. Raul paused to look around.

"I think he was looking for a way out. And I suspect I can see what he saw. Look."

A rock fall had left a climbable slope. It had clearly been there for some time because plants covered it thickly, growing from between the cracks. Raul went towards it, then stopped again.

"The trail meets another of cob." He moved forward, searching around, looking around until he reached the rocks. "His trail has gone. I can only assume they followed him. I do not see any sign of limbs ripped off, so I suggest we continue to follow the cob trail."

Rodon nodded his assent.

"Fine. One of you keep your eyes on the top. I do not want a cob to surprise me while I am climbing."

He shouldered his long-arm once more and jumped onto the rocks, pulling himself up on branches and using all four limbs to scramble up the heap. Near the top he slowed and peered nervously at the way above him. He risked a quick glance backwards, saw Rodon with his long-arm to his shoulder scanning the skyline and, satisfied, went back to climbing. He reached the top, pulled himself over and disappeared from view.

Berwick exchanged glances with Rodon. They waited. A minute or two passed. Rodon continued to cover the top while Berwick anxiously scanned the bushes and rocks around them, his ears listening for any sound.

Then Raul's head appeared at the top of the rockfall. He gestured for them to come up one at a time. Rodon nudged Berwick who briefly objected.

"Take it as an order," said Rodon.

Berwick climbed up. He went quicker than Raul.

"Were you trying to worry us disappearing like that?" he asked.

"I was just making sure I was alone up here," he said. "And we are alone for as far as I looked. Cover Rodon."

Berwick watched the ground below while Raul looked behind them. Once Rodon had climbed up to the rim, they took stock of their situation.

The ground was covered in low vegetation. Over in one direction was a flat topped rocky hill with steep sides. In the other, was a closer and lower hill which obscured anything behind it. Between the two the land undulated gently with an occasional rocky outcrop.

"Which way?" Rodon asked.

"Towards the hill. At least that is the way the cobs went, so I assume they were still following him."

"We should see where the Tafa's guards went as well then. She's bound to ask," said Rodon.

Raul nodded and looked back across the bowl of rock. He was thinking about the first trail he had found, plotting its direction forward across the bottom of the bowl and looking at the rock walls for where it could have come out. He pointed.

"That could be where they climbed out. There are some rocks near a ledge over there."

"What makes you think they left the bowl?"

"I assume someone watched them leave, or they would have told us they disappeared in the bowl."

Berwick nodded his head.

"So shall we take a walk around the edge and see if I am right? We can come back to Grafton's trail."

They walked around the lip of the hole in the ground. As they went they looked into the bowl. They could still see the cobs watching them, but they had not moved. They could not see any others.

When they reached the place where Raul suspected the soldiers could have climbed, he started to search around. He soon found it.

"They were here. And they went in the opposite direction to Grafton."

He looked off into the distance. Then he began to follow the trail.

"We should go back to Grafton's," said Rodon. "He was alone."

"I know. I just want to follow this a little further."

The two men followed behind him. He had walked about a hundred yards and stopped.

"They bunched up here. They had been walking in single file, like us. But they came up together here."

He looked around some more.

"And then they started walking again."

He followed the track further.

"Wait," he said.

He walked on and came back. He began to look around in other directions, bending over. He went back onto the other side of the trail and looked there and looked back the way they had come.

"What be the matter?" asked Berwick.

Raul did not answer at first. He was still trying to make sense of what he saw.

"I think they started to run. In different directions. And some seemed to start running backwards."

"So where be they now?"

The plants grew up to waist height. Raul started to follow one of the new trails. The other two broke away and started to make their own way through the bushes, looking at the ground.

Suddenly Berwick bent down.

"I've found something. It could be blood."

The other two joined him. There was a large dark stain on a stone.

"It looks like something was dragged a short distance," said Raul. "And then the trail stops."

"Perhaps the cobs picked them up," Berwick suggested.

"There are no other tracks."

Puzzled, they began to look again.

Berwick bent to look under a branch. There was something behind it. He had to bend down further.

It was an arm, a right arm, still in its sleeve. It had been ripped off at the shoulder. There were gashes on the upper arm and blood all over it. A long-arm lay nearby.

He called the others over. There was a ring on the finger. Rodon removed it. It bore the symbol of the fountain which they had seen at the Tafa's palace. He put it in his pocket.

"Cobs have been known to tear delf apart," said Raul. It was almost an accusation. "But those look like claw marks. Not the hands of a cob."

"So if they were attacked and were running back to the rocks, we could suppose they be all dead," said Berwick.

"And we should look for Grafton."

"If they got a group of armed delf, I don't see much hope for Grafton. They said he wasn't armed."

Raul picked up the long-arm and looped its strap over his shoulder. They hurried back to where they had come up over the edge and found what they had assumed to be Grafton's trail. They kept an ever more watchful eye. If something had attacked the delf, it might also be watching them.

"Lead on," said Rodon.

They went in single file as before, with Raul leading the way.

"It be so quiet," said Berwick. "Be we in Limbo again?"

As he said it, a breath of wind blew past them and he looked up to see the grey clouds drifting.

They found one more long-arm before they reached the hill, ten minutes later. They climbed its side following a zig-zag route which the cobs had taken. On the other side a plain stretched out into haze. About a mile away across a flat stretch of ground, broken by a couple of large rocky outcrops, was a higher hill than the one on which they stood. At its highest point stood a stubby tower and rising from its roof was the unmistakable flower shape of a light funnel. All three of them recognised it.

"It is short for a light tower," said Raul.

They looked around the rest of the horizon, tracking past the wide flat top which seemed to be one of many in that direction, past the near circular bowl.

"More towers," said Berwick.

They counted eight towers in the distance scattered across the plain. They were wide at the base and grew progressively narrower towards the top.

"I think they are just rock," said Raul.

There was no obvious pattern to their distribution in the landscape. Three were relatively close to one another, but the others were dotted at irregular intervals.

The sky behind the rock formations was clearing. The sky which showed through the grey cloud had a pink hue.

"I assume the trail leads for that light tower?" Rodon asked.

"Of course," said Raul.

They moved on, their long-arms at the ready. Raul was watching the outcrops between them and the light tower.

"I do not like those," he said. "I suggest we give them a wide berth. I am sure the trail will go straight to the light tower. If we find nothing there, we will come back."

"Agreed," said Rodon.

They left the trail and worked their way out into the open bushes. Berwick was nervous. It was uncomfortable country to be in. The bushes were high enough to cover anyone, or anything. He kept looking behind him nervously. Raul and Rodon looked calm, but he could tell they too were on edge.

As they passed the first of the outcrops, they all instinctively looked at them. They saw they had been right to make the detour. A group of cobs were coming out from among them. They loped on their knuckles. One climbed to the top of the rocks and looked back the other way. Another started to bark at them.

"That be a warning call," said Rodon.

"They are threatening us?" asked Raul.

"No. It be the warning they'd usually give each other."

Several were edging out into the scrub towards them. Raul lifted his long-arm to his shoulder.

"I could get them from here," he muttered.

"Don't," said Rodon. Even as he did so the cobs stopped and all joined in the barking.

"I don't like this," said Berwick.

Then the one at the top of the rocks started to bark. It was still looking the other way. The cobs below barked ever more frantically, then they turned tail and disappeared amongst the rocks.

"What scared them?" asked Berwick. He could feel a cold sweat break over him. Then his eye was caught by a movement in the distance. It came from the sky. Something was coming from the tops of the tall rock formations they had seen in the distance. At first he thought it was smoke, then he thought it looked like a flock of birds wheeling up into the air. The others had seen it too.

"What is that?" Raul asked.

"I don't know," said Rodon.

The natural instinct was to go back to the known safety of the collapsed cavern, but that was also towards the unknown birds. They began to walk towards the light tower faster now although none of them had spoken to the other. Berwick looked back over his shoulder. The swarm of whatever it was had grown larger. It was coming closer and seemed to be coming in their direction. Was it heading for them?

There were two swarms. He could make out individual shapes, but there could have been dozens of shapes in them. Judging from the distance, they were too large for birds. They began to run. They were nearing the second outcrop now and the hill bearing the light tower was much closer.

Berwick looked behind him again. He was shocked by how much closer the flock was. A group broke away and started to fly lower. He saw his companions slow down and turn to look. He tried to make them out. They did not look like birds, but more like lizards or dogs. They appeared to be pale blue, with darker, brownish undersides to their wings.

Then they swooped.

Rodon was the furthest back. His long-arm was raised and he fired at one. The flying thing spun in the air, tried to flap then fell to the ground. The others pulled out of their dive and flew to the side. While Rodon was re-loading, Raul and Berwick took the chance to fire into the air. Another creature was hit and fell.

Then they were running again. Berwick had known fear like this before. It was like one of the delf's demons swooping out of the sky at his fleeing back, but there had only ever been one of those at a time. Here there were perhaps thirty or more and he did not know what they were.

He heard a whooshing sound and knew they were coming again. He turned. Two were almost upon him. Black bulbous eyes stared blankly at him from snub faces, fanged mouths open. He ducked and lashed out with his long-arm. He struck one of the creatures, but the blow made him lose his balance and he fell. It probably saved him. The second carried on past him as he went down amongst the bushes. He still had his long-arm and he rolled, looking around him.

It had made no sound, but he saw the one which he must have hit. It too had fallen, but had picked itself up. It was the size of a dog, but it reared up on its hind legs. He saw claws on all four feet. The wings had been folded back against the body. Its mouth was open, but it kept its distance. Berwick raised his long-arm and fired. The head exploded. Then he looked around again. There were others in the air around him. He tracked around and shot at two,

192

hitting one. This gave the others pause for a few moments and he was running again.

He saw the other two. Rodon was running, Raul had just taken out another. There did not seem to be so many now. Then he realised that some of them had gone back to the first outcrop where they had seen the cobs. There was a pack on the ground near them.

He had no more time to look at the rocks because there were more bird dogs coming at him. He changed direction suddenly, running at an angle to meet Raul and Rodon. He heard the swoofing of wings behind him and turned to face it, long-arm raised. He fired at the beast at almost point blank range, ducking down instinctively as soon as he made the shot. The creature let out a squawk of pain and dropped into the bushes. He could hear it thrashing on the ground, but he did not stop to inspect it.

He reached Raul. They stood back to back watching the circling creatures. Rodon took the chance to run over.

"How far to the tower?" Rodon asked, his back to it.

"Three hundred yards," said Berwick.

"Damn."

"Let's see how far we can get like this," said Berwick and they started to move like some six legged animal towards the funnel tower.

Their attackers seemed to sense what they were doing. They ceased their circling and started to lose height. Raul fired at one and missed. The others gained in confidence. Down they came again, claws outstretched. They came faster than they could reload. Two fell, but three others came down on them. Raul used his pistols as they creatures came closer, then the trio beat at them with their long-arms as the creatures fluttered madly around them. They tore at jackets and faces, then they were on the ground and snatching at the legs of the delf and the men. They wielded their long-arms like clubs. One creature was knocked sideways, stunned and the other two backed away out of reach.

There were more in the air. Raul moved his jacket out of the way with one hand, his other gripping his long-arm's barrel, and pulled out a pistol again. He fired twice. The first one dropped one of the creatures on the ground, the other missed as the creature dodged away into the bushes. He held his fire, not wanting to waste ammunition on a hidden quarry.

Some still circled, but others flew down to land a little way off. The men and delf could see the tops of the bushes moving as the creatures came towards them, unseen, along the ground.

Rodon fired twice into the air.

"Run!" he said.

All three broke and sprinted. The funnel tower was still an impossible distance away. With each mad step they expected to feel claws ripping at them, claws which they had seen were strong enough to remove an arm. They dodged through the bushes.

"Stand and fire when I say," Rodon panted.

They ran a few more steps.

"Now!" he said.

They stopped and turned. The guns of the men fired at the airborne attackers. Raul watched as several came bounding out of the vegetation and fired his pistol. He emptied it and pulled out his second, firing that too.

Some of the creatures from the rocks appeared to be forming up to join those near the light funnel.

"I be out of bullets," said Berwick.

"Me too," said Rodon.

Both shouldered their long-arms and pulled out their pistols.

And then came the noise.

It was a deep booming ring. It throbbed and rose. It came again. And again. And then it began to increase in tempo.

The creatures stopped, momentarily confused.

"It is the light funnel!" said Raul.

They needed no common instruction, they turned and fled for the tower. The strange booming continued. It grew louder as they approached. The creatures were screeching confusedly. They tried to fly towards the tower, but seemed repelled or frightened by the noise.

There was a door in the tower. It was open. They crashed through it slamming it behind them and only then did they turn around.

It was a small round tower. Down the centre hung the narrowing bronze stem of the light funnel with a collection station at the bottom. Next to it stood a man in a torn jacket and behind him were two cobs holding rocks. The man was holding a stick in his hand with which he had clearly just been striking the funnel.

"Hello," he said. "Are you looking for me?"

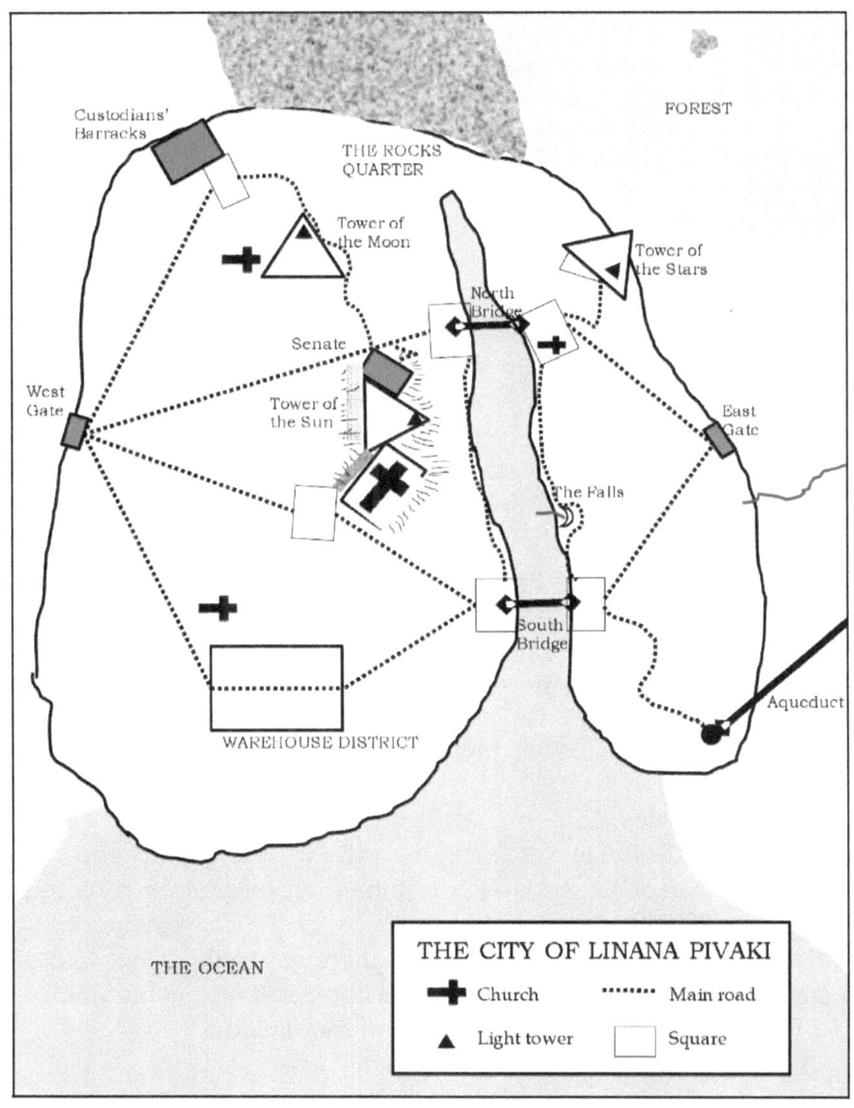

Custodians'
Barracks
THE ROCKS QUARTER
FOREST
Tower of the Moon
Tower of the Stars
North Bridge
Senate
West Gate
Tower of the Sun
East Gate
The Falls
South Bridge
Aqueduct
WAREHOUSE DISTRICT
THE OCEAN
THE CITY OF LINANA PIVAKI
Church
Main road
Light tower
Square

31

EVEN AS THE armies stopped moving on the plain beyond the city, a stirring became apparent once more on the far side of the bridges. The wolfman army was on the move again. As their first ranks began to march across the two bridges, the Knight Wardens formed up and began weaving sun wraiths.

Many of the senators had left the inverted pyramid of the senate hall to watch what was happening from the roof terrace. They saw the wraiths tearing into the ranks of the wolves so that they seemed to be making little headway across the bridges. Fitzwarren turned to Henry Clifford.

"We seem to be having better luck than Kallick did. The wardens are holding them."

"Kallick would have had to fight them on a broad front," said Giles who had stayed with them. "Here they are funnelled into a gap."

Clifford nodded.

Some wraiths were sent over to the far side of the gorge to wreak havoc amongst the wolves waiting there to cross. It took four wraiths before the creatures began to dissipate. They melted away into buildings and behind walls until there was only a thin line of them constantly replacing their burned comrades on the bridges.

"Excuse me, sir," said a voice behind the senators.

A young custodian officer stood there.

"Senator Clifford, the marshal would like to see you."

Clifford cast a glance at Fitzwarren and Giles and followed the officer across the terrace to where the Marshal of the Knight Wardens was standing. General Wootton was with him. Both looked troubled.

"We wanted to confer with you before we talk to the rest of the senate," said the marshal.

"You are an old soldier and have a better understanding of military setbacks."

It was Clifford's turn to frown.

"What setbacks?"

"We have killed hundreds of these creatures with the sun wraiths," said the marshal, "yet they keep coming. I have never seen such disdain for the wraiths. They keep marching into certain death."

"So why does sound like bad news?"

"We do not have enough light sponges to keep them at bay for much longer."

So that was it. They were running out of light. While their stocks held, they could hold off the beasts. What hope did they have after that, Clifford did not want to guess.

"Do what you can, general. I have faith in you," said Clifford.

The general looked as though he was going to say something else, but thought better of it, saluted and went back down the steps. Clifford, Fitzwarren and Giles returned to watching the progress of the battle.

It was as the general had described. The wolves kept coming across the bridges.

"There are indeed fewer wraiths," said Fitzwarren.

"They are being more careful in their use," said Clifford.

None of them remarked on the more obvious fact: slowly, Wootton's legion was being forced back.

Giles noticed several senators slip away in the hour that followed as they watched helplessly from the citadel walls. Never in his life before had he watched a battle, yet been unable to influence its outcome in some way. He considered his next move. Defeat looked inevitable for the legion and he needed to escape if he could. They had not come here to be caught up in this.

Clifford's knuckles were white on the balustrade. His face too was pale as he watched in silence. He seemed to be a different man to the one who had hosted them at dinner on their first night in the city. Fitzwarren was pacing, yet unable to take his eyes from the spectacle below them.

Suddenly the pack of legionnaires at the western end of the bridge collapsed and the wolves poured through like water through a child's dam of sand. They formed a broad front along the square by the bridge and there they stopped.

The two forces stood watching each other.

"Now it ends," Clifford murmured. "What are they waiting for?"

"Look!" said Giles.

They followed his arm to where a wolf was moving through the bridge bearing a white flag."

"Now they have us at bay, they offer to parley," said Fitzwarren.

"We must go down," said Clifford.

Fitzwarren hesitated, but followed when he saw Giles was going with Clifford. The other senators who were still left went too.

The flag of parley whipped in the wind which was also urging on the swirling flames in the burning buildings of the Old Quarter. There was a stillness as the wolf soldiers stood back, a dark, impassive line. The flames caused a dull glint on their dark mail and some could see it reflected in the animals' eyes.

Then their ranks parted. They gave way to reveal a quite striking contrast. Walking through them were tall, pale faced beings with golden helmets and breastplates. They wore white kilts with a long sword at their side. Each had a spear in one hand and a round shield in the other. Spreading from their shoulders were white feathered wings. They marched in front of the wolves, forming a tightly packed formation, impassive to the wind.

There was a stirring from the weary soldiers and citizens of Linana Pivaki. There had been rumours of a vengeful God, but now they were seeing the evidence for themselves. Here were angels, so close and clear that feathers could be seen riffling in the wind. There were angels in the streets of Linana Pivaki. The citizens watched in silence for something to happen.

Then a voice called out from amongst the angels.

"Who comes to parley with the host of the Lord?"

Clifford looked about him. There was fear on the faces of the few other senators around him. Most had fled to their homes to await whatever doom the night might bring.

If this truly was the army of the Lord, then surely they would not strike him down as he would have expected of those wolf soldiers. He felt emboldened by the inaction around him, by the fearful looks which the other senators gave him. They clearly expected him to be their spokesman. He turned to Fitzwarren and handed him the axe. Then he pushed his way through the soldiers in front of him.

The distance between the two forces was about forty yards. It felt to Clifford that it took a very long to cross that open space. He could feel the wind on his back, a strong gust seemed to push him forward. He wondered what he would do when he reached the angels; he wondered if these were the last moments of his life and what it would be like to leave it.

As he approached, the angels parted. They gave way like water gives away for a hand and they closed behind him again. None of them touched him as he made his way through their ranks, walking in a space that moved with him, until the last one parted and he found himself in an open square surrounded by angels who all turned to look inward.

In the centre of the small square was a man sat upon a large wooden chair. He wore a crimson robe and a clergyman's cap. His hair was long and dark and his face was square with strong features and prominent brows.

"Who be you?" asked the man.

"I am Senator Henry Clifford."

"Do you speak for the people of this cesspit?"

"I speak for the people of Linana Pivaki."

The man stood.

"I don't care for its name. It be a nest of vile corruption and I be the sword in the right arm of the Lord. He has sent me to purge the worlds."

"What are you purging?"

The man's eyes bulged.

"What do I purge?" he asked too quietly. "Be you so sunk in your iniquity?"

Clifford could not think of an answer that might help.

"My lord," he asked, breaking the silence. "May I ask who you are?"

"Where be Silver and those who came with him?"

The man did not even sound as though he had heard Clifford's question.

"Silver?"

In his surprise, Clifford was briefly dumbfounded. He regretted repeating the name. "He is our guest," he said. "I cannot give him up to you. Take me instead."

The man raised an eyebrow.

"So there be honour in you yet. I will not harm them. They have done the Lord's will. Where be they?"

"Close by, my lord."

"Call for them. I want them here."

Clifford wondered if he was supposed to return through the angels to find Silver. He half turned, thinking the angels would give way to him, but they remained immobile.

"Call them," said the man with emphasis.

Clifford nodded and turned around. Then he called out.

"Silver! Lord Giles!"

There was another silent pause. He did not know if anything was happening. The man had sat down again and was staring at him.

"Lord Giles! Jack Silver!"

Then his hair stood on end as the words were echoed by the angels all around him. It sounded just like a chorus of his own voice.

In the silence that followed, it began to rain, lightly at first. It took several long minutes before he saw the angels moving around something that he could not see below their shoulders and wings. Then the final angels parted and Silver and Giles entered the square. Silver looked fearful yet full of wonder. Giles could not hide a wary look in his eyes.

As soon as Silver saw the man on the throne, he ran towards him, collapsing on his knees in front of him.

"Your Grace!" he said. And then he began to sob and could say nothing more.

So it was as Silver had said, thought Clifford. This was the Archbishop who had come out of Limbo.

"Stand up, Silver," said the Archbishop. "And Lord Giles. I did not know it was you who had come with Silver, I only knew someone had remained loyal to the Order. It be good to see you."

The Archbishop stood and folded Lord Giles in his arms. Then he placed a hand on Silver's shoulder.

"You have been faithful to me. Faithful to the Lord."

"I have tried to do your bidding," Silver said.

"What should I do with this city, Silver?" the Archbishop asked with a great sigh. "Should I spare it? Be there any virtuous men here?"

"I believe there be some," he replied. "But it be filled with devils and devil lovers and the cursed offspring of their coping." The last words were spat out.

"And it be by means of those accursed that I be here. The Lord turns evil on itself once more."

"The senator here be a good man, Your Grace," said Giles. "He has looked after us as guests."

The Archbishop looked at Clifford approvingly.

"Just now he offered his life in exchange for yours."

The Archbishop sat back, his chin in his hand and thought for a while. Then he beckoned Clifford to him.

"What say you, Clifford? The Lord be merciful and forgiving. The Order may yet thrive. It simply needs to prune away the corruption and stand tall in creation."

"We are good Christians, Your Grace," said Clifford.

"You be not so," the Archbishop said gently with a shake of his head. "You be fallen, but yet the Lord will pick you up and take you to His bosom once more if you would but repent of your sins and ask for forgiveness, for your sins are vile in His eyes."

"We will repent if we have done wrong," the senator replied.

He was thinking quickly, trying to read this man. He was still trying to understand the whole catastrophe that had befallen his city in one day. Yesterday he would not have called himself a superstitious man. Yet here he was faced with angels and warrior wolves which had marched out of Limbo and defeated the unbeatable legions of the Republic. He had a duty to uphold and he was now the people's last line of defence. He was his own last line of defence.

"The people of Linana Pivaki are a good people. They have created an empire here in the south and rule it."

"But do you rule it or be you ruled?" the Archbishop asked.

The rain began to fall more heavily now.

Clifford had not seen them approach, but he found he was now flanked by two angels. They were taller than he by a head, broad and muscular. Although fair of face, those faces held no emotion.

They grasped his arms and lifted him up. Clifford gulped in air. They had lifted him so easily, they were gripping him tightly and he felt pain in his arms. The rain ran off them as if they were made of stone, but Clifford could feel it soaking through his tunic, could feel the wind chilling him as it whistled around them. They carried him towards the Archbishop who thrust his head forward.

"Do you rule or be you ruled?" he hissed. "You consort with devils! You have bred a mongrel people, half devil, half human."

"It was not the people of today who made the puoli!" Clifford said. He was trying not to show the pain he felt. He could feel his arms being crushed. Already his hands were numb. "But they were only made from the lowest people. And they were made so that our armies could swell and conquer in the Lord's name."

"But you *lie*, senator," the Archbishop said softly, stating the obvious. "I have felt the dreams from the spawn of a new generation of these monsters. They have powers to pierce Limbo and cross the worlds, if they had but time to hone their powers."

The senator was thinking. His head felt light. Who was the Archbishop talking about? He remembered some university professor years before who had been dismissed because he had married a delf. He was a doctor now, or a philosopher. Perhaps he had children.

"We could find them. Bring them to you. All the puoli are in the old quarter, where you came. Perhaps they are all dead."

"No. They be not dead. They serve me in their sleep, for thus does the Lord turn all of Satan's feeble rebellions against him. They keep the gates of Limbo open. I did hear two voices, but I have only heard one of late."

He moved in his seat and his eyes which had been looking across the city focused again on the senator.

"I will tell you how the men of the Order can stand tall again," said the Archbishop. "You must rid yourself of sin. You must cut off the poisoned limb."

"We will seek forgiveness," Clifford replied, then he winced. The pain in his arms was like rods of steel being pushed up inside his bones and muscles from his wrists to his shoulders.

"The devils must be consigned to darkness," the Archbishop said. "They will be given unto the pit and the ocean will purge them from the world."

What was he saying? Clifford wondered, a frown creeping across his face.

"They must all die," said the Archbishop. He gestured to the gorge behind him. "The abyss which we crossed, that will be their abode. Once they are all gone, you, the descendants of the Order, shall begin a new covenant with the Lord."

"You are saying that we must kill all the delf?"

"Killing devils buys a great reward in Heaven. They be not human. They have tricked you for centuries. They have fed your pride and greed until you were enslaved to their ways. You be so under their spell that you even wield their sorcery."

Clifford stared, stunned at the Archbishop. Kill the delf. He disliked them, they were a thorn in his side, but *kill* them all? But another voice in his head came to him clearly. There was no argument, it whispered. Either the devils died or the whole city would be destroyed. This great warrior bishop was holding out an olive branch. He would spare the descendants of the Order.

Had Clifford and his ancestors not kept them as pure as they could? Had they not made sure that the Christians were a separate people from the delf still? And of the puoli?

The Archbishop looked at him with narrowed eyes.

"They have blinded you. Go. Pray. The Lord be forgiving. Three days and three nights you shall have to decide whether to turn back to the Lord or to forsake Him entirely. Go now. Come back to me within this time or the city will burn."

The angels released him and he dropped to the ground, landing heavily and falling. The Archbishop was sitting back in his chair.

"I had thought I was giving you an easy choice," he sighed. "Remember, Senator. God be merciful."

Then he held up his hand and made a gesture and the angels behind him moved apart. A man limped out from between their ranks. He held one arm cradled against his body, there was a cut across his forehead and a livid bruise underneath his left eye. His clothes were torn and bloody. Henry Clifford recognised his son immediately.

"Edward!" he exclaimed and struggled to stand. Despite his injuries, Edward ran forward and put out his good arm to his father, helping him to his feet. The Archbishop nodded as they embraced.

"I have hope, Senator. Surely such gallantry as your son displayed, misplaced though it was, be the vestiges of a gift from the Lord?"

He made another sign and the angels moved away from the father and son. Walking backwards, they moved to surround the Archbishop. Then they filed back into the main body of the army until the angels with the Archbishop in their midst had vanished. There remained only the menacing dark mass of wolf warriors standing impassive in their black chain mail facing the last of the city's defenders. Then the Archbishop's host turned about and marched back across the bridges to the old quarter.

32

THE CLIFFORDS, FATHER and son, were in their living room. Henry had bathed his son's wounds and now they sat quietly, looking out over the gorge and the waterfall. Where they were was sheltered from the wind, but they could see it whipping at the water, sending much of it backwards as spray. As they looked, it was briefly lit as the sun appeared below the dark clouds which had hung over the city all day and the fragments of water shone bright against the side of the gorge which was now in shadow.

"So what are we going to do, father?" Edward asked eventually. His arm was freshly bound and in a sling. Only the cuts on his face were still visible, those on his arms and chest were hidden by the loose, clean shirt he wore.

The senator was staring vacantly at the waterfall. At Edward's question, he stood and went to the window and looked out to the left, towards the bridges.

"They're still there," he said. He shook his head. "I just thought: maybe they had gone. Gone as suddenly as they came."

Edward thought his father had aged. He said nothing. His father took a deep breath.

"There is only one thing we can do," Henry said. "We can avoid extermination."

"You can't mean that!" There was surprise as well as anger in Edward's voice.

The older man turned to look at his son.

"Edward, for centuries the legions of Linana Pivaki have marched without fear. My whole life, your whole life, we have done what we have wanted, gone where we willed, traded for what we wanted."

His eyes turned back to the silent masses lined up beyond the bridges in the old city.

"Our power meant nothing to them."

"But there must be something we can do!"

"You talk like a young man. You've already forgotten what it was like to fight them. They were like the ocean. Some of the waves may break on you, but the sea keeps on coming. You cannot stop it. The Archbishop has given us a choice and it is a clear one."

"They're our friends! We cannot murder them!"

"They have never been my friends. Acquaintances, yes, but they have schemed against us in the senate."

"Father, you enjoy the schemes. You've always loved debating, but now you're just giving up."

"I am not giving up!" the senator snapped, rounding on his son. There were tears in his eyes. "I am trying to protect my people. The delf die anyway. The legions have tried and failed. We senators must now do our part. We are meeting in the morning at Fitzwarren's. After that, you must be ready to do *your* duty."

Captain Benedict found Lord Giles by the falls, watching the spray tumble into the depths of the gorge.

"My lord, we have known each other a long time."

"Speak freely, Benedict."

"I do not like this. The Archbishop tried to destroy Outreterre."

"His Grace had wanted to weed out the corruption in Outreterre, the same corruption we came here to seek help against. As vain a hope as that has turned out to be. But we be on the winning side at the moment, although caught between Hell and the Devil. I have little love for these devil lovers. We will have no help from them against the delf. Yet to leave now would be madness. His Grace wields great power and he trusts us and values us. That be to the good. We can influence his decisions. We bide our time. Have someone look to our horses. I want them ready to ride at a moment's notice. We will wait to see how this could end for us."

"Very well, my lord. I will see to it."

The dusk had just given way to night. The streets were empty and a heaviness lay in the air despite the thick wind which blew amongst the buildings. It felt as though a storm was building.

Two men were walking down the street in the south of the city. At irregular intervals, one of them would point at a door and the other would make a small mark on the door frame, using a pot of paint.

Then there was a muffled sound of commotion which became suddenly louder as a crowd burst onto the street at the far end. They carried sticks and swords and guns. They stopped at the first marked house and someone at the front hammered on the door. Others in the group flowed past and towards other houses.

The door opened and those at the front moved quickly. They grabbed the delf who had opened the door, pulling him onto the street and going into the house. The delf was pushed to the ground. Arms and weapons were raised in the air, then brought down. Then there was a gunshot from inside the house.

At that, the mob speeded up in its movements, washing around the street. Frightened faces appeared in some of the windows. The crowd continued to try the marked doors. None of them were being opened any longer. Then came sounds of rending wood as axes and cudgels smashed them in.

Streets away in the centre of the city where the villas were large and strongly built, Senator Clifford sat gloomily by the light of a number of candles. He heard a distant knock and voices as a servant opened the street door. He raised his head at the approaching footsteps and Fitzwarren came in.

"I am glad I found you," he said. "Where is Edward?"

The senator shook his head.

"In his room. He still hopes to do the impossible. He wants to rally the remains of Wootton's Legion to defeat the army of God. I know I should be proud of his stubbornness, but he's a fool."

"We will all die if he tries anything," Fitzwarren exclaimed. "We are under a truce!"

"There's nothing they can do. They will realise it soon if not now. You're coming to the meeting tomorrow?"

"I think our meeting is superfluous," Fitzwarren replied.

"Why so?" Henry asked.

Edward had entered the room behind them. Fitzwarren smiled at him and put out his hands to grasp his shoulders.

"My boy, I'm so pleased you're safe. I could not believe it when I heard you were missing. God is merciful."

"Why is the meeting superfluous?" Edward asked, repeating his father's question.

"Have they gone?" Henry asked in disbelief.

"No, but the people have made the decision for us," Fitzwarren said. "There are mobs in the streets."

"What are they doing?" Edward asked, although he knew what was coming. He had a sick feeling in his stomach.

"They are doing as God's messenger demanded. They know they will surely die if they do not."

"This must stop!" said Edward. He started to leave. His father put a restraining hand on his arm.

"Try to stop it and they'll kill you. The decision has been made for us. It is inevitable. Let it happen now. They die or we all do."

"These are my own. I've grown up with them, fought with them, drunk with them, laughed with them. If they're not my own, who is? Delf, puoli and man. We support each other. I will desert them only in death."

He shook off his father's arm and walked from the room.

33

RAUL, BERWICK AND Rodon stared at the lightly built man in the woollen coat who had just let them into the stone light tower.

"You're bleeding," he said. "Let me help you."

They realised they were. Their sleeves were torn and their faces and hands were cut.

"They can't get in," the man added. "At least, they tried to before and couldn't."

"What about those?" asked Raul, pointing at the two cobs.

"They're mine," said Grafton. "Well, one is. The other seems to be a local, but he's quite friendly."

"And you be Hugh Grafton?" asked Rodon.

"I am. Did the Tafa send you?" Then he frowned. "Where are you from? You're not from Linana."

"That we be not," said Rodon. "But the Tafa wants your safe return. And that of her men."

"Ah. That last won't be possible. They didn't have your discipline, I'm afraid. And I'm not sure how we're going to get back either. It might not work a second time."

"We will think of something," said Raul.

Grafton looked at him and smiled. "We will," he agreed.

Berwick went to a narrow slit window and peered out.

"What are they doing?" Raul asked.

"Some be returning to the rocks," Berwick said. "But I can't tell if it be all of them."

They heard a thump reverberate down the funnel. Grafton struck the side of the light funnel twice and a flurry of wings reached them as the creature which had landed on the edge of the funnel took flight again.

"So how did you get here?" Rodon asked Grafton. "You be not even armed."

"I was lucky. They took longer to see me and then a herd of animals appeared which offered richer pickings than my scrawny frame. But after two more arrivals, the harpies are beginning to show more of an interest."

"Harpies?" asked Berwick.

"Just my name for them. I thought it fitting."

Raul was standing in one spot, turning and looking up at the tower around him.

"It looks old."

"It does, doesn't it?" Grafton agreed. "I would say centuries. The cobs say it's very old, or as close as they can come to saying very old. They call it 'always'."

"Do you know where we be?" Rodon asked.

"No. But I do know where we're not."

"Be it Limbo?" Berwick asked.

"I hadn't thought of that, but no, I don't think it is. I think this is another world."

"But there be cobs here."

"And a light tower," said Grafton. "But there's more. You'll see it later. At nightfall, if the sky is clear. Is it still cloudy?"

Rodon frowned. "Why?"

"I will risk a look outside. Would you hold the door for me?"

Berwick lifted the latch and opened the door slowly while Grafton stood close to it. Once it was open enough, he quickly looked out.

"Still cloudy, but there is clear sky too now, look."

He pointed up and they followed his finger. The cloud was grey, tinged with pink, but in a gap, they could see sky.

"It be green!" exclaimed Berwick.

"Interesting isn't it?" said Grafton.

He pulled his head back inside and Berwick closed the door, dropping the latch as he did so. Grafton turned to look at his three visitors.

"When I said this was another world, I must say I would have expected some surprise, not simply a challenging question."

The three exchanged looks.

"We've seen much. It makes for an open mind," said Berwick.

Grafton raised an eyebrow.

"Look, we need to find a way to get away from here," he said. "I don't think that simply charging across the open ground is the way to do it. The harpies appear to learn quickly and they'll be ready for us." He looked at Raul. "I don't suppose you can weave can you?"

"Weave? Light you mean?" Raul asked.

"Yes."

"No."

"Just a thought. You're Unama delf aren't you and I…well I just thought I would ask in case you could. The collection engine is stiff, but I think it would work again."

He moved across the room to the far wall where there was a door.

"And look what I found in here."

The door opened with difficulty, the wood was warped and heavy and scraped across the uneven floor. On the other side was a small room with walls and roof made entirely out of stone. The only light was from two narrow windows and a small hole in the roof. Below the hole was a circle of blackened stones which had once been used as a fireplace. A wooden chest with a large lock stood on one side, next to one of two low broken frames with scraps of rotten material hanging from them.

"Those look like they were once beds," said Rodon.

"Not been used for a while though eh?" smiled Grafton. "And see down here."

Grafton knelt down and pointed to the base of the wall, where it was thickest. They crowded around to look. Carved onto the stone was the rough symbol of the sun behind a cloud. Grafton looked at Raul.

"Do you know what that means?"

Raul hesitated.

"It means something secret doesn't it?" Grafton said.

Raul made a non-committal noise.

"I was married to a delf," said Grafton. "I have read delf texts from Linana Pivaki. This means there's something hidden. It's a sign to other delf, others who know the light lore."

"I know little of the light lore," said Raul.

"I've made it my study to find out what has been forgotten in Linana. I haven't had a chance to look around here yet. It can't be anything sophisticated. This building is too roughly made, although I might be wrong."

"What be in the chest?" Berwick asked.

"I don't know," said Grafton. "It's locked and I've been reluctant to break it."

"Perhaps the hidden thing be a key," said Rodon.

Grafton started to feel around the stones. Once or twice he found a loose one and groped around inside with his fingers with a look of disappointment. He stopped and looked around. Behind him, a roundish stone stood next to the wall. With difficulty, he rolled it over to the other side where he had stood before and stood on it. He began to feel around the stones again. He reached up, spreading his fingers wide and following his hands with his eyes. The other three and the two cobs watched him silently.

"Go back a moment," said Berwick.

"Why?" asked Grafton.

"I thought I saw something odd. Just a bit further back, no a bit further. There!"

"Yes, I saw it," said Grafton excitedly.

There were three stones one above the other and all three had moved when he touched one. He carefully stepped off the rock, moved it to the right until it was under the suspicious stones, then climbed on it again. He felt around them with his fingers, then slowly began to pull them out. He kept pulling and drew out what appeared to be a slab of rock. The three stones had been placed along one thin edge.

Grafton studied it, turning it over in his fingers. Then he put his fingers on the opposite edge to the stones and pushed. The slab opened like a book. Grafton looked up at them smiling, then turned back to it.

"There is writing." He squinted at it. "I, Velkuri the Mage built this tower...I gathered the light of the Cradle...It is the light of creation...the light of new beginnings...It is the light of possibility."

Grafton looked thoughtful. "The light cradle?" And then he smiled. "Of course."

"A mage?" said Berwick. "That makes it hundreds of years old."

"Do you know about the mages?" Grafton asked him.

Berwick caught Rodon's eye. Rodon liked to think he was a good judge of character. He watched when others talked. Now here was a man who was married to a delf. He seemed to embody all that he and Berwick hoped Unama and Outreterre could be. It felt as though they were on the brink of something important. It was a time for trust. He nodded to Berwick to go on and his face relaxed. Rodon suspected the younger man had been thinking the same as he.

"The last mage was trapped in Limbo," Berwick continued. "We found him there. He returned to Unama and helped to make a peace between delf and men. He defeated the hosts of Limbo with the light of hope."

"Really? You have been to Limbo?"

Berwick nodded. "We all have."

"You've all been to Limbo? Which explains why you took being here so calmly. And there we were thinking Outreterre would rot from within with its own lack of adventure. And this mage you met. Was he called Velkuri?"

Raul shrugged. "We just knew him as the Mage."

"But even so, a mage built this. A mage came here."

Grafton was looking around the simple room with renewed wonder. "Where are we?" He looked at the others. "Perhaps you will understand how we all came to be here."

"The light needle?" said Raul.

"Yes. It's what comes of an adventurous mind. I've used it before, but this has never happened until now. The only difference was that many of the cobs were asleep. I have read that the light can be used to amplify dreams, although," he hesitated, "you probably knew that. I think they were dreaming and we followed their dreams here."

"A cob's dreams can follow the light?" Raul scoffed.

"Why not? They are the dreams of a sentient being."

"But don't you need someone to pull you through to another world as well?"

"So I have read. But you can tell me more from the sound of things."

"It be true," said Rodon. "Although the Mage did not seem to need it."

"Well then. I am not a mage, so I can only think that the cobs of this place were dreaming of them too. They seem different to wild cobs. They're more like my own. So how did they come to be here?"

He pursed his lips at the faces looking at him. Only Berwick gave a slight nod.

"All this is fascinating," said Raul. "But we have work to do and we need to take you back to the Tafa."

Grafton smiled.

"It is fascinating and I must come back here. But yes, we need to leave. We have no food."

He led them back into the funnel room and stood so that he could see the rocks through one of the small windows.

"We only need make it to the rocks over there, I think."

"But there be your harpies waiting there."

"I think there are tunnels. The cobs would never survive against the harpies if they had no way of avoiding them. From what they say, I think there are underground ways which they can seal against the harpies."

"But you said yourself we would not survive another run outside," said Raul.

"Perhaps a short one. And if there were distractions. That herd of animals I saw. I've seen it each evening I've been here, so I'm hoping it will come back. We've only a few hours to pass. I'll use it as best I can."

"You talk like a scholar and I too have studied the ways of the delf," said Rodon. "Why be there only one keeper station? All the other light towers I've seen have three, one for each of the sun, moons and stars."

"True, but here I think this Velkuri only wanted one. You'll see soon. Well, as we have time, shall we try that chest again?"

All four of them returned to the room with the beds. The cobs followed quietly and watched them.

"Do you want to open this?" Raul asked.

"Oh yes," said Grafton.

Raul pulled out his knife and tried to prise at the lock, attempting to lever it open, but it would not move.

"We could blow the lock," he said, putting his hand on the butt of his pistol.

Grafton shook his head. "That could damage it. And you may need that bullet. I hope I have something useful on me. I always carry a thing or two."

He pulled out a small leather wallet from an inside pocket of his jacket. He untied the cord around it and rolled out the wallet. It contained an assortment of small tools: tweezers, sharp ends, hooks, an L shaped device.

"I like to poke around at things," he said. Then he selected one of the tools and knelt down by the box. He put the tool into the lock and prodded. His hand made small movements and his eyes looked into space, moving around as he visualised what he could feel.

He smiled.

"Nothing too complicated. I thought it was going to be something infernal."

They watched him for some minutes.

"There is no need to watch," Grafton said. "In fact I think I'd prefer you didn't. This will take as long as it does."

"Sorry, but there be not much else to do," said Berwick.

"We could see if there be anything that will help us get to those rocks," said Rodon. "Let's have a look outside."

34

BERWICK KEPT A lookout for the harpies while the other two went around the building to see if there was anything of interest. They found it quickly. Wedged into the crook of the two rooms with large rocks at its base to hold it in place was a large wooden frame. Steel sheets had been laid across it. These were rusting badly, but otherwise intact. Rodon and Raul looked at each other quizzically and started to roll away the rocks to free it up. It took both of them to move each one.

The frame was still wedged into the corner, but now they could move the other end and Raul looked behind it.

"There are handles," he said. "And there are parts of more of the frame. There used to be sides."

"But what be it?"

Raul shrugged.

Berwick could make nothing of it either.

"A fence?" he suggested.

Just then, they heard Grafton call out.

They went inside and found him with a leather bag on his lap. He was just pulling his hand out of it. In it, he was holding a light sponge.

"Velkuri said he gathered light. This must be it. Still here and still full of light. It's fascinating."

Grafton stood and took the bag with him into the funnel room. He looked at the sponge in his hand again, then back at the base of the light funnel where it entered the pedal station. One of the cobs became a little agitated when he looked at it and the one with him copied.

"Why are you so nervous?" Grafton asked them. Then he crouched down and undid the flap on its side. It was stiff, but opened. Grafton put his hand inside and pulled out another sponge. He weighed it for a moment, then slipped it into the bag with the rest of them.

"We should take these with us."

The rest of the afternoon passed slowly. Grafton poked around the tower happily. All three helped from time to time, although they did not know what they were looking for and Grafton could not tell them. In the end they gave up, appointed the first person to take watch, while the other two sat by the wall, each with a long-arm resting against a shoulder, and went to sleep.

Later, Grafton woke the other two. From the light coming through the window slits, it appeared to be evening. He was smiling.

"Come and take a look outside," he said. "There are no harpies about, so we should make a move as well."

They saw he was wearing a backpack and had one of the spare long-arms from the Tafa's guards over his shoulder. He unlatched the door and made a noise to the two cobs who had come back inside. They loped over and stood next to him, scanning the sky.

Berwick, Rodon and Raul stood up, shaking the sleep from themselves and went to the door. There was something very odd about the light. Berwick could not work out what it was, but as he stepped past the door, he realised what it was.

He had never seen anything like it.

It was as if a smoky veil of light had been thrown across the sky from horizon to horizon. Far, far away, but vast, a nebula lit up the night. Shades of crimson drifted onto purples like swirling dyes frozen in water. Darker smoke leaked into the centre casting green and pale blue shadows and the whole was jewelled with thousands of sparkling stars caught up in the cosmic clouds.

The three of them turned open mouthed to Grafton. He smiled at them.

"Behold," he smiled. "The light cradle. And final proof that we are...somewhere else."

He pointed away to their backs. There was a cloud of dust.

"The herd is coming. Now come on. Let's get over to those rocks."

The wild cob hooted at Grafton, then it took the other cob around the back of the building. They all followed.

Seeing the rocks had been moved from the frame, the wild cob muttered and turned to look at them all. Then he took hold of the frame and pulled suddenly. The jerk from its strong arms freed it. The cob gibbered to the other and the two lowered the frame into a horizontal position above their heads. They held it there for a moment, then leaned it on the wall. The wild cob looked at Grafton. Realisation dawned.

"It's a shield!" Grafton said.

"What?" asked Raul.

"They use it as a shield against the harpies."

Two of the cobs, Grafton and Berwick took the weight of the frame while the other two held their long-arms ready.

They broke into a jog as soon as they were clear of the funnel tower. They moved awkwardly with the ungainly iron covered frame above their heads. They could see the rock towers of the harpies in the distance and as they watched, a cloud of harpies rose from each of them. There must have been hundreds. At the same time, others rose up from behind the nearer rocks where they had seen the cobs.

"They were waiting for us," said Berwick.

With his arms above his head, he felt exposed, even though he was holding the shield. It only provided cover from above. Raul and Rodon were readying their long-arms. Berwick had never seen cobs look frightened, but these were clearly tense. Their lips were pulled right back to reveal their teeth and their ears had flattened against the sides of their heads as they ran.

They were not going to reach the cover of the rocks before the harpies descended on them. The creatures were circling now.

"Stop while we give them a volley to think about!" said Rodon. The two men stopped, briefly jerked by the cobs who wanted to keep running. Raul and Rodon each raised his long-arm to his shoulder and fired at the harpies. Two screeched and fell from the sky, but the others kept coming.

"Again! Fire!" called Rodon.

They did so. The harpies pulled away again, too far away to waste ammunition by firing.

"Go now!" said Raul.

They ran again, fear was on them as the once distant cloud of harpies came ever nearer. The rocks were still too far away. Grafton was at the front.

"Here they come!" he said, looking towards the sky. "Keep moving! Cover the sides."

Raul threw the strap of his long-arm over his shoulder and pulled out both pistols. Rodon did the same. The long-arm was better saved for distance shooting and they were unlikely to have a chance to reload.

The first they knew how close the harpies from the rocks were was when they thudded into the top of the shield. They could hear the skidding of claws on the metal, then there was a flurry next to them. One of Rodon's pistols fired, its sound louder than usual under the metal roof, and the first of the blue creatures spun away. Just as it did, two more came from the other side. There was no chance for Raul to fire and they both came underneath the frame. One seemed confused by the confined space. It squawked and flapped madly, flying into the wild cob at the rear before emerging into clear space. The other slashed wildly with its claws.

Afraid to fire in case he hit one of the four holding up the shield, Raul clubbed at the beast in a frenzy. He felt a sharp pain in his right hand, then warmth as blood ran down his arm, but the harpy was on the ground. The first had gathered itself and was hopping towards them, its wings outstretched. Raul pointed one pistol at it and fired. The second harpy flew back and clipped the first as it came up. They gained a few moments of respite.

The rocks were closer. There were thuds above them again. Two more harpies skittered off the shield at the back and joined the second. They launched themselves at the cobs' backs. The cobs howled and let go of the shield with one arm to try to fend off their attackers. It unsteadied Berwick and Grafton and pulled them backwards. They came to a halt as the frame dropped on all of them.

There was confusion and terror under the shield. More of the creatures were dropping out of the sky, some sliding off the metal, others landing on the ground next to them. The cobs were still screeching. The wild cob reached around and caught the wing of its tormentor and pulled it in front of him. Its claws ripped at his back, but then he had it and his own hand was grasping at the harpy's throat, held away from his body by his long arms.

Grafton's cob was having more trouble. It was flapping its arms uselessly behind it, screaming. The screaming continued even as Rodon fired at point blank range at the creature's head and it fell back from the cob.

Grafton and Berwick flung the shield away from them. It knocked away some of their attackers, but now they were completely exposed. Unshouldering their long-arms, Grafton started to raise his to his shoulder, but Berwick used his like a club.

This was close range fighting and there was no time to aim. He swung madly. The creatures hung back. There was more pistol fire. Berwick could barely understand what was happening around them.

Then suddenly the harpies above them pulled up into the higher air where the ones from the rock towers were flying. In the pause they heard a sound like distant thunder and saw behind them in the distance the dust lifting into the air. It was the herd Grafton had seen on the other nights, but much closer now.

They took the chance of the respite and ran hard. Suddenly Grafton realised his cob was not with them. He looked behind and it was curled up on the ground near the bodies of the fallen harpies. He turned back.

Raul's eyes opened wide with astonishment.

But one of the harpies had also noticed the lone man. Perhaps it thought this was easier prey than the herd for it swung around in the air and dived.

Raul stopped, swinging his long-arm around and up at the harpy as it dropped out of the sky. Grafton had yet to see it. Raul tracked the creature as it dived. It was much bigger than any bird he had shot at. He fired.

It only clipped the harpy, but it was enough to knock it off its course. It fell, rather than dived to the ground and rolled to its feet a few yards from the wounded cob.

Raul was running back now. Grafton had seen the harpy and stopped. The cob lay motionless between them. He was unaware of Raul behind him. In a moment, the long-arm was up and Grafton fired from the waist. The harpy was flung back just as Raul reached him.

"Come on, leave the cob!" he spat.

"It's still alive," said Grafton.

"Who cares?"

"I do," Grafton replied and he heaved the creature up, pulling one of its arms around his neck.

Raul did not care about the cob, he wanted Grafton out of the open.

The others were at the rocks now watching the sky and the three still a hundred yards away.

Raul watched Grafton struggling for a moment. He eyed the cob with disgust, then reluctantly took its other arm. He could smell it as they dragged it between them as they ran for the rocks.

When they reached the others, Raul dropped the cob. Grafton let it go more gently.

The wild cob loped over and sniffed its fellow. Then it looked at Grafton for a moment, pulled the unconscious cob over his shoulder and ran around the back of the rock.

They followed it in time to see it nimbly climbing and disappear into a horizontal cleft.

"Keep a watch on the sky," said Raul.

It was hard to concentrate when he felt at any moment a creature could descend on him. His neck was prickling.

He reached where the cob had climbed. There were regular worn places in the rock. He struggled to pull himself up, but could see how a cob with its long arms and strong fingers would have managed it with ease.

He tried again and pulled himself into the cleft. He crawled to the back and realised a wide crack extended part way across. He could not see where it went.

He pushed himself back out, looking for a moment at the nebula. The others had their backs to him. He dropped off the cleft onto the ground.

Raul, Grafton and Berwick were watching the harpies, but they were in the distance and below them was what had attracted them. A large herd of four legged beasts was galloping and the harpies were attacking them, diving in relentlessly, harrying the sides of the herd from all directions. He watched with them for a moment, then told them about what he had found.

With parting glances at the spectacle, the three followed him around the other side of the rock.

"Here," said Raul to Grafton. "I will help you up. Now go to the back. Do you see?"

"You go next. I can climb up on my own," said Berwick.

Between the two of them, they easily launched Rodon onto the ledge. The other two followed. Grafton had already disappeared down the hole. When they too had jumped down, the darkness closed around them.

"Damn, I can't see!" said Berwick.

"Wait until your eyes become accustomed," said Grafton.

They were in a passage made of earth and stone. But then there was the sound of stone dragging across stone and it went dark.

"Who did that?" Berwick asked.

"Don't worry," Grafton said. "It's the door. Our friendly cobs have locked us in to stop the harpies from following us. Does anyone have a light?"

"I have a candle," said Raul. He lit it and the first thing it lit was the two cobs standing by the entrance watching them. Then they jumped forward and past them and went off into the darkness.

"Follow them," said Grafton.

The four of them ran down the passageway, trying to keep up with the cobs, following Raul's candle and attempting to avoid injury on the roughly carved tunnel. They were briefly aware of side passages opening up as they rushed past them.

"Where does this go?" Berwick panted.

"The right way," said Raul.

It was a disconcerting flight through the dark. Grafton struck his head and fell back onto Rodon behind, who held him up and pushed him forwards. Grafton staggered, put out his hand, then was on his feet again and moving forwards.

There was space around them quite suddenly. They could feel the darkness opening up and the walls moved away from Raul's small candle. Raul stopped.

"What be the matter?" Rodon asked.

"The cobs have stopped." Raul paused. "And we are not alone in here."

Berwick looked around. He could just make out pale glowing circles. He realised what they were just as Raul said it.

"There are cobs in here. They can see us. There are many of them."

Berwick saw one enter the edge of the field of light given off by the candle. It looked at Raul and seemed to be sniffing him. He could see Raul stiffen, then force himself to relax. The cob came closer to him, looking at him. Then it moved down the line sniffing each one of them in turn and gazing at them with its pale green eyes.

Raul had lowered his candle when the cob went back to him. It studied him for a minute. Raul stared back at it. Berwick knew that Raul had never been so close to a cob before and not killed it. He looked down at his other hand and saw that it had moved to his belt and was touching the butt of his pistol. Then the cob croaked at him. Raul did nothing, but stayed looking at it. The same croak came again.

"Do you know what it is saying, Grafton?" Raul asked.

"I think it is saying 'fire'," he replied.

It croaked again.

"I think it knows you be delf," said Rodon. "

It croaked and rasped.

"'Always fire'," said Grafton. "I think it's talking about weaving light from the funnel. Do you think it knows about wraiths?"

"Or they remember the mage," said Rodon. "But they don't live that long."

"No, but they pass things from one generation to another," Grafton said.

"Cobs do that?" said Raul in disbelief.

"Of course, why not?"

"They are just animals."

"To you. Because they do not look like you. I know of no other animal with a language."

"Are you saying the Mage brought them here?" Berwick asked.

"That is one possibility. Can you think of another? We know a mage called Velkuri was here. Perhaps there were others."

Grafton turned back to the cob. He coughed and cleared his throat, then made his own rasping sound.

"What did you say?"

"Hopefully I asked where my cob was."

A cob came out carrying Grafton's injured cob over his shoulder. He laid him on the ground. Grafton bent over him.

"The pity of it. He's dead."

Then the cob which had brought him in reached out and tugged Grafton's sleeve. It barked, then made off for the other side of the cavern.

"I'm going to follow him."

"I do not believe this," said Raul. But he, Raul and Rodon followed.

They dodged along a tunnel which wormed its way through the ground. They had to bend double for most of the way and each of them banged their heads and caught limbs on protruding rocks as they tried to keep the candle lit and follow the cob.

Eventually they saw a crack of light ahead of them and made for it. The cob stood by it and pushed.

"Hold this," said Raul and passed Berwick the candle. He held it up as Raul felt around the edge of the crack. Both he and the cob pushed. When it gave, it moved slowly, rolling away from the widening entrance.

Outside, they could see the familiar sight of the bowl into which they had first come. They were looking out one of the sides. It was completely dark now, but the bowl was well lit by the green and blue glow of the nebula.

"It is there," he said, pointing to the right. "That is where we came in."

He stepped out onto a ledge and swung himself down, his legs dangling until they found a purchase beneath him. Then he let himself drop. The others followed him.

The cob stood above them. It coughed more sounds at them.

"Did it say something about sleeping?" Rodon asked.

"Yes," said Grafton. "Always fire and sleeping. Something else too."

The cob repeated the sounds and touched its head. Grafton smiled.

"I think it's talking about dreaming," he said.

"Can we go now?" asked Raul.

Grafton paused and made a kind of whimpering sound. Then he turned back to the others and started down the side off the bowl.

They made their way along the bottom. The nebula gave off plenty of light by which to see, especially after the darkness of the tunnels.

They reached the pile of stones beneath the entrance through which they had come and climbed up it. There was no one inside, but the light needle still stood sentinel.

Grafton stopped at the blurring of the cave walls and tried to see what was beyond. He could see only rock. He took a step forward, but Rodon put a hand on his shoulder.

"That is Limbo," he said. "I have been there before and I don't want to go there again. The Tafa wants your safe return, so if you want to go in there, you can do it after we've returned you."

Grafton smiled at him.

"Very well. But you must tell me more about it."

Grafton walked on and they gathered around the needle.

"We need to close this way between the worlds," Rodon said to Grafton. "Can you do that?"

"I hadn't realised I could open it," he said.

"We'll need to dream it back to Naadu. That be all. Isn't that right Raul?"

"Something like that," he said.

"So we'll need someone who knows Naadu well. Who would dream of home."

"Let's get some of the guards," Grafton said.

"I'll go up and get some," said Rodon.

He began to walk up the tunnel. He could see the entrance ahead where the door had been opened. He noticed the dry smell of the passage, so different from the smell of vegetation of the other world, but as he reached the open air, the dryness of the passage was replaced by a damp smell. The sky was obscured by a thick, wet fog. He stepped out, but stopped abruptly, then ducked back inside the passage, his long-arm already in his hands.

Boxes has been tipped over and the canvas shelter had collapsed on top of them. Patches of dry blood dotted the ground, together with long-arms and scraps of clothing. There was no sign of their guards however. Rodon took a quick look around. He climbed up onto a rock and surveyed the area around, but could see nothing through the fog save for the rocks which faded into the grey. He was alone.

He went back to the camp and the tunnel mouth. He was about to re-enter the tunnel when he heard a sound and whirled around. It had come from under the canvas. He put his long-arm to one side and, pulling out one of his pistols, moved silently over to collapsed shelter. He whipped up a corner of the canvas. It was all he could do to not shoot. A dead harpy lay on the crates in front of him, a gaping exit wound in its back. Then a crate tumbled forward from a pile. He lowered his pistol and shoved it into his belt. Sam Atana was lying sprawled half underneath some boxes. His face was covered in blood.

"I heard...you walking," he said, dragging the words out.

Rodon went over to him.

"Help me," he said in a rasping whisper.

35

ATANA WAS STILL cradling a long-arm and there was a pistol and a blood smeared sword on his lap. The puoli was barely conscious. As he went closer, Rodon could see why. Sam's right arm was hanging from his shoulder. There were deep gashes in it and other claw marks up his front. He had clearly lost a great deal of blood.

"What happened?" Rodon asked. As he did so, he picked up a piece of rag that was lying on the ground behind him and began to tie it around Sam's good arm as a tourniquet.

"Flying...flying things...from..." Sam coughed. "From the tunnel." He took a wheezing breath. "Thought you were dead."

"Where be the others? Where be the other guards?" Rodon demanded.

Sam rolled his eyes and coughed.

"Water," he said.

Rodon took the flask which he was carrying over his shoulder and held it to the puoli's lips, letting him take a few sips before moving it away.

"Not too much now," he said. "Where be the guards?"

"Dead. Maybe some got away. They surprised us. Just came out." He paused, panting for breath after so many words.

"I'll get Grafton," Rodon said.

Minutes later, Rodon had fetched the others. Grafton cradled the puoli's head in his arms and tried to wipe away some of the blood with a rag which he dabbed in water. Sam was barely conscious and his breathing had become irregular. Rodon, Berwick and Raul stood around helplessly.

"So that was where the harpies went," said Berwick.

"What do we do now?" asked Raul. "Stop up the hole so no more can come through or leave it open so they can go back?"

"We need to close it off," said Rodon.

"How can we do that?" Berwick asked.

"What happened before – with the Mage?" Rodon asked, half to himself. "It was about dreaming of the place wasn't it? The light amplified the dream. He thinks that be what happened to move him there in the first place. We need someone to dream of here. Or of Naadu."

"And what's happened to Naadu? Where are those harpies now? They could destroy the city. We need to warn them."

Their conversation was stopped by a sob. Grafton was sat with his friend's lifeless body in his lap. He breathed deeply and looked up at them blankly.

"Was this my fault?" he asked. "I let those harpies in."

"It was the cobs dreamed you in there," said Raul. "You didn't know what was going to happen."

"I be sorry for your loss," said Rodon. "But we need to warn Naadu about the harpies, if it be not too late already. The way to that world needs to be closed now."

Grafton looked down at the ground. He had only just found that world with its amazing nebula and now they were going to seal it off again. The body in his arms told him why it needed to be closed.

"Yes, you're right."

"What do we do first?" Rodon asked.

"If we need a Naadu delf to dream it back here, we need to go back to Naadu City. But we need to seal off that doorway before any more come through."

They piled crates and rocks against it until the doorway was completely hidden behind them. Grafton insisted on wrapping Sam in a sheet and covering him with the canvas held down by rocks and boxes. He did not want the harpies to return and find him.

Then they took up their weapons and walked out down the path which they had first taken from the city. The fog still lay thick across the rocks. They kept their long-arms ready at all times, every moment expecting a swarm of harpies to descend on them out of the mist.

The only sound was the crunch of their feet on the gravel. The fog deadened all other sound.

"It be like we be in Limbo again," Berwick whispered.

The track began to drop until it reached the paved roadway. This they followed until they came upon a delf leading a horse loaded with sacks. They greeted each other, but did not stop.

"He did not look like someone who has seen harpies descend on his city," Raul said.

As they went closer to Naadu, they met other delf and there was nothing unusual about their demeanour. The city appeared normal when they reached it and they made their way to the Tafa's palace. While they did receive strange looks, it appeared to be because of their long-arms which they held at the ready rather than slung over their backs.

The Tafa was pleased to see them, but immediately asked after her soldiers. So Grafton recounted their story. He showed her the ring from the hand they had found. She nodded when she saw it. Rodon noted that Grafton said nothing about their finding of the Mage's light tower. He ended with the plea for help to reseal the tunnel.

"But where are these harpies you describe? Were they lost in the fog?"

Grafton shrugged.

"That is all I can assume," he replied. "Naadu is still shrouded in fog. When it lifts, you may yet be attacked. We do not know how many have come through, but we saw hundreds of them in there."

"And you need someone who can *dream* of Naadu?" she asked, perplexed. "And you must go back into the cave?"

"Yes, back to the needle. We must dream it back here to seal the way to the other world."

She smiled. "I have already lost a good many of my soldiers to these creatures. I think you took it in there, you can bring it back. I want that needle where I can use it."

She looked hard at Grafton.

"And what do you suggest I do to protect the city?"

"Position your best marksmen around the streets. Put them in groups. If any harpies appear, people must go indoors. I don't know how safe they'll be, but it will be safer than being outside." He gestured at Rodon, Berwick and Raul. "These men held them off with disciplined gunfire. I saw your other soldiers break and run. They are all dead."

The Tafa frowned at the criticism of her troops, but said nothing.

"I will send my steward with you with some guards to see for himself."

The three were stood ready and they watched as the Tafa spoke to Eudinasis. Then he called some more guards. These were not like the ones who had accompanied them before. Grafton recognised some of these guards as ones who had found him and Atana in the desert. They were experienced desert riders rather than palace guards with watchful eyes and skin like sand.

The travellers and Grafton walked on ahead. This gave them the opportunity to talk.

"She didn't seem to believe us about the harpies, but there be a lot of soldiers," said Berwick.

"Perhaps it be for our benefit," said Rodon. "I think we be still her guests."

"Surely she means us no harm," said Grafton, frowning.

Rodon raised an eyebrow. "I be not so sure, but if she can use us to get what she wants, she will."

The fog had still not lifted as they left the road and started along the rocky track that led into the tumbled upper reaches of the escarpment. Eudinasis called out to them with cross petulance.

"What are you looking for?"

"Harpies," said Grafton. "We told the Tafa about them. They came from out of the tunnel in the rock and have already killed a dozen of your comrades."

"Why are you looking up in the air?" Eudinasis asked.

"Because they fly," said Raul.

"We were told it was just wild cobs."

"They are the least of your worries," Raul replied. "These harpies hunt cobs."

When they reached the entrance to the cave, nothing had changed. There were still the overturned crates, the canvas covering Sam's body and the dried patches of blood on the ground.

"We need your help to move the needle," said Grafton. "Then we can seal off the tunnel. Could you come down with us?"

"No. You will not seal the tunnel," Eudinasis said. "You will retrieve the needle and we will make the entrance secure, but it will not be sealed."

"I don't think that be wise," said Rodon quietly.

"I did not ask you," said Eudinasis. He smiled, but only with his mouth. The eyes were serious. "The land beyond that tunnel belongs to Naadu now."

Berwick was not used to anyone talking to Rodon in that way, but Rodon seemed unmoved. He went over to where they had placed the harpy and covered it with a horse blanket. He pulled the cover off and displayed its strange corpse to the delf guards. Its mouth was open, showing sharp teeth and Berwick noticed something was caught on the claws of a bloody foreleg. He preferred not to think about what it could be.

"This be what we warned you about," Rodon said.

"Now we need your help," said Grafton. "You are all from Naadu aren't you?"

The delf nodded.

"Then we would like as many of you as possible to come down with us to the needle and think of home. I know it sounds unusual, but it is the Tafa's will you would be doing."

Eudinasis was still studying the harpy. He prodded the body with the butt of his long-arm.

"You said there were more of these?"

"Yes. They live in a place on the other side of this tunnel. That is why we need you to help us seal it up. We must not let any more through."

The steward looked up from the harpy.

"I am sending no more of my soldiers into that hole. You go in and bring out the needle. I have no trust in you or your people. Bring out the needle or we will shut you in there."

Grafton looked around helplessly at the others.

"Come on then," said Rodon.

The others hesitated, but he beckoned them to follow.

"Watch the sky," said Raul to Eudinasis as they entered the tunnel. Berwick could not tell if he was offering a sincere warning or was mocking him.

"Could you dream of Naadu, Grafton?" Rodon asked him quietly as they walked down the tunnel.

"I have been here a while. I could try."

"It seems to be our only chance of success."

When they reached the end of the tunnel, it was night in the rock bowl. To their surprise, a group of cobs were squatting around the needle. Some were asleep. The others stood up as they saw Grafton approaching and made soft grunting noises.

"Be they yours?" Rodon asked.

"They are. But it's not all of them."

"You will have to make do. Let's see if we can make this happen. Can you tell us what you did last time? We'll need you to sleep."

"You will need someone to pull you as well," said Raul.

"I think we can rely on the Tafa for that," said Grafton.

"If we can't seal it by using the light, then we'll just cause a cave in and block the passage."

"But that would leave the way between the worlds open," Grafton said.

"And what would happen then?" Rodon asked.

Raul paused. "I do not know," he said eventually. "It simply feels wrong."

"We will worry about that if we need to," Rodon said.

Grafton explained the workings of the light needle to them.

"This is not going to work," Raul said.

"It worked last time," Grafton retorted. "We have to try it."

He lay down on the floor. He gestured to the others to do the same thing. Even the cobs curled up on the floor. Then he sat up again.

"You must not go to sleep," he said. "I don't know what would happen if our dreams competed. We could end up in Unama."

"We will just lie here," Rodon said.

"I will need your help if I am to sleep. I need you to turn this small wheel here gradually as the cobs in the big wheel go faster."

Grafton placed a light sponge into the chamber. He gestured to the cobs.

"Up wheel, up!"

Four of them stood and climbed into the wheel. Grafton lay down. He did not think he would sleep, but he remembered his experience with the shaman. Perhaps he could meditate and that would work. This was all a step into the unknown.

The cobs started to walk. Rodon turned the valve slowly. The cobs speeded up.

The wheel clunked as it turned, the sound increasing to a regular fast beat as they moved up into a run. Grafton felt it lulling him, his mind drifted into the rhythm of it.

Berwick could see a glow begin to form just out of his sight from near the end of the needle. It grew in brightness, then a sharp blade of light stabbed across the cave and out into the bowl.

They lay on the floor, waiting. Grafton was riding the beat and he felt he could sense the glow from the needle at the background of his awareness.

Then the light faded, the cobs slowed and they all opened their eyes. They were still in the cave.

Grafton sat up.

"I'm sorry," he said.

"It does not seem right to me," said Raul. "We were always surrounded by light when the Light Doctor did it before."

"Last time we were too, but the needle did not behave in the same way."

His eyes moved in his head, searching for an answer. He stopped looking inwardly and began to look around the walls of the cave.

"Unless..."

The others watched him.

"I know you need to think, but we must hurry," said Rodon.

"Yes, yes," said Grafton only half listening. He was searching the walls of the cave in the same way he had searched in Velkuri's light tower. "Here!"

The others peered over.

"You see it? Glittering? Perhaps the light from the needle struck some of this rock. The light passes through it and back."

He could see the others were not following him. He gestured to Raul.

"Raul said that the light was all around you when you travelled with it?"

The others all nodded.

"So my tight beam of light, no matter how refined it is, may not work. It needs to be diffused somehow or it does not touch me."

He smiled.

"That is my hypothesis. So now we will test it. Let's move the needle so it is pointing at this part of the wall. There seems to be a concentration here."

Together they shifted the machine around. All except Grafton. He was scraping away at the wall. He cut something out and put it in his pocket. Then he ordered the cobs once more into the wheel and they began their walk.

Grafton placed another two sponges into the chamber, shut it, nodded to Rodon who had taken up station at the valve wheel again, and lay down.

Raul checked up the tunnel, half expecting to see Eudinasis on his way down to see what they were doing. There was no one, they still had time.

The clunking of the wheel notched up. Grafton lay with his hands by his sides. His eyes were closed and he had slowed his breathing. If this worked, it would be an exciting discovery, but he would need to know what the mineral was. He could show Rua. It was her calculations which had led to the designs of the funnels on the needle.

The wheel was reaching its optimum speed. He felt himself following the beats of the wheel gears. Then light was all around him. He could feel it through his eyelids. It seemed to lift him and he was riding the light. There was something like purple cloud all around him. Was he inside the nebula? Then his world lurched and for a moment he felt he was spinning and falling.

When he opened his eyes he saw sky, daylight and the roofs of buildings. The cool of the cavern was gone and was replaced by a thicker, warmer humidity.

Berwick sat up and looked around. It was not a part of Naadu he had been in before. Grafton was standing. Someone, a delf, was coming towards him, an expression of wonderment on his face, but a gun in his hand.

"Hugh!" said the delf. "Where did you come from? I was just thinking of you."

"Alai…" Grafton's voice drifted off. "Where is Rua?"

Alai's face dropped. "I do not know. But they are looking for her."

"What do you mean? Why do you have that gun?"

"Oh, Hugh, terrible things are happening."

Rodon and the other two were standing up.

"This be not Naadu," Rodon said.

Grafton took a deep breath and turned to the three who were still gathered next to his needle.

"No," said Grafton. "We're in Linana. I couldn't help myself. I was thinking of home."

36

JACK SILVER TREMBLED as he paused behind the Archbishop at the ruined gate to the Tower of the Stars. The unnatural light floated through its archway. The Archbishop had almost gone through the entrance when he turned on him.

"Oh you of little faith, why be you afraid?" he said sternly.

Silver shook himself and walked in behind his master. His eyes were wide as he entered the courtyard, every moment expecting to feel something which he never did. Once he was through the gate, the light changed to a flat grey.

He looked around. Right in front lay the bloody corpses of the custodian guards who had attempted to stop the entry of the Archbishop's army. A few dismembered wolf warriors were scattered amongst them.

He looked further. Walls and towers lay in the dust, but around them were lines of bodies, stretched out as if asleep. He walked over to the nearest ones and looked at their faces. They were a man and a woman, but they had the outlandish mix of features of the corrupting devils. Their faces looked troubled and were not the faces of people at rest. He prodded the one closest to him with his foot.

As he did so, the ground shook violently. Startled, he fell across them. He panicked, flailing his arms in an attempt to pull himself off without touching the puoli.

He felt a hand firmly grasp his own.

"Calm yourself, Silver," said the Archbishop in a voice which gently reproved. "The quakes be stronger here, so stay away from the walls if you feel they may crush you. But they have not crushed me."

"Be they alive?" Silver asked.

"These creatures? Yes, but they dream deeply. It be something like the devils in the pit all those years ago, Silver, where we made a thing out of despair. *Their* dreams combined can make a gate into

Limbo. I would never have thought it, but then I would never have believed someone would breed men with devils."

"So we be in Limbo now?"

"No, Limbo be there," the Archbishop replied, pointing to the mist on the far side of the courtyard. "This be still one of their temples, but now it be a bridge into Limbo."

The ground shook again, a weaker tremor than before. The Archbishop walked away from Silver, looking down at the puoli as he went.

"Your Grace," Silver asked. "Be you looking for something?"

"Someone," he said. Silver hurried to catch up with him, nervously looking at where he was putting his feet, fearful of stepping on one of the bodies.

"When I was in Limbo, I reached out in my dreams. I found you, I found others I knew, but they turned away. But there were others. I could hear their dreams, feel the shadows of their thoughts in Limbo. These puoli here, their dreams be slight, unfocused things. They reach beyond this world, but only reach Limbo. But there were two that I felt, stronger than all the others." He looked at Silver. "All the puoli be here, you say?

"Yes, Your Grace. They told them they would be safe here." He smiled.

"Then they be here somewhere. I will know them. I will smell their dreams."

He continued to walk, stepping over the bodies, unmindful of the intermittent tremors which sent dust, grit and the occasional stone from the walls. Silver followed, looking alternately at the Archbishop and the puoli. The Archbishop worked his way across the courtyard, up and down, looking to his left and right as he went, then turning once he reached the wall.

In this way, they came to where the light tower lay across the ground. The funnel was resting on its rim, the tall tower behind it in a trail of massive chunks of masonry. The Archbishop stopped at the funnel and looked down at where the shining rim lay resting on the ground. Silver looked and turned away quickly. It had fallen across the body of a young woman, cutting her in two. He was grateful that her lower half was partly hidden under the funnel.

"That be not her, although she be close."

He walked towards the misty gate to Limbo. He walked slowly along the rows. Suddenly he stopped. He cast his eyes about him and then rested them on Rosa.

"This be one," the Archbishop said. "Remember where she lies. There be another, although I can no longer sense her."

He turned away from Rosa and looked at the half of the courtyard he had not yet inspected. "The other must be here still."

"Why be you so interested in them, Your Grace?"

The Archbishop did not look at him and his tone was if he was thinking aloud.

"Their dreams felt as if they were stretching across Limbo. I think they could see Christendom. They be different somehow."

"Do you think they be..." Silver hesitated. "Do you think they be blessed?"

"No. They be cursed. But they be also cursed with the seeds of their own downfall. These be always the signs that the Lord has given us. I believe we can use their dreams to find our way back into Christendom."

""But what if they be dead like that woman we saw under the stone?"

"No, I think she be alive. I could feel her the last time I slept. It was as if all these," he gestured at the sleeping puoli, "were but a weight leaning on a door. But it was these two who turned the handle."

"It be another girl?"

"Yes."

"Shall I arrange for this one to be moved to a place of safety?"

"Do not touch her. I want her to keep dreaming this same dream as these others."

In truth, there was much the Archbishop did not understand and he was loathe to meddle with his bridge to Limbo.

"She be quite safe in here. The devil lovers' resistance has ended."

They continued their searching, reaching the middle of the courtyard without finding anyone, then continued up and down the further side. Still they had found no one.

"Don't follow me so closely," the Archbishop snapped. Obediently, Silver fell back a few steps. The Archbishop was looking more closely at each puoli now, pausing a little longer. Silver was afraid to say anything, feeling the Archbishop's agitation.

At last they reached a breach in the side wall and here the Archbishop stopped. He looked out through the mist into the open country on the other side of the wall.

"She was here," he said. He looked around him, then back out through the wall. "And she was dreaming. I can smell the odour of the dream. So she was still dreaming as she went through. How could that be?"

"Sleep walking?" Silver ventured in a small voice.

"Yes, perhaps," said the Archbishop. "But all I know is that she be not here." He looked out through the gap in the walls again. "She be gone into the wilderness. She must be found."

Silver felt emboldened that he was able to talk again. He had felt ignored at this moment of triumph over the city, jealous that he was not the subject of the Archbishop's attention.

"I will find her!" he said. "I will find her for you. I will take my men and search."

The Archbishop turned kind eyes upon him.

"Once more the good servant speaks. Yes, Silver. You shall find her. Take your men and bring her back. Through her, we will enter the old world and once we have fulfilled our purpose here, we shall purge that world of corruption also."

The angel was tall and silent with powerful mail clad shoulders. The only others accompanying Silver were Dent and Boyce. The angel was larger even than Dent. Silver did not take them through the courtyard of the Tower of the Stars. He wanted to keep that a special experience between himself and the Archbishop. Instead, he led them around the outside of the walls, clambering over the rock and small bushes as the wind gusted around them. The angel followed uncomplaining. Unnerved by the occasional tremor, the men kept well away from the walls until they reached the gap which he had seen from the inside.

They looked at the ground to see if they could see any tracks. None of them were trackers and they looked in vain. They looked around.

"If she was asleep, she can't have gone far," said Dent, the larger of the two.

"She could be awake now though. She's probably hiding."

"We could call for her? Pretend we want to help her," he suggested.

"We don't know her name," Silver snapped. Dent shrugged.

"I would have made for that wood over there," Boyce said, pointing down the slope to the trees which crowded together thickly.

The vegetation looked closely packed as they approached it, with no easy way in. Boyce jogged along it and stopped at a dark gap. He went inside and came out a minute later.

"Over here!" he called.

The other three joined him. The angel was an unnerving silent presence.

"She could have gone in here. I can see where I would have gone if I'd been her, but the ground's too dry to leave any marks."

"Well follow it through where you would have gone," Silver said. "See where it goes."

When they emerged from the trees, they were a little downhill of the city, but they could still see it above them, beyond the wood, while behind them, Akus was visible. The wolf soldiers still pinned Kallick's legion against the river.

"And where from here?" Silver asked. He had been hoping to find something and was disappointed to have nothing to show for himself.

Boyce looked around and rubbed his chin in obvious thought.

"Well there be two ways, I'd say," he said. "Along the ridge here to nowhere, or away down there to Akus. She wouldn't go there now though. When did she leave?'

"We don't know. So she could have left before His Grace arrived."

They sat in thought for a while. Finally Silver made an impatient noise and stood up.

"What do you think?" he asked the angel. The angel stared back at him, unblinking. Silver took a deep breath. "We'll look in Akus."

Two angels stood on either side of the main road as it entered the town. Boyce and Dent looked at them nervously, but Silver walked between them confidently and the angels ignored the men and the angel who walked with them.

A gang of men stood in the street. They looked to be townsfolk and they were shouting angrily at a three storey building on the edge of the town.

The volume increased as a man was dragged from the building. He was older and looked like a puoli. He was thrown to the ground and kicked.

Silver approached them.

"You there," he called out. They did not hear him at first and he had to repeat himself. Several closest to him looked up, took in the confident demeanour of the three men and their clothes, but mostly the tall, blond angel who walked behind them. Their sudden silence was infectious and soon, the whole mob was looking at Silver with fearful expectation.

"I be looking for a puoli," he said. "She came this way." He decided he would make it definite. He did not want to sound as though he was in any doubt about the situation. The men all looked at him, but none spoke.

"Tell me," said Silver again. "Have any of you seen a puoli come this way. The Archbishop would smile on anyone who provided information."

One man, with a beard and a weight about his belly, looked at the men on either side of his to build his confidence, then spoke.

"Your lordship," he said. "All the puoli went up to the old quarter. There's none about now. Just these delf and we're seeing to them for you."

Silver looked down at the man they had pulled from the building and realised he was indeed delf. He was grizzled and aging and he looked at Silver with wide eyes.

"There was one who was not in the old quarter," Silver said. "She is loose and dangerous." He hoped he sounded authoritative.

"Your lordship!"

Silver realised he was being addressed by the delf. The man with the belly gave the delf a kick.

"Stop bothering him!" he said.

"Your lordship! I can tell you if you save me!"

The man was about to kick him again, but Silver put up his hand.

"Wait," he said. "What would you tell me, devil?"

"I have seen a puoli. She came here. Two nights ago."

Silver walked closer. The men about him were frowning. He felt Dent, Boyce and the angel behind him.

"Who are you?" he demanded.

"I am Tibo," he said. "I trade in horses for the caravans."

"And who was this? What be her name? Where did she go?"

"Her name is Rua Grafton, your lordship. She is a puoli. She wouldn't say where she was going."

"Then why did she come to you?" He snapped his fingers and Dent had grabbed the delf by the scruff of the neck and pulled him up. Tibo's hands reached up to Dent's single hand around his neck, but Dent slapped them down.

"She wanted horses," he said.

"And you gave them to her?"

"I know her father. She said she would bring them back."

"Them? Did she take more than one?"

A wildness entered Tibo's eyes. He realised he had said more than he had intended.

"She took two," he said.

"Why? To keep one rested?"

Tibo hesitated, then nodded quickly.

"There was two of them, wasn't there?" said Boyce.

Tibo's eyes darted to Boyce, then to Silver, the angel and Dent. He did not know where to look.

"Tell me and you shall be saved," said Silver.

Tibo looked around him again. Then he nodded. What harm could it do, he wondered.

"Who was it, this other?"

"One of you sir," he said. "A man."

"Be you lying to me? Who was he?"

"I do not know, sir. I had never seen him before. He looked foreign, sir."

"Foreign? Like me? Did he look like me?"

"No, no, sir. Not like you. I have never seen clothes like he had on."

"What were they like?"

Tibo had entered too far now, his chin was shaking so much, he could barely speak.

"Just different clothes, sir."

Silver did not want to enter a conversation around clothes.

"And where were they going?" he asked. He was feeling pleased with himself now.

"I do not know," Tibo stuttered. "Just to find her father," she said.

"And where be he?"

"I do not know. North. Maybe still in Naadu," he said.

"So she went that way," Silver pointed. "Along the escarpment or on the road?"

"Escarpment," Tibo gasped.

Silver bent his head close to the delf's face.

"Are you lying to me, devil?"

Tibo shook his head.

"That is all I know, your lordship."

Silver stared him in the eye for a few moments, searching for a flicker that would betray the lie, but saw none. Then he stood back, satisfied and nodded at Dent. Dent dropped him and Tibo lay still.

Silver started to walk away. As he went past the large man with the beard, he looked at him.

"Kill it," he said.

After the first couple of kicks, Tibo did not call out any more.

The Archbishop was pleased with Silver's news. He took seven of Giles' men. Five he sent along the road below the escarpment. The other two accompanied Silver, Dent and Boyce. They took extra horses so that they could move faster, alternating between horses to give each one a rest from carrying a rider. They rode away with little preparation. Giles' men were pleased to be out of their compound after being virtual prisoners. Those on the road were given instructions to watch the heights and to keep track of Silver's party at regular intervals.

They galloped away under a sullen grey sky and the wind brought the smell of the sea as it whipped about their ears. They rode with little talk and took their food as they rode. They only slept when it became too dark to see and then they ate a hurried supper before wrapping themselves in coats and blankets. They rose again at the first glimmer of dawn, mounted and rode off again in search of their quarry, although Silver was aware that they followed only the most basic of trails.

240

<h1 style="text-align:center">37</h1>

SOLIMO WAS PEDALLING. It was true, he realised. He often used to sing as he collected light, but he was thinking too deeply. He was inside himself and did not see the sunlight falling across the room from the high windows of the funnel room.

He looked up at that light and the bright blue of the sky. He saw the sun edge into view. He continued pedalling and he watched it out of the corner of his eye as it moved fully into the window. It was a huge ball of fire. In comparison, the balls the keepers could weave were nothing.

He would find out more. The Light Doctor had died before she could finish teaching him. He needed to know more, then he would be armed against temptation, or have a better understanding.

A voice came to him in his memory. It was the Mage's as he lay gasping on the ground after he had funnelled hope through his own body, before he disappeared.

"Of course, you could find the books," he had said. "My light tower is still there. You have something of the mage about you, Solimo. Given time."

Were his books really there? Was there still a place in Unlembien where his light tower stood and contained the books the Mage had taken there centuries before?

Those books belonged in Unama. They were the lost lore. It had diminished since those times. Mondo and Esella were trying to help him, but they did not know enough. He needed the advice only the mages could give him and they could only pass that on through their books of lore.

He had to go to Limbo.

Solimo lay on his bed and looked at the three candles he had arranged into a triangle on the table against the wall. He tried to look into the centre of them, seeing the candles only peripherally.

He let his mind wander.

He had been to Unlembien with the very same men Rodon and Berwick who had come a few weeks before. They had called it Limbo. He had had adventures there with Raul and with Charlie. He often wondered what Charlie was doing. He had been a child back then, but they had become friends. From time to time, they glimpsed each other in dreams, but they never managed the same connection they had all those years before.

Solimo knew it was because he was afraid. Thinking of Charlie made him think of that time in the impenetrable darkness of the Pits. There he had been starved of light, time had slowed and he had given in to despair. Although he had found hope again, he was still haunted by the darkness and shamed by how he had lost himself.

He was no longer aware of his surroundings. There was merely a glow of candlelight around his thoughts.

He had shared that experience of Limbo with many. Rodon, Berwick, Raul and those other men of the Order; Colman who he had saved and the two who had died, John Biston and Ned Smith. The Light Doctor had died too. He had not been there to comfort her. And of course there had been Charlie and his father, Richard. He was a man who had lost himself too before he came to Unama. What had happened to him?

Solimo's thoughts spread into Limbo and he was back amongst those landscapes. He realised he was lying on a plain of dust and stones and in its midst was a dome of darkness, while around it were the outer works of the Mage's light tower.

Something had happened to the tower for it to be blanketed by the dark. Then Solimo knew the answer. He had done it. He had dreamed of the darkness and dreams made Limbo. He had created his own torment, just as the Mage had done.

38

THEY HAD BEEN riding in silence for a while. Rua seemed comfortable with the silence, but Charlie wanted to talk to her.

"What was your mother like?" he said at last. Rua took a deep breath and for a moment he thought she was going to be angry. "I'm sorry," he added quickly. "I shouldn't have asked."

"No," she said. "I like to talk about her. I don't think my father does though. I think he misses her too much. I talk about her to Rosa all the time. We talk about everything."

"They're cool those kinds of friends."

"Cool?"

"I mean, it's good when you've got friends you talk about everything with."

"She understands me better than anyone."

"So what was your mother like?"

"Father met her at the university. He was a great scholar. He's interested in everything: in history, in geology, in botany. Being interested in light lore led him to an interest in medicines. And they met in the library when they both wanted to look at the same book. He suggested they look at it together and took it to a reading bench. It wasn't really a book. It was more a collection of paintings of plants all bound up. Each one had a description of it and its uses, whether it was ornamental or herbal or medicinal or good in cooking. It talked about the best ones for lining light funnels. I remember her telling me how she let him turn the pages and watched how the light from a high window shone down on the book and she saw the book reflected in his eyes. She said they started turning the pages over at the same time..."

She looked across at Charlie from under her eyebrows.

"I'm sorry. I'm boring you."

"You're not. I like stories about how people met. I hope I have a good story about how I meet my wife."

"You're already a traveller. You will meet her travelling."

Charlie's heart leapt and he merely managed to grunt a reply.

"So you want to hear more?"

"Yeah, go on," said Charlie.

"What my father didn't know then was that she was the granddaughter of a shaman."

"What's one of those?"

"They're a kind of...a wanderer. Delf. They have a special relationship with the light. There's more light and more sun here than I think you will have seen in Unama. In Linana we often have clouds in the afternoon, but out here in the desert, there are often no clouds and the sun is hot. These last few days have been very unusual." She took her eyes off the cloudy sky and continued her story.

"There were never many shaman and I haven't seen one since I was young. They live out in the desert and over the years when Linana's power was growing, they were seen less and less often. Mother said they did not like the light which the Senate made into a weapon. They did not understand it."

"You mean the sun wraiths? But I've seen those in Unama."

"Yes. But that's all they use. They're woven here by the Knight Wardens of the Light. They're the heart of Linana's power across all the lands eastwards and south. But they're not interested in the rest of light lore. That's what my father is trying to rediscover before it is lost forever. So although father and mother were smitten since that first time, they were drawn together more by what mother's grandfather had taught her. He said shaman go from the bright light into the darkness of caves deep in the desert. And in there they are said to create their own light."

"Really? How?"

"I don't know."

"Oh," said Charlie, disappointed.

"He said he made light after being in the dark long enough. He just imagined it."

"Weird. Have you tried it?"

"No. But you can dream light can't you? I have wondered about doing it."

"We should have tried in the cave on our first night out here!"

"He said it was better to be on your own. He said it's easier to create your own world."

"I can understand that. I spent a night camping under the stars in a forest in France on the edge of the Pyrenees a few weeks ago. Those are mountains. I lay there in my sleeping bag and all I could see was the stars and the moon shining on the snowy summits of the highest mountains. It was cool."

"You were cold?"

Charlie laughed. "Yes, I was actually. My sleeping bag's not thick enough for that altitude. I was wearing everything I had with me!"

The track led them to the edge of the escarpment where it dropped steeply to the coastal plain. They rested their horses on the cliff top. The wind had relaxed to a strong breeze which ruffled their hair. They could clearly see the road running along the base of the escarpment. Charlie frowned.

"Hey look," he said and pointed. A group of riders were galloping northwards along the road. "They've got spare horses with them."

"Get down!" said Rua. "Have they seen us?"

"I don't think so, look, they're still going forward."

"I'm not sure. Let's go," said Rua. There was fear in her voice.

"What's the matter?"

"I don't know. It's the dream I had. I don't want them to see us."

Charlie shrugged and walked his horse away from the edge and back out of sight of the road below.

"They can't get to us up here can they? Is there a way up?"

"I don't know. I suppose they could climb. There are places where they could climb if they left their horses behind. I just had a feeling that's all and I have learned to respect those feelings."

"Yeah, I always realise after I've done something stupid that there was a warning bell in my head telling me not to do it."

She smiled. "Something like that, yes."

When the evening came on, they pitched camp under a tall, leaning rock which gave the impression of some shelter. The clouds were thickening up and Charlie eyed them with distrust.

"I feel a need to make some sort of shelter," he said. He looked around. "I could make a wall, but I'm not sure about a roof."

"Well while you're thinking about construction work, I'll put some food together."

"How about some of your stew?"

"No, I do not want to light a fire."

"You still worried about those riders?"

She nodded but said nothing. Charlie let it go and started prowling around looking for rocks. Rua watched him amused as he began to gather stones and put them in a line.

"You remind me of my father, fussing about with those stones," she said.

"You should never criticise your father," he said putting on a deep paternal voice.

"You see those hills way over there?"

He turned to see where she was pointing.

"Those ones on the horizon?"

"My father built a wall over inside a cave just to keep us separate from the horses."

"What were you doing over there?"

"Looking for lichens that need hardly any light or water."

"Whatever crumbles your biscuit," Charlie said.

She gave him an odd look and they both returned to their tasks.

"Supper's ready," she said.

"I'm building a house," he said.

"So I can see." She was laughing at him.

"You won't be laughing when it stops you getting wet. I reckon I can build it up to the rock if we sleep close in underneath it. Then it won't be too high and fall over on us. Which would be unfortunate."

"I'd rather get wet than be crushed by one of your walls. Are you sure you're competent?"

"You're cheeky. I'm from Derbyshire which is full of dry stone walls and I must have climbed over half of them one way or another. I'm sure I can remember something about how they're built to knock up something half way stable."

"Well I'm going to eat. You can do what you like."

"You'll eat your words when I've built you a cosy little cottage with two floors, a freshly swept doorstep, a pantry and its very own light tower."

"You are strange."

"And you're from another world, so don't get me started."

Rua threw a hunk of bread at him which he caught nonchalantly and began to eat, sitting down next to her. She yawned as he was eating. He yawned too.

"You need to sleep. You've hardly slept since you came here," Rua said.

"I know. I am knackered. But I can wait a few hours. I'll take first watch again," he said. "I need to keep building my wall extravaganza. I can watch that you don't start dreaming while I'm making it."

"And I look forward to waking up to your master work."

He found the work quite absorbing. When he started, he had light to see, but eventually he realised he could see no longer, so he found his head torch in his backpack and put it on.

The wall was coming along nicely. He had found some large rocks which gave him a good start as they sat quite high. He filled in the gaps in the base with smaller stones, of which there were plenty lying around. He tried to make the rest of the wall two stones deep to help provide some strength. He thought he could smell rain on the wind, but he had some way to go. He was beginning to wonder himself if he really needed to build anything, If the rain came from the sea, which felt most likely given the prevailing wind, the rock under which they were sheltering would keep most if not all of it off them. But he had promised a wall and it now became a kind of proof of his worthiness.

He had used up all the stones near their camp and he had to wander further, coming back with armfuls which he laid on the ground carefully so that they did not rattle too much and wake Rua. She looked peaceful. He turned away and went in search of more stones.

He felt as though he was becoming quite skilled at this. He was looking for particular shapes, but finding a place for anything he found, filling up his pockets and his hands as he went. His head torch flashed across the ground, picking out stones which he gathered and took back to the camp. He was on his way out to forage again when she whimpered, but he was already too far away to hear her.

He was muttering to himself now as he worked. "Come on Charlie boy. Just a few more. The west wing's coming on nicely. It hasn't been rebuilt since the fire in the days of King George. The National Trust will be delighted. Perfect shape. Look at that. Nice. Now what else? Yep, those'll do – "

He stopped and looked around. He had heard something. His torch flicked across his surroundings as it followed the movement

of his head. Then a thought occurred to him and he turned it off.
He felt a cold rush sweep over him. If he had just heard something.
If that something was people, chances were that they would know
exactly where he was. He must move, but he had ruined his night
sight with the torch.

He tried to breathe as lightly as he could so he could listen.
There was nothing. He took a step backwards. Then another, and
another. He felt exposed. His hands were still gripping two rocks
and there were more in his coat pockets. He felt weighed down. He
was not even sure in which direction the camp was any more. His
eyes were adjusting to what little light there was.

He listened again. Perhaps he had imagined it. There was
nothing there. He became aware of a glow above him and looked
up. The moon was riding its way through to the edge of a cloud.
Suddenly it broke through. Unmistakably and about as far away as
he could throw, two men were standing quite still and looking in his
direction. Just as the cloud covered the moon again another
movement caught his eye to their right.

He turned and ran. He had got his bearings in the moonlight and
his eyes were adjusting. He definitely heard other movements now;
others were running in the darkness. Then there came a crump and
a muffled cry. It sounded as though one had fallen over.

The moon re-emerged, brighter than ever. Another sound came
from the direction of the camp. It was a cry from Rua. They had
reached her before him! There seemed to be movement all around
him now. He had no idea what he would do when he reached the
camp. He realised he was still carrying the stones.

He could see his wall now. It looked pathetic. But there was a
glow coming from behind it. He dodged around it and there was
Rua. She was still lying on the ground and seemed to be asleep, but
behind her where the rock had been, and still was, was misty grass
in daylight.

Stunned, he turned around. A man appeared right in front of
him holding a vicious dagger. The man stopped, looking wide-eyed
at the mirage next to Rua. She was moaning again. Then the man
looked at Charlie and lashed out with the knife. Charlie threw up his
hand and it caught the edge of the blade. Then, before he knew
what he was doing, he threw one of the stones at the man with his
other hand. It flew wildly past the man's shoulder, but it was
enough to shock him. The second stone caught the man square on

the chin and knocked him down. Charlie did not wait to see what happened next. Feeling the warmth of blood trickling down the back of his hand onto his sleeve, he grabbed hold of Rua and dragged her into the mist.

39

IN MOMENTS, THE two were in Limbo and Rua woke with a start. The misty gap, now dark behind her head, faded. She looked around startled and puzzled.

"How are you here?"

Charlie was breathing hard and he could feel his heart racing.

"You were dreaming. We were being attacked. I carried you into Limbo."

"I thought there was someone coming. I needed to get away."

"You mean you dreamed that deliberately?"

"Yes, I – "

Then she saw his hand.

"You're hurt."

He looked at it for the first time.

"Yeah, he cut me, but it seems to have stopped bleeding. But time pretty much stops in here." His mind went back to the attackers. He could not get the image out of his mind of the man lunging at him with a knife. "Who were they? I saw one. I think he was a man, not a delf."

"Things are not right," she replied simply. She looked around the grassy plain on which they found themselves. Hills rose up in the distance under a flat, grey sky.

"We need to get back. Can you get us back?" Charlie asked. He was worried now. He had acted without thinking before. It had not occurred to him that the hole would close behind them. "There must be a way back."

"I have been here before," she said. "But the other times there has been something coming. A wolf creature coming for me. Something called me here before, but this time I came on my own and there is nothing here."

They both scanned the empty horizon.

"I don't think I recognise it. I thought I must have been everywhere in Limbo."

"Limbo is endless. We create it in our dreams. You can never go everywhere."

"*We* create Limbo?"

"Of course we do. I have been exploring Limbo all my life. I am a first puoli. It is our curse and blessing to often sleep between the worlds."

"Did your Dad know this would happen?"

"He said he did not think about the consequences of his love for my mother. But he was fascinated when it did."

Charlie looked about him at the empty grasslands. He felt very small and the sense of it was becoming quite oppressive.

"So how do we get back?"

"I suppose I dream us back," she replied.

"But it's dangerous to dream here. What you dream, you create. I did it once. I made a bully from my school. And that's how the mage made the army I told you about. He had nightmares and they were still there when he woke up."

"So do you want to stay here for the rest of your life then?" she frowned. "I do not."

"No, no, but we need to do it safely."

He yawned suddenly.

"You are tired," Rua said. "You should sleep first."

"I don't trust myself not to have nightmares of those men. I can wait. Can you go back to sleep? I'll try to tell what you're dreaming and if it doesn't look good or something starts to appear next to me that isn't a way back, I'll wake you up."

"I will try."

She curled up on the grass and closed her eyes.

"Charlie?" she said. He loved the way she said his name. "It is hard to sleep in such a big place. Could you sit by me. Let me lie against your back? I'll feel as if I'm somewhere."

"Sure," said Charlie, trying not to sound as enthusiastic as he felt.

He sat down and she pushed up against him until they were leaning on each other. Her touch made his back tingle and he felt her warmth all through him. He closed his eyes to savour the feeling. She pushed against him gently. He could hear her breathing. He tried to make his breathing match hers.

"Charlie?" she said again. It was softer this time. He felt a hand touch his. He touched her fingers and they gently wrapped around each other. Then she sat up and moved in front of him so that her back was leaning against his chest. He wrapped his arms around her and she leaned her head back on his shoulder. He felt her hair on his cheek. "I feel safe with you," she said.

"I feel safe with you too," he replied. "Funny isn't it?"

"What's funny?" she asked. It was a different tone. He opened his eyes. His arms were still around her and for a moment, he did not notice what was strange. Then he realised he was still leaning on something. He turned around. He was leaning on Rua, yet Rua was in his arms.

"Charlie?" said the Rua in his arms.

Rua behind him sat bolt upright. Her eyes were wide.

There were two Ruas.

His head reeled. He must have fallen asleep. He must have dreamed.

"Charlie," said dream Rua and nestled back contentedly into him.

Charlie felt himself going red. He could not even look at the real Rua. He was acutely aware that dream Rua was lightly stroking his arm. He sat rigidly waiting for the thunderbolt to strike him. Somewhere in his mind, the thought occurred to him of how strange it was that acute embarrassment could trump being stranded in Limbo.

A slight smile tugged at the side of Rua's mouth as understanding dawned.

"You went to sleep didn't you?" she said.

"Yes," he said, his voice barely audible. He tried again. "It was just a dream." This time it was too loud.

Real Rua reached out a hand to touch dream Rua.

"Is she real?"

"Yes," said Charlie. Why didn't she say more? Why didn't she hit him or shout at him or something.

"She seems to like you," she said. She almost sounded as if she was enjoying herself. "It's a bit creepy."

Did she mean it was creepy that she suddenly had a double or creepy that the dream Rua should like him?

Dream Rua did not seem to register real Rua. Real Rua leaned closer to dream Rua, inspecting her.

"She is not like me. She is too smooth. She does not have this mole," she pointed to one on her neck. "She is not me. But she is quite amazing."

In his head, Charlie agreed that Rua was amazing. He felt like a murderer standing over his victim as the victim's family entered the room.

"Are you alright?" she asked him suddenly.

He nodded.

"Yeah. It's just…I'm…I'm sorry."

"There is such power in Limbo, if you can create just by dreaming. Why did the mage not dream his own army?"

"He didn't trust himself." Dream Rua was still stroking his arm. He wished she would stop. "He was afraid of what he might dream. You need to be able to control what you dream about. And that's pretty hard. As you can see."

"I have some control in my dreams. That's why those wolves scared me. They weren't from my dream." She looked at dream Rua. "What happens to her now? What shall we do with her? Is she alive?"

He put his hand on her hand firmly to stop it from stroking him.

"I don't know. How could she be? But then, I've seen what creatures of Limbo can do. They are real enough."

"Well I will need to dream again if we are to go back."

"Do you think you can?"

"I've been doing it all my life. Meditation and dreaming are very close together."

Charlie eased himself out from behind dream Rua and stood up. He walked away to give real Rua some space in which to relax. Dream Rua followed him passively. He was horrified she would think this was how he liked girls to be. He had dreamed her without personality. It was the look of her. Dream Rua had none of the real Rua's cheeky intelligence.

He sat down on a rock and the dream Rua snuggled into his side again. He did not have the heart to push her away.

"Are you real?" he asked. "Can you think? What are you thinking now? What's going on inside there? Is there anything even inside there?"

She said nothing.

His eyes wandered around the horizon of Limbo. Like much of what he had seen before it was monotonous, except for one patch of sky on the other side of one of the far hills. There, it seemed to be night, although it did not reach far up into the sky. Rather, it reached somewhere on the far side of the hill. He frowned and was curious about what it was.

He looked back at Rua. She was lying on her back and fidgeting. She did not seem to be asleep yet. How far were those hills? Did he have time to get there and back before she slept? If he was quick.

He stood up and started to walk towards the hills. Dream Rua followed him. He started to jog.

"Charlie," she said, but she did not run.

He could feel the dry grass brushing against his boots. He looked back at Rua. Dream Rua was watching him forlornly, but the real one was lying still.

The ground had started to rise now. The darkness was hidden from view. He kept turning back to look at Rua, torn between curiosity and the fear of being left behind, trapped in Limbo like the Mage had been.

He was nearly at top of the rise. He stopped at the top and looked onto a landscape that was familiar. It was flat, apart from a few rocky outcrops, and without vegetation. It reminded him of where they had found the Mage's light tower, but where it would have been was instead a shifting dome of darkness. It was disturbing, frightening, yet fascinating. Charlie turned again to see Rua in the distance. She was maybe half a mile away. As he looked, above her head, he saw something misty. She was dreaming.

He did not even look back at the dark shape, he simply started to run. "Fool, fool!" he said to himself over and over. The mist was growing. He was still a long way away. The Mage was trapped in Limbo for nearly six hundred years. What would he do in that time? He lived lifetimes as he ran, thought of possibilities, of his parents of his friends left behind, of exploring Limbo and becoming as mad as the Mage.

He could hear his breath now. He was panting hard. He must keep his feet, don't even think of falling over.

"Charlie."

He could hear dream Rua.

He was swearing with every footfall. He ran past the dream Rua. The mist was still there! It was still growing with Rua under it as he reached her, panting. He stood trying to catch his breath with his hands on his knees. He wondered where it would bring them out or what the time was, whether the men were still there.

He looked at the sleeping Rua, then at dream Rua. She was watching him. He pondered whether he should go through first and checking that it was safe, but was more concerned that the hole would close behind him, separating them. Perhaps he could peer through, but what if it closed when he was between the worlds, half in each? He looked through the opening as if it were a window. He could make out rock, but nothing that clearly showed where they were. There was nothing else for it. He bent, put his arms under the sleeping Rua's shoulders and, pulling her as gently as possible, he stepped backwards through the mist.

He felt the air change. It was like stepping outside. He could feel air, there was a different acoustic to the silence of this night. Then he realised dream Rua had followed them out.

"You must go back!" he said.

"Charlie!" she said and looked sad. Then the mist began to fade and Charlie realised it was too late. Rua stirred. Charlie smiled at her broadly.

"You're amazing," he said. "You did it."

She smiled. "I cannot wait to tell father." Her face darkened. "What is she doing here?"

"She followed us. There was nothing I could do."

"She followed you, not me. Now what are we supposed to do with her?"

Charlie had no answer to that.

"I suppose father will be interested to see her. Are you sure she is harmless?"

"Rua, I'm not sure of anything. She could spontaneously combust after a month for all I know. All I know is they seem to get created with what you give them when you dream them. That's why the ones the Mage dreamed were full of hate for the delf."

Dream Rua had sidled up to Charlie and was now leaning against his shoulder. He tried to move away, but she held on.

"Don't be nasty to her," said Rua.

He could not tell if she were teasing him. He decided not to reply. Instead he looked around.

"We aren't at our camp. We've drifted inland. The location can move once you close the bridge. Or that's what I've heard. We could be anywhere."

"We are not though. The sea is that way. And not too far. You can tell from the sky and the wind, unless it has completely turned around. Dawn is not far away. Oh, your hand is bleeding again."

Charlie looked at it. Blood was flowing out of his hand and it was sore.

"Press on it and hold it up as high as you can above your heart. That will help stop the bleeding. I could put something on it, but need to get back to the escarpment."

At least they were safe from their attackers for now, whoever they were and whatever they wanted.

They walked towards the coast, smelling it on the wind. Dream Rua walked very close to Charlie and he tried to pretend she was not there, yet also wanted to show that he was not uncaring. As a result, he achieved neither and he was unable to tell if the real Rua was amused or annoyed by it all.

They reached the heights above the coastal plain and sat down.

"I recognise this. The camp must be a little further on," said Rua.

"It all looks the same to me," Charlie replied.

"Don't you remember that outcrop back there," she said pointing southwards." I remember its shape."

Then she lay down and looked over the edge which led down steeply.

"Yes. I can see some."

"See some what?" Charlie asked.

"Verenedon. It's that plant down there. If you mulch up the leaves it helps to stop bleeding. I think you need some."

"But how are you going to get it?"

"Climb down," she said matter-of-factly. "Father always used me to get his samples. I've climbed far worse than this. I could almost walk down to that."

"Rather you than me."

Despite her boast, she did take things slowly, carefully trying out footholds and ledges and feeling for loose rocks, of which she found a few. Charlie watched her descend, but it made him feel uneasy, so he moved away from the edge and sat down. Dream Rua sat next to him.

He heard something and looked up. As he did so, riders came around the side of the outcrop Rua had pointed at only a few minutes before.

"Stay down there! Someone's coming!" he called out. Then he stood up and grabbed dream Rua's hand.

"Run!" he said.

Dream Rua looked confused. "Charlie," she said, pleading.

The horsemen had clearly seen him.

"Come on!" he said. She would follow him. He started to run. As he ran, he realised she was not following. She was standing still, confused, watching him run away.

"Charlie!" she called out.

He paused, stopped, turned. He changed his mind a dozen times in a fraction of a second. He had to lead them away from the real Rua.

"Come on!" he called back.

Then he was running again, as fast as he could. He reached a cluster of rocks. It was their campsite. Dream Rua was not with him. He looked back and saw her still watching him go. The riders had slowed down as they approached her.

"She's not real anyway!" he said under his breath.

He swallowed a feeling of guilt and clambered into the rocks, coming out into the open area near which they had camped. He could see the leaning rock, but there was no sign of the horses. Their saddles were there, but he could not see their bags. He swore; the men must have taken it all. Then he saw strange dark patches on the ground. It looked like blood. Surely he had not bled that much. He found a knife, possibly the one which had cut him. He picked it up and held it nervously in front of him. He was expecting the riders to appear at any moment. Where were the horses?

Then he saw a head. It lay against a rock and at first he thought it was a stone caught in a shadow, but a second look showed it was clearly a bearded head with eyes and mouth wide open.

He staggered back and looked away and saw blood splashed down a rock behind him. Terror was growing in him now. Where were they? What had happened? Where were the horses? He whistled softly. Amazingly he heard a whinny. He looked around and could see nothing. He took up one of the saddles and balanced it on his shoulder, then he moved quickly towards the sound, turning every few moments to look behind him. Still there was no one there.

He reached the edge of the rocks and could still see nothing. Something came out of the rock at him. He leapt back, raising his knife, his stomach suddenly weightless.

It was the horse. He realised what he had taken to be a single rock was actually split down the middle so that it was like a narrow tent. The horse had been inside the cleft.

He talked to it quietly, threw the saddle over, tightening buckles and the cinch, then jumped on. Where were they? Perhaps they were waiting for him. Then three riders appeared. Charlie took one look at them, dug in his heels and was off.

He rode inland. He did not know why except that something told him that going along the ridge line would make him easier to follow. He looked over his shoulder. The riders were hesitating, then two started after him. The other jumped down to look at their camp. He called out something Charlie did not catch. Charlie looked back again. Both the other riders had turned around and had gone back to the camp. Perhaps they had found the blood too. Charlie would never know. He rode.

40

THE WIND WAS behind him and the rising sun was low and in his eyes. He hoped it would at least dazzle his pursuers too. He had no idea where he was going, he had no plan. He simply rode.

The ground moved beneath them, gravel and sand. Then rocks loomed out of the dawn at him and he twisted around them. He found himself riding downhill slightly. The rocks increased in number and became a forest of rocks. He was forced to slow down and wind amongst them. He turned left and right, but kept on, moving inland.

It was quiet with only the sound of the horse. He kept on going, following wherever it was easiest to go. His only thought was to put as much distance between himself and Rua as he could and to bring his pursuers with him. Then a thought occurred to him. He did not know what had happened to Rua. He did not even know why they were being pursued by these men. This was the first time he had had to think and he decided he had not made a good job of things. He did not even know whether he was being followed or not.

He stopped his horse and turned around in the saddle. Nothing. Nothing to see, nothing to hear. He stared at the rocks, inhaled deeply through his nose and held it for a moment. Then let it go. He needed to know he was being followed. If he was not, he needed to go back for Rua.

He looked around for some kind of vantage point. Just ahead, a taller, lumpier rock stood up a little way from the broken maze he rode through. Its top was angled upwards a few degrees. He found his way over to it and dismounted, walking around the rock until he found some handholds. He pulled himself up and looked around for where to put himself next. He heaved, resting his knee on a small ledge, fumbling with his fingers and found himself on top of the rock. He bent over as he walked to its highest point, afraid to show himself.

He could see to the edge of the rocks and to the open desert beyond which contrasted with the dark cloud blowing in from the sea. He stood there for minutes, looking for movement. The rocks lay before him like a crazy-cracked pavement whose cracks had widened over time. Then he glimpsed something. Something moved behind a rock, passing across a gap. He saw only one. He watched for a few more minutes, but saw no other movement. Someone was certainly behind him and he had just lost some vital minutes of advantage in looking out. He could not tell how far they were behind him: it was hard to judge amongst these rocks, but he thought it would be no more than half an hour.

He went back to the way he had come up, trying to let himself down. He climbed a few steps, then turned around and jumped, bending his knees as he landed. His horse was waiting patiently and he mounted up and went on.

The rocks spread across a valley and he saw from its sides that he was reaching its end. He began to climb and left the stones behind him. Ahead of him was open desert once more, but he could see a different shading over to his left that showed a canyon.

He cantered out. The horse was happy to let go after its careful stepping amongst the rocks. He needed to lose his pursuers now in whatever way he could.

The canyon ran parallel to the rock valley in which he had been riding for the last few hours. Disconcerted to be out in the open, he decided to make for the canyon and hope to find a way down.

Something made him turn around. As he did so, he saw not one, but two horsemen appear. They must have seen him because they started to gallop. Charlie immediately pressed his own horse to go faster. When he looked again, they were gaining on him. His previous estimate of half an hour had been way out.

There was a gunshot from behind him. Surely this was not how it ended, here, alone in the desert. There were more shots, but he was near the canyon now. The horse veered close to it and he rode along its side, looking for a way down.

He saw a slope, a steep one of loose stones and stopped the horse. He looked down it, frantically wondering if the horse could do it or if he should dismount. And suddenly the horse bucked and whinnied and crashed to the ground. There was a flurry of tumbling and rolling and bruising. He realised he had rolled over the horse's head. The horse lay twitching at the top of the slope and he too lay dazed for a moment. Then he picked himself up, staggered and ran for the slope.

He scrambled down the rock face, sliding on the loose stones that littered the sides of the valley. His weight carried him down. There was no chance of stopping, he simply skittered and tumbled. He put out a hand and propelled himself away from a larger boulder. He skidded the last few steps, then he was on firm ground again.

He looked up at the top of the cliff. He could not imagine how he had come down. He would not have even have thought of climbing it. As he looked, the two horsemen came into view. They did nothing, said nothing. He could hear his heart pounding in his ears. Then one of them looked down to his right. Instinctively Charlie looked that way as well. The third horseman had finally made his reappearance. He stood a couple of hundred yards away where the canyon turned a corner.

Charlie could not go up, he could only go forward. He started to walk away, watching the horseman who stood still, watching him in turn. Charlie's walking speeded up, then the horseman kicked his heels into the horse's flanks and it started to trot. There was nothing for Charlie to do but run.

He did not stop to see where his pursuer was, he just looked for somewhere to go. Ahead, maybe a hundred yards, the canyon took another bend and a rockfall similar to the one he had come down formed a slope up to the sheer rock. The man's horse would have difficulty on the slope. He thought no further than that.

He was sprinting now. He could hear the horse behind him. It was galloping. He could feel his legs stretching out, reaching desperately for speed. At any moment he expected something, an impact. He turned. The horse was upon him. The man's arm was raised and carried a sword. Charlie pushed away with his right foot in a sudden change of direction and the horse thundered past him.

Charlie was off again, forcing himself to go. The horseman reined in his horse. He was a big man with broken teeth. Charlie thought he could see every bead of sweat, every hair follicle, every mark on the man's face. He was still running. They were at forty-five degrees to each other. Charlie's focus was on the mound of stones. The rider was so intent on Charlie, he did not seem to have thought about where he was going. To the man, Charlie was simply running scared.

The horse was bearing down on him again. The sword arm was raised, the man's teeth clenched as he swung. Charlie realised the horse was going to cut in front of him, blocking his way to the stones. The horse was there, Charlie had no chance. He stopped suddenly, staggered forwards and everything became slow. Charlie pushed his weight backwards and fell as the sword cut down through the air. Charlie watched it pass mere inches in front of him.

He rolled, stones digging into him. Picking himself up, he dodged around the back of the horse as the rider struggled to turn it again. A few steps and he was on the stones and higher than the horseman. He picked up a handful and started to lob them at the rider. The first missed, but the rider swayed to one side and the horse skittered in response. His next one hit the rider on the shoulder and the man cursed. He swapped the sword into his left hand and groped for the pistol in his belt. Charlie threw a larger stone. It struck the man just below his eye. His right arm let go of the pistol and went to his cheek. Charlie followed up with another stone and another. One went wild, but the next hit him in the chest and the one after smashed straight into the man's nose. He howled and fell from his horse.

Charlie was no longer thinking. He rained stones down on the man on the ground. He had to stop him drawing the pistol. At last he drew breath and paused.

The man lay still on the ground. The horse had moved a little way off. Charlie was breathing heavily. He walked warily down the stones and towards the man, thinking that at any moment he would jump up. He weighed a rock in each hand as he went forward.

When he reached the rider, Charlie was shocked. The man's face was a mess of cuts and bruises and blood had covered the lower half of his face and beard from his broken nose.

Charlie bent down and picked up the pistol and pointed it at the inert body while he prodded it with his foot. He was a dead weight. Had he killed him? He was afraid to check his pulse; afraid that the man would suddenly grab him, but also afraid of what he might discover.

He looked up at the higher ground. The two others stood watching him. One seemed to raise something. The gunshot had gone off before Charlie realised what was happening and he dived for cover on the ground. The next hit the ground near his head. On the third, he saw the body next to him jerk. He jumped in surprise, then realised a bullet had just struck the man. If he had not been dead before, he was now.

Charlie lay still to see if they would fire some more. They seemed to be waiting to see if he was dead. He looked at the horse and saw the rider's long-arm still in its saddle holster. He leapt up and ran to the horse. Two more shots rang out, but they missed him by a long way. He pulled the long-arm out, unhooked what he recognised was a satchel containing powder and shot, and dived back to the ground away from the horse.

He had watched long-arms being used and reloaded often. He had played with the lever mechanism which, on a well looked after weapon, would unscrew the breech in a single turn. He had always loved the movement of it. While he had done all of that, he had never fired a long-arm before. His father had told him it kicked more than the odd hunting rifle he had used occasionally. He took aim at the two men on the skyline. He knew he would not hit them, but he them to know he could fight back.

He took a bead on them and squeezed the trigger. He saw a spit of dust below and to the right of the riders. He tried again, adjusting his aim to compensate and fired once more. This time he saw the ground near the top of the rocks on their right. It was clearly enough of a threat to the two riders who turned and rode off back down the rocks. He watched them go, then stood up and stretched. He replaced the long-arm in the holster. Then he unbuckled the man's belt. He sheathed the sword in the scabbard which hung off it and tucked the pistol back in its holster.

He looked at the man. He wanted the coat, but it felt wrong to take the coat of a dead man. He hesitated for a few seconds, then bent down and rolled the man out of it, not without difficulty. Nights were cool and he would need it. He fingered the bullet hole in the chest, then rolled it up and tied it behind the saddle.

He crouched next to him looking at the man's bloody face. He did not know why he did it, beyond feeling as though he should do something. He picked up two small stones and put one on each of the man's eyes. Then he grabbed a handful of sand and let it flow from his fist onto the dead man's chest.

"Sorry," he whispered. "But you were trying to kill me. I didn't mean to."

Then he stood and climbed onto the horse. He had to find Rua.

41

RUA HUGGED THE cliff. All she had heard was Charlie's warning that someone was coming, the dream Rua's plaintive cry and Charlie's next shout from further off. Charlie had gone. Where, she did not know, but she had no time to think about it because the next thing she heard was horses' hooves.

She pressed herself into the steep slope, not even daring to look up. She had a bad feeling about whoever it was.

"Well now, my pretty," said a voice.

"Be careful," said another. "She be a witch."

"Charlie!" came dream Rua's cry.

Rua felt a strange sense of responsibility. She wondered if that was somehow a part of her up there. She cared about what could happen to the dream Rua. But another part of her told her that was no person bewailing Charlie; it was just a figment of his imagination made real, or at least given physical form.

"Who be Charlie?" came the first voice.

"It must have been the one who ran away."

"Who be Charlie?" the first voice asked again, this time more harshly.

"Charlie!" said dream Rua.

There was a slapping sound.

"Charlie!" she said again.

"She be mad," said the first voice.

"She be possessed by Satan," said the second. "Tie her up and put her on one of the horses."

"What about this Charlie?"

There was a pause. Rua was relieved. Charlie was not there, but she did not know where he had gone.

"Ledbetter, you can help me take the bitch back to the city. Boyce, take Dent and Cokes with you and find that man. Bring him back, or kill him, whichever is easier. His Grace only wanted the girl. Then catch up with us."

"Sure, Mr Silver. He be only in those rocks. He didn't seem to be armed."

She heard what she assumed was three of the riders leaving. It sounded as though there were now only two, the one who seemed to be in charge and the one called Ledbetter.

"You hold her. I'll fetch the rope," said the leader.

"Charlie!" said dream Rua.

"Gag the bitch! And hold her steady. She won't hurt you."

"You said she was a witch!"

There was a moment's hesitation. "That she be, but she can't harm you. Now hold her steady while I tie her."

She heard muffled cries from the dream Rua and muttering from the men. Then she heard them talk to each other as they lifted her onto what she assumed was a horse. She had a sudden realisation that what was being done to the dream Rua was really meant for her. Charlie clearly was not far away and she feared for him. What would she do if Charlie was killed? She had brought him out here.

"Right," said the leader again. "Make sure she be tied on properly. Where be Boyce?"

"Silver, look. There be someone coming back."

There was the sound of a horse returning.

"Silver. We found Fycher's head." The man was almost gabbling.

"What are you talking about?" said the leader, Silver.

"His head. There be blood all over the rocks. We couldn't find a body."

"Did that witch kill him? Show me."

"How could she tear off a man's head?"

"What about the man? Where was he? And where be the others."

"There was no sign of anyone. There was no body. Just his head. And that man. He rode off inland. He had a horse. He be gone."

"Well find the bastard and kill him. Tell Boyce I want that bastard's head. He doesn't kill the Order. Show me. Ledbetter, bring the bitch."

Rua heard the horses moving off. She was frowning. What had they been talking about? Who was Fycher and what was that about a head? But Charlie still had a horse, he had got away. But then she felt a pang. He had left her behind. He had escaped on his own with no thought for her. She felt sick and dug her fingernails into the rock.

She stayed where she was. Silver had said he was going back to Linana. She decided to take advantage of the situation and find somewhere safer to hide. All it would take was for someone to look over the edge and they would see her. What should she do? She dared not go up, so the only other course of action was to continue down as she had planned. As she went, she passed the verenedon she had seen from the top. She pulled off some of the leaves and stuffed them into a pocket in the pouch on her belt. Then she carried on. Every few moments she looked up nervously, expecting to see someone peering over the edge, but no one came.

It was looking up which made her lose her concentration. Her fingers slipped at the same time as a foot and suddenly she was sliding down the steep slope. Panic gripped her. She grabbed out wildly with her hands. She felt a pain in her thigh, but then she caught her hand on a stone and managed to arrest her fall.

The sound of dislodged stones rattled on for a few more moments, then the only sound was of her breathing, fast, and to her ears, loud as she lay on the rock. Had there been anyone to hear her fall? No one called out. No head appeared over the top of the escarpment.

She looked around. There was still a way to go. Her trousers were ripped on her right leg and there was a long cut. It did not seem to be bleeding too much, but she would need to see to it.

Rua felt very exposed as she made her way down the last section of the escarpment and felt relief when her feet reached level ground. Then she ran to a lump of rock and gravel which appeared to have fallen from the top. It gave her some cover from prying eyes above. She found its shelter and sank down behind it to consider her next move.

She had no horse and no water or food. Her father was days away on foot, but that seemed to be her only choice. She knew there were places to find water. Or perhaps their saddles were up at the camp. But something had happened there. She wondered if this Fycher was one of the ones who had attacked them. She had been asleep. Could Charlie have done it? She realised how little she knew about him, but he had not seemed like a killer.

She had heard no further noise from above. She could only assume they had all gone by now. What would her father do? She knew her first priority was water. She knew she should check at their camp, but she was afraid to go back up. She walked along the base of the escarpment until she was well past the camp and any potential pursuers were behind her.

She found a little water trickling in a shaded gulley at the base of the escarpment. It tasted of dust and her stomach was grumbling. She did her best to ignore it. She drank what she could, but it was shallow. Taking the verenedon from her pocket, she chewed it and rubbed the pulp it onto the cut on her leg.

Then she stood and looked for a way back up the escarpment. It looked steep, but she knew from past experience that there were ways up. You just needed to be patient and not go straight up.

She stood back and surveyed the rock. It was like looking at a drawing of a maze: she would see a good place to start then follow it up, only for it to turn into a dead end. There were many places where there was a place from which to start. She looked at the where the stream came out of the rock. That looked to be the way.

She was able to walk up the first section, just putting her hand on the rock to steady herself. She was a third of the way up before she needed to use both hands and face the rock. There was only one section where it was true climbing and she had to dig her fingers into small crevices in the rock. She had done it before, but her leg throbbed as she put her weight on it for a moment. Then she was past that section and able to scramble again, hugging the rock, but still with a thin ledge on which to rest.

She was still relieved when she reached the top and was once more on the plateau. She scanned the horizon for the rocky hills she recognised. They were so far away. What else could she do. There was nothing else to do but walk. There she would find shade and shelter and hopefully supplies. She did not dare think what she would do if her father's cache was empty.

The sun went behind the cloud from the sea before midday so she was spared the direct heat of it, but the air felt close as though a storm was coming. Thoughts ran through her head. She thought about who those men were and what had happened to dream Rua. What was the dream Rua? It was amazing that in Limbo, dreams could create reality. And what of Charlie? Where was he? What could have happened to him?

Her thoughts went to her father. She wondered what he was doing and what his reaction would be when she told her story. But what if she could not find her father? What if she never even reached Naadu? She could die alone in the desert, here in the middle of nowhere. Would anyone find her bones if she did?

But she was not going to die. Those hills were already closer and she was going to get there. She concentrated on every step and the faint crunch her boots made as she walked.

Eventually, without noticing, her thoughts faded and she was simply walking. Every stride took her closer to her goal and she walked in a straight line across the desert. The hunger faded and the thirst which came on eventually was a background annoyance.

The sun went down and she continued walking. The moon lit the night and she could see perfectly. The stars swept over her like a shawl and sometime during the night she reached the dark cave opening which she knew would be there. She walked straight into it as if it had been her own home back in Linana.

She was so tired. She wanted to sit down, but knew she should not. She could feel the cold of the desert night crawling into her. Inside the cave mouth she turned right and felt the rock. Quickly finding the slab which came away in her hand she groped behind. It was all done by feel and the canvas bag touched her hand. Although she knew it would be there, she felt amazement at its presence at the same time. Silently she thanked her father for his secret caches in the desert.

She heaved the bag down, pulled out a flask of water, took a mouthful and rolled it around in her mouth as her father had taught her to relieve the terrible dryness. Then she spat it back into the bottle. It might need to last a long time. Then she drew out the leather lined bedroll, snapped it open, crawled inside it and was asleep in moments.

Charlie did not relax the whole way back through the rock maze. He was expecting the other two pursuers to ambush him at any moment. Even when he reached the open desert and could scan an empty horizon, he was still tense. Once, when the sun was low, he thought he saw figures ahead of him in the distance. He had gone slowly, deliberately giving them time to get ahead, so he decided it was probably them. He watched them for a while, trying to decide which way they were going, but they were too far away to tell. He could only assume they were going away from him.

He found the place where he had left Rua behind. There was no sign of her and no sign of any presence. He was expecting evidence of a fight or some kind of struggle. He had feared finding her body. He went back to the campsite. The head had gone, but he found a small mound of freshly dug soil and over it, a cross of stones had been laid. Soil had been scattered across the patches of blood and the other saddle had also been taken.

He searched for Rua. He looked around the stones, under every leaning rock. He called her name, time and time again. He even scrambled down the escarpment, hoping to find signs of her presence, but there was nothing.

He could only assume one thing. They had taken her. They had taken both her and the dream Rua and gone back to Linana Pivaki.

He sat on a rock on the edge of the escarpment and looked around him at the empty desert and the distant sea. How had he come to be here? He remembered the craziness of his visit to Unama and how he had accepted it all. But this was a different place. What he had experienced before had become normal in his memory. This was fresh, new. This was frightening. He had no idea what he was going to do or how he could ever go home. He looked at himself in an oversized coat and hat that had belonged to a dead man.

The horse turned to him, shook its head and looked away.

"What?" he said to the horse. "What do you think I should do because I'm buggered if I know."

He was tired. His choices seemed as barren as the land around him. There was nowhere to go, no one he knew, no way home.

But he did know. They had taken Rua. Rua had brought him to this world and perhaps Rua could take him home. In his mind he saw her look at him with her inscrutable brown eyes. He had to find her. He did not know how and he did not know what he would do when he did. He would worry about that later. What he did know was that he had found from his time on the road alone or with his father that sometimes there was no use over-planning. Things just happened.

He stood up. The horse looked at him.

"Come on horse. We're going back."

Rua was diving into the dark. She could see the darkness moving past her, rippling away from her as she went down into the depths of the dark.

And when she awoke, it was to darkness. It was as if she had not opened her eyes. And an idea came to her.

Rua moved her head to look at the mouth of the cave. The moon had set and the stars were hidden in the cloud, but there was a feeling of light beginning to creep into the night. She peeled back the blankets, rolled up her bedding, took the canvas bag and walked deeper into the cave.

She knew she needed to be away from the light to imagine her own. In the depths of the cave it was cool and she sat and contemplated the darkness.

She had rarely had this solitude before, this opportunity to be alone in the silence without even the distant hubbub of the city outside her window. What could she really do with her dreaming? After all, she had travelled through to Charlie's world and found Charlie.

She sat and breathed deeply, slowing herself down, emptying her mind. It was difficult at first; thoughts tumbled through it.

Charlie. He was strange, but she liked him. He was from another world, but had travelled in hers to places which she knew only from stories. She smiled at his youthful confidence.

He had dreamed of her, or something like her. It was touching. He seemed to like her, to find her attractive in some way. That in itself was attractive. She thought of him smiling and laughing and of how he had saved her from the star tower. He had saved her. She realised now she had taken that for granted because she had been so caught up with what was happening to her city.

She thought of the glowing star tower and of the creatures which had come out of it. Charlie had told her about his other world and about his father. They both shared adventures with their fathers, although their fathers sounded very different. She wanted Charlie to meet her father. And she wanted to meet his. And his mother. He still had a mother. She remembered her own mother, the Shaman's granddaughter. She remembered her soft hands and voice and her eyes gazing at her. She saw those brown eyes now and then, unbidden as thoughts came and went, they were Charlie's eyes.

She focused on the eyes. They became as large as the darkness around her. Gradually her thoughts slowed and faded until she was barely aware of thought and she did not know if her eyes were open or closed. She was floating in the darkness. There was no sound and certainly no light. She no longer noticed the hard rock under her.

She waited in the dark. She did not think about what she was waiting for. She did not even know. She simply waited.

There were spots first. They crept out of the darkness, fading in and out. There were circles of colour and white around her. She could not tell if they were inside her head or outside of it. She opened and closed her eyes, but she still saw the dots. They were splashing all about her. Some came and went as flashes, but others came slowly. And as time went on, although she could never have described a length of time, more and more of the spots of colour appeared more slowly, like a cloud condensing into form above the mountains and more and more of them stayed for longer.

They began to overlap, blotting out the dark, until she could no longer tell whether there were new ones coming and going or whether all of them were staying and piling layer upon layer. The colours blended and as more and more of them mixed, the colours faded into white.

Then she was no longer surrounded by darkness, she was surrounded by white. White light.

She gazed into the light. It was inside her head and outside of it, but it illuminated nothing. She could feel it lapping at her like something tangible. She could feel it inside of her, but there was no touch on her skin.

She wished Charlie could see this too. This was her amazing thing. She realised now she had a gift. She had something huge inside of her. She felt like she was floating into it. She was reaching for something. Where had the thought of Charlie come from in all this blankness? It was like it had come spinning at her out of the white and she had taken hold of it.

Even as she thought that, the thought became firmer and gained a shape. She held onto it, she was riding the thought of Charlie into the whiteness. It was swirling now like a thick fog on the mountain tops as the clouds smother them. And like that cloud, shapes formed out of it as if left behind by the cloud, but they were not the shapes of rocks. They were the shapes of people. Seated people. In a room. The only light was a low fire and the stars in a clear sky through a window behind them.

"Richard," said a voice, a deep, calm voice. Then it became a little louder. "Richard, wake up. Someone is here."

The older man was looking at her with great wonder. It was he who had spoken. The vision shimmered and for a moment, Rua thought it would vanish. The second man opened his eyes and blinked in surprise. He looked right at her and she could see a face that was familiar. The eyes and eyebrows were unmistakable.

"You are Charlie's father," she said.

If George had not seen it with his own eyes, he would not have believed it. Was this, he wondered, what the appearance of angels was like to the ancients? A sudden opening of the air and the arrival of a young girl. Was this how angels came to people in dreams? Charlie had told him that dreams linked the worlds and now he had seen it happen.

After she had recounted her story, Richard seemed in no doubt about its veracity. He was agitated and moving about the room, emotions pouring across his face. He stopped.

"So you don't know where he is now?"

"As I said. I'm not even sure what is happening, only that creatures have been trying to come out of Limbo and now they are here. And there are men too, the ones who attacked us in the desert. They were real enough. They did not speak like Linanans. I heard them talking to each other. They were calling each other by name. One called Fycher was dead. Maybe Charlie killed him."

"Charlie couldn't kill someone."

"I couldn't see what was going on. Then these others, Boyce and Ledbetter and Silver and Dent, took the other Rua."

"Who did you say?" said Richard, turning suddenly.

"Dent."

"No, the other names. Did you say Silver?"

She nodded.

"I knew a Silver. But surely it couldn't be the same one. You say this is another country."

"He was a foreigner."

"Yes, and there are things coming out of Limbo again. We have to get back. Can you take us back?"

"I hope so. I do not know. This is new to me. I have never done this before. And you were dreaming of Charlie too. Our dreams met."

"I have been dreaming of him," said Richard agreed. "Since George first called me."

"You mean you could be stuck here, just as Charlie is stuck there?" George asked.

Rua shook her head.

"I don't know."

George realised there were tears in her eyes.

"Could you try to go back, to take me with you?" asked Richard. "We have to find him."

"I will try, but I didn't mean to come here."

"Solimo would say that the worlds must be close."

"May I come?" George asked.

Both looked at him.

"I'd like to come. I want to help."

He opened his hands.

"I want to see this place."

"We need to get there first," said Richard.

42

RODON, RAUL AND Berwick were sat around Grafton's kitchen table. Rodon was looking thoughtfully at the table top and absent-mindedly twirling a spoon backwards and forwards in his fingers. Raul was staring into space, somewhere in front of the row of pans hanging from the opposite wall, while Berwick sat shifting in his seat. Then he suddenly pushed his chair back and paced across the room. The other two snapped out of their staring and looked at him.

"What are we waiting for?"

"There be rioting in the streets," said Rodon calmly. "We can't just go out into it."

Raul grimaced and shook his head.

"Grafton told us this was a place where delf and men lived side by side. It did not take much to put the lie to that."

"What be Grafton doing anyway?" Berwick asked. "He said he'd be an hour."

"Have you seen his study? It be full of papers and books. It was always going to take longer than an hour to pack them away safely in case the house was attacked."

"He be remarkably calm for a man whose daughter has gone missing," said Raul.

"He keeps himself busy."

"I will go to see what he is doing," said Raul.

"Perhaps I should go," said Rodon. "You be also rather agitated and he be upset enough already."

Raul shrugged and Rodon stood and went through the door towards the shop front. It was dim because the blinds were still down. Grafton was kneeling behind a rack of shelves which was standing at an angle to the wall. On the floor in front of it were boxes and bottles. Grafton was putting something in place on the floor.

"Ah, just in time," he said. "You can help me put all these things back on the shelf."

"What do you down there?"

"Just sealing up the hole. There are several in the house. This one is proof from fire as well."

Rodon looked at what appeared to be just another part of the tiled floor. There were no obvious marks.

"Be the join here?" he asked, thinking he could see a difference in the plaster around the tiles.

"Try it," Grafton smiled.

Rodon bent down and put his fingers into the gap between the tiles and tried to prise the tile up from the floor. It was difficult when he did not even know if he was trying to move it the correct way. He looked at Grafton who was smiling faintly.

"You might as well stop now," he said. "That's not the right place anyway." Then the smile faded. "I wanted to see just how hidden I could make them. It started as a game I played with Rua about hiding things."

Rodon tried to think of a reply, but he was disturbed by a loud clattering at the door. Grafton started and frowned. With the blinds down, it was not possible to see who it was. He stood up and started to move for the door.

"Be careful," said Rodon. "It could be a mob."

"Mobs don't knock, even that loudly. Wouldn't there just be a stone through my windows?"

There was a banging again, then a huge crash as the door burst open in a splintering of wood. Grafton stood back and Rodon leapt to his feet. Six men stood there, the largest with an axe which been just applied to the lock. The others all had pistols at the ready and they raised them when they saw people inside the shop.

"What do you want?" Grafton asked. "I was about to open the door."

"Who be you?" asked a weasely man with whiskers.

"This is my shop. Who are you?"

"You didn't answer my question," said the man, walking up to Grafton until he was stood too close to him. "And who be you?" he asked Rodon. "You look familiar."

It was only then that Grafton saw there were others out in the street, a crowd of creatures which stood on two feet, but which had the heads of wolves and dark eyes. He felt the hair rise on the back of his neck.

The other men had advanced into the room. Two each covered Rodon and Grafton with their weapons while another watched the door.

"He looks like Rodon," said one of them.

"And you be Lord Giles' men," said Rodon, deciding he might be able to play the advantage of this.

"So what if we be? What do you here?"

"You know these people?" Grafton asked, trying to mask his wavering voice.

"Not personally," said Rodon.

The weasel brushed past Grafton and walked up to Rodon.

"What do you down here, Mr Rodon?"

Rodon did not respond.

"And who be your friend?" asked the weasel.

As Rodon looked at Grafton, he too noticed the wolves outside. Any further thoughts evaporated in the horror of the sight.

"You walked into my shop, I thought you would know who I am."

The weasel turned back to him.

"You be Grafton? We heard you were away."

"I came back."

"Then we need to talk to you. And you too, Mr Rodon."

Rodon frowned at the small man and the small man looked away, pretending he was turning to his men.

"Take them back."

Then the internal door to the house opened and Raul was there. He looked startled.

"A devil!" exclaimed one of the men lifting his weapon to fire. It all happened quickly. Rodon had dived at the man, knocking his arm as the gun went off. It was loud in the enclosed space and it was immediately followed by the sound of glass breaking as the bullet struck jars on a high shelf.

"Get out!" Rodon shouted.

Raul shut the door instantly. Two of the men rushed it, but it was already bolted.

"Go round the back!" the weasel shouted to two of the others. "Take the wolves!" Then he turned to Rodon who was sprawled on the ground, wrestling the man who had fired.

"Devil lover," he spat. "Lie still and put your hands on your head or I'll make a hole in it."

Then he turned to the axeman and nodded his head at the internal door. The axeman set to it with great thuds.

Grafton was still wide eyed.

"Sit down there," said the weasel. "On the floor."

Grafton hesitated for a moment, then complied.

The man who Rodon had felled rolled away from Rodon and stood up. He seemed uncertain as to how to treat him.

"Hurry up with the door," said the weasel, his voice calm.

Rodon lay face down, his forehead pressed against the cold tiles. He felt completely powerless. Seconds ticked by, marked only by the axe in the wood.

Then he heard shouts, heard the door unlatch, and a clearer voice.

"There be no one here, he be gone."

"Search the house."

"Already doing it," the voice called back. "But there be something else you should see. Out the back."

Grafton took an involuntary intake of breath. The light needle! The weasel saw Grafton's expression and a slow smile crept across his face.

"Something interesting be it?" he said.

Raul and Berwick were running across the rooftop terraces. They had grabbed what little they had. At the end of the block of buildings, they stopped at the hatch that led to the interior stair. Raul lifted it, listened for a moment, then let Berwick through before following him inside and pulling it closed behind him. He pushed a bolt across, grateful it had been left open. Then they descended through the empty house. As they went past open rooms, they could see chests and wardrobes had been opened and some clothes were left strewn about.

"Left in a hurry," said Raul.

They reached the bottom of the stairs, found the front door and paused.

"How many were there again?" Berwick asked.

"Six."

"That be five at most if only one guards Rodon and Grafton. They won't be expecting us to go back into the house behind them."

"I would not assume that."

"What else can we do?"

"Wait?"

"They might kill them."

Raul nodded grimly and Berwick opened the door so that they could peer out. Then he pulled his head back quickly and turned to Raul, his eyes wide with fear.

"What did you see?" asked Raul.

Berwick tried to understand what he had seen.

"I don't know. But there be more than five of them."

"What?"

"Look!"

Raul peered out. There were wolfmen in the street in front of the house. He pulled back in horror.

"That is too many, whatever they are. There is nothing we can do here. We must save ourselves for another day. We cannot help them if we are dead."

Berwick knew it was true. Raul pointed at the narrow alley between the houses opposite.

"That way," he said. Berwick nodded. Then Raul opened the door and ran. Berwick was right behind him. They were quickly across the road and charging down the alley. It reached a T and ran down the backs of the other houses. Raul turned right, further away from the wolves. He could see it was a dead end. He had led them into a trap. No, there at the end was another alley leading away from this one. He hoped it led out onto the next street. They dodged down it. As they reached the houses again, he looked back and could see dark heads bobbing in pursuit.

In moments they were out on an empty street. Smoke was rising from several places in front of them and there was a sound of distant shouting. They had to run.

The wolves came bounding out of the alleyway. There were four, then another four behind them. Raul pulled out one pistol, then he stopped, aimed at the closest wolf and fired. He saw the beast's shoulder kick back before he was running again. The wolf kept coming.

The road led downhill. They reached a junction and the noise became louder. Just down the street was a crowd of people, they made for them, hoping to lose themselves. The crowd was chanting.

"Devils! Devils!"

They were looking upwards and following their gaze, Berwick and Raul saw with horror that there were two people, two delf, perched on window ledges above the street. They had ropes around their necks and hands could be seen, gripping them as they writhed to free themselves, shouting, eyes wild.

It was too late to turn back now and besides, with the wolfmen behind them, there was nowhere to go. They barged on through the crowd, Berwick first with Raul behind him, head lowered in the hope that he would not be noticed. They were almost through when a hand grabbed him by the arm. He tried to shake it off and turned to face his attacker. The man saw his face and was about to shout when they were both pushed to the ground by the force of bodies.

There was different howling and calling out now and screams of fear. The wolves were tearing into the crowd indiscriminately. The man had let go of Raul. Raul looked around for Berwick and saw his face looking back for him on the other side of the crowd. He was clear of them. He could run, the way was clear. For a moment, Raul thought that he would. In that madness, he would not have blamed him. He was only an ironhead after all. Raul watched him. Berwick was looking around, searching for him. Then he looked down and their eyes met. He did not even look away at a path for possible escape. He came back. The mob was no longer watching the delf in the windows, it was panicking. They were pushing and shoving against each other and those that could were fleeing.

Berwick dodged two as they ran past him, almost knocking him to the ground. He reached Raul and put out his hand to help him up. Just as Raul took hold of it, Berwick let go and jumped back. Surprised, Raul dropped to the ground. Berwick whipped out his pistol and discharged it over Raul's head. There was a wolf above him. Its head whipped back with the impact at point blank range, but it stayed standing. The man who had taken hold of Raul was scrambling to stand. As he did so, he dug his foot into Raul's belly, but he was barely on his feet when he was struck by the beast's arm, its claws raking across his face. The man screamed and stumbled into another wolf which lashed out. He dropped to the ground like meat.

Raul rolled and another body fell on him, a small axe narrowly missing his head as the man dropped it. Raul snatched at it and hacked at the legs of the wolf that was still standing over him. The axe bit deep and the creature reeled and fell, its foot half severed. Then he was out of its way and pushing himself up to stand, ready to run.

The street was complete in confusion now. The mob was dispersing and the wolves were chasing individuals and dismembering those they reached. There was blood and bodies everywhere.

Raul and Berwick were together again and together they fled. But as they passed a wolf, it dropped its dead victim and sidestepped into their path. Berwick shoulder charged it and Raul swung the axe deep into its neck. The head flopped and the beast staggered to one side. Then the two of them were running again.

43

THE ARCHBISHOP SAT in his chair and looked at the young girl in front of him.

"She does not look like a witch," he said. "Be you a witch, girl?"

"Charlie," she said quietly.

"It be all she bloody says," said Boyce. "She be mad, Your Grace."

"A sure sign that the devil has possessed her!" said Silver.

"And this Charlie," the Archbishop asked, "he was with her you say?"

"We chased him off, Your Grace. He was a coward. Left the girl to us."

"So much for Charlie," mused the Archbishop. "Has she slept?"

Boyce looked puzzled. "No," he said.

"Good. She will be tired. I have prepared a room. See she be comfortable and that it be dark. I want the room watched at all times. If anything happens let me know, whatever the time."

"If what happens, Your Grace?"

"You will know if anything happens you should tell me about," said the Archbishop.

Boyce and Silver led the girl away.

Giles had said nothing throughout the whole exchange.

"She doesn't add up to much. Just a scrawny half breed."

"She be my door to Christendom. I have felt her dreams. I know they can pass through Limbo. We will ride her dream, tether it and enter Christendom."

"What will you find there?"

"Our destiny, Lord Giles. The place that was once our world has become corrupt and it is our lot to be the Lord's instrument."

The next morning, dream Rua was brought before the Archbishop once more.

"She did not sleep?"

"Not at all, Your Grace. She stood in the room all night. Stood, Your Grace," Silver repeated. "And all she did was to call out for this Charlie. She be bewitched."

The Archbishop studied the girl standing forlornly in front of him.

"Perhaps it be this Charlie who be the witch. You say he killed Fycher and the others?" He stroked his chin in thought. "Take her away. Make her sleep." He watched them go, then turned to Giles.

"Bring me her father."

George and Richard were coming back from the village shop just before it had closed. They had bags of food in their hands.

"Why did you buy that kitchen knife?" George asked.

"I didn't want to go empty handed into whatever's there."

"Would you use it?"

Richard shrugged.

"If there's one thing I learned from being there last time, you never know what you might find yourself doing."

They walked a few more steps. Richard's comment strongly suggested something revelatory and perhaps disturbing. George pondered how to pose his next question. In the end, he decided that being blunt was the easiest approach.

"Did you kill anyone last time?" he asked.

Richard did not reply at first. George wished he had not asked.

"No I didn't," Richard said. "But I tried to."

They walked into the pension and smiled at the owner, a busy looking widow.

"Do you think she knows Rua's in the room as well?" Richard asked.

"A middle aged man and a retired priest with a young girl in their room? It would make her day."

"I could pretend she was my daughter."

"She looks nothing like you," said George. "I think we just keep quiet and if we need to leave, we do it when she's out."

They tramped up the stairs and stopped outside the room.

"Are you sure this is the best way to help Charlie?" George asked. "What about your wife?"

"I emailed her. She'll get it in the morning. I know she'll kill me, but she would want me to find Charlie."

"You say she's been there too?"

"Yes, but she tries to forget all about it."

George looked directly at Richard.

"You want to go back don't you?"

Richard raised an eyebrow. The priest was uncomfortably perceptive.

"Am I that obvious?"

George smiled.

"I've missed it," Richard said. It was a kind of relief to admit it. He realised as he said it that he had felt ashamed at the way he felt. "I've never felt so alive. Yes, I've made a career change, but... Much of my time there was terrifying, you know? Why do I want to go back?"

George nodded.

"But then I felt so free. And I'd never felt so close to Charlie before. It was like...him and me."

He paused and looked at the door handle.

"Some days I want to explode. It's not something I can talk to anyone about, but it made me who I am today. When people asked me how I got the idea for the career change, I tell them..." He smiled. "...I tell them the idea came to me in a dream."

He looked at George in a way that reminded him of Charlie when he was being cheeky.

"So I'm not lying am I?"

Grafton was stood in front of the Archbishop. He was trying to show outrage rather than fear.

"Why am I a prisoner?"

"You be not a prisoner, Mr Grafton, you be in our care. As you realise, this be a dangerous time to be in Linana Pivaki. You be safer with us that you could be out in the streets of the city. You should be pleased to be here, protected by my cohorts and the walls of this fortress. But I be curious, Mr Grafton. We found an engine outside your house. I have taken a look at it myself. It looks impressive. Would you care to tell me what it is?"

Grafton did not know what to make of this man out of Limbo and the army he commanded. He inspired fear, yet Grafton's intellectual curiosity was also piqued.

"Who are you?"

The Archbishop's eyes narrowed, but he accepted the question, sitting a little straighter as he responded.

"I be Archbishop Sibbald and I come like Jonah to Nineveh bringing the Lord's wrath if you do not change your ways."

"Where do you come from?"

"I come from God. And the Lord commands you to answer my question."

Grafton felt he had pushed his own questions as far as he could. He did not understand what was happening, only that his city was in the grip of this man and his unnatural army. Now he needed to provide answers.

"It is only something I made to help in the mines to the north."

"But what does it do?"

"It makes holes in the rock."

"But it uses light does it not?"

Grafton looked wary.

"Yes, I know a little about devil sorcery," said the Archbishop, seeing Grafton's look. "Do you understand what you tamper with, Mr Grafton?"

"I don't know what you mean."

"You play with the sorcery of Satan!" the Archbishop exploded. "What does your engine do? How do you work it? What were you using it for?"

"I told you, it is simply a tool for the mines."

"Then how did you come to be here? We heard you were in the desert, yet you suddenly appear in this city, with this great engine. How did you enter the city?"

"Through the gates."

"Liar! The gates be guarded. We would have seen you arrive! How did you come to be here?"

Grafton could not think fast enough. He could not construct a lie that worked. He lapsed into a fearful silence, his mind locking up.

"I can make you talk, Grafton. Making someone talk be very easy. Oh it does not have to hurt you. You have a daughter."

"She is missing."

The Archbishop smiled without feeling and shook his head. A chill struck Grafton at his core.

"You know where she is?"

The Archbishop nodded to Benedict who left the room. Grafton looked around, agitated. She was here. Where was she? And then she came in.

They led her in easily. She did not look herself. There was a glassy look in her eye. He ran to her. No one stopped him, but the Archbishop shot out an arm.

"Do not touch her!" he said.

"She's my daughter!"

"Do not touch her," the Archbishop hissed. An angel stepped forward and pinioned his arms behind his back.

"What have you done to her?" he cried, wincing.

"We have done nothing, Grafton. The question be what have *you* done to her? How have you bewitched her?"

"Charlie?" came the dream Rua's plaintive voice.

"Who is Charlie?" Grafton asked.

"Who indeed? Your familiar?"

"No, you misunderstand. Something has happened to her. I have nothing to do with this. Rua, Rua speak to me."

She ignored him.

"Rua, what has happened? Rua!"

"If you value your daughter's life, Grafton, you will tell me about your light engine. And there be still time for you to seek absolution for your sins before the Lord."

Grafton stared at the girl he thought was his daughter. There were tears in his eyes and he longed to hold her and comfort her. She looked so lost and helpless. Something terrible had happened to her. She looked different somehow.

"Take the girl back to her room," said the Archbishop. "And take him away too. Let him think before I talk to him again."

As they led him away, Giles moved closer to the Archbishop.

"He looked to me as though he was telling the truth. I don't think he has bewitched her."

"I agree. But they be both witches and I will know the truth of this engine before they burn."

<h1 style="text-align:center">44</h1>

SOLIMO STOOD BEFORE the gates of the darkness-entombed light tower. He had made his way across the plain. The drawbridge was down, the entrance beckoned. He slowly made his way through, but inside he was confronted by the unlight.

There was a distinct boundary between the light and the dark. He looked at it fearfully for a time, trying to make out what it was, whether he could see through it. He tossed in a stone and it disappeared, but he heard it land on the ground. Tentatively he brushed at the darkness with a fingertip. He felt nothing at all. If he had closed his eyes he would not have been able to tell whether his hand was in the dark or the light.

He tried to remember how they had entered the Mage's light tower before. They had walked across the outer yard and climbed a set of steps which led to a door, a room, a larger room with a staircase rising out of it to successive landings. With a quaking heart, Solimo realised that if he was to retrieve the Mage's books, he was going to need to find the whole way as if he was blind. And back out again.

He stood in front of that darkness for a long time, unable to enter, yet unable to turn back either.

"Well Solimo," he said at last. "Just try it. You can always go back."

Before he lost his nerve, he stepped forward and was immediately swamped in darkness.

He moved his hand in front of his face, but could not see it. He felt compelled to check all his limbs were still there, even though he could feel them.

He put his hands out in front of him, carefully feeling with each foot before placing his weight on it. In this way, he came to the wall. As he touched it, he lurched back in his shock. Then, knowing it would be there, he felt it again. It was reassuring to have something solid to touch. He could work his way along this. The steps were to the right, he remembered. He moved to the right, still feeling with hands and feet until he reached them. He went over to the wall side and started up the steps, hugging the wall.

He was gaining a little in confidence. Holding onto the wall and climbing the steps gave him a shape to imagine, but soon enough he reached the top of the steps and he had to grope about again for the door, reaching across empty space once more until he found it. The door opened as he turned the handle. He felt the closeness of the building around him as he entered.

Here he paused. He was inside the tower. He thought he could probably find his way out again, find his way to the gate because he knew the darkness ended in the courtyard. But inside would be all dark as far as he knew. Too dark. This was madness, he could not do it. He had tried, but making such a distance while being effectively blind was too much of an obstacle; too much for anyone. This was nothing to do with the time he had spent in the Pits, this was just common sense.

Then he was backing out. He was reversing out of the doorway and had his foot on the top of the steps. And there he stopped himself.

"Hold on," he said aloud. "Stay still and breathe."

He forced himself to breathe in slowly through his nose and exhale through his mouth.

"It is only darkness. Think of light. Remember what it was like."

He forced himself to remember the inside of the light tower. He returned to the first room inside the light tower and groped along its walls until he reached the second room. His knee bumped something and he breathed in sharply and reached down to touch it. The edge of something wooden. He had found some furniture. He carried on and was relieved to reach the staircase. Nothing had changed and he had remembered it all correctly.

The stairs rose in a spiral. He could feel the curve of the outer wall. It was disorientating to climb steps blind while forever turning. Then he found the landing and was once more in space with nothing before him. He remembered the steps continued up the far end of the landing and he waved his arms around until he found the balustrade and worked his way along that. He found the next set of steps and went up.

When he reached the second landing, everything changed. He noticed at once that the nature of the darkness was different. Now he could almost see it. There was something about it, some kind of substance. And it was moving.

He had never known darkness that moved before. The blackness was filled. It shifted in front of his eyes. There seemed to be whirling things. He could not tell whether he could hear them or feel them, but he knew they were there. His body felt tense as if at any moment something would come flying into him, knocking him over, cutting him, taking hold of him and picking him up, flinging him into an abyss.

He was rooted to the spot. He had come in this far, he had begun to calm down, to become more confident, but now it that confidence left him.

He shrank back against the balustrade. He had to go down again, get out. He leaned to find a handhold. There was nothing there – his foot slipped on the top step and he tottered forward to avoid falling down the steps and landed, sprawling on the stone floor. He felt it cold against his cheek.

He fancied he could hear something moving in the darkness. He felt like a child again when the night magnified every sound and the mind would conjure others out of the air. Sweat prickled all over him like an icy breeze has just passed over him. He listened intently. Was anything coming? There had been no nightmare hordes outside the tower, but could anything still be inside? Could it see him?

He closed his eyes. It was turning him mad staring into utter darkness. He did not know how long he lay like that, but he heard nothing coming, only the sound of his own panicked breathing. He concentrated on that and gradually it slowed.

He thought back to his time in the Pits. His despair had not set in immediately; he had been able to keep it at bay for a while, no, for longer than that. How had he done it?

Mondo had said he had not heard him singing much. Why was that, why did he not sing? He had sung in this light tower once and the Mage had heard him. If he sung now, who would hear him?

Suddenly he did not care who heard him. At least it would be an end to this agonised waiting. Whatever was there would come for him. And then... He did not know. He pushed himself to his feet.

He began to sing. It was feeble at first. Somehow without light he had no reference point for volume. It was an old song, from the south coast sailors. He paused at the end of the first stanza and listened. There was no call, no footsteps, no answering song. He continued into the second stanza, louder this time. It was about sailing into the heart of a storm on the way home. It was relentless, beating time as the sailors worked rhythmically, as he had always imagined, but fiercely as the wind and waves beat against them. As he reached the end of the song, he realised the sailors did not reach home, not in the song. It left them still furling the sails and lashing down the cargo. Surely they made it home though, he thought, they wrote the song.

He put a foot out, touching the ground gingerly, expecting nothing to be there. It touched firm ground. He reached out his hand, slowly, tentatively. It touched nothing. He rocked forward on his ankle, shifting his weight and moving his other leg to follow. His whole body was tense. As his back leg came forward and down he put it on the ground lightly, not trusting there would be anything there. But there was.

He rested. Two steps. How far did he have to go? How many floors was it? It could be thousands of miles; it could be around the corner. Anything could be around the corner.

He lifted both hands and held them out in front of him, feeling for what could be there. How would he find the way into the Mage's rooms if the hidden door had been shut? It was hard enough when they could see.

Nothing had come for him. Perhaps it was waiting, but it had not come for him yet. Perhaps he could do this. He had come this far. He was at some more steps. Up those he went to the next landing. Was the room he and Charlie had found on this floor?

Charlie, that cheerful bright eyed boy to whom everything had seemed so simple, everything had been possible to his young mind. And what things they had accomplished! Through the Mage, they had overcome the Archbishop's legions, but that had only been possible as he funnelled the hopes of man and delf through him. Hope. It was a powerful thing. The Mage had said it was part of the instinct in living things to survive.

What did he hope for? He hoped for an end to this darkness for a start. He hoped for peace with the Order. Perhaps it was because he had no dealings with the people of Outreterre, but he had the young Charlie's faith that it would all work out. It had to. He came to another staircase, felt the stone wall with his outstretched hands and began to climb.

He hoped he would find the books of the Mage. He would find them. Time was on his side, it slowed right down in Limbo, so there was no need to rush this crawl in the dark. It would end. One day he would look back on all this, one day soon. It felt like forever, but it would end as all things did. Perhaps the candles would still be lit in the Mage's rooms. He would do it. He was a Light Keeper.

Solimo could see his hands. A small glowing ball, a tiny white flame was hovering just above his open palms like a firefly. It lit the creases of his skin. It was a wondrous and precious thing like a jewel. It was the most amazing jewel he had ever seen. It did not sparkle, but stayed constant, a tiny light in the darkness.

He bent close to it looking into it, longing for the light against this darkness around him. It cast only a little light, yet it filled his heart and he felt a warmth flow through him and his hope grew.

Then, smoothly, without any fuss or pulsing, the spark in his hand grew. He cupped it with both hands. Now he could see his shadow, the hands in front of his face and a light inside them. He could see the stones on the wall.

Marvelling, he brought his hands towards him and the flame grew further. He could see the steps under his feet now and the walls around him. He was casting a shadow.

Solimo smiled. It was a smile of wonder and of joy and as he did so, the light grew stronger yet. The whole stairwell was lit now and he could see. He circled his hands around the ball of light. He could feel nothing. There was no warmth, it was simply light. A thrill ran through him. This light grew with his emotions. He had created it.

Slowly, he parted his hands. The ball split into two, one half following each hand. At the top of the landing he stopped and looked around. Shadows stretched and leapt as he moved his arms. He followed a corridor, found more stairs and eventually found himself in a room which felt familiar. There was a chimney breast and near it on the wall, a small image of a cloud obscuring the sun. He was in the right room. He began to tap on the wall, the light moving backwards and forwards as he moved his hands. And the door slid open to reveal a staircase going up.

He could not believe it. He could hardly contain his excitement. He was there. He was finally back in the Mage's rooms. There they were: the tapestries on the walls, the two long tables. And the books, the missing books from the Mage libraries which had been hidden away, trapped in Limbo for centuries.

It was so bright, it was like daylight, yet outside the windows it was pitch dark. Solimo moved to the closest table and looked at the book which was open. There would be time to read these. He walked slowly down the tables. Several books were open. He stopped at one of them because a title had caught his eye. It said *The Black Sun of Unlembien*. He read down the page.

As he read, he realised he had not made the darkness in which the Mage's light tower was shrouded. Someone else had done so, someone who had access to these books. It could not have been the Mage because he had left, which meant it could only have been one person, the one who had been left behind. The Archbishop.

His body had never been found when the Mage destroyed the nightmare legions, The Archbishop who had led the army had not been the real Archbishop. This meant that he has possibly never left the light tower. He could be there now, hiding, watching. No one had challenged him. Surely the Archbishop would not have let him in this far if he had been present. That was what the darkness, the black sun, had been. It was a defence and he had breached it.

Something made him turn around and when he did so, he saw he was wrong. The Archbishop *had* left a last line of defence and now he was trapped. Blocking his way out of the room were two tall, winged warriors wearing armour on their chests. They were head and shoulders taller than Solimo. Their faces were impassive, but they were both coming towards him with swords.

The light in his hands died. The room was plunged into darkness.

To have come so far...

He could see the Light Doctor's face in his mind in these, his last moments. He saw Mondo and Esella too. He had failed in the final test as he had failed before. He had said he could never be a Light Doctor. He had told them all along that he was nothing more than a healer. He opened his arms to accept death, spread them wide. He was afraid of the dark, he was not afraid of death. He was afraid of what he might do with power, he was not afraid of wielding the power. If this was death, then let it come quickly. Why did these soulless angels not strike him?

"I am here! Can you not see in the dark? Here, I will help you!"

The light sponges were in the bag around his shoulders. As always, there was a small glass bowl in the pocket of his long coat.

He had always refused to weave a sun wraith, but now perhaps was the time to do it. He did not want to die in the dark, he wanted to remember the light of the sun.

He slipped his hand into his bag, pulled out a light sponge. He took the bowl from his pocket. Then, with one hand, he squeezed the sponge into it.

As the light dripped into the bowl, the room was drenched in sunlight. Warmth filled his heart as the sunlight filled his soul. He remembered the sunrises and the sunsets, the light and shade as the clouds passed over the hills and under the sun. The high summer sun with its yellow vibrancy; the low winter sun which shone soft and golden.

In his palms the flame grew again. The angels stood gazing at his outstretched arms as the sun wraith formed as a ball over the glass bowl. These creatures of Limbo had been formed out of desires and fears. That was what drove them. They were without soul, without heart or mind. They were born with a purpose which was not their own. They gazed on sunlight they could never enjoy and on a light of hope they could never feel. Theirs was an empty existence.

They stared at the ball of the sun as if drawn to it, then both of them walked towards it. For a moment, Solimo saw the light of the sun reflected in their dead eyes. It formed itself into an echo of Solimo, its arms outspread and leaning forward, it took the angels in a fiery embrace. The Limbo-born were consumed as the wraith hugged them tighter. By the time it had faded, the angels were charred and twisted on the floor.

Solimo stood in the Mage's room for a long time.

These puppets of the Archbishop's had been shown hope and had destroyed themselves. Or had he done it? Had he taken a life or given oblivion? Perhaps he had given them some comfort as he had done to the dying at times in Unama.

Where the essence of the light of the sun had shone from the windows, the unlight of the black sun had been burned away. Once more there was a view of the plain outside and he knew how he could burn away the rest of it.

Solimo sat down in one of the chairs and looked around at all the books. He had forgotten how many there were. He had thought he could carry a few back with him, but he would either have to be selective or to keep coming back. He was sitting in front of the book which described the black sun and it reminded him of the Archbishop once more. If he had been here, where was he now?

He raised himself from the chair and went over to a window. Over towards a low line of hills two things caught his eye. The first was a localised patch of mist. The second were the bodies and weapons scattered in front of it.

45

EDWARD CLIFFORD LEFT the house in the evening. He headed straight for the quarters of the custodian guard. Mobs of men were prowling the streets armed with cudgels, axes, swords and guns. They looked angry; a few looked frightened. They would look him over before nodding at him, smiling or saluting. He returned none of their signals. He was appalled at how quickly the first city of the Republic had descended into anarchy.

At first he saw nothing more than the mobs. He had passed the senate house and was nearing the Tower of the Moon when he heard gunshots. He drew his pistol. He found the source of the sound when he turned a corner.

Barricades had been thrown across the street. They were made up of a couple of wagons and piles of boxes and furniture. Men were squatting behind them taking occasional shots over the top. He peered down the street and could see another barricade sixty yards down it. He could only assume it was manned by delf. There were a few bodies in the street between the two and a couple more behind the barricade. One wounded man was being tended to.

A bearded man caught sight of him.

"Hey, captain! Come to help? We're trying to get one of those delf off the roof. He can see behind the barricade. A few of your boys are here already!"

"Where?" Clifford demanded.

"Just down by the wall. I told them to – "

Clifford did not wait to hear the rest of the sentence but bent low and ran along the barricade until he found the two men in question. He recognised them, but did not know them well. They were older, experienced men and were reloading their weapons with practised ease.

"What are you two doing here?" he demanded.

"Come to get the delf, sir."

"On whose orders?"

"I didn't know we needed any, sir."

"You are soldiers under the command of General Wootton. As custodian legion, your duty is to protect the people of this city. You will return to the barracks at once."

"Lots of the boys are out too, trying to round up the delf."

"There have been no orders. You will stand down at once and return to quarters. And anyone you see on the way too."

"But sir, we're needed here."

"We won't win a war by fighting our friends, soldier."

"If they were our friends, they'd die to save us. We'll all die if they don't."

Clifford pointed his pistol into the man's face, inches from between his eyes.

"Do as you are ordered soldier or I swear I'll blow your brains out."

"I don't think I can take your orders any more, Mr Clifford," said the man.

The gun went off and the man's face was torn open, the back of his head exploding onto the wall. His friend fell back in shock, his mouth open, his face splashed with blood and more. Clifford turned the gun on him, his face set firm.

"I'll go, sir." He stood and with a last glance at his dead comrade, scampered back up the street.

"What's going on here?" came a voice from behind him. Clifford whirled to find the bearded man running bent double towards him. He saw the dead man and Clifford's gun. "What are you doing?"

"Dismantle this barricade," said Clifford. His voice was stern. There was anger in him, but he felt remarkably calm.

"What? Are you mad?"

"Dismantle it and go home."

"Go to hell."

As Clifford's gun fired again, the man's face wore a look of surprise as he slumped backwards. Another man nearby looked across in shock and made to raise his long-arm, but was beaten to it by Clifford's weapon. There were others behind the barricade, but they appeared to have no stomach for a greater fight than shooting at a distance. They ran off.

Clifford tucked the pistol back into his belt, raised his good arm and stood up.

"Hold your fire!" he called out to the delf barricade. He pulled at
a crate and a table and they slid down, leaving him a place over
which he could climb. He kept his arm in the air and his other hand
visible in his sling. He did not want the delf to think he had a
concealed weapon.

A bullet whizzed into the wagon next to him.

"Hold your fire!" he said. "I want a parley!"

"Come on then. Stand in the middle," a voice called back.

He walked forward, feeling very exposed in the empty street.

"That barricade is no longer manned," he called out. "Who is
your leader? I need to talk to him."

Suddenly another shot rang out, immediately followed by a
second. He flinched.

"Hold your fire!" he called.

"You had better come over here," a voice called from the delf
side. "Your own kind are shooting at you."

He ran for the barricade and scrambled at it. Arms pulled him
over. He found himself surrounded by delf. Their faces were grim,
desperate and fearful. He was led at gunpoint to a house. Inside was
an older delf with large, sad eyes and his grey hair tied behind his
neck. He was wearing an old legionnaire's jacket.

"What do you want? I hear you are killing your own men."

"They did not obey orders."

"What were your orders?"

"To dismantle the barricade and leave."

The old delf raised an eyebrow.

"And why would you do that?"

"Why?" Clifford repeated, incredulous. "Where is this getting
us?"

"It will get you killed, will it not? Our death sentence has been
read out. But we will not go without a fight."

"And neither will I. I don't know who this Archbishop is and I
fear his army. But no army is invincible and I haven't seen enough
of it to give in now."

"Brave words, captain, but what are you suggesting?"

"We need time and in this city, we have no time and we don't
know who our friends are."

"Are you suggesting we leave?"

"Isn't that better than being holed up in ever smaller corners?"

"Ah. This is just another way of being rid of us. Send us out to die in the open."

"What is your name, soldier?"

"I am no longer a soldier. My name is Keti. I fought for Heywood's Legion."

"Then you know all about a fighting retreat and where you can lead your pursuers. We leave as a fighting force, but take the elderly and the children with us. If you're going to fight, fight your way out of this city."

"You say, 'we'. Are you coming too?"

"I am. And as many of the custodians as I can muster."

"Much of the custodian legion is already behind our barricades." He looked at his jacket. "As you can see. Some of us are still guarding the city."

"Then I will bring men to help us. Men I can trust."

The old delf soldier looked at Clifford.

"I will see your words are passed on. But we would need more than men."

"I will go back and gather weapons, food and wagons. Together we can make a plan to defeat these beasts."

"You have more hope than I."

Clifford looked out at the barricade.

"You are not without hope. It is how you direct that hope that is important. This here can only have one outcome. I'm offering the possibility of more."

Clifford made his way with even greater haste and vigilance to the barracks. He was uncertain what kind of reception would greet him when he arrived, wondering what news the soldier would have taken with him, assuming he had even really gone there.

Whenever someone looked at him, he thought they would know him for the officer who had murdered three men at the barricade. He tried not to think about it, but he did. He had killed three men in the space of a minute. He realised his main concern was that others would kill him for it. He felt no remorse. It had been necessary.

When he reached the barbican gates of the custodians' barracks, he saw that there were ten wolfmen lined up outside. One of Giles' men in a long brown coat was sat behind them, his head resting on the wall, his eyes closed and a long-arm lying across his knees. Clifford moved back behind the wall. He would try the night gate.

He worked his way around the streets until he came to the small door hidden in an angle of the barracks wall. He watched it for a time, but there appeared to be no one guarding it and no beasts. Either they had not discovered its existence or they saw no need to guard it. As a captain, he had a key and he took this out ready before walking quickly out of cover. He unlocked the gate and went inside.

The gate opened into a small terrace just off from the main courtyard. He was struck by the unusual quiet as he went. Normally there would have been a unit drilling in the central courtyard, there would have been shouts and voices echoing around the buildings, but there was only silence.

He found some men in the mess hall. Some were eating, but most were reading or talking quietly to each other. A few simply sat and stared. He looked in a couple of barracks and found the same thing. He was surprised at how few soldiers he found. Even without the delf and puoli, there should have been more. He saw a sergeant he recognised, a tall, barrel of a man with long moustaches.

"Where is everyone, Buller?" he asked him.

"Some slipped off home to their families, sir. Others went to kill delf."

"How did they leave?"

"I suspect the same way you got in, sir."

Clifford gave him a questioning look.

"Sergeants have a key too, sir."

"And why did you stay?"

The sergeant let out a deep breath.

"I hadn't had any orders. I don't know what to do. We're not used to losing battles, sir. I don't know how to do it."

"We've not lost yet. Round up all the men you can. Bring them into the square."

It took almost half an hour. The men seemed to shamble in for something to do, pleased to be given some direction. There were well over a hundred and they stood around like a crowd, waiting for him to speak.

"Buller, make them look like soldiers."

"Sir."

Buller marched to the front of the crowd.

"Custodians! Attention!"

Most of the men snapped rigidly upright. Others were slower. A few did not move. Buller walked smartly up to one and pressed his face close to the other's. Then he grabbed the man's right ear and tugged.

"What have I got in my hand, soldier?"

"My ear, sergeant."

"Shall we test it again? Custodians! Attention!" he bellowed into the man's ear, then let go. The man stood upright, arms by his side.

"Good. Now you look like soldiers again," said Clifford. "Most of you will know me. I am Captain Edward Clifford. Someone said to me today that the soldiers of Linana Pivaki don't know how to lose a war. But who said the war was over? We have been bested in a battle. Now our city and our very way of life is being threatened.

"We have been a great city for nearly four hundred years. Four hundred years has seen the empire and influence of Linana spread across the lands. Is there anyone with whom we do not trade? Have the roads and borders not been made safe because of our legions?

"I look around me now and something is wrong. I look at this legion, a legion that has had the honour this last year of guarding protecting our capital and something is missing. This city was not made great through men alone. This city was founded on a union of men and delf, and indeed puoli. That union has been strengthened by centuries of strife and prosperity. Can that achievement really be undone in a single night? I thought I fought amongst men, amongst warriors, protectors of their countrymen. Am I wrong?

"We have been bested in a single fight, outfoxed by a force we have seen now for the first time. But soldiers do not give up. They find weaknesses and they exploit them."

He looked over the assembled men. They were listening.

"This Archbishop has threatened our people and is holding us to ransom. We have let him. We can change the terms of the current situation by leaving the city and taking the delf with us. With the delf out of the city, it is no longer in the power of the city to give up the delf to the Archbishop's wolves. They must come for us."

He peered at them, trying to see the fear in their minds.

"You fear death? You fear being caught in the open like Kallick's legion? We know now that gunshot will not kill them, but we know we can still burn them and maim them. We will use ourselves as the bait, but we will lead them to their destruction. And some of us will die. But if we do, we will die not as weaklings hiding away from friend and foe alike, but staunchly staring death in the face."

He stood up straight.

"Who is with me?"

There was silence. Some of the men had a light in their eyes, but others were hesitant, fearful, waiting on the reaction of their fellows. He walked up to the front rank and looked a soldier in the eye.

"Are you with me? Are you a man?"

"I am a man, sir," he said.

"Are you for hiding away for the rest of your life, ashamed to look your family in the face? Afraid to walk past the houses of the friends you betrayed? Or are you a true protector of the city and people of Linana Pivaki?"

He stared at the man, waiting. The man looked straight ahead, trying to avoid Clifford's eyes which were boring into his.

"I'm with you, sir," he said quietly.

"I didn't hear you."

"I'm with you, sir," he said louder.

Clifford patted his arm.

"Good man. A hero of the custodians even before he lifts his arm, he risks standing alone." He turned to the next man. "And you?"

"I'm with you, sir."

He walked along the line, staring each man in the eye and from each one he received the same answer. At the end of the line he walked amongst the assembled ranks.

"Who's with me?"

Arms and voices were raised.

"I can't hear you, Wootton's," he bellowed. "Who is with me?"

A hundred voices and more roared their response.

He turned to Buller and said quietly. "Now we give these men something to do before they change their minds."

"We need to remove the guards on the gate," the sergeant said. "I'll need some men, a couple of old gun carriages and some timber."

Clifford looked at him quizzically. "Take what you need."

It was evening before the men of the custodians began to leave the barracks by the night gate in groups of three or four. They vanished into the streets, making their way further up the city by taking different routes through the streets and laneways.

At the main gate of the barracks, the man was slouched on the bench while the wolfmen stood still and menacing. There was a hammering on the gate and the man stood up, surprised.

"Quiet in there!" he called.

The hammering continued, then the gate swung in, opened from the inside. The man drew two pistols and peered at the gate while the wolves lined up facing the entrance. Suddenly, from the entranceway, a group of men ran out slashing with swords and axes. The wolves immediately moved forward, raising their own weapons.

The soldiers fell back inside the gate before any blow could be struck and tried to push the gate to, but the wolves were in the entrance and pushing the gate aside. The lone Melion man peered from behind them and saw what appeared to be a fence advancing towards the wolves' flank at speed. A line of upright wooden poles had been fixed across the front of two gun carriages which had been lashed together. The stockade crashed into the wolves, knocking two down and trapping the others against the stone wall behind them. Immediately, arms brandishing axes and halberds appeared, below the fence and over the top. They slashed at the legs of the wolves and at their necks before they could free their own arms. The lone man from Giles' contingent turned and ran. He was barely half way across the street before two crossbow bolts struck him in the back and he fell forward and lay still.

The wheeled stockade was pulled back after a minute. The wolves were still struggling to move, but none was able to rise. The soldiers moved in mercilessly, severing limbs and decapitating heads until there was only a pile of black body parts against the wall.

Clifford could tell the men felt bolder for their action and having seen a group of their enemies destroyed. Now the larger units of men carrying packs of food and heavily armed with pikes, axes and swords as well as long-arms, began to thread up into the city.

Clifford himself was leading twenty men and they found their first mob within ten minutes of the barracks. Several dead delf already lay in the street and another group was being shoved towards the mob. When the crowd first saw them, they gave a cheer, but their faces changed when the soldiers lined up into two ranks, and lifted their long-arms to their shoulders.

"Let the delf go," Clifford called out in a clear voice. "Go back to your homes."

There was muttering and shuffling amongst the group.

"What's going on?" asked a man, taller than the others and well-dressed.

"We're bringing law back to the city. Go home. I'm not telling you again."

"There's only the angels' law," the man said. "We're saving ourselves. What are you doing? You could not save us."

"Let the delf go. Come up this side of the street," Clifford said to the delf, pointing to the left hand side where they were clear of the guns. The delf looked between Clifford and the tall man with fear in their eyes.

"Do nothing," the well-dressed man said. "They won't fire if the delf are among us."

He turned his back on the soldiers and walked towards a delf who was still being held by the arms. He began to raise a pistol towards the delf's head. Clifford's own pistol fired and the man dropped to the ground, clutching his ruined shoulder and screaming in pain.

This was a moment of truth. His men had just seen him shoot a man. Would they support him?

"I can shoot you all one by one if that's how you want it."

There was muttering from amongst the others. Clifford wanted to turn around, to make sure that his men were still with him, to look at their faces. Out of his peripheral vision, all he could see was that the raised long-arms did not drop. There was some muttering from the front rank of the mob, but the delf were released. They ran for the shelter of the soldiers. Then the mob began to disperse. One helped up the well-dressed man and they hobbled down the street.

Two streets on, they rounded a corner. The street was filled with delf of Wootton's legion. There must have been nearly two hundred of them led by a tall sergeant with a great axe over his shoulder. The two units stood facing each other for a few moments, then each gave a cheer and they ran together hugging and patting each other on the back. They were a legion again.

46

THERE WERE NO watchmen at the gates surrounding the two great wooden sheds of the warehouse district and they stood as darker hulks against the night sky. Soldiers quickly smashed the lock and forced the gate of the great compound in the south west of the city and fanned out inside the walls.

The warehouses stood on one side of a single road with a gate at either end. On the other side of the road were stables and wagon yards. Several lights showed from inside the upper storey of the stables. Clifford called his officers and sergeants together. He looked at two of them.

"Rouse the stable hands. Harness up as many wagons as you can find, then start bringing them to the warehouses. Put saddles on the horses too. They'll need to do double service. The rest of you, start preparing supplies."

The soldiers and delf dispersed. They had collected many of the people as they went through the city until the soldiers were heavily outnumbered by the families with them. Clifford had armed as many of them as he could with weapons taken from the mobs and from the dead in the streets, wolf and soldier alike.

A group of children with a few of the older delf, were shepherded into the side of the nearest warehouse. The warehouses were cavernous wooden structures supported by a forest of pillars. Amongst the pillars were the goods ready to be shipped out to the empire or traded in the city itself. On the one side were bales of cloth, on another a stack of crates and further over were rows of sacks. There were metal canisters and jars of pottery both rough and workaday as well as ornamental.

Above it all hung a higher floor filled with bales of hay and sacks of grain, brought up by a great crane which jutted out from the front of each warehouse.

Within minutes, potential supplies were being found from amongst the goods and carried towards the great doors. As they piled up, a young delf came running in. He was directed towards where Clifford was trying to ascertain what was inside a stack of sealed wooden boxes.

"The first wagons are ready," the delf said. Clifford nodded, then called over to some men at the front of the warehouse.

"Turner! Open the doors. Start loading what we have as they bring the wagons over."

The great doors rolled open with a rumble which sounded loud in the night. Clifford winced, and as he did so, he realised how quiet the night had become. He knew they would have to work very quickly if they were to succeed.

Wagons were soon rolling out of the warehouses along the street. Clifford began to walk up the road, exhorting everyone to work faster. As he reached the second warehouse, a wagon came out of it carrying a full load of tall, pottery jars. The men driving the wagon were chuckling and smirking. Instantly suspicious, he waved his hand at them to stop.

"What's in the jars?" he asked.

"We thought they'd be good for carrying water, captain," said the driver.

"What's in them?" Clifford insisted.

"Vezi," the man said.

"Ditch it, now. We can find water elsewhere."

The soldier was slow to respond.

"*Now*, soldier. We don't have much time."

The man called over a couple of his fellows and they began to heave the jars off the wagon. Satisfied his orders were being carried out, Clifford moved on. He heard a crash of breaking pottery behind him. The men were looking clownishly at a puddle of the spirit as it spread across the cobbles from a broken jar at their feet.

"Just get it out of the way!" Clifford called.

He continued back down the row of buildings. The roadway was full of horses.

Then he heard a commotion ahead. There was shouting and men began running for the gate through which they had come, weapons glinting from the scattered lanterns. His hair prickled and he drew his sword, then began calling men behind him.

He met Buller coming towards him.

"Don't worry, sir, it's the delf."

Out of the darkness came a great crowd of city delf. Keti was at the front still in his old legionnaire's jacket and he shook Clifford's hand.

"We brought who we could, but most were too afraid to come."

"We have what we have," Clifford said. "We need to leave soon. We will have to make do with what we can find from here in a short time. Have your people help."

The delf went out to assist and more wagons began to line the road. There were not many, but he realised they could not take much longer. Keti was standing by him, frowning.

"Wagons will be too slow, once we get into open country."

Clifford looked at him. He knew he was right, but they needed as many supplies as they could if they were to stave off hunger as well as pursuers.

"Captain, our first priority is to escape from the city. Our second is to survive once we are outside of it."

Regretfully Clifford nodded.

"Start loading up the children and make for the gates. For the rest we will just have to take what we can on horseback. We leave in ten minutes."

Clifford found himself a horse and gave the order for the eastern gates of the warehouse quarter to be opened. The convoy of wagons, horses and people started to move forward. The leading horses had begun to leave the gates when shouts of panic erupted from the front.

Shots were fired and people started to run back inside the gates. Clifford spurred his horse and galloped towards them, but the horse was skittish. He regretted the loss of his military trained horse. As he did so, the first wolf soldiers marched through the gate. Even in the darkness he could recognise the shape of them, the mass of them as they hacked at everything in their path.

Soldiers fired at the animals despite their previous experience of its ineffectiveness. Clifford wheeled his horse. He needed to organise a defensive line. To his relief, a body of pikemen was already moving forward. Even as they did, he was aware of how pitifully small a group they looked as more and more wolves poured through the gates. The phalanx drove into the wolves and pushed back the centre, but to the right of them, the wolves began to encircle them.

"Pull back!" Clifford bellowed, but it was too late. Their line of retreat was already being blocked. The pikemen began to move in the only direction they could: the interior of the nearest warehouse.

Hundreds of the wolves were coming now. He caught sight of Keti who was marshalling unarmed civilians back and into the warehouses to make room for the fighters to move in the street. Clifford felt sick. He had made a trap for them all. Their only hope was to pull everyone back out of the warehouse district to disperse into the streets. And what would become of the delf?

A couple of bolts of flame passed over his head as crossbowmen fired a few paltry burning arrows into the enemy host. He gritted his teeth. It was not over yet and they would take as many of the wolves with them as they could.

They had lined up the wagons across the road to form a kind of barricade. It slowed the beasts down, but did not stop them. There was a crash, then another as two were overturned, spilling the contents of the tall jars across the ground.

"Keti!" Clifford called. "Get everyone out of here who isn't armed. Just get them out."

But there was already screaming coming from the nearest warehouse and people were streaming out.

"They're in the warehouses!" someone called.

The creatures had filtered around the back of the buildings and found a way in. They were in danger of being surrounded.

He drew his sword and fought back tears. They were not for himself, but for the people he had hoped to save.

"Fool! Fool!" he snarled at himself. He should have listened to advice. The plan was ridiculous. How could they have hoped to escape the city? Even if they had escaped the walls, they would surely have been overtaken and destroyed on the plain.

People were fleeing past him, making for the western entrance. He saw soldiers amongst them. He let the first ones go as he stood in his misery. Then he shook himself and moved his horse into the way of the others. He levelled his pistol at the next two, a man and a delf.

"Stand and fight!" he shouted. "You're not dead yet!"

The dark melee was suddenly lit by a bright light as a sun wraith rose over the fighting and swooped into the wolves. The solitary wraith lifted Clifford's spirits. There were Knight Wardens amongst them, however few there may be. It seemed to put new heart into the frightened soldiers before him and they turned back to the fighting.

For a few moments, the tide of beasts appeared to halt, but then it began again, pushing the thin line of soldiers back. From his vantage point on the horse with the fading light of the wraith, he could see a sea of black wolf heads pouring through the gates and into the buildings.

Then there was another glow, but this did not come from the sky. It was a blue glow and it came from the ground amongst the wolves near the wagons. It was fire. Something was on fire on the ground. And he remembered the vezi, the inflammable alcoholic spirit which had been spilt across the road just where the fire arrows could have landed.

The fire caught on the wagons and he saw some of the wolves take the flame. Then there was more fire, this time from the interior of the warehouse.

He could see beasts aflame. They would walk a few paces then appear to lose purpose and blunder into their fellows. He rode forward, an idea forming. It was desperate, it was stupid, but when hope was all but lost, it did not matter.

He rode into the beasts slicing at them with his sword, but his horse was terrified, its eyes rolling back and it kicked out as blades and claws cut into it. Clifford fell, landing heavily on his wounded arm. He gritted his teeth and picked himself up.

"Into the warehouse!" he said to the men around him. "Follow me!"

He led the custodians inside amongst the stacks of goods. The heat was already strong. The group of soldiers looked at their leader, expecting the next order. Out of the corner of his eye he saw the wagon loaded with vezi. It had been pushed over to the side of the warehouse behind them.

"Just get them to follow us," he said.

The wolves needed no encouragement. They came on. The fire was spreading quickly and had started to lick at the walls. Sparks were rising.

The piles of goods and racks and shelving broke the flow of the wolves and slowed them down. The soldiers began throwing things in their path from around them. Clifford grabbed the arm of one of a group next to him.

"Come with me. There's vezi on that wagon. Pour it out! It burns!"

They ran for the wagon. The first jar they simply tipped over the side where it smashed, the spirit spreading quickly across the floor. Another was offloaded and grappled awkwardly to an aisle by two of the troopers.

"Get a lantern!" called one to another standing nearby. Then they laid it in on the ground and started rolling it forwards. Some soldiers were being pushed back by the mass of beasts ahead of them. The jar began to pick up pace.

"Out of the way!" called one of the rollers. The jar ran up against the legs of the soldiers in front. Several fell backwards over it. The others turned to face what they thought was a new threat to see it smashed by a descending wolf axe. Then the lantern was thrown into the puddle and a blue flame leapt up. Soldiers and wolves alike caught light. The fire caught onto clothes hanging from a rack.

There was a wind inside now as the air warmed and flowed and Clifford became aware of the ceiling being on fire. Of course, the hay was baled up and stored in the upper floor. It too was alight.

The inside of the warehouse was lit orange and red and shadows surged around the walls. Carrying as many jars of vezi as they could, they made for the rear of the warehouse. A single small door was at the back. An axe swiftly broke the lock and they were outside in the cooler night air. But the open door created a draft and they saw the flames inside fanned by the breeze.

He saw more flames now. They were leaping from the roof of the warehouse onto the one next door. They ran down the rear of the warehouses. They found the back door of the next one and smashed some of their jars and spread the contents around.

The seething crowd of beasts was packing tightly into the cathedral-like vastness of the warehouse. As they moved, they pushed over stacks and walked over the heaps of spilled cloth, sacks and bottles. Blazing timbers and gouts of fiery straw fell from the roof. Some of the wolves had become walking torches.

The heat was intense. Smoke roiled out of the roof, throbbing red within from the flickering flames. Clifford looked about him. He could still see some of the custodians fighting, but there were so few now. He saw Buller rallying a group of weary, desperate soldiers. All of them were wielding axes. They were sweating in the heat and grimy with soot and dirt and blood. They simply ran forward into the wolves, hurling themselves at the wall of them. Many in the front rank of beasts fell, but there were more behind them. He saw Buller's body drop, his head removed at a single stroke while his comrades fought on. Only two were left to retreat as a crowd of the wolves came on. Then there came a great creak and a section of the grain loft floor fell in one great fiery section, a crashing sheet of flame. Men and wolves disappeared beneath it and a wall of hot, displaced air billowed out in all directions. Stoked by the sudden onrush of wind, the flames roared higher and the heat seemed to redouble in intensity.

The fire was everywhere now. It was impossible to see across the building from the smoke. Blackened bodies appeared momentarily through the reek, then were hidden again. Clifford dropped to the ground, his eyes stung and were running with tears. He was coughing so hard he thought he would choke. There was no air. His left arm was agony and he clutched it to him. He tried to crawl across the floor, but it was filled with broken goods and burned and splintered wood, some of it still smouldering. He froze as a great, black leg passed him and his back tingled with the expected blow, but it never came as he lay covered by the smoke.

Then arms were dragging him. He cried out in pain and he felt a sharp stab and warmth running down his leg.

He regained consciousness outside. He was being sat up and someone was binding his leg. He inhaled the clearer, but still smoky air and was spluttering again, hacking coughs wracking his body.

"Get it out of you, captain," said a voice he recognised as Keti's. They were outside the gates to the warehouse which were still open. Through them he could see both buildings, now alive with fire and their doors shut.

"What's happening?"

"We got them. They're burning in the warehouses. They just kept walking into them. We locked them in. What now, captain?"

"They know we're here now," he said. "Help me up."

"I don't know you can," Keti said.

"Then you can support me. Get me up."

Keti pulled the captain up and Clifford could see him better now. There was a deep red cut across his cheek and beard and his face was blackened. But through it, the whites of his eyes shone out.

"Can you stand?" Keti asked.

There was still a pain in his leg.

"I can't stand on my leg."

"That does not surprise me. You have a hole in your calf, but you will live."

"Gather who you can. We have to fight now. We can't outrun them. Bring fire. Move everyone up to the gorge. We take the fight to them."

47

BERWICK AND RAUL joined a crowd fleeing the city and heading for a gate on the coastal side. They appeared to be mainly men and women, but they thought they saw delf amongst them, cloaked as many were against the wind from the sea.

They were jostled and carried along by the crowd, but everyone seemed too set on escaping from the anarchy to be curious about who their fellows were.

Once out of the gates however, the two of them slipped away and into the trees. Keeping out of sight, but just inside the forest edge where the vegetation was a little thinner, they made their way quickly. They were soon around the side of the city. They watched the walls for movement, but all eyes seemed to be turned inwards, for that was where the enemy was.

Had they only paused for a minute or two they would have met someone they had known before.

They made their way over the ridge to the north of the city. Here the bones of the escarpment had exploded from the ground, forming a jagged spine of knuckles and fingers of rock. It ended in a sheer drop and a jumble of rocks which formed a natural wall to the northern part of the city at the head of the gorge.,

The followed a handful of locals along a narrow path which led along ledges and tracks that would have been difficult for goats. Once out of the rocks, they slipped away from the Linanans who more interested in their own flight than the actions of a couple of strangers. Now they had found a flat chunk of rock with the city before them, the forested ridge behind and the plain to their left.

"What be happening?" Berwick asked.

Raul looked down from their vantage point above the city and shook his head.

"The city is out of control."

Raul turned and scowled at him. "You know, for a moment when we arrived, it looked as though things were different here. I let myself think that this place was different."

"But they didn't build this city out of this hate. Something has happened."

"You happened. Your kind."

Berwick thought of answering, then looked back at the mobs in the streets and the smoke drifting across the rooftops. He did not feel as though he had an answer for Raul. He changed the subject.

"So how be we to get Rodon?"

"Not through that. Your friends would string me up as soon as look at me."

"We can't just leave them to it."

"Berwick, I do not know what you want to do. You cannot stop a murderer in Collenium, yet you think you can stop a civil war in Linana Pivaki?"

Berwick knew Raul was right. He hung his head and felt like a raw recruit again. There must still be a way to find Rodon. He looked inland at the old quarter on the far side of the chasm. Even from where they stood, they could see wolves on the bridges and the on the far side. There was no way they could move safely through the city and certainly no way they would be able to cross the chasm. That only left one way.

"We'll have to outflank them and come in through the rear. I'll have to go in on my own. If I be not with you, I reckon I'll be safe from the wolves."

"I will not argue with you about that," said Raul.

He could leave now. This was his chance. It had never been his battle. He had done what he had said he would do and led the two men to Giles. He could go home to Esella. And the baby. She would ask him about this journey, about what had happened. About what had happened to Berwick and Rodon. He would not know. Someday, perhaps he would. Berwick was not even looking at him. He could practically see the thoughts going through the soldier's iron head. He was still a boy really. Only a foolish boy would have risked himself as he had done to pull Raul out from under the wolves' feet when he had a clear path of escape. Why should he help him try to kill himself again? And for what? Grafton? He hardly knew the man. Just because he had married a delf. True, he was unlike other men. He seemed to accept delf without question while still acknowledging their difference. As for Rodon, he had been the cause of death and torture to countless delf. He had only changed his mind when he had witnessed the madness of the Archbishop and seen the Light Doctor die defending a human farmstead against the nightmare legions. He owed these people nothing. He would go home and tell Esella he had left them to fight their own wars in a country where their long lost cousins had shown their true colours.

Why was that Berwick ignoring him now? He did not even seem to think Raul should come with him. Did he think the delf would simply leave now? What did he think of Raul? Why had he even come back for him? He was outraged. Did Berwick have such a low opinion of him? His sudden anger flooded out of his mouth.

"You expect me to go now do you not? Or just to wait here while you go off on your own?"

Berwick turned back with a look of surprise on his face.

"No," said Raul. "No, I have come this far. I will go with you. I need to pay back that bastard Rodon for staying behind."

"While we got away?" Berwick asked. A smile was playing around his mouth. He was an irritating boy.

"I will not owe anything to a man," Raul spat.

Then Berwick shook his head in bewilderment, stood and shouldered his long-arm.

"Then let's find a way out of this city and down onto the plain."

The Archbishop was fuming. He paced in silence to the far wall, then turned to look at the man. He was one of Giles' men and his face was pale.

"They have burned my wolves?" the Archbishop demanded. "*Burned* them?"

"There were many casualties on both sides, Your Grace," the man said.

"But they dared to burn the warriors of our Lord?"

The frown slipped down his face like a visor.

"I will bring in the wolves from the plain."

"Your Grace, they are watching over the remains of the legion," said Lord Giles.

The Archbishop looked at him as though he were a fool.

"Then we will destroy the legion first. We will finish off these sinners quickly. They have had more than enough time to save themselves. This city be damned. It be foul, it be stinking. This be an empire of the damned and it *will* be destroyed. I will wait no longer. I will send them all to the fires of hell."

Even as he spoke, the wolves on the plain surrounding Kallick's legion began to move.

As Edward's force moved up through the streets, they met people, human and delf fleeing in terror. Fire seemed to be springing up in many parts of the city and dark smoke was drifting across the sky bringing an early evening.

The guardsmen were armed with pikes, swords and torches, axes and spiked clubs. It was not long before they were confronted by a crowd of wolves. They were running down the street, loping grotesquely on two legs.

Edward formed up his troops with pikemen at the front. As the beasts came on, they lowered the pikes and charged at the animals. Some were skewered by the pikes, but others came on, running under the sharp points. Their teeth and claws fixed on the guardsmen, but other soldiers came from behind, swinging swords, axes and clubs.

Edward was held back by Keti. He shouted orders, but there was nothing he could do. His troops were locked in a combat which would end in the death of one side or another. It was a struggling mass of bodies. He could only watch at the hacking and clawing, as the bodies fell and were walked upon.

Then he realised the movement had eased, the men were hanging back, at a loss. There were no more wolves to fight. He limped up to his men. They looked at him with wild eyes, their faces glistening with sweat and blood. Too many of them lay on the ground, still or groaning. Surely they could take no more of this?

"They're spent already," he said to Keti. "And who knows how many wolves there are."

"We'll fight them all!" one of the men said, his teeth gritted as he walked amongst the wolves. He had overheard Edward's remark.

"Not at this cost," Edward said under his breath. The man did not hear him. He had turned back and was hunting amongst the wolves for movement.

Edward turned to Keti who was watching him. Edward shook his head.

"We must do something else to force them back," he said.

"How will we do that?"

"We fire the city. The fire will drive them back."

"But we will have no city."

"What will we have if they overrun us?"

48

THE ARCHBISHOP TURNED back to Grafton who stood, pale faced and confused by a table. His fingers played idly on its surface. He kept his eyes on the Archbishop. This one was unpredictable, he thought. There was no knowing how he could react to the most seemingly innocuous remark. Grafton was a clever man, but he was paralysed with fear for his daughter and fear of this man. When he tried to think of how he could escape from this situation, he could see nothing but the Archbishop standing before him.

The clergyman clasped his hands in front of him and a friendly smile floated up into his face from under the skin. For a moment, Grafton felt relief: this man meant him no harm.

"Mister Grafton," the Archbishop said, then paused and studied Grafton. "I understand you be an educated man. That you taught at the university." The Archbishop smiled again. "Before your downfall." Then he frowned and looked past Grafton's left ear. It was a small frown as if he had momentarily forgotten something of little importance. "Before you married a devil." He looked at Grafton once more. "Whatever could have possessed you?"

The smile had gone now and the Archbishop was staring into Grafton's eyes. Grafton did not know whether to meet the gaze or look away. He met the gaze. Perhaps if he looked into the eyes of this madman he could try to read what was in his mind a moment before he spoke and somehow gain an advantage.

"Where be she now?" the Archbishop asked.

Grafton's head spun. Did he already know the answer? Surely he did. He knew other things about him. There could be no harm in telling him.

"She died." Grafton's voice came out unprepared; half whisper, half croak.

"And be now in Hell," the Archbishop said gently, "where she waits for you." His gaze moved across the room to Rua. "And your daughter."

Involuntarily, Grafton's eyes flicked towards her.

"It need not be long before you be reunited."

Then the Archbishop's tone changed. He relaxed and strolled away.

"Now, I would like to ask you once again about this engine of yours which we found in the street. It be an impressive device. What does it do?"

His voice was light. Grafton said nothing.

"We found light sponges with it," the Archbishop continued. "I know what they be. I know how they be used, but I must admit, this be new to me. What be it?"

Grafton hesitated.

"Hmm?"

Grafton cleared his throat.

"It is merely something I was experimenting on. I like to...play with things."

"This be serious play. The devils don't play with their sorcery. I have seen it here too. So, tell me. What does it do?"

He looked at Grafton, then, without moving his head, he spoke again, but not to Grafton.

"Cut off her little finger."

"No!" Grafton said, but the guard had lifted her hand to his knife and her finger dropped to the floor.

"Charlie!" she called again, but did not flinch. There was not even any blood.

"Rua, I'm sorry!"

"She took that well, Mister Grafton. Your daughter has the false strength of Satan in her. Only witches do not bleed. Would you like to see her burn?"

Shocked, feeling sick with fear and anger, Grafton gushed out the answer the Archbishop wanted.

"It cuts rock. That is all. I was helping in a mine. Nobody here was interested in my work, but the Naadu were. That is all it does. It burns the rock and cuts it. I was playing around. I did not have a use. I was just playing with the light out of curiosity."

The Archbishop held his eyes. He held them for half a minute, then he began to nod.

"A cutting tool. Of course. So simple. Then you will show us how it works. I have it outside. You can show us now. Bring the girl."

Henry Clifford sat with his head in his hands in the room. He had closed the curtains. He wanted to close out the world, but the noises of the city had changed too much. He had never noticed its background noise before. It had always been there. But it had changed now. There was no regular murmur and bustle; now there was silence punctuated by shouts and gunfire.

Then there came a rattling on the front door. It turned to banging. Someone was pounding on it. The mob had come for him. He had expected them. Sooner or later they would blame their rulers for what had befallen them.

The banging stopped and there was silence once more. He lifted his head from his hands. That was not the silence of a mob. Mobs were never silent. They needed noise to keep up their courage.

"Henry!" called a voice from outside. "Henry, are you inside?"

It was Fitzwarren. Clifford roused himself. By the door to the hallway, a short barrelled long-arm was leaning against the wall, a bandolier full of bullets hung on a peg above it. He picked up the long-arm and went to the front door.

"Henry!" came the voice again.

He drew the bolts, turned the handle and opened it slowly, the gun pointing through the gap.

"Good God, Henry. It's only me. Don't shoot."

Clifford opened the door fully.

"What are you wearing?"

Fitzwarren had on a helmet and breastplate. He had a brace of pistols in his belt and a kindling axe in his hand.

"Off to war, Fitzwarren?" Henry asked.

"I'm leaving."

"And going where?"

"As far as I can. Others are leaving too."

"They will find you."

Fitzwarren looked at his old friend and the gun in his hand.

"I thought you might go down fighting. Edward is."

"Edward? Where is he?"

Suddenly Clifford realised there was more he could do than sit at home and wait for the mob.

"They broke out of the barracks," said Fitzwarren. "He has fought his way up through the city. They are at the North Bridge now, waiting for the wolves. Or perhaps the wolves have already come. Are you coming with me?"

"No," Clifford muttered. "No," he said, louder this time.

"Then, goodbye." Fitzwarren held out his hand and looked Clifford in the eye. "I don't know if we'll meet again."

Clifford took his hand, but said nothing. Fitzwarren let go of his friend and quickly walked away down the street. He did not turn back. Clifford watched him go, then he went inside and lifted a heavy bandolier off the hook. Resting the long-arm in the crook of his arm, he pulled his front door closed behind him and walked up towards the bridges.

One of Giles' men jogged into the room and leaned into his ear.

"My lord, I thought you would want to know before we brought him in. We have found Mr Rodon."

Giles liked to think that little surprised him, but this did.

"What, here?"

"Yes, my lord."

"Show me."

Giles followed the man out and found three other Melion soldiers guarding Rodon, his wrists tied.

Rodon did not look surprised to see him. He looked at Giles with the same expressionless face he remembered from many years' experience. Rodon was an intelligent man and a capable soldier, yet here he was bound and guarded.

"Well, well, Thomas. I be astonished to meet you here. Did you follow us?"

"In truth, when an embassy sends itself to new lands, it be wise to ensure the message be agreeable to the state."

"Of course. The manor lords be no longer trusted. I had forgot."

"And you consort with a suspected murderer."

"Do not you worry, Thomas. He has been under the watchful eye of my men at all times."

Giles smiled and clasped his hands. He would surprise Rodon yet. He made his next sentence sound as everyday as possible.

"His Grace will be pleased to see you after all these years."

"His Grace? The Archbishop?"

Yes, that moved him. And what was that he saw in Rodon's eyes? Not fear, surely. Guilt?

"Why yes. Did you not realise? He be here."

For Rodon, everything fell into place.

"So the wolves be his own Limbo dreams."

"So it appears. And he has angels too. God be on our side," smiled Giles.

"You cannot believe that. He be –" Giles detected hesitation. "He be not well."

"You mean he be mad? Oh yes. Quite mad and with an army which be holding this great city to ransom."

"I tried to turn him from his course to save Outreterre before."

"Yes, I remember you telling your tale after the battle. It did not work of course, but Outreterre thanked you for your actions."

"So why do you side with him now?"

"In the circumstances, it be the most convenient strategy. Be you alone?"

"There was only time to arrange a passage for myself."

Giles chuckled.

"You be not used to lying, Thomas. Well, I think it be time you and the Archbishop were reacquainted."

<h1 style="text-align:center">49</h1>

THE DARK CLOUDS massing in the sky gave a false impression of lateness in the day which made Raul and Berwick hurry all the more. They would alternate jogging with walking, feeling exposed as they crossed the landward plain. They could see a small town ahead of them and agreed they should skirt around it away from the river and look for a small boat on which they could make their way into the city.

The town looked deserted, but they could see bodies in the streets which clearly showed that it shared the troubles of the city.

They came upon the wolf army quite suddenly. The town stood above the river's floodplain and the dip in the topography hid them until almost the last moment. Even then, the first thing that they saw was the remains of Kallick's legion with its back to the river while around it, in a motionless crescent, stood the ranks of dark wolves.

Raul and Berwick dropped to the ground. They looked at each other wide-eyed. It was the stillness of the wolves which disturbed them the most. In the ranks of the other army, a wall of flags half way into the mass of men and delf rippled broadly in the wind. Filling the ground between the two armies were the dead. Toppled and broken were six cannons, the barrels ripped from their carriages lay like amputated limbs.

"That be the end of that then," Berwick muttered.

Raul shook his head and gestured a short way downstream to the dam across the river. Behind it stood the reservoir, its high earth banks rising a little higher than where they lay and covered in bushes and young trees. From its eastern corner, the aqueduct flung itself out across the open ground in two layers of arches until it reached the landward walls of Linana Pivaki.

"We can cross the river that way. Avoid the wolves."

Berwick needed no further convincing. They ran, bent double below the brow of the rise. Reaching the dam, they paused and looked around. They were now about a hundred yards from the two forces which were still facing each other. The wolves were motionless, but there were signs of movement amongst the men and delf soldiers.

The two surveyed the next part of their route. They needed to cross open ground to reach the bush covered front of the dam. They felt naked as they went over the top of the slope on their bellies. Berwick had his face planted in the grass and stalks of it tickled his nose and poked into his eyes. He was in two minds as to whether to just run as fast as he could before he reached cover or to crawl slowly, exposed to anyone who might turn their head in his direction and see their dark shapes on the grass.

"The eye catches movement," Raul had counselled, and so they were crawling inch by inch. Berwick felt his fingers dig into the soil and under his nails and he pulled himself forward, pushing with his toes. As he did so, he peered towards the two armies.

He was glad there was some movement in the legion's camp. There seemed to be more towards the rear. It was not hurried, but it was reassuring. Had they been still as well he would have felt more obvious.

They were over the crest now and heading down towards the front of the dam. The bushes at the top were thinner and lower than those further down, but they were still welcome cover. Perhaps he could get up and run just that last little way. It was such a short distance.

Then his peripheral vision caught some movement. Already it had become instinctive to look at the wolves. Something was different. He could sense Raul had noticed it too. The wolves were stirring.

"They've seen us!" he whispered.

"No."

Raul was right. None of the wolves were moving towards them or even looking in their direction. Their attention was fixed on the ranks of the legion. The legion appeared to have noticed it too. Amongst their ranks there was a flurry of movement as if someone had put a stick into a group of ants.

The wolves began to move towards the soldiers.

Tears were running down Grafton's cheeks. He did not understand what had happened to his daughter. She was not herself. He desperately wanted to hold her and comfort her, but he was being held strongly by one of the angels. She had not even winced when the Archbishop's men had struck her, but he could not bear it.

"And you say you use cobs to turn the wheel? Cobs? Could men do it?"

"They would need to be trained to work together, to work at the same speed," said Grafton looking at the ground. He could no longer make himself meet the Archbishop's eyes.

"Soldiers can march in time," said Lord Giles. "If a cob can do this, so can a soldier."

"Show me," said the Archbishop. "Lord Giles, have four of your men come to us."

The light needle was set up on the terrace outside the Tower of the Stars facing across the gorge to the rest of the city. Lord Giles' four men were stood waiting next to it, looking at the machine with childlike curiosity.

"Instruct these men," said the Archbishop.

Grafton swallowed and spoke quietly, but precisely.

"You must start slowly, the sponges need time to warm up. You must all go at the same pace. That is important. Keep up the speed and go faster as I tell you to."

His box of light sponges had been brought too and next to it was the bag he had been carrying from the tower of Velkuri.

He took a light sponge from the box and loaded it into the chamber.

"Start walking," he said. "A little slower."

The men were struggling to keep the same pace. Benedict stood by the wheel.

"Come on," he snarled at them. "Cobs can do this."

A fifth of Giles' men appeared. He was carrying a drum. The captain took it from him.

"I took the liberty of having Roper search for one of these."

"Well done, captain," said the Archbishop. "I could always be proud of the men of Melion."

The captain passed the drum to Grafton and the angel let go of his arm.

"Beat that to the time you want. They can march to a drum."

Grafton took the drum and started to beat it. Sure enough, the soldiers were more comfortable with it and began to march together and speed up together. The big wheel groaned, but ran smoothly on its bearings.

All at once, a jet of light shot out from the needle. It leapt out of the square and struck a tall building on the street below. The stonework began to melt and fall away.

The Archbishop was triumphant.

"A marvel, Grafton. An engine that can harness witchcraft. But how could we use such a cursed device? If it burns rock, it can burn a city can it not?"

Grafton realised what he had done and stopped drumming. He sank to his knees. Confused, the soldiers began to slow in disorder, the light went out.

"No matter," said the Archbishop. "Turn it on the city. Burn it!"

He looked at Grafton.

"As for you, I think you have shown us all we need."

"Build a pyre for this man's daughter. Out on the terrace where it can be a beacon of their destruction."

"You promised!" exclaimed Grafton.

"I don't keep promises to witches. You will burn too, soon enough."

Edward stood at the edge of the chasm. The city was burning behind him where they had set it alight to trap the wolves. On the far side of the bridge, he could see more of them massing. He turned to face his men. They looked back at him grimly. He looked from face to face, resting for a moment on each one. In their eyes he saw determination, but he also saw fear, and worse, he saw hopelessness. He saw men and delf who would fight to the death because there was no alternative.

Two cannon were drawn up behind them, dragged onto small terraces which overlooked the roadway to the bridge. They would remove the heads of too few wolves before they made it over the bridge and closed with his weary force.

He walked down to the bridge and stood in the middle of the roadway. On the far side, he could see wolves still joining the mass already gathered in the streets above the chasm.

He heard footsteps behind him and then Keti was at his side, looking across at the enemy too, but saying nothing.

"Perhaps we should make a stand on the bridge," Edward said. "It's a narrower point to defend. We could march to the far side and fight them as they force us back."

"We could throw a few over," Keti said. The wind was ruffling his hair and he pushed it out of his eyes.

Then they were silent again. Edward's eyes drifted over the scaffolding which stood in three places along the left hand side.

"Keti." He said it quietly, an afterthought.

Keti looked at him.

"Could the cannons hit the cables?"

When Rodon was brought in, the Archbishop forgot about Grafton. He went pale and the room fell silent. Silver and Giles understood the relationship that had once existed between these two men. Rodon had been the trusted retainer and confidant who had deserted his master to warn the peoples of Outreterre and Unama that the Archbishop was unleashing the nightmare legions on those lands. Giles had respected Rodon, but Rodon had turned into a mewling devil lover who was weakening the power of the manor lords in favour of a burgeoning trading class.

The Archbishop's face was calm as he approached his former friend. Rodon watched him impassively.

At the last moment, the Archbishop thrust his face into Rodon's.

"Judas!" he hissed. "I nurtured you. Taught you everything, yet you betrayed me to the devils."

Giles wondered if Rodon would say anything. He remembered what Rodon had told the manor lords afterwards about how he had tried to turn the Archbishop from his course a number of times, but that he had seemed obsessed. Giles could see that now. Yes, the Archbishop was mad, but it would only be another madman who would attempt to reason with him.

Rodon said nothing in reply. He looked directly into the Archbishop's eyes.

"Still the same gruff dog he ever was," Giles murmured to the captain.

The Archbishop's hand whipped around and slapped Rodon hard on the side of the head.

"How dare you look me in the eye, worm! You be not fit even to crawl upon the ground. How great be the Lord that he delivers my enemies to me. One by one you shall fall. A fire awaits you in this life and the next."

Not knowing what to make of the sudden movement amongst the wolves in front of Kallick's legion, Berwick and Raul pulled themselves on. With their attention fixed on the wolves, they reached the bushes in no time. They did not wait. Still on their hands and knees, they moved faster, careful not to brush past the plants and make the foliage shake. They breathed easier as they reached the thicker undergrowth towards the bottom of the slope. Soon they would be across and would be able to make their way down the far bank of the river.

A distant cry sounded. It was immediately followed by more shouts and the sounds of clashing metal. Raul and Berwick exchanged a glance. Fighting had clearly broken out again. Suddenly there was a blur of movement next to him. Raul hurled himself back before he could think. There were figures in front of them, coming at them from the trees. Berwick's hand had moved to his pistol when he heard a voice.

"Wait!" it cried.

The figures paused. Raul was picking himself up. A large delf stood over him with a spade. Others were eyeing them suspiciously.

"We nearly killed you!" hissed the one in the middle.

They were wielding axes and shovels and Raul could see only strain in their eyes.

"Come with us. We need all the hands we can get now," said the delf in the middle again. The large delf pulled Raul to his feet and they were ushered through the bushes to a large hole in the ground.

"We are almost ready to blow it, but we need to move these boxes in."

"We be not from the legion," said Berwick, looking around and trying to understand what was happening.

"I can see that," said the lead delf. "Grab a box and pack it into the hole." He saw their hesitation. "Do it now, or it will be all over for the legion. Can you not hear the wolves are attacking? Kallick is relying on us.”

“What are you doing?” Raul asked.

Berwick realised. “They be going to blow the dam,” he said. Immediately he picked up a box and carried it into the hole. It was a cave cut into the face of the dam. Already the inside was lined with boxes.

“How did you get them here?” he asked.

“Swam across the river at night,” one of the delf said. “We floated them on small rafts. I hope it is enough.”

As they carried the boxes, there came a slithering from above them. Berwick looked up startled as a wide-eyed, pale faced man covered in mud and grass skidded down through the trees.

“The top is ready. We must blow it now. They’re being forced against the river.”

“We have one chance,” said the leader. “Blowing it early will help no one but the wolves. Grab those boxes. They are all going in.”

“But the legion will be washed away too!” said Berwick.

“Not all,” said the delf next to him.

They worked without talking, packing the boxes into the opening against the back wall. When they were all away, the leader pulled the end of a fuse from under some leaves and took it into the cave. He was gone a few moments before emerging again.

“This one first, then the top.” He turned to the man who had come from the top. “I will light this now. Light yours and join us on the bank.”

“You be going back?” said Berwick.

The delf stared at him.

“I know not who you are, but Kallick’s legion stays together. If this dam does not break, we will join our comrades and fight and die with them.”

“That is suicide,” said Raul.

“That is loyalty. You are not the legion. Go where you want.”

Then they were gone, grabbing their tools and making off into the bushes.

Raul looked at Berwick.

“For a moment I thought you were going to join your soldier friends,” he said.

Then they were running through the undergrowth, no longer trying to hide. They came out of the bushes and reached the far bank. The aqueduct stretched above their heads. They went under it, slowing as they climbed to the top of the bank and slipping in their hurry.

On the bank from which they had come, the wolves were closing around the remains of the legion. It was being forced into a smaller and smaller space.

At the top, Berwick was already on his way towards the city, but Raul called him back. His hunter's vigilance had noticed something. On the bank a little way back from the dam wall, a small rectangular boat had been moored.

"We take it down the aqueduct," said Raul. "It will lead us right into the north east quarter of the city."

They jogged back to it. Raul climbed in while Berwick was untying it. Raul looked around and Berwick cast off, jumped into the stern of the boat and picked up the oar. Then he started to paddle towards the viaduct.

There was a dull thump. The ground shook violently and a brown explosion bloomed in front of them. Bushes and dirt were thrown up and out from the front of the dam. Small waves rippled across the surface of the reservoir from the centre of the wall.

Berwick felt like he was bracing himself for something. Then it came, a louder explosion than the first. From the top of the dam wall, water, dirt and rocks were thrown into the air. He put up his arms, squinting at what might come down. A rain of spray and dirt pattered into the water and around them. There were larger sploshes, then Berwick flung himself backwards, the paddle dropping from his hand as a rock landed in the boat between him and Raul.

As the debris settled, there was a sound of rushing water. A small breach had been made in the top of the dam and the lake was beginning to flow over it.

"That won't do anything," said Berwick, then he looked around for the paddle. It was floating in front of them, its lighter weight carried it ahead of them and towards the breach in the wall. Raul turned and looked at him.

"Paddle with your hands," said Berwick. "Turn it towards the aqueduct."

A lazy current was pulling gently on the boat. It was caused by the sudden flow of water to the centre of the dam. They were being pulled slowly but surely towards the front of the dam, but away from the channel to the narrow aqueduct. They dipped their hands in on the right of the boat, trying to turn its nose. As they moved forwards, Raul at the front could see the fighting. The plan had failed. The legion was doomed. There was a fair flow of water pouring over the front of the dam, but it was never going to flood the valley. They managed to turn the boat and began to paddle it towards the mouth of the aqueduct. As they moved closer, Raul could see the river muddying from the new waterfall.

What he could not see was the damage being done to the front of the dam by the eroding cascade as it stripped away more covering of the already weakened dam wall.

It gave way without warning.

The only sound was the water. It was moving faster now as it poured, out of sight, from the new breach below the surface. The boat began to move away from the aqueduct once more. Then the whole centre of the dam crumbled, sinking away in an instant. The surface of the reservoir had given way beneath them and they were caught in a torrent as the water rushed towards the gap.

On the bank below them, the legion was fighting on. Then as the churning brown water boiled angrily towards them, they broke and fled back towards the river. As he gripped the sides of the boat, Berwick saw them leaping onto the wagons and sprawling onto what he realised were rafts. Then they were picking up speed caught in the inexorable pull of the violent waterfall.

The wolves followed the men and delf into the water which swirled around them wildly. They hacked as they moved and soldiers were cut down as they ran. Others turned to fight, even as they retreated, but the wolves' advance had gained momentum now the defence had broken apart.

Nothing was going to stop them going over the waterfall now. Their boat was turning as it neared the edge. Berwick gripped the sides. He felt his stomach drop, then his world was water and noise and confusion. It was tipping and he closed his eyes to the spray, but his mouth was already full of water, he felt its cold cloak around him and they were spinning. For long moments he could not tell which way they were going, nor what was happening.

The face of the dam was not quite straight where the vegetation had once grown, but had now been stripped away by the force of the water. They had slid down it in the flood. The boat was full of water and he was soaked. He looked forward and saw Raul gripping the sides and grimacing, his face and clothes dripping. As they hurtled around, slewing sideways, he became aware of others in the water.

There were both men and wolves. The men called out to them or swam or floated, grabbing onto what they could. The wolves flailed as if trying to run, unable to cope in this new element. There were hundreds of them in the water. Some lashed out at men as they floated past them, but they were unable to control their direction.

They were still moving quickly, but the ride had smoothed out somewhat as the flood carried them downriver. Wagons and rafts accompanied them and there were many bodies floating with them, some hanging onto flotsam, others face down.

They bore down on a wolf. It was struggling in the water and as they came closer, they realised it was almost swimming in its attempts to reach a weary looking delf. At the front of the boat, Raul rose unsteadily to his feet, picking up his long-arm by the barrel as he did so. He swung it hard at the wolf's head which jerked to one side, Raul lost his footing and fell backwards heavily into the boat. Berwick reached out and grabbed at the hand of the delf in the water. He reached him, but the grip was slipping. The wolf was moving slower now. Berwick reached over the side with his other hand. The delf's face was trying to hold on, but his grip was loosening. Berwick reached further, grabbing the delf's wrist with his other hand, then gripping again. He had him. Now all he had to do was haul him in. He felt arms around his legs. It was Raul pulling him back. Together they pulled the delf into the boat and he lay in the bottom gasping as they floated amongst the wreck of the two armies.

The wolves struggled less now; they simply floated with the current down the river towards the smoking city. The wolves began to stamp. They began together, quietly at first, but it increased in volume. Edward stood ready as Keti marched at the head of sixty pikemen and brought them down to the bridge. When they reached him, he took shouldered an axe and despite Keti's remonstrations, led the soldiers onto the bridge himself, trying in vain not to limp.

He needed to do something against the stamping, so he started to sing. His voice floated out over the space around them and was lost. But the rank behind him heard and the song caught until all sixty were singing. It was picked up by those watching. It was a marching song, plain and simple, but he could not bear their own silence in the face of what would come at them sooner or later.

The phalanx of pikemen reached half way. The wolves had begun to stamp louder. It was all the stranger because they made no other sound, but stood tramping on the spot, watching with their dark eyes.

They were three quarters of the way across. Edward had not expected to get this far. He began to wonder what to do, how far to go. He did not need to think for long. The wolves began to move. Like iron filings pulled by a magnet, they swarmed down between the parapets of the bridge.

As they came, a narrow beam of bright light shot out from the far side of the gorge. It hit the corner of a building next to the senate and soon afterwards there came a strong smell of burning as the masonry began to melt.

"What is it?" Keti asked.

"I don't know."

As he said it, fire leapt up inside the building as timbers were exposed and caught light.

Clifford could not afford to be distracted.

"Double!" shouted Clifford and the men broke into a run, pikes down.

They hit the wolves hard and drove at them, the full weight of the phalanx pushing against the dark crowd. At the back, more wolves continued to join the crowd and the horde pressed forwards against the men and delf. Gradually, Clifford and the soldiers were being pushed back.

As they went, he could see more and more wolves piling onto the bridge and the more that came, the faster they were moved back. Two pikes snapped. The wolves at the front were being propelled forward by their fellows.

Half way again and the pikemen were finding it harder to keep their feet. Then the cannons started to fire. The first ball sailed harmlessly over the beasts, bounced on the far wall and dropped into the chasm. The second ploughed into the wolves, but still they came on, walking over the fallen.

50

CHARLIE SAW THE smoke before he saw the city. It had been visible from miles away as he trekked across the top of the escarpment, a drifting grey cloud rising into the clouds as it blew inland.

Now he was close, he could see it billowing up and glowing red from the fires beneath it which were still out of sight. The tangled forest was ahead of him and he was coming to the gap from which he and Rua had stood and looked back at the city only a week before.

He was looking out onto a different city. Much of it was obscured by the dark smoke, but he could see the flames now as they danced among the buildings.

The ruined Star Tower, which lay closest to him, was just as it had been, lit by a dull flat light. Although there was smoke around it, none appeared to enter it. It rolled past as if held off by a wall.

Charlie left the horse tethered at the edge of the forest, just inside the trees where it could not be seen. He wondered what to take with him. How long would he be gone? He took some dried meat and put it the pockets of the long coat. There were two bandoliers of bullets in the saddle bags, one of which was partly empty. He put them both on, but they were heavy. He took off the partly filled one, feeling comforted by the weight of the full one. He took one of the pistols and slipped it in his belt. Lastly he pulled the long-arm from the saddle.

He looked across the open ground between the trees and the walls. Nothing stirred. He could see no movement in the Star Tower either. Smoke still rose from the city behind and there was the sound of gunfire. He felt a dead weight in his stomach. He did not know what he was going into and could not believe he was walking into a war. He had been there before, but then he had been a child, an observer. He hadn't really understood what was going on.

He lifted up the long-arm in both hands and looked at it, wondering if he would need to use it. It made him feel both stronger yet more vulnerable. If he had a gun, he was more of a threat to someone else. He shrugged that off. Had he not been chased down when he was unarmed? He decided he was better off with the long-arm and the pistol hanging by his side.

He patted the horse's flank.

"Someone'll come and get you," he said. Then he looked out to the city again before sprinting, zig-zag, across the open ground until he reached the stones. There he dropped, breathing hard. He rested the long-arm across his knees and looked towards a pile of rubble where the walls had broken. He looked above him too, half expecting someone to be watching him from the walls, but there was no one there.

He crawled along the ground. The long-arm was heavy and awkward, slowing him down, but he was afraid to give it up. He moved on his elbows, pushing himself with this toes and looking ahead, pausing every few moments to listen.

When he reached the breach, he could feel his heart in his ears. He removed his hat, pulled himself up the stones and peered over the top. There in the flat grey light lay hundreds, probably thousands of bodies. Across the middle was the broken tower and his stomach lurched as he saw legs protruding from under the stones.

Towards the rear of the enclosure hung the misty entrance to Limbo. He recognised it now. It was the origin of the grey light which lit everything in a flatness without shadow. As he looked at it, the ground shook and his heart missed a beat. He had forgotten about the earth tremors.

How would he find Rosa? Seeing no one standing, no one indeed who appeared to be alive, he stood up and walked warily through the gap in the wall. Even as he did so, the ground shook again and it continued to shake as he walked. He looked down at the closest faces for Rosa. None were Rosa or what he remembered Rosa as looking like. He had only met her that one time. She had been tall and long haired with the same oval eyes as Rua, although her eyes were not like Rua's. He stopped and looked around. It was going to take a long time to find her and all that time he was vulnerable.

He cast his eyes across the whole tower courtyard, hoping her face would leap out at him from the hundreds. His eye was caught by the way into Limbo. It was a larger entrance than the one through which he and Rua had escaped.

He walked towards the whiteness of the Limbo gate, casually looking at the sleeping puoli as he passed them and stepping over their bodies. When he reached the gate, he looked at the mist. What lay beyond it? He walked closer until he had reached the edge and could look in. He could see nothing. He moved a step closer. Behind him, the courtyard still appeared to be full of mist. He thought again of what had come through the gate, then he stood back and turned. He shivered. He needed to find Rosa quickly. After that, he was not sure.

He had not gone far when a voice called out.

"What are you doing?"

He froze. Two men were standing inside the main gate watching him. He could not think of an answer. His hesitation seemed to have decided them. Each was raising his own long-arm.

"Who be you?" they asked.

He was five yards to the left of a tumble of rubble from the central tower which had leaked out to the side of the main collapse. He altered his course.

"Stop! Who be you?" they called out again.

His heart was thumping. The ground shook as he was about to leap behind the stone and he ended up losing his balance and falling rather more quickly than he intended. He pulled the long-arm from over his shoulder.

"Come out or I'll fire," called one of the men.

Charlie's back was pressed against the wall. He had to keep the men away. They would not know him and he could not explain himself. Thoughts were flashing through his mind, but they came to an abrupt stop when the gunshot cracked and he heard the ping of the bullet on the fallen masonry by his head. There was a gap in the stones next to his head through which he could see the two men. They were hesitantly walking very slowly towards him as if they were trying not to make any sound. His anonymity gave him some protection. He rested the barrel of his long-arm on the stone and pointed it through the hole, aiming at the ground in front of them. Then he fired.

They stopped as the dust kicked up in front of them.

"Don't come any closer!" called Charlie, trying to sound confident and menacing. As he reloaded frantically, he tried to work out which of the two looked to be the leader. He saw one look at the other and decided it was the one who had stayed looking ahead. He aimed low. He thought of the big man who had tried to kill him and who now lay dead miles behind him. He did not want to kill this man, but they might kill him.

The men raised their long-arms, one after the other.

"Come out you bastard," said the leader.

Charlie fired. Even as he did so he wanted to take it back, to not have fired. There was an instant cry of pain. Both men were on the ground. He looked again. They were moving. Both of them were moving. Charlie felt some relief, but also fear. What had he done? Now they would really be after him. Then he saw the blood and the man groping for his leg, perhaps his shin. The other was looking nervous.

"Get out!" called Charlie. "You're both in my sights. Get out or I'll fire again."

Even as he said it, he wondered what he would do if they did not leave.

The man on the left took the hint. He raised both hands and raised himself onto his knees.

"We'll go," he said. Then he took the groaning man under the shoulders, taking hold of the long-arm across the injured man's chest with each hand, and dragged him away and out of the gate.

Charlie relaxed, but only for a moment. He had to assume they would be back and that they would return with more men. He needed to find Rosa.

He had to remember where they had been sleeping. She had been nearby. They had not been far from the breach in the wall, so he worked his way along from there in increasingly large concentric semi-circles. Some of the puoli did appear to be sleeping, so much so that he walked with a light tread for fear of waking them. There was an unnatural silence about the whole place.

There was something strange about the puoli too, something about their sleeping which made them appear to be dead. He paused and looked down at the one next to him. He had a yellowish, bony face. Perhaps they were all dead. Charlie watched him. The realisation prickled up his back that the puoli was not breathing. None of them were. If they were dead, there was no point in trying to find Rosa. But it had been days, how could the bodies look so fresh?

He bent closer and reached out his hand slowly, afraid to touch the man's skin, afraid that the puoli would suddenly waken at his touch and grasp his hand. He swallowed and touched the puoli's cheek, pulled away, then touched it again. His face was warm. They were alive, but suspended.

Then he remembered his previous time in Limbo. Time had slowed down so that days could appear to pass in Limbo where much less time was happening in the worlds. So Limbo had leaked into the Star Tower. He shivered again, although he was not cold, and moved on. He hurried now, scanning to left and right.

She found her about twenty feet from the Limbo gate, directly in its centre. He bent over her and put out his hand. She too was warm.

"Rosa," he whispered. "Rosa, wake up."

She did not stir, she did not breathe. The tremors had no effect on her. He shook her gently.

"Rosa," he said again.

She did not move.

He looked around, replaced the bullets he had just fired from his long-arm, then hung it over his shoulder. He put his hands under her arms. She was a dead weight. Where should he take her? Out of the courtyard, away from the influence of Limbo. That had woken Rua and he could only expect that to have the same effect on Rosa.

He began to drag her towards the breach on the wall. It was difficult. He had to manoeuvre his way through all the bodies. As he did so, he would look up at the gate, expecting at any moment to see someone coming through it and all the while trying to think what he would do if and when they did.

His way was constantly blocked by the bodies on the ground. Once he tried to drag Rosa across the bodies, but it seemed somehow disrespectful, as if they would know what he was doing. He continued to drag her down the rows of bodies, which meant moving away from the break in the wall. At the furthest point, he looked up again. There was a figure in the courtyard doorway.

He knew there was something wrong. The figure looked too tall to be a man and there was something behind it. It was tall and powerful and was wearing a shining gold breastplate. As it moved forward, Charlie realised that what was behind it were wings. It looked like an angel.

Charlie knew it was not human. He knew he was looking at something from Limbo. He laid Rosa on the ground, lifted his long-arm and fired. The angel was some distance away and his shot missed. He was nervous about shooting with so many puoli nearby. The angel kept walking towards him. He took out the pistol and, holding it steady in both hands, fired again. The angel jerked, then started forward again. He looked. He had hit it, surely. He was close to the wall now. He started to drag Rosa across the bodies. He had no time for niceties.

The angel was moving more quickly. Charlie was almost at the wall. He put Rosa down and aimed his pistol again. He fired. This time he saw the hole appear in the breastplate, but the angel did no more than pause. He fired again and the same thing happened. He picked up Rosa and started to drag her up the stones, but the angel was closing in now.

It was large, far taller and broader than a man. Its beautiful face was impassive beneath its curled, blond hair. It moved with menacing grace.

Fear gripped Charlie. His heart was pounding, but he was looking for something, some other weapon. To his left, in the lee of the fallen tower, the stones had fallen in such a way that a large slab hung across a heap of stone like a small roof. As the angel came on, he heaved Rosa across to the stones and half rolled, half flung her underneath it, then stepped out in front, grabbing two fist sized lumps of stone as he did so. They had served him well before.

He launched the first one at the angel. It flew wildly past the thing's head. He took the left hand one in his right hand and threw again, as hard as he could. The stone crunched into the angel's left cheek. Its head kicked back, but its expression did not change. Still it came at him. Hopelessly, he stood across the fallen Rosa and emptied the pistol into the chest of the angel. Each ball made a hole in the breastplate and the angel shuddered with the shock of the impact, but it would not fall, it would not die. It extended its arms, its blank eyes staring into his face.

Then there was a noise, flapping, a sound of wind and something blue swung in front of him. There was a brief moment of scrabbling and what at first appeared to be a large blue bird had crashed into the angel, passed in front of Charlie and was away, lifting up towards the far side of the courtyard.

For a moment, Charlie stared at the angel. It had been decapitated. With only the stump of its neck, it had been reduced to little more than Charlie's height. It had been knocked out of the line of its path and continued in a kind of stagger, its arms held blindly in front. It tripped on rubble and tumbled into the heap of stones. There it continued to squirm silently, swimming clumsily on the loose stones.

In disbelief, Charlie looked about for the blue bird. He saw it soon enough. It was perched on the far wall. It was the size of a large dog. It had folded back its wings and was holding the angel's head in its front paws. Putting its head on one side, he saw it take a bite from the head of the angel. He dropped a ball into the breech of his long-arm, then tipped a measure of powder in to prime it. As the creature pulled its own head back and moved the angel's head around and tried another bite, he wound the breech back into position. Next he would reload the pistol, but then the bird squawked and tossed the head to one side. It fell to the ground, bounced, rolled and stopped. Then the flying beast raised its head and looked around. Its eyes rested on Charlie.

With barely a second's pause, it pushed itself off from the wall, its wings outspread and glided towards him. Charlie lifted his long-arm. He had one shot and then he would be unarmed, one shot before the angel reached him.

As the creature hung towards him, he followed it with the gun's sights, pulling his left hand back towards him to better support the barrel. He waited a moment longer, then fired.

With the explosion of the pistol, there came a screech. The creature crashed onto the ground by his shelter, flapping wildly. Desperately he grabbed at rocks and hurled them at the thing. The animal screeched again, then leapt into the air. It circled dizzily, then whirled back in a wide circle, apparently confused by the gun going off so close to it. Then it looped around as if to gain some air for another pass at Charlie – and vanished through the Limbo gate.

Gingerly, Charlie stood up and watched the misty gateway, waiting for it to come flying back at him. He waited and watched, hardly daring to breathe. Maybe it would come back in a few more minutes; maybe it would never return. He could not keep watch on that gateway for ever.

Then a cold rush went down his back as his hairs stood on end as a thought occurred to him. There could be more. He whirled and scanned the courtyard. No, he was alone with the puoli.

He knelt down again and reloaded both pistol and long-arm, glancing around him as he did so. Once that was done, he lifted Rosa once more. When he was almost at the wall, he looked out across the open ground towards the forest.

There was no sign of his horse, but perched amongst the trees on the edge of the forest were dozens more of the same large blue creatures.

51

RICHARD AND GEORGE were sitting quietly in the shadows of the room. A candle was burning low in front of Rua who was sitting cross-legged on the floor.

"It's no good," she said, turning around. "I cannot concentrate. I am thinking too much. When I did it before, it was quite dark. But I know you are there, it is hard for me to relax."

"There are shutters outside," said George. "We could close them and we should go outside."

"But we could miss her going to sleep."

"Maybe you need to sleep too," said Rua. "Charlie told me you did that before, you all tried to dream the same dream."

"We tried to think the same thing, to think of home or a person. But we had the light then. Solimo, the Light Doctor, even the Mage. They all used the light from the sponges when we dreamed. We don't have any."

"I have never needed the light to travel to Limbo. Dreams don't need the light. I know you can follow the light or simply follow your dreams. I am first generation puoli, so my dreams are strong."

Rua lay down on the floor. A little awkwardly, Richard lay down too, head to head so that he was lying in the opposite direction. George closed the shutters and lay on his bed.

"I'm glad the bishop can't see me now," he said.

Despite his worry, Richard grinned.

Richard's thoughts wandered restlessly. He kept thinking of what could have happened to Charlie. He thought about what Rua had said about the dead man called Fycher. And then his thoughts tumbled about Unama, Solimo and everything he had told them about dreams, the light and Limbo. He kept trying to settle his mind, to focus on Charlie, but he was too tense and trying to relax was only making it worse. He gave up on trying to relax. That was when he went to sleep.

He was in Limbo again. He was walking down the crumbling slope to the Mage's light tower. He was with Charlie and Raul and Berwick and the other soldiers. Then he slipped. He reached out to stop himself sliding down. He felt a hand grabbing his.

"Help me!" he called out, pulling on the hand and sitting up.

All the blood had drained from George's face and he was gripping Richard's hand. Rua was sitting up.

"It didn't work," she said. "We are only in Limbo."

Henry Clifford saw a narrow blade of light stretching above him and parallel to the ground. He was running under its arm as it moved across. He turned to see what it was pointing at and saw it hit the corner of the Senate house. Pieces of it began to fall away, slip down itself like treacle. This was new devilry.

He reached the chasm. He had heard the cannons begin to fire, their dull roar like thunder over the quiet city. It was only as he came around the side of the buildings which bordered the chasm that he could hear the shouting from the troops on the bridge.

The soldiers were formed up around the mouth of the bridge. There were pitifully few and merely the two cannons perched above them. They were firing into the midst of the black crowd which was filling the bridge now, pushing against a few dozen soldiers who were steadily giving ground.

Suddenly the bridge rocked. One of the cables fixings had been carried away by cannon fire. He realised they were deliberately trying to destroy the bridge.

He saw Edward standing to the back of the phalanx of pikemen who were the last line of defence against the oncoming wolves. He ran towards him.

"Edward, what are you doing? You can't destroy the bridge!"

"We have no choice."

"But at the expense of history?"

"Bridges can be rebuilt."

Edward jumped forward and put his good arm on the back of the nearest soldier.

"Shoulder to shoulder. Our strength is in our comrades!"

Edward was no longer listening to him. Henry felt like an irrelevance. He had tried to save the people. He had tried to save the city, but Edward in his obstinacy had ignored him and risked everything. There was no longer anything to be gained from playing the politician. Edward had forced everyone into being soldiers. Yet here they were, being forced off the bridge. The last redoubt was about to fall.

Many of the wolves and the last soldiers on the bridge had been knocked off their feet by the snapping of the cable. The wolves had briefly lost their momentum, but others from behind were piling over them. The few remaining pikemen were finally forced off the bridge. They were pushed to one side. The wolves' way forward was now clear.

Henry Clifford cast about for a weapon. His long-arm was going to be of no use here. Just behind the pikemen an axe lay on the ground where it had been discarded or dropped. He ran forward and bent to pick it up.

"Father! What are you doing?"

The bridge was still swinging and it was hanging at a dangerous angle where it had lost its support. Then another cannonball struck the opposite cable support.

As Henry straightened, he looked back at his son. Wolves which had made it over the bridge were already running for him.

"For the Republic!" he called out. Then he turned and raised his axe, swinging at the head of the closest wolf. The axe lodged in the beast's head and it fell, but as he went to free it, he was toppled by a blow from a spiked mace. The senator crumpled like a sack being laid on the ground. Edward had no more time to think about it because the wolves hit the pikes.

Behind them, the bridge slowly fell away like a tongue lolling out of a mouth. As it went, hundreds of dark shapes spilled from it, dropping through the air into the gorge and out of sight. The bridge itself swung back, timbers rippling off, and smashed into the side of the gorge.

There was no pause from the near bank. Some of the wolves had made it across and the survivors of the custodian guard fell on them in vicious hand to hand fighting, buoyed by the knowledge that there was no longer an endless stream of their attackers.

The course of the little boat had steadied, but it still rushed headlong on the flood, bearing Raul and Berwick and the delf soldier with it. Around them were wolves bobbing helplessly and Kallick's soldiers clinging to rafts and flotsam. Ahead of them, the northern walls of the city were coming closer. They could smell the smoke which poured out of the city over their heads. They gripped the sides of the boat, neither of them comfortable riding fast moving water.

"Do you have a plan?" Berwick asked.

"No."

Most of the wolves had stopped struggling and were simply being carried by the water. They watched some of the soldiers in the water kick their way to the bank, but for some, the current was too strong. Those on rafts were faring better. With the combined strength of those on board, they were able to reach the bank. They saw some jump ashore with ropes and haul the raft in. Those ashore then began to run down the banks, throwing advice and ropes to their hapless comrades.

Berwick tried to steer towards one soldier, paddling with his hands. Raul and the delf they had rescued leaned over the edge and as they reached the man in the water, they bent and grabbed him under his armpits, falling back with him across the boat.

He was delf too and he panted and coughed up water.

"You are safe now," said Raul.

The delf kept shaking his head until he could speak.

"Safe? Do you know where this river is going?" He took their puzzled frowns for an answer. "If we do not reach the shore soon, once inside the city we are all following the wolves over the Falls of Linana."

Berwick and Raul looked at each other.

"What do we do?"

"Paddle!"

The right bank was closer, so all four began to paddle towards it. At first they were out of time with each other, but then they began to stroke the water together.

The city was closer, but so was the bank. A tree was leaning over the water. If they could get close enough to it, they would be able to reach out and arrest their movement. All four stopped paddling, ready to reach for the nearest branch as it loomed at them. The first delf stood and jumped. Just as he did so, the gauntleted arm of a wolf came over the side. The little boat rocked and they instinctively lowered their arms to hold on. The wolf's other arm appeared and then its head. Still holding onto the side, Berwick leaned back and kicked the wolf solidly on the snout with both feet. It fell back and away from the boat, but the branch had gone by now, the first delf they had rescued still hanging from it and starting to inch his way along it to the bank. Now nothing of help lay between them and the dark tunnel in the rock under the walls where the river flowed.

None of them was speaking now. They watched as the tunnel mouth came closer, waiting for something. Darkness descended and for a few moments they were blinded. Then they noticed shafts of light as they passed under drains. By their dim light, they saw that a stone walkway ran along each side of the river. It was partially submerged because of the volume of water. All three knew what they would have to do.

"The left bank!" said Berwick, so they would be paddling with what he hoped were their stronger right arms. They were frantic now. They could see light ahead of them and they did not want to be in the boat when they reached the end of the tunnel.

With a grinding sound, the nose of the boat hit the walkway and slowed. The delf was in the front and he bounded over the bow, onto the walkway where the water was still about his shins, and tried to hold onto the boat. The other two were on their feet, about to climb out too, but no longer paddling. The boat was slipping around so that it was almost side on to the flow. They could see things floating towards them but they were just shapes in the gloom. Berwick jumped and landed sprawling, with water in his nose and mouth, but he had gone before Raul had had a chance and the force of his jump had pushed the boat away and out of the delf's hands.

"Raul!" he shouted.

Berwick scrabbled to his feet, spitting out water. The other delf was with him as they splashed after the boat. It had swung right around so that it was floating backwards. They could dimly see Raul's shape in the stern.

They felt so helpless. The boat was picking up speed. They saw Raul straighten up, then they lost sight of him altogether. Had he jumped or fallen in? The boat continued. Light hit it as it emerged from the mouth of the tunnel and for a moment they could see it bobbing on the water against a mist of spray. Then it was gone.

Berwick stopped dead in his tracks, the delf beside him. He could not believe it. He leaned over gasping, his hands on his knees. Raul was gone. What would he tell Esella? He should have been the second one to jump.

"Move over!"

The voice came from his right, from over the churning of the water.

Raul was hanging by both arms from a beam running below the roof of the tunnel. He swung and landed with a splash on the walkway, falling awkwardly onto his knees.

Berwick knelt down beside him and hugged him.

"You delf be truly full of magic!" he said.

Raul pushed him away gently and pointed to some steps against the wall. They led onto the beam and across the other side to some more steps. It was a bridge.

They stopped just long enough in the tunnel to see wolves in the water in helpless silence following the boat over the falls. Then they started searching for a way out.

"If there be a walkway, there must be a way into here from the street," said Berwick.

"They use it to clear the tunnel of debris after storms," said the delf.

Not far from the bridge, they found a narrow access tunnel. Hearts still rushing from their ordeal and dripping with water, they took it, following the steps up to the surface.

Richard, Rua and George stood up and dusted themselves down.

"Incredible," murmured George. "And they call it Limbo?"

"The delf call it Unlembien," said Richard. "It's the world between the worlds. It was the Order who called it Limbo. Unama I could understand. This place....never."

They were in a cleft of the hills on the edge of a stony plain. They walked out onto the plain and a tower of stone stood there.

"What is that?" George breathed.

"It's the Mage's light tower," said Richard. "We're back. Look, this may have been my fault. I was dreaming of this place."

"I was too, at least, those hills are familiar," said Rua. "It was where the wolves came from."

They walked further into the plain, feeling extremely small. They kept their eyes on the huge light tower, while Richard was searching nervously for any sign of the nightmare soldiers who had surrounded it the previous time he had been there.

Solimo turned a page. For some reason, even though he was engrossed in his reading, he had just thought of Richard.

As Richard and the others walked, the perspective changed, the land behind the tower moving into view. A smudge of white caught his eye. He squinted. There were dark shapes on the ground in front of it.

"Look! What's that?"

As he spoke a speck emerged from the white and flew up into the air where it circled.

"It's a bird," said George.

They kept walking towards the light tower. The bird flew down and alighted on the top of the funnel itself.

"That's a very large bird," said Richard.

It pushed off from the funnel lazily, spreading its wings as it glided towards them.

Richard swung his backpack off, rooted inside and pulled out the kitchen knife. It was at least a foot long and had an eight inch blade.

"What are you doing?" George asked.

"It's big and it's coming for us. Have you ever been attacked by a bird protecting its nest? And that one's big."

The creature was clearly heading for them now.

"That's not a bird," said Rua.

"I wish I had a shotgun," Richard said. "Put your bags over your heads. Run for the tower."

It was the closest cover there was, but the creature was coming in too fast. It had four legs and its claws were outstretched. Richard held his backpack in front of him like a shield and had the knife ready. He was running in front of the other two, hoping their moving target would be harder to hit.

The harpy swung in, talons raking at the bag. Richard cried out and slashed with the knife. He connected and cried out as a claw cut his arm. Then the harpy was away. It was carrying his bag. It dropped to the ground with it and started to tear at it with its jaws.

"Work around it. Anyone got a coat or a towel?"

George pulled a small blanket from his bag and handed it to Richard. Richard wrapped it around his left arm.

"I feel naked without that pack."

The animal found salami in the backpack and took bites out of it.

Solimo looked up from his book. He had heard a sound. Until he heard it, he had not realised how complete the silence was. He stood and went to the window. Down on the plain he saw four people moving. He looked again. Not four, but three and some kind of animal. It was sitting on the ground and the other three were moving away from it. He watched with interest.

He had good eyes. Was it just because he had been thinking of Richard that one of them looked like Richard? It was hard to say at this distance. Had he dreamed him up?

The harpy noticed the three of them moving again and it dropped the salami. This time it did not fly, it ran along the ground like a dog.

Richard knew with some animals it was good to look big, with some it was good to play dead. His gut told him not to play dead to this one. He put up his arms and ran at the creature roaring. It leapt at him and Richard thrust his left arm in its face. The teeth bit through the blanket and he cried out in pain again, but stabbed at it madly with his right.

It howled and let go and stood back snarling at him.

"Run!" said Richard.

The other two were hesitating.

"Just run! Now!"

They ran and Richard followed. The beast jumped off too. It was close, but it ran in an ungainly way, slowed by its folded wings. George was tiring quickly. He would not be able to run far.

Richard turned at bay. All he could see were the jaws of the animal.

At the same time the animal jerked its head up. It spread its wings as if to take off. Over Richard's head, a fiery wraith had floated. It hovered in front of the harpy. The creature eyed it up, then it seemed to decide it was no threat and it made to run at Richard again. In a blink, the wraith was on the harpy, there was a smell of burning flesh, and the creature lay dead on the ground.

Richard turned to look up at the light tower. Who had sent it?

The wraith hung in the air. George watched it with fascination.

"How is there a sun wraith here?" Rua asked, not expecting an answer.

Richard was walking towards the gate again, the other two caught up with him.

"Is this safe?"

"Somebody up there likes us," said Richard.

They reached the gate and were about to go through when someone emerged from the door above the steps and ran down to meet them.

"It is you!" said Solimo. "Are you real?"

"How am I supposed to answer that question in this infernal place?" said Richard.

The two of them hugged.

Richard turned to the other two who were watching the meeting with puzzled looks on their faces.

"Rua, George. This is Solimo."

Edward Clifford was exhausted. Around him, a dozen or so men and delf of Wootton's legion had collapsed or were leaning on their weapons catching their breath. The last of the wolves that had made it over the bridge lay twitching on the ground.

Clifford leaned for a moment on the parapet above the gorge, watching wolves churning in the water below the falls. A soldier so blackened with soot it was impossible to tell whether he was delf or man ran up and saluted.

"Captain, we think we've cleaned out the lower city, sir. We cleared fire breaks and forced the wolves into the amphitheatre. Then we threw in bombs and blew them to pieces."

"Good work, corporal. How many are you."

"Eighteen sir. But that includes citizens, me and the walking wounded."

"Good God."

He looked around at the few left from his detachment.

A saw a troop moving up the street towards them.

"Here they come now."

The soldier frowned.

"No sir, they're not ours. I left them organising the residents to put out the fires."

There were thirty or forty of them and they stopped and stood to attention. Two came forward carrying a stretcher. On it lay a tall delf. His face did not have a spare ounce of flesh on him and his hair was cropped short.

Clifford recognised him and snapped to attention.

"General Kallick! We thought you were dead, sir."

"Not yet, captain. Where is General Wootton?"

"I cannot say. I last saw him before the wolves first took the North Bridge."

"How many guards do you command?"

"Not even thirty. We think we have contained the wolves on this side of the gorge. The South Bridge still holds. They've sent no more across. Maybe he's out of wolves."

"Maybe. What say you that we take the fight to him. I am expecting more of my legion to come up behind us and some may have entered the old quarter on the river if they were able to avoid the falls. We have one hour to rest, arm up and wait for any more survivors. Then we cross the South Bridge."

"Sir, what about the people?" asked the corporal. "Can we use them?"

"The people turned on each other corporal. I don't even know why I'm fighting for them."

"It was not all of them."

Clifford sighed. He was past caring.

"Find who you can. Arm them as best you can. We'll march with them in the middle so they can't run away."

The corporal called to three or four of the exhausted troopers waiting by the bridge. They heaved themselves up and, going with the corporal, dispersed into the streets.

An hour later and a force of sorts had been mustered. To hide their numbers from watchers on the other side of the gorge, they had gathered in a square closer to the Senate. The Senate itself was still burning. Citizens were labouring with buckets in a chain gang, but smoke drifted from the roof and windows.

More of Kallick's legion had reached the city so that between them and the remains of Wootton's custodian guard, there were over two hundred regular soldiers. Their numbers had been swollen to more than double that with the addition of a motley citizen militia. They were armed with weapons which had once been used by custodian guard.

Non-commissioned officers were trying to arrange the militia so that they were between a vanguard and rearguard of soldiers.

Kallick and Clifford were watching from the corner of the square, the general leaning on a crutch.

"Are we reduced to this?" Clifford asked.

"We are the Republic's only hope. By the time any other legion hears about what has happened here, the city will be ashes and the Archbishop could be reinforced. My worry is that he has left us alone for so long since the fall of the bridge."

"I have set up the regulars as pikemen," said Clifford. "We cannot trust the militia to hold their positions and without that, we will be destroyed. They will be better to hack and slash at close quarters."

"Agreed. The main body will advance down the street towards the Tower of Stars. Put some skirmishers under Keti. Arm them with bombs, pistols and axes and send them around the side streets to worry at their flanks." The general sighed. "I wish I knew how many he has left."

"We can comfort ourselves that whoever is directing their attacks is not very sophisticated. So far it has simply been frontal assaults with overwhelming numbers."

"But there is much a general can do if he cares little for the lives of his troops."

Kallick ran his eyes along the ranks of his new command.

"I think that is enough curling of the pig's bristles. It is still a pig. I feel I should say a few words to them."

Kallick went to a balcony on a first floor window from where all could see him. The numbers were impressive, the faces less so.

"Soldiers of the Republic! Yes, you are all soldiers now. You all know how important this battle is. The enemy has been shaken by our counter attacks and now we must strike while he is off balance. You are the last chance for Linana Pivaki. Your children will talk of this day. 'My father was there, my mother was there,' they will say. "They saved this city. I am proud of them.' Now is the time you earn that pride, that you earn the gratitude of children yet unborn. Be strong, be fierce and we will throw all these beasts into the gorge! Today a new legion is born. Today I name you Hope's Legion."

He had hoped for a cheer, but only a few voices were raised and they faded into the nervous silence of the others.

He nodded to the front ranks which were made up of troopers from his own legion. They began to sing. It was a song to lift the spirit, a marching song. The tune was simple and even the militia began to pick it up.

"Sound the advance!" he called.

A trumpet blew, orders were shouted. Hope's Legion began to march.

Dusk was falling as they reached the South Bridge. There were no wolves in sight and the bridge was empty. Veterans scanned the buildings on the far bank, but the less experienced began to think the victory had already been won. They must have burned, drowned and buried them all.

The front ranks reached the far bank. When they did, Keti turned to look at Kallick with a questioning look. Kallick nodded, Keti signalled to a group around him and they broke away from the main column. The broke up into small units and ducked off to the right down alleys and side streets.

The legion marched along the top of the gorge where the street was wider than those amongst the buildings. Clifford looked back and could see the rear guard, made up of the remains of Wootton's legion leaving the bridge. They were all across now. He felt uncomfortable. This was too easy after the heavy attrition they had suffered. He wanted to order a retreat, but he knew the general was right. They needed to keep up the momentum of their earlier attacks. In those, they had used luck and their knowledge of the city. In this he felt they had thrown away their use of luck and the local knowledge was only a weapon for the skirmishers. They were walking into the unknown and all of them were tired.

A murmuring began to run back through the ranks. The vanguard had turned a corner. He heard a shout and they came to a halt, the militia stopping untidily behind them.

He went up to the front. There he saw that his worst fears had been realised. In their fatigue they had been focused on the wolves, but the Archbishop had held back some of his troops. They had forgotten about them because they had not taken part in any of the fighting.

Lined up across the street, faces blank, breastplates gleaming in the last of the sun, stood the angels with bright swords drawn. They did not move, they did not look as though they cared whether they lived or died.

It was going to be like starting again. It was like having to wake up, just as you sink gratefully into your bed after a very long day. Hope's Legion was not going to be a legion for long.

52

THE BIRD DOGS were still sitting in the trees. They had not moved since the last time Charlie had looked at them, hoping they had gone. He kept low and crawled back to where he had left Rosa. She was still sleeping. He sat in the lee of some rubble and slowly pondered his next move.

Rua was amazed by the Mage's rooms. She could barely listen to Solimo and Richard recounting their stories. Instead she wandered around the room looking at the tapestries and opening books at random, excitedly scanning the contents. How her father would love to see all this! George seemed to be torn between the two as well.

"So you think it's the Archbishop?" Richard was saying.

Solimo opened his palms.

"I can think of no one else. We left him here with these books, he used the Mage's nightmares against us, so why would he not dream some of his own?"

"But that meant he dreamed while he was here."

"From what I have read, the Mage could have done this too, but he was simply afraid. That is what he told us."

"Then what can we do?"

"I think there is a way from Limbo to Rua's city."

Rua turned sharply.

"To Linana? Is it near here?"

"Yes, you can see it from up here. Look."

Solimo led them over to the window and pointed to the patch of mist.

"Those look like bodies."

"The Knight Wardens would have fought them," said Rua.

"That's where that flying creature came from," said George.

"I have never seen one of those before. That was not from Linana. It must be from Limbo," Rua said. "But if that is a way back, we must take it while we can. I had wanted to find my father to help us understand all this. But he is safe in the desert somewhere and now Solimo can help us. And these books."

It took a few moments for Solimo to realise that his first reaction to Rua's faith in him had not been doubt.

"I will do what I can to help you," said Solimo. "I am a Light Keeper."

"You never used to weave sun wraiths," said Richard.

"No. I wove my first one here. It was that or be killed by two of the Archbishop's creatures. I have few sponges left."

"And you know what they are," Rua said. "You know how they were defeated before."

"The Mage used himself to funnel hope. I do not even know how to begin doing that. He said even he had never done it before."

"Would the Archbishop listen to a priest?" asked George.

They turned to look at him.

"I mean, he is an Archbishop, so we have something in common even if he doesn't value my lowly rank. But is there a doctrinal argument I could use?"

"I don't know," Richard answered. "You're the priest. All I can say is that little he does seems very Christian to me, although I could say that about a lot of Christians in the old days, and he's pretty medieval in his thinking."

"One thing is certain," said Rua. "We are getting nothing done here. I've been gone for days. Anything could have happened. And," she said looking at Richard, "Charlie is still there somewhere."

"He is. Come on Rua. You two don't need to come."

"I said I was coming and I'll see it through," said George.

"And if Charlie is in trouble, I will come. And if I can help your city, I will."

Charlie was surprised no one else had come into the courtyard of the Light Tower. Perhaps the wolves had moved on and he had been dealing with only those who had been left behind. There was only one way to find out. Leaving Rosa behind, he sidled up to the main gate, moving from cover to cover.

Reaching it, he looked out and immediately pulled his head back. Parts of the far side of the city were in flames and smoke was rising into the already leaden sky. The terrace in front of the gates was full of people and there were crowds in the square below.

Slowly, he peered around the gate once more and looked more widely and more carefully.

There were two pyres and next to each stood another angel holding a burning torch. His stomach lurched. Rua was on the one closer to him. Was it Rua, or was it dream Rua? He stared at her. It was dream Rua, he was sure of it. Any sane person would be terrified up there, but she simply stood.

So who was on the other? He hoped it was not Rua. It was a man. Who was it? He stared harder.

It looked like Thomas Rodon. How could it be Rodon? Weren't they across the sea where the Order never went?

Neither pyre was lit. There was also a machine, like a large cannon, or no, narrow funnel on wheels. There were men in long coats standing near it. Then he noticed that one man was being restrained by two of the others who had hold of his arms.

The Archbishop had been pacing up and down until Hope's Legion entered the square below the terrace. Then he turned to Captain Benedict who was with the Melion soldiers by the light needle.

"Have that engine ready for my command."

Benedict picked up the bag from the top of the box, removed a couple of sponges and placed them inside the chamber.

Grafton saw what they were doing. They had taken one of the sponges they had found in the light tower below the nebula.

"Not that one!"

One of the Melion soldiers shoved a long-arm into his belly and Grafton doubled up, collapsing onto the ground.

The four soldiers mounted the wheel, the drummer started a slow beat and the soldiers began to march.

The Archbishop leaned on the edge of the terrace parapet and looked at the battalions of angels confronting the last hope of the city.

"What be this raggedy army that dares to confront the Lord's angels!" he said with a disdainful smile. He turned to Giles. "Have you ever seen anything so pathetic?"

In truth, Lord Giles was impressed by the determination of the citizen army massed at the far side of the square below them.

"You have to admire their bravery, Your Grace."

The Archbishop rounded on him.

"Bravery? It be not bravery! It be impudence. It be arrogance. It be overweening pride to think they can challenge the Lord's vengeance."

He turned to Benedict.

"Let them see their city burn behind them!"

The needle was pointed at the city. The soldiers had settled into a regular pace and the machine was throbbing. The needle end began to glow and Benedict gripped the handles on the bulbous end.

Light flashed out from the needle, but this time it was different. This time, it came out like a spray, widening as it crossed the gorge in shifting shades of green, blue, purple and crimson.

The light needle swept across the city and Charlie gaped. As the light passed across his vision, what he saw changed, sometimes imperceptibly, sometimes dramatically.

One moment, the city was in flames, in another it was a ruin, or completely overgrown. There were different people in the streets, wolves, humans, delf, angels, puoli. He saw his father dead and alive, he saw each of his friends or saw them not. He saw angels flying, falling, standing, fighting. He was surrounded by angels, or he was alone. He saw Solimo in the distance. There was Rua, the real, true Rua, standing smiling in front of him, walking away, or sitting on a chair looking at him. Time could have frozen, for in a few moments, he saw everything that could be, possibilities flowering and closing in infinite number.

The whole city appeared to have stopped, were they seeing what he was seeing? There was a silence about everything with only the sound of the crackling flames and the roar of the falls to disturb it. It was as if everyone was holding their breath, all poised on the edge of a decision, suddenly aware that where they placed their next footstep, where they looked next, what they said, what they did could change everything.

The light needle, glowed red, Benedict let go of the handles with a cry. Its barrel started to wilt, then the whole needle collapsed in on itself, crumpling like a ball of paper. The great wheel tipped, scattering the soldiers onto the ground.

At that moment, it began to rain; great spots of it. Charlie could feel them land on his hat.

The Archbishop turned on Grafton.

"What did you do?"

His eyes were narrow and he did not move them from Grafton's face when he said the next words.

"Burn the witch!"

Perhaps Grafton had been trying to persuade himself that it was not going to happen, but at this, he suddenly wrenched himself free.

"No!" he shouted.

The two men either side went to grab him again, but the Archbishop waved them back.

"He will burn anyway. He can do it now."

Grafton ran for the pyre, but the angel standing next to it had already set its torch to the wood.

Crouched behind the gate, Charlie realised who the man was. Rua's father was about to die saving a copy of his daughter. How could he make him realise? He found he had moved instinctively to the middle of the gateway. There was nothing he could do. He could take one shot, maybe two before they either shot him or he had to take cover. And then what?

"Charlie!"

Dream Rua had seen him.

"Charlie!" she called again. With a sick feeling, he realised it sounded like pleasure at seeing him rather than the horror of her impending death.

Heads turned to look at him. It was too late to hide.

Silver looked at the two soldiers who had discovered Charlie in the Tower of the Stars.

"You said it was a spy. It be the sorcerer from the desert!"

"He must have killed the angel!"

The two knew what had happened to Fycher and now the angel they had sent in had not returned. One was already injured. They were thinking twice about how to deal with him. Their hesitation was enough for Charlie to turn back into the Tower of Stars and run.

Benedict jabbed his finger at the four men from the wheel and the drummer.

"You! With me!"

He ran for the gate with the others close behind him.

Grafton had turned when his daughter called out to Charlie. She was looking at someone. He saw a figure in a long coat standing in the gate to the Tower of the Stars. The flames caught quickly. He tried to run through them, his hands in front of his face, but the heat forced him back. Then he felt a great blow and was on the ground with the angel standing over him.

Charlie was sprinting for the breach in the wall. All he knew was that he had to escape. He was jumping over puoli, ducking behind rubble. His back was tingling expecting a bullet at any moment.

He could hear the voices behind, but he was at the breach. He stood there for a moment looking at the trees and realised there was no escape through the wall. He had forgotten about the winged creatures. Two of them stirred. They had seen him. There was a ripple of movement as all of them opened their wings.

Rosa! He could not leave her. The fallen tower lay between him and the gate. It would give him some cover. He dashed back.

"Where is he?"

"Behind the tower. Spread out. Keep low."

He reached the pile of stone where he had left her. She had not moved. He pulled her up and over his shoulder. She was slight and he could manage it, but his two paths of escape had been cut off.

Then other shouts came from the men.

"Look out!"

"Up there!"

There was rapid gunfire. He heard screaming. The harpies were flying over the wall and through the gap. Distracted by the men, they were ignoring Charlie off to their left. He thought of going back to the breach, but that would be running straight into the line of fire from the men and the harpies might see him. He half stood and looked around.

There was a way. The gate to Limbo stood unguarded behind him. It was the only way. Limbo was his chance for escape and Rua and Rosa his only hope for return.

The gunfire and shouting continued. From some of the shouts and harsh shrieking of the animals, he could tell the men were having some success. He had to go now before they turned their attention back to him.

With Rosa over his shoulder, and stepping around the puoli as best he could, he made for the misty portal.

"Stop where you are."

Charlie looked to where the voice was coming from. A man was pointing a pistol at him. His hair was shaved to his scalp and he was one of the toughest looking men Charlie had ever seen.

From a doorway opposite the short road up to the terrace, Raul, Berwick and the delf came running. They had armed themselves with discarded weapons. Had somebody been looking their way, they would have been exposed to view for a couple of seconds, but everyone was distracted by Charlie, Grafton or the two armies facing each other in the square.

The terrace was above head height to them, but Berwick and the delf gave Raul a leg up and he hauled himself over the balustrade. Now he was hidden by Rodon's pyre.

He scrambled up the faggots, his knife was out and he was cutting Rodon free. Rodon began to turn his head.

"Now we are even," Raul said and slipped a pistol into Rodon's hand. The angel had its back to him. He pulled an axe from his belt and threw himself at the angel. The axe caught the angel in the back of the neck, half severing it. It staggered around, clutching at him, but Raul dodged back, then ducked in again under its arm and swung up into the angel's chin. The head kicked back and the angel toppled, the head barely attached. And Raul was running for the next pyre. Flames were leaping up it now, the air around it rippling in the heat. Giles, Silver, Boyce and the two remaining soldiers were raising their guns. Then Rodon leapt from the pyre firing the pistol Raul had given him. Berwick and the delf they had saved from the river were charging up the roadway as fast as they could.

Then harpies came flying from the gateway.

Benedict looked Charlie over as he pointed the pistol at him.

"They talked about you as if you were some whoreson berserker with a liking for severing heads," said Benedict. "But I just see a scared boy with some nasty little friends."

The man started to move so that he would be between Charlie and the Limbo gate.

"If you've got any hexy tricks, don't try them on me. I'll put a bullet in you before you can do anything. Who be the girl? Why don't you put her down?"

"She's just a friend. Don't hurt her, she's done nothing."

"One of those half-caste bitches? None of them be leaving here. I should shoot you now. I know you be here with Rodon."

There was something moving in the mist. Benedict saw Charlie's eyes flicker.

"Don't even think of running through there. You wouldn't get a yard."

A shout came from behind Charlie.

"They've flown outside, captain!"

"Go after them. I've got the lad."

There was definitely a shape in the mist now, he did not know whether to look at the emerging shape or the man with the gun. The shape became clearer for a moment, then backed away. There were more wolves coming through. Even that line of escape was a death sentence.

Then it was coming again.

"Eyes on me, boy," Benedict snarled.

Charlie tried, but the shape was clearer now. It was a man, it was...

"Drop the gun," said the shape.

Both Benedict and Charlie looked now.

Benedict saw a kneeling man pointing a long-arm at him. Charlie saw his father.

Benedict fired from the hip, unaimed. The shot went wide. Richard's did not.

Benedict spun away, hit in the chest, his pistol fell on the ground. He stayed on his feet for a few moments, his eyes wide and staring, then fell back onto a puoli.

Richard stayed kneeling, sighting down his long-arm, but both his eyes were open as he looked at the fallen man. Then Charlie saw his father's eyes flash upward and widen. The gun lifted as he did so and he fired once, twice. There was a screech, cut off in the middle, then Charlie heard the harpy land heavily. He turned to see it lift a wing, before it lay still.

The second shooting seemed to shake his father out of a daze. He stood up and came towards Charlie, who still had the unconscious Rosa over his shoulder. There was further gunfire outside the wall.

"Come now," called Richard. Charlie started to move forward, but he realised his father had not been talking to him. There were others coming through the mist.

Charlie could not believe his eyes. First there was George McClure, then Solimo, then Rua.

Rua ran to him.

"You have Rosa!"

She had her arms out.

"I was trying to get her out."

He wanted to hug her, but he still had Rosa. It was not how he had envisioned their reunion. He laid Rosa gently on the ground. She knelt down to look at her friend. The moment had passed.

"I didn't know where you were," he said. He needed her to know he had not run away. "I thought maybe they'd got you. So I had to come back. And I thought if they were after you, maybe they were after Rosa too. I didn't know what to do..."

He almost felt tearful. His father gave him a one armed hug and over his shoulder he saw Solimo giving him a warm smile which was full of concern.

He remembered everything that was going on.

"Outside, there's...I don't know what...the Archbishop, Rodon..."

He realised just how confused he was.

And then the shooting came louder than ever.

There was complete confusion on the terrace. The Melion men were caught between the sudden frontal onslaught that had freed Rodon and an aerial one from the rear. Three of the Melion men came out though the gate after the harpies.

There was fury and indignation on the Archbishop's face.

The flames from dream Rua's pyre blazing behind him, he raised his sword like a cross and roared at the angel battalion.

"Destroy the pagans! Deus vult!"

Immediately, the ranks of angels began to move forward. Hope's Legion had been waiting too, but at this, the pikemen lowered their weapons and advanced swiftly, aiming for enough momentum to push the angels back. The two sides met with shocking force, but the angels were larger and heavier and the momentum did not last. Pikes were snapping and Kallick's force was being driven back.

A ball flew into the air from the angels' flanks. It landed amongst the angels. A few seconds later, the bomb detonated. Angels were blown apart, but their advance was relentless.

Raul was nearing the Archbishop. Rodon was close behind him. There were others coming from the gateway now. They looked familiar, he frowned, then his legs were knocked out from under him. Rodon had tackled him. He was about to curse him when he saw the Archbishop throw up his arms to protect himself. The harpy which had been diving at Raul tipped a wing to alter its course and grabbed the Archbishop's robes, lifting him up. He was too heavy for the animal to carry far and it dropped him into the flames of dream Rua's pyre. The priest cried out in pain. He floundered to free himself, his skin burning, his clothes catching alight.

The angel which had lit the pyre lumbered to free its master. Grafton, still groggy from being knocked to the ground by the angel, raised his head. He knew he was too late to save his daughter, the fire was raging. With a roar of anguish, he charged at the angel. It tripped on a log and crashed headfirst into the flames. It dislodged a flaming bundle of sticks which rolled on top of it. Its arms and legs ploughed up and down and it rolled out of the flames, but it was now a walking torch. It blundered towards the balustrade and tipped over.

The Archbishop was still scrabbling, then he felt himself being pulled. Rodon had thrust his hands into the flames and was dragging his former master from the pyre.

Raul was on his feet. What was Rodon doing? Now the Archbishop was clear of the fire, Rodon was rolling him and wildly patting him with his bare hands to smother the flames.

A shot rang out. Rodon convulsed, then fell across the Archbishop. Raul turned in horror to see Silver holding a pistol in both hands. Raul was still holding the axe. He threw it and it lodged in Silver's ribcage. With a look of surprise, Silver collapsed to a sitting position, blood pouring from his mouth.

There was an old man. Raul did not know him. It was George McClure.

George had removed a small vial from his pocket. He put his thumb in it and rubbed it on Rodon's forehead.

"Through this holy unction may the Lord pardon thee whatever sins or faults thou hast committed."

"What do you?" asked the Archbishop, the words struggling out as confusion reached through his pain.

"I'm giving the last rites. I will give you extreme unction next."

"But yours is a Godless world."

"Oh no, Your Grace. I see the Lord everywhere. He is in my heart. Look around you. Is he in yours?"

Raul ran over and knelt beside Rodon. He gripped his hand and his shoulder, shaking him.

"You cannot die, ironhead. I will not be saved by some human. I will not owe my life to one of your kind."

"Live with it," Rodon said through gritted teeth. "Go back to your family. Prosper. I've made my legacy."

He coughed hard and his fingers tightened around Raul's fist.

"Why did you save that bastard?" Raul asked. He was brimming with disbelief.

Rodon screwed his eyes up with pain, then opened them.

"He was my friend. Everyone should have a chance to redeem themselves."

"Not him. Not in exchange for you."

But Rodon's grip had already loosened. Raul let his hand fall onto his chest. He realised he was crying. He would never understand humans. Berwick came up and put his arm around Raul's shoulders.

Grafton was on all fours, his head on the ground in his hands, his body wracked with sobs. A girl came up to him. Slowly she crouched beside him and touched his shoulder.

"Father?"

Grafton turned his head.

"How?" he said. Then he was sobbing again, sobbing and clutching his daughter to him.

Edward Clifford was trying to rally the militia. They knew they were being forced back. The occasional bomb thrown into their midst was having little effect. Although the militia had not come into direct contact with the angels yet, Clifford could see that the phalanx would soon collapse. It would be up to him to prevent a rout.

"Hold the rear. Stand your ground!"

He was shouting orders he did not believe in. They were outmatched, outclassed and merely delaying the inevitable. He had seen the wonder of the futures displayed to him. Every other man and delf had stood amazed. What effect of the light it was, he did not know, but all he could see in his mind now was Linana Pivaki in ruins.

A man from the militia broke from the flank and started to run, two others started after him. Clifford stepped into the path of the first and pointed his pistol at the man's face.

"Back into line. Your fellows are relying on you to watch their backs."

The man hesitated then reluctantly returned, the others moved back into the line. The shouts and clash of arms from the front was loud, but Hope's Legion was steadily giving way.

George had moved over to the Archbishop. He touched the oil to his forehead.

"Through this holy unction may the Lord pardon thee whatever sins or faults thou hast committed."

"Do my angels fight?"

"Are they your angels, Your Grace? I had thought they were the angels of the Lord."

"I prayed for them and they came to me."

"But you created them? Forgive me, but you seem to take pride in them? Do they not obey you?"

"They obey the word of the Lord."

Solimo came up by his side.

"Let me see his burns."

The Archbishop's eyes widened in horror.

"Take that devil away. Do not let him touch me."

"What is a devil that shows mercy, Your Grace?"

Four men came running up to the terrace. Berwick raised his long-arm, but the delf at the front held up his hand. His other held a round ball.

"I am Keti." He was looking around at the carnage, the bodies of men, angels and harpies littering the ground."

"The Archbishop is dead?"

"Badly injured," said Solimo.

"Then who do these angels obey? They are forcing us into the gorge. It is almost finished."

"There must be someone directing them," said Berwick.

"Maybe there is," said George.

He picked up the Archbishop's sword, looked at it wistfully for a moment, then ran down the road that led up to the terrace.

George McClure was running into the square. The rear rank of angels turned to face him. He did not think about what he was doing, he simply felt impelled to do it. He grasped the sword in both hands raised above his head, holding it by the blade so that it formed the shape of a cross.

"Stop!" he shouted. "Deus vult! Stop fighting!"

Nothing showed on their faces. He had heard the Latin war cry of the crusaders shouted before he came out of the gate. God wills it. Now he understood where it had come from.

"In the name of the Lord, lay down your weapons. Deus vult!"

The empty eyes of the angels in the rear ranks turned on him and raised their eyes to the cross of the sword. Their movements slowed. Now they were looking towards him and had stopped their advance.

Emboldened, he stepped towards them. They parted to let him through.

"In the name of the Lord, lay down your weapons. Deus vult!" he called again, more clearly now.

As he moved forward, more and more of them stopped. They slid their swords back into their scabbards or laid them on the cobblestones of the square. Then he had reached the front ranks and all that was before him were the amazed faces of Kallick's pikemen.

53

KALLICK, CLIFFORD AND George surveyed the angels from the terrace.

"What do we do with them?" Kallick wondered.

"They obeyed you, Father. Could you order them to destroy themselves?"

"They obeyed the word of the Lord. Perhaps you could order them to do that yourself."

"If they obeyed our orders," Kallick wondered, "could we use them as a weapon? It will take a while to fill the hole left by the loss of two whole legions."

"Not a weapon to be trusted if anyone could invoke the name of the Lord to use them," said Clifford.

"Yes, I think you'll find most people suggest God is on their side," George smiled.

"Wouldn't they fight back if we tried to destroy them though?" Kallick asked.

"Perhaps we could maroon them on an island," said Kallick. "Or sink the ship on the way. What about Limbo? The gate is not yet shut."

"It will be soon, the puoli are gradually being carried out of the Tower of Stars and distributed around the city," said Clifford. "They are waking up. The focus created by them dreaming in the same place is already so weakened the gate is beginning to fade."

Berwick was looking at the bodies of the Melion men. Frowning, he went up to Raul who was talking to Keti.

"Have you seen Lord Giles? He be not among the dead."

Raul shook his head.

"He was here when it started, I be sure of it," Berwick said.

He sighed.

"Ah, I came for Silver anyway."

Silver sat where he had taken the axe in his chest, his lifeless eyes still open.

"Would Giles go back?" Raul asked.

"Why wouldn't he? He's broken no laws, and even if he had, there be only me that knows it. He will be a thorn in my side for a long time yet."

"You see what I mean," said Raul turning to the veteran soldier Keti. "You are back to where we are now. At each other's throats and pretending we are at peace."

"Not quite," said Keti. "When the light did not shine on us, there were certainly some who chose to walk in the darkness, but many sought out the light again."

He looked across at Clifford.

"He will be a greater man than his father."

"That be every son's dream. And his sadness if he achieves it," said Berwick.

Keti smiled and limped over to Clifford and Kallick.

Solimo stood up from administering to the Archbishop and joined them.

"Why be you letting them close the way to Limbo?" Berwick asked. "That would be a quick way home if the way to Kunnaslaki be still open!"

"Not at the expense of these puoli," Solimo replied. "Holding onto a dream for days as they have done is exhausting. And I am not leaving so soon. There is healing work I can do here."

"What about the Mage's books?" asked Raul. "Is that not what you went for in the first place?"

"It is. But I know where to find them and perhaps they are in the best place for now. I do not feel ready to be a mage just yet."

"Is the Archbishop dead yet?" Raul asked.

Solimo smiled despite himself.

"Those wounds will always give him great pain. He will not be able to walk or feed himself for some time, but with the proper care, he will not die of them."

"Do you mean your care?" asked Raul in disbelief. "And I thought Rodon was mad."

"What greater torture than to be cared for by those you would destroy?" Solimo smiled. "Who knows where that may lead?

Rodon's last wish was for the Archbishop to have a chance at redemption."

Raul shook his head and walked away. Berwick smiled at Solimo.

"You be very wise."

Solimo bowed his head.

"No," he said.

There were many bodies in front of where the North Bridge had stood, men, delf, wolf. Clifford tried to remember where his father had fallen. They had been so close to each other when it had happened, but Edward had been powerless to help him. He was so tired, but he had to find him.

A wolf was lying across the senator's legs. Henry Clifford's eyes were still open. Edward tried to make out if, in death, his father's face still wore a particular emotion. What would he have wanted his father to be feeling at that moment?

He dragged the half animal carcass from his father and then knelt beside him. The older man was still gripping the axe and, with some difficulty, Edward prised his father's fingers from the shaft. Then, sitting back on his haunches, he did what he had never done with his father in life. He kept hold of his hand.

Grafton clambered through the rubble of the Tower of the Stars and out through the tumbled-down wall. He was sick of looking at the destruction of his city. The clouds had cleared and a new moon was shining as brightly as it could. A fresh smell was rising from the plants and from the earth after the rain.

He walked down through the forest until he came to the open rock. There he could turn his back on the city. Far below, the waves glowed unperturbed in the moonlight and inland, the dark mountains lifted their summits to the stars in vain.

He turned over in his mind what he had seen when the sponge from the other world had been placed in the needle. He had a memory of a confusion of images, there at the same time, yet each visible fleetingly. Others had seen it too, but no one could make any sense of it. He knew he had stumbled upon something important, but what was it? The answer lay back amongst the harpies and the castaway cobs. He breathed in deeply and exhaled. He felt comfortably insignificant below the teeming stars and he felt more curious and more excited than he had ever felt before.

Rua found Charlie and his father leaning on the balustrade above the gorge and talking quietly. They noticed her come up.

Richard smiled.

"If you'll excuse me, I just need to talk to George about something," he said.

Charlie winced inwardly, but gratefully, at his father's tactfulness. Was he that obvious?

"How's Rosa?" he asked as his father walked away.

"She is well. It's going to sound rather silly, but I have given her some calming herbs and sent her to bed."

"More sleep?"

"Good sleep this time."

Charlie laughed and there was a silence between them that longed to be filled.

"Did you come back for me or for Rosa?" Rua asked at last.

Charlie wondered if jealousy or simple curiosity had driven that question.

"For you. But I thought you'd like it if I tried to help her."

She smiled.

"I let you down in the desert," he said. "I ran away."

A small frown settled on her forehead.

"You did not," she said. "You led them away from me. And besides, what else could you have done against them?"

They fell quiet again and looked out over the gorge at the city. There were flames dancing from the warehouse district in the east to the streets which had deliberately been fired in the west. And in the nearer streets which faced across the gorge, there was a swathe of damage where the light needle had cut across the buildings.

The people had come out of hiding. They were inspecting the destruction and trying to control the fires.

"You will need a new senate house," said Charlie.

"We will need to make many things new. Much has changed. This doesn't feel like my home anymore."

That silence again.

"What will you do now?" Charlie asked. He tried to make it sound nonchalant, as if it were just simple curiosity.

She narrowed her eyes.

"I don't know. I would like to learn more about the light. Perhaps I could find the shaman. Or your friend Solimo could teach me. Maybe I could go back to Kunnaslaki with him."

Charlie felt jealousy rise within him.

"But then I would still be a long way from you," she added.

Charlie looked at her. His heart surged. She smiled at him.

"I'm afraid I do say a bit more than just your name though."

He felt himself going red. Her face turned more serious.

"I came back for you too," she said.

He was taller than her by a head, so when he put his arms around her, she nestled perfectly against his neck. He kissed her hair. She tipped up her head and when he looked into those eyes, everything else vanished. For a few moments, time stopped. The dead, the grieving, the lost, the guilty and their burning city were no more. All of them vanished from the face of the worlds during that first kiss.

Free ebook: Tales of the Delf

Being able to build a relationship with my readers is one of the best things about writing. It turns it from being a lonely occupation to a sociable one. Occasionally I send newsletters with details on new releases, special offers and other bits of news relating to the Light Funnel series and other books.

And if you sign up to the mailing list, I'll send you *Tales of the Delf*. This is an ebook of short stories from Delf folklore from both before and after the coming of the Order. It provides some extra colour on Delf culture and light lore.

You can get it free by telling me where to send it. Just go to http://eepurl.com/clgE5j.

Enjoy this book? You can make a big difference

For independent authors, honest reviews are a powerful way of bringing their books to the attention of other readers.

If you've enjoyed this book, I'd be very grateful if you could spend a few minutes leaving a review (it can be as short as you like) at your favourite retailer.

About the author

Find out more about KA Barron at www.kabarron.com. You can also connect with him on Twitter at @kabarronauthor, on Facebook at www.facebook.com/kabarronbooks and if you feel like it, send him an email at kevin@kabarron.com.

Also by KA Barron

Novels

Light Funnel

A father in despair. An ancient destiny. A darkness that can change everything.
Fear has kept ancient enemies apart for centuries, but the Archbishop has made a discovery which will overturn the balance of power.

Falling between worlds, young Charlie Denham and his father Richard find themselves on opposite sides when war looms. The descendants of lost crusaders now face a decisive conflict with the Delf who wield demons of fire.

As darkness pours from the earth and armies gather, Richard and Charlie will face the nightmare from a lost past which threatens to consume both worlds. They must find each other, and escape the approaching storm, if they are to have any hope of staying alive or returning home again.

This is the first volume of the *Light Funnel* series.

Later books in the series will be:
    Light Cradle
    Light Mage

Kevin Barron writes in other genres too. Here are some more of his books.

Travel and humour

Into the blue

Half-planned travels of an amateur vagabond

Kevin Barron feels guilty if he stays at home and does nothing. His solution is to visit other countries and do nothing there instead. An added benefit is that writing about it gives him something to do at home.

Lose your ticket before you've even set off, find out what whalers think of Greenpeace, dodge dive-bombers, meet dangerous truckers, interview a tennis star, witness horror, walk all night, fish for your dinner, watch sunsets in the wilderness, ride legendary highways, stargaze in the Rockies, hitch-hike through the outback, be rescued by an angel, become Robin Hood, escape from Colditz.

This collection of stories covers more than a decade of travel, so throw your backpack over your shoulder and head off...into the blue.

Wandering home with an amateur vagabond

When you leave, at what point do you start going home? And when you leave and don't come back, where is home?

Moving to another country for a while provides an excellent opportunity to travel on the way. Having threatened The Big Trip for years, Kevin Barron finally takes the plunge and, as a result, finds that the idea of home is not as clear as it used to be.

Kayak in the rain, meet an Aboriginal elder, make conversation with a grumpy barber, kill sheep, crash a car, eat entrails, be in the Middle East on 9/11, ride legendary highways, find yourself face to face with an elk, get lost in the African night, have the best view at Shangri-La, fight a fire, be ill on an overnight bus, search for intruders, flirt, haggle, dance, joke, eat, hike, misunderstand, leave home and return.

This collection of stories follows those of Into the blue, so throw your backpack over your shoulder again and set off on the never ending journey home.

Tales of Socks and Splendour

The Grumpete is a disgusting yet warm hearted character who lives alone in a land beyond the Ocean of Spleg. Embarking on an adventure one day, he encounters the Kazza Princess in a distant castle and their lives are never the same again.

Join the foul-bummed Grumpete and the kimmering Kazz as they shine, explode, wander, flatulate, burn, run, reproduce, eat and fight their way through a series of far-fetched adventures in glorious nonsense verse.

Whether read out loud or quietly to yourself where no one will find you, these fast-moving and humorous poems are sure to entertain children of all ages...apart from perhaps those of a delicate disposition.

Business

How to Run Facilitated Workshops
A pragmatic guide to successful meetings

Are your meetings a waste of time? Get productive.

We've all had those moments of wondering about the point of meetings. People wander off topic, take over, tune out...

Perhaps you have run some workshops, but want some ideas about how to deal with specific situations.

In today's fast moving business environment, you need to make the most of people's time, energy and knowledge. This book is aimed at people in organisations who have limited time and budget to achieve their objectives, but need to be inclusive, consultative, yet efficient.

It provides pragmatic advice of immediate use to both novice and experienced facilitator. It can be read end to end, or you can dip into it depending on your need.

The book is packed full of advice and techniques to help you prepare for, run and follow up on facilitated workshops. Not only is the process described, but there is advice for dealing with problems along the way, notably managing behaviour that can kill productivity and collaboration. There is a focus on planning the workshop and setting out the agenda. A set of sample agendas covering a wide range of project scenarios is included.

With the advice in this book, gleaned from twenty years of experience in industry and consulting, you can pre-empt problems and be well on the way to saving time and achieving usable outcomes that will accelerate your projects.

Kevin Barron has worked in industry and consulting for more than 25 years. He has led teams, worked on projects and delivered training across many sectors including banking, media, retail, wealth management, telecommunications, transport, IT services, utilities, local and national government, and manufacturing. He has facilitated hundreds of workshops in the UK, Australia, New Zealand, Sweden and Germany. He is also an experienced business analyst and agile practitioner.